FLIGHT FROM VIENNA

PETER R AUER

ISBN: 0615980198
ISBN 13: 9780615980195
Library of Congress Control Number: 2014904468
Peter R. Auer, Washington, DC

This book is dedicated to my parents, Lili and Rudi Auer, who gave up a great deal to be together and to eventually gain freedom.

ACKNOWLEDGEMENTS

I AM INDEBTED to my wife, Carolyn Schiller, who taught me to enjoy and appreciate the importance of historical fiction and who consistently encouraged me to write the story of my parents, Lili and Rudi. I am grateful to her for listening each evening to the story *Flight from Vienna* as it unfolded and for providing invaluable, good-humored feedback until the process had been completed. I am also thankful for her willingness to participate in the research process both here and in Vienna. And, finally, I am particularly indebted to Carolyn for her meticulous editing and proofreading, without ever suggesting it to be a chore.

TABLE OF CONTENTS

FOREWORD

THIS STORY IS about Rudi Auer and Lili Gruen in Vienna from 1932 to 1934. They would become my parents. While the fundamental components of the story are factual, the minor characters and events are fictitious.

Much of this story comes from what my parents shared with me during their lives, my father sharing much more than my mother, who preferred not to talk about these years and several others following. I now believe that memories of those years were too painful for her to share, even with me, with whom she was very close. I became determined to write this story because of what I was not told rather than because of what I was told.

First trained as a historian and involved in education for half a century, I decided to write this so that it may become a contribution to Holocaust literature. Holocaust literature needs to be as complete and comprehensive as possible to help curtail anti-Semitism, which again seems to be on the increase in Europe, curtail future Holocaust denial, and to prevent human beings in the future from committing major atrocities against other human beings.

I also wanted to write this story for my grandchildren in order that they might understand how their great-grandparents fell in love and lived a period in their lives.

Looking back to those years, one recognizes with some consternation the relatively widespread existence of anti-Semitism, which was reacted to only sporadically and by small groups of people at any one time. Why was there no concerted opposition? Why no call for the fundamental recognition of human rights in Vienna? Why so many ostriches with their heads in the sand?

1

CAFÉ LANDTMANN, VIENNA, AUTUMN 1932

RUDI AND LILI had agreed to meet outside Café Landtmann, next to the Burgtheater, at 4:45 p.m. on this particular day. Rudi had never been to Café Landtmann, as he thought it a bit highbrow, but Lili had been there often, especially for their wonderful ice cream and pastry dishes. This classic Viennese coffee house had been in existence since 1873 and had boasted many celebrities as regulars, including Sigmund Freud, Gustav Mahler, Marlene Dietrich, and Romy Schneider.

It was raining heavily, so Rudi, who was a little early, took a seat at a booth where he would clearly see Lili as she arrived. He observed the somewhat luxurious interior with the plush-upholstered seating, the elegant chandeliers, and the beautiful wooden floors. He became a little anxious already a couple of minutes after their agreed-on meeting time. Rarely was she late. As if to announce her entry, there was a heavy thunderclap at the very moment Lili entered, shaking out an umbrella. Rudi rose from his seat as an immaculately dressed waiter in a dinner suit smiled at Lili, took the umbrella, and placed it in a stand near the front door. Rudi took Lili's right hand and kissed her gently on the cheek. As they sat opposite one another in the booth,

Lili let out a big sigh, glad to have finished work for the day and pleased to be with Rudi.

Rudi ordered a piece of Mandelkuchen and coffee for Lili and Wuerstel mit Senf and a beer for himself, as he figured this would be his dinner while Lili was expected home for dinner with her mother and brother, Walter. After having demolished one sausage, Rudi produced a draft article he had written for the university.

"Would you proofread this for me, please, Lili?"

"Of course, but my writing is probably too Viennese for the university folk," she explained with some laughter.

Her joyous disposition soon changed as she began to read.

The article was about the rise of Hitlerism. It argued that the National Socialist Movement, led by Hitler, constituted a huge future threat to Austria and probably to the rest of Europe and Russia as well.

"Where did you get all this information from, Rudi?"

"I got much of it from reading recent copies of the *Voelkischer Beobachter*, the Nazi daily journal. Hitler, who dominates the National Socialist Movement, sees Germans as a 'chosen people,' a superior breed who deserve an enlarged Volkstum. Hence, Hitler's got the idea that Germany and Austria should be rid of all people who were not of the Aryan race, healthy of mind and body. Aryans should breed prolifically and constantly increase their Lebensraum. As a first step, Austria should be annexed and this Anschluss achieved as soon as possible. And all non-Aryans expelled."

Lili hadn't read half the article when she looked up, somewhat grey in the face.

"Is this true?" she queried. "What could this mean for all the Jews in Vienna, thousands and thousands of us? No one thinks of us as Jewish; we are all Viennese. We have been Viennese for generations."

"Unfortunately, Hitler's viewpoint regarding the superiority of the Aryan people is gaining considerable momentum in Germany, and I think, to some extent, also in Austria," exclaimed Rudi.

"Surely not also in Austria?" questioned Lili.

Rudi took her hand in his and continued. "Some mutterings around campus have focused on blaming Jews for the economic depression from nineteen twenty-nine and all the misery that has flowed from that. The Jews, many argue, control most business, and that is pulling everybody else down."

"I know that many businesses are run by Jews, and most of these are indeed very successful because Jews are generally very hard working, and many also are bright and well educated. They deserve to do well, and they don't prevent others from being successful," Lili went on.

"Yes, this is certainly true," agreed Rudi. "Unfortunately, it seems often to be the case that people who are not particularly successful blame their lack of success on those who are seen to be successful. In any event, there is clear evidence that anti-Semitism is on the rise dramatically in Germany and, to some extent, in other parts of Europe as well, including Austria."

"What could this mean?" asked Lili, somewhat concerned.

"Well, while I don't foresee any Nazi takeover in Germany in the near future—and hence a threat to Austria—I have been reading about the rise of Nazism in Germany, the relentlessness of Hitler in his pursuit of power, and the increasing support he seems to be getting. And having just read parts of his book, *Mein Kampf*, I realize this man is a madman. His ideas are really scary...very scary. If he himself believes all the things he has written and wants to implement even some of these ideas, we really need to keep a close eye on his attempts to increase power unto himself. If he were to gain power in Germany, it would certainly not be wise for any Jews, or, for that matter, any other non-Aryan Germans or Austrians, to remain here in Austria. I don't think your family has anything to worry about at this time, but I think it very important to follow political developments in Germany. It is this message that this article is really trying to get across," concluded Rudi.

Just then there was heavy pounding of boots, some yelling, and whistles being blown, which suddenly stopped as two young men were thumped against the outside wall of the café. Everyone in the café gasped. The head waiter with a loud voice requested, "Everybody, please remain in your seats."

"What's happening, Rudi?" asked Lili with a little concern.

"I don't know yet," he responded as a waiter returned from the window and walked passed Rudi and Lili.

"What was that about Herr Ober?" asked Rudi.

"Just a couple of Nazis from the university being apprehended; they were apparently apprehended for harassing a covered woman coming up from the train."

After normality resumed and in response to prompting from Rudi, Lili complimented him on his writing, suggesting only a few punctuation changes. As they quietly finished eating, she reflected on their discussion with considerable ill ease, wondering whether anti-Semitism could ever reach a level in Vienna where Jews felt compelled to flee their own city. As they were about to leave their table, Rudi ran his right forefinger over Lili's plate to capture the last remnant of almond cream. She gave him a disapproving glance.

"Sorry," he said, as he gave an innocent shrug and a little smile.

As the waiter gave Lili her umbrella, Rudi asked him to save the same booth for the same time tomorrow. Lili smiled approvingly and hooked into Rudi's arm as they left the café. It had stopped raining, and Rudi walked Lili home to her Ring Strasse address. He kissed her on the mouth then on the forehead before watching her disappear behind the ornate gate.

—◈—

THE NEXT DAY, Rudi met with Heinrich, the editor of the *Wiener Universitaet Zeitung*. "I like it a lot," declared Heinrich with a knowing smile. "It will be published in next week's edition, and I'm sure there will be some quite varied responses."

Rudi sauntered off to a lecture, somewhat self-satisfied that the article had been finished and submitted. He couldn't concentrate well on the lecture as he sat reflecting on Heinrich's comment that the article would elicit quite varied responses. He hoped there'd be no particularly negative responses. His mind also led him to wonder about how Lili's day was going, and he hoped that their discussion the afternoon before was not too alarming for her. Becoming increasingly fond of Lili, Rudi was looking forward to meeting her again that afternoon, and he was somewhat bothered by the fact that they came from such different worlds. He was brought up in a Catholic working-class family in Kärnten, having spent little time in towns any larger than Villach, before coming to Vienna. Lili was from a wealthy, well-connected Jewish family, established in Vienna for generations. Rudi was nineteen years old, and Lili was twenty-seven. The day before at Café Landtmann, he felt a little inadequate, and this day he thought he was not sufficiently well dressed for that august establishment, so he walked back home to iron the best trousers he had and put on a clean shirt. Satisfied with what he saw in the mirror, he wiled the next couple of hours away before sauntering back to Café Landtmann, where he sat outside near the front entrance to await Lili's arrival.

He already spotted her some thirty metres away. He recognized her by her elegant gait as she walked toward him, her dress tight to below the hips then flaring out midcalf. *Very nice*, he thought. They hugged at the front door and walked inside, their waiter from the previous day showing them to the same booth where they sat before. They held hands across the table as they exchanged small talk. A lull in their conversation afforded the waiter an opportunity to take their orders. Lili wanted a piece of Streuselkuchen and coffee, and Rudi ordered goulash and a beer. Lili would, that evening, have dinner with her brother, Walter, after their participation as "extras" in the production of *Die Fledermaus* at the Vienna Opera House. Walter and Lili were extras three or four times per week during the opera season. They loved their involvement, now in its third year, having become familiar with many different operas and able to speak occasionally with some of the singers. Rudi had never been to the Vienna Opera, though he had been to a symphony at the Wiener Musikverein. He was quietly trying to envisage what it would be like to participate in crowd scenes at the opera when Lili asked, "Did you submit your article?"

"Yes," said Rudi. "And I'm pleased to say the editor liked it a lot. Did you mention the contents of the article to your mother yesterday evening? What did she say?"

"You wouldn't really want to know, Rudi."

"Yes, I really do want to know. What did she say? What did she say?"

"She said it was a lot of Quatsch."

"What is Quatsch?" Rudi asked impatiently.

Lili had no intentions of sharing all her mother had said, as this would likely make Rudi very angry and possibly provide considerable strain on their relationship. Lili just said that her mother was not aware of any increase in anti-Semitism in Vienna, and, in any event, they were nonpracticing Jews, and nearly all their business acquaintances and friends were also nonpracticing. Rather, they all actually celebrated Christmas, taking great pride in selecting and decorating Christmas trees and purchasing presents to exchange during a number of festive gatherings in each other's homes. Speaking about this Hitler madman and his fanciful views was a lot of Quatsch, just nonsense, her mother argued. Rudi should not concern himself with happenings in Germany and should concentrate on his studies here in Vienna. Rudi had an inkling that this was not all that Lili's mother had said, but he did not want to push it.

Lili's mother, Hedwig, had indeed said a great deal more. She expressed her disappointment, even disapproval, that Lili was interested in Rudi at all. He was, after all, still a boy—far too young and unsophisticated for Lili. She should become involved with one of the many young Jewish businessmen, acquaintances of the family, very eligible, and who would love to become involved with her if she were amenable. There were many Jewish men who would make Lili a wonderful husband and father to her children and would be able to provide a life at the standard to which she had become accustomed and deserved. Rudi was just a country boy, son of a mere stationmaster, with little understanding of the comings and goings of the world, undoubtedly ignorant of life in Vienna and indeed anywhere else. Anyway, it was not appropriate for Lili to be courted by a Catholic, even if he were of the appropriate age and of sufficient standing. Rudi was simply not of the right standing. It was a matter of class. Lili should just forget about him.

As Rudi mopped up the last of the goulash sauce with the remaining bread and wondered how he could ensure that he and Lili spend time together again soon, Lili asked, seemingly out of the blue, "Would you like me to show you around the opera house this Saturday afternoon? I could arrange to give you a private tour." Lili knew that several tours would be given by guides whom she knew, and she could surely go around alone with Rudi.

"That would be very nice," he replied.

Lili placed a hand on top of his and went on, "Perhaps we could meet by the Strauss statue in the Stadtpark, and I'll bring a couple of sandwiches for lunch."

"That sounds great."

"Make it at noon," she suggested. "That'll give us a little time before we go to the opera house."

Feeling very comfortable with each other, Rudi and Lili, hand in hand, turned into the Ringstrasse, and, with barely any further conversation, arrived at Lili's home. They parted with a passionate kiss and exchanged waves as the gate closed behind her. Lili had planned this meeting for a number of days because she had something important to tell Rudi, and the park would be a good place.

2

RUDI, 1913–1931

RUDI WAS BORN on 8 December 1913, into a working-class family in Boeckstein, a small town in southern Austria. His father, also named Rudi, was a railway worker of meager means. He was a man of small stature but large aura. He was a joyous man, a gregarious person who was liked by a lot of people. Rudi's mother, Maria, was tall and elegant of disposition and a more earnest sort—a good Catholic who was more solitary and took life much more seriously than her husband did. She "wore the pants" in the house. Rudi was an only child who grew up to hold a deep respect and love for his parents. His father was posted to different railway stations, and hence the family moved a number of times, including to Sattendorf, Annenheim, Klagenfurt, and Villach. Rudi, therefore, attended different schools, and his mother took him to the local village churches where, with each move, she quickly became settled into the congregation. This was probably a factor in Rudi developing into a restless, unsettled soul.

Rudi the elder was not very interested in religion and certainly not the devout believer his wife was. Whenever he could, he tried very hard to find excuses not to attend with Maria and his son. Though he believed in a God, the younger Rudi was likewise not interested

in organized religion. He learnt from early on at school that, histori-
cally, religion was the cause of considerable hatred between peoples
and the underlying cause of numerous wars. He was also soon able to
make excuses not to attend church services with his mother.

A very intelligent boy, Rudi often found school lacking in interest and challenge, and hence, generally found it boring. With
minimum work, he retained above-average grades, and his teachers
consistently reported that his level of achievement would improve
if he only "tried harder." Characteristically, he would listen to his
teachers with only half an ear and would finish his work quickly.
Teachers generally reported that he was often talkative and disrup-
tive, unable to apply himself appropriately to his studies. At other
times he was just looking out the window, contemplative, thinking
about many things, some related to school, many not. With time
on his hands, he often distracted others from doing their work and
enjoyed devising pranks and taunting teachers. Rudi loved to col-
lect insects in bottles and observe their behavior. He also liked to
allow them to mysteriously escape in the classroom. Half a dozen
escaped wasps can cause quite some commotion, he discovered.
He was once observed during classtime in the schoolyard, feeding a baby bird that had fallen from its nest. On another occasion
he was sent home because he had a baby red fox, which he had
rescued from beside the road, hiding under his pullover. This red
fox became Rudi's pet and was to live under his bed for a couple of
years and was walked every day, much as a dog is walked. Rudi was
aware that a fox should be in the wild rather than cooped up in a
small apartment, so one day he took it to the edge of the woods,
bade him good luck, and let him go. Rudi missed his pet a great
deal and was convinced that he sighted his fox several times over
the coming months.

Playing marbles in class and constructing and throwing quite
elaborate paper aeroplanes often brought laughs from his peers and
scowls from teachers. He liked to use glue to paste a teacher's text-
book to his desk or permanently close the teacher's desk drawer. His

proudest prank was to hook up a dead rat to a string and, via some primitive apparatus, have it travel along the chalkboard rail behind the teacher's back. The whole class was threatened with punishment, but nobody would say who the guilty party was. Rudi owned up to save his classmates from what he thought would have been unfair punishment, and his parents were called to the school. His mother was highly embarrassed and annoyed with him; his father saw the humor in the situation and offered some hollow rebuke, though he smiled inwardly. Rudi was deprived of meeting with friends after school for a couple of days. The punishment was worth the pleasure he got from the prank, the break from boredom, and a little comic relief he believed he provided his classmates.

Why are so many of my teachers so boring and the subject matter they are trying to teach so uninteresting? Why, in high school, would I be interested in the Peloponnesian War, he thought, *or in the stories of Gilgamesh?* "What's the use of learning Latin verb declensions and conjugations?" he asked one of his teachers. He was never going into the priesthood; he'd never need to speak Latin. There were only a couple of teachers who seemed to have understood where Rudi was coming from. One was Herr Henning, a young, tall, dark-haired, athletic-looking art teacher whom he got on well with; the other was an older, Jewish science teacher, Herr Birnbaum. Herr Birnbaum took some care to counsel Rudi as to how to cope with a boring school situation and how to minimize getting into trouble.

Some teachers were quite relieved when, from time to time, Rudi would play hooky. He never seemed to just hang out; rather, he'd arrange to meet a friend to go hiking, skiing, or swimming. Or he would sometimes just spend the day hiking or swimming himself. Rather than ask questions of his parents regarding his absences from school, teachers often just ignored these, happy to be rid of him for the day.

In addition to hiking, skating, skiing, and swimming, Rudi played handball and was active in athletics, gymnastics, wrestling, fencing, and canoeing, either at school or within the community. Not a star in any of these activities, he was generally very competent and enjoyed the human interaction these activities afforded him. He was really a well-rounded sportsman with an athletic physique. He was handsome and spent much time with girls during his teenage years. There were, however, no serious relationships during his years at school, as he was more interested in participating in outdoor activities, especially skiing and skating in winter and swimming in summer.

Rudi learnt to ski from an early age, his first real outdoor shoes being a pair of ski boots. When he played hooky at school and on weekends, he would frequently go skating or skiing, sometimes by himself, other times with friends. During high school, Franz was a close friend of his for several years, and he and Rudi would spend countless days together skiing or hiking. Rudi and Franz were true buddies, often together out of school time and sometimes playing hooky together. They freely shared their thoughts and feelings with one another and had no secrets. They regularly planned day trips together, most often in the mountains. They were both excellent skiers. They were often having such fun that they let time get away from them and frequently returned home later than their parents expected, each time getting an earful and sometimes receiving some form of punishment. They spent a lot of time skiing on the Gerlitzen, where they also spent many days hiking in summer, when they also often went canoeing or swimming in the Ossiachersee or the Woerthersee.

On a Saturday in April 1931, they were ski touring on the Gerlitzen and having an exceptionally enjoyable time. There was excellent snow cover with twenty centimetres or so of powder on a firm base. The sun was shining brightly, yet it was unusually cold. Rudi and Franz were having a whale of a time, skiing off the beaten track, making new tracks between the trees, jumping over logs, not another human to be seen, though they saw a fox bounding in the distance. They stopped for a picnic lunch. It was eerily quiet. "Das war wunderbar," said Franz, puffing a bit and grinning from ear to ear.

"Yes, it doesn't get better than this," replied Rudi.

They sat on a log, sharing cheese and ham on rye bread sandwiches their mothers had prepared and finished munching on a couple of apples. Rudi took out a block of chocolate, which they shared. They strapped their skis back on again, skiing joyously between the trees until they came to a more open but undulating area with excellent opportunities to jump over ridges. They delighted in each jump, gaining confidence by the minute, some jumps keeping them airborne for eight to ten metres. They would take turns going first and wait below a jump site to watch the other. They both fell several times as they gained a little too much air or lost their balance. They would dust themselves off, laugh a lot, and keep going.

They agreed to do one more jump before making their way home. Rudi was watching from below as Franz came over a jump, no more difficult than most others before. Coming off the jump, something happened. He saw Franz higher than usual and skis in the air above his head. He crashed and somersaulted several times, his skis and stocks becoming somewhat tangled. When he came to a halt, there was no movement. Franz lay sprawled on the snow, motionless. "Franz, Franz," yelled Rudi as he herringboned as fast as he could towards his motionless friend. "Gott in Himmel, Franz, sag' was. Franz, Franz, bist du verletzt?"

Reaching Franz's side, Rudi saw there was no motion. One of Franz's skis with a broken tip lay on one side; both poles lay by his side, one hand without glove. He had blood coming from his mouth. Rudi screeched at the top of his lungs, "Hilfe, hilfe, bitte, hilfe!"

Two skiers who had been skiing just above and a little to the left of Franz and Rudi heard the plea and arrived at the scene. They quickly took off their skis, and, with Rudi looking down over a motionless body, one asked, "Was ist dein Name?" After he told them, one man instructed, "Stay here, Rudi. Put your jacket over his chest. Keep talking to him; don't stop talking to him, and we'll go down and fetch a doctor."

Rudi put his jacket over Franz's chest and sobbed as he tried to speak. "Franz, Franz, what happened? Franz, talk to me. Please, Franz, say something. Talk—talk to me. Bitte, bitte, Franz, talk to me," he pleaded as he put the glove that had been dislodged back on his friend's hand. Rudi felt Franz's face. It felt cold to the touch. Rudi rubbed his face and arms. There was absolutely no movement. He put an ear to Franz's mouth and nose to ascertain whether he was breathing. He tried to find a pulse in his neck, in his wrist. Nothing! Rudi feared Franz was dead but still hoped against all signs. He sat on the snow shivering, sobbing, and wailing beside Franz and gently caressing his forehead, all the while trying to converse with him. "Where is the doctor? Where is the damned doctor?" Rudi sobbed.

About forty-five minutes after the accident, a doctor and an assistant arrived. He bent over Franz and affirmed, "Er ist tod. Es tut mir wirklich leid, er ist tod."

"Gott in Himmel, how can that be? It cannot be; it can't be," Rudi cried as he collapsed to his knees. He had lost his best friend.

Rudi was guided slowly down the mountain and taken to the hospital in the valley. Soon his best friend was wheeled past him on a gurney, a sheet covering his entire body.

"It was a freak accident, Rudi; the tip of his right ski pole went through his heart. He had no chance. He died instantly," the doctor exclaimed.

Rudi cried and cried late into the evening as Franz's and his parents were notified; each arrived at the hospital within minutes of one another. The crying continued into the night as hospital staff tried to comfort two distraught sets of parents and one distraught teenager.

Rudi was heartbroken. He felt he had lost half of himself. Now with whom could he share his feelings, his dreams, his hopes, his fears? He felt very alone. He felt empty, depressed. He remained so distraught, he was unable to attend Franz's funeral and felt terrible that he did not attend. His teachers appeared generally understanding and were very lenient about Rudi getting his school assignments completed. Mr. Birnbaum was the most sympathetic, making special efforts to understand the impact of Franz's death on the boy. He encouraged Rudi to complete his school assignments so that he would graduate with his "Matura" at the end of the year as scheduled. Rudi was so depressed and disinterested in his schoolwork that, at the arrival of the summer holidays, it appeared most likely he would not complete his final exams.

Rudi invariably spent summer school vacations at home, his parents never having sufficient money to take family holidays or even to send him on a summer vacation elsewhere. Rudi generally helped his father, who was the stationmaster at the Annenheim train station. Annenheim is a pretty, picture-postcard village on the northwest banks of the Ossiachersee, where the water reaches temperatures of over twenty-four degrees centigrade—great for swimming and other water sports. The villages along the lake's shoreline were invariably inundated in summer with holiday makers mainly from Austria's larger towns and cities, especially from Vienna.

Rudi the elder, understanding his son's grief at having lost his best friend in a skiing accident only months earlier, gave the boy all sorts of tasks to keep him from brooding. Rudi swept the stationhouse and waiting room, emptied rubbish bins regularly, cleaned out the guttering, and watered the potted plants of red geraniums. When his father was busy greeting return summer guests, Rudi collected the spent fare cards and naturally wished them a nice vacation. He often carried suitcases and other travel bags a few dozen metres or more than two hundred metres for guests staying in local guest houses and hotels. He was frequently given a few groschen for his efforts.

When it was quiet, he would go by himself or meet up with some friends on the banks of the Ossiachersee. There was always something to do: swimming, canoeing, sailing, fishing, or just enjoying an ice cream from a nearby stand. When he was alone, he'd wander a few hundred yards to find a quiet spot to sit on a log or dangle his feet in the water. He'd pass the time watching all sorts of fish peacefully swimming by; some he knew were trout. He'd think about school and how far behind he was with his assignment work.

Would it really be worthwhile doing all this hard work I'd have to do to be ready for my Matura exams? he thought. *Don't know whether I'd cope with another four years of school after that. I know it's uni, and I know it would be a great experience being in Vienna and living away from Mum and Dad. And I think I'd really find studying law interesting. Perhaps not. I'm sure I'd be homesick. It would be so much better if Franz were still here and we'd be in Vienna together. I miss him so much. God, I don't know…I don't know what I should do,* he fretted.

Just then, from under a low-hanging branch, a visitor arrived. "Servus, Rudi." The greeting came from Herr Henning, Rudi's art teacher.

"Guten Tag, Herr Henning. How did you find me here?"

"Your father told me you'd be around here somewhere. How are you? I just wanted to check up on you. Um, that sounds wrong; I wanted to see that you were OK. I know how upset you've been these last months after the loss of Franz."

"That's very nice of you. Yes, I miss Franz a lot. He wanted to become an engineer, you know, and we were planning to room together in Vienna next year. I don't know whether I can do it now… you know, without him. And I have so much catching up to do with my schoolwork, especially with mathematics and science, that I'm not sure I really want to try."

There was quite a long pause, and then Mr. Henning said, "You know, lots of teachers have been concerned about you and will go out of their way to help you get to the Matura exams and do well. Your mathematics teacher is a very compassionate man and will provide as much help as you need to pass. And your science teacher, Mr. Birnbaum, would do anything for you except sit for the examination himself."

"Yes, I know Mr. Birnbaum cares a lot about me; he's been very nice to me," Rudi said with a hint of a smile, remembering the many times Mr. Birnbaum encouraged him. "We'll see," he said as he threw a small piece of stick out into the water, watching small ripples radiating out in circles.

Mr. Henning and Rudi stared out into the water. It was a warm, very pleasant afternoon with just the slightest cool breeze coming off the lake. "Do you know Mr. Birnbaum well?" asked Rudi. "I have always liked him for some reason."

"Well, I've only been at the school for five years, and he had been there for quite some years before then. He's a very serious, very conscientious teacher who has always had everybody's respect. He also has a wicked sense of humor," Mr. Henning concluded with a chuckle.

"He seemed different the last few weeks…seemed to have something on his mind. Is he worried about anything? Do you know?" Rudi enquired.

"Yes, as a matter of fact, something has been on his mind. As you probably know, Mr. Birnbaum is Jewish. His family comes from Germany. Most of the family members live there, some in Prussia, others in Bavaria. They are all becoming deeply concerned about the rise in popularity of Hitler and the Nazi Party and how that may affect them."

Rudi interrupted: "What are they worried about? Hitler's an Austrian, isn't he, and somewhat of a madman?"

Mr. Henning responded, "Yes, Hitler is both. He's basically a thug, and most of his followers seem to be thugs. He's a very dangerous man for all of Germany, as he appears to be an absolute megalomaniac, pushing to becoming German chancellor. He is ruthless towards people who get in his way. Hitler's Nazi Party is gaining more and more seats in Parliament each election, and it seems that it will soon dominate German State Parliaments and the Reichstag."

"Is it because of the Nazis' anti-Semitism that Mr. Birnbaum's family is becoming anxious?" queried Rudi.

"Yes, the Nazis hate Jews, whom they have mainly blamed for the poor economy in Germany, the high level of unemployment, and any other problems Germany might have. If Hitler had his way, he'd drive all Jews out of Germany and out of Austria, for that matter, because he has designs on someday annexing Austria and forming one supernation of pure Germans—a master race." Mr. Henning paused.

"He wrote about all this in his book, *Mein Kampf*, didn't he? Have you read it?" asked Rudi.

"I read some excerpts a few years ago when the second volume was published," replied Mr. Henning. "Apparently the book has just become very popular in recent months and received a lot of support in Germany. It advocates the development of an expanded Germany as a country of a master race of perfect blond specimens." After a pause, he quipped, "You'd be perfect, Rudi; I wouldn't pass the test with my dark hair."

"So what might happen to Mr. Birnbaum's family?" Rudi asked with a serious tone.

Mr. Henning responded, "I think the Birnbaums and many Jews are becoming increasingly worried that there could be a deterioration of their way of life in Germany as Hitler gains more power and actions against Jews increase."

"No wonder Mr. Birnbaum has seemed somewhat preoccupied recently. Please pass on my best wishes to him if you see him during the vacation," Rudi concluded.

"Yes, I will. I must away," said Mr. Henning as he stood up. "You look good, Rudi. Look after yourself now. Servus."

As his teacher turned and walked away, Rudi said, "Thank you for finding me. Auf Wiedersehen." Just at that moment a fish jumped out of the water and made quite a splash as it plopped back in again. Gulls were circling overhead.

Rudi felt a little uplifted to think a teacher had come especially to see how he was faring. He got up and walked back to the Bahnhof, eating an ice cream he purchased on the way. His father, surprised that he was away so long, enquired, "What kept you, Rudi? Did Mr. Henning find you?"

"Yes, Father, he came just to see how I was doing. Really nice of him."

"Yes, that is very nice to have a teacher go out of his way to see you. I'm sure that all your teachers would help you catch up with your work. I can see you passing your exams in December, just needs a little effort. And you'd be off to Vienna. Your mother would miss you a lot. I wouldn't. Sorry, just kidding! What did you two talk about other than school?"

Rudi explained, "Well, I had noticed that Mr. Birnbaum seemed somewhat unhappy and preoccupied recently, and I asked Mr. Henning if he knew anything. Apparently all his family lives in Germany, and they're Jewish. They fear the consequences of the Nazis gaining increased power and possibly kicking them out or forcing them to flee."

"Yes, Rudi, the Nazis are terrible bastards, wicked people," he said with some anger in his voice." Rudi had never heard his father use such language, and he surely wouldn't use it in the presence of his wife. He went on, "I think that all Jews—others too, but especially Jews—need to be very fearful of Hitler and his mob. Jews are increasingly being targeted for ridicule and are being harassed, and there have been incidents of brown-shirted youths beating them up. I also read an article in the *Voelkischer Beobachter* the other day that was full of hatred and vitriol against the Jews."

"What's the *Voelkischer Beobachter*, Father?" asked Rudi.

His father answered, "It's the newspaper of the NSDAP—the National Socialist German Workers' Party, the Nazis. The hatred towards Jews and others expressed in this paper is unbelievable. You rarely see that paper here in Austria. It was left on the train, and the cleaner brought it to me. He had never seen it before. Mind you, the Nazis are already making trouble at Vienna University, according to something I read in our paper the other day. I will not share that with your mother." After a pause, the stationmaster continued, "Yes, I think Hitler wants to take over Austria too, you know, so Jews here in Austria need to watch out as well. Terrible bastards," he repeated as he moved to the station gate on hearing a single whistle indicating the arrival of a passenger train.

Rudi followed his father, ever charming and welcoming to visitors to Annenheim, and he soon found himself carrying a couple of pieces of luggage and following a family to their hotel or a Pension. He was to act as porter many more times this summer period. He also had time to do some swimming, canoeing, and sailing with some other young people but still missed Franz very much. *What would Franz expect of me?* he thought over and over again. This summer dragged on much more than previous summers had, and he soon found himself actually wanting to be back at school.

The teachers were all pleased to see Rudi again and, from the commencement of this final term, offered to help him catch up with his studies. Rudi was so taken aback by their generosity of spirit that he quickly determined he'd give it his best shot. He worked very hard, harder than he had ever done before. He passed Matura, the Gymnasium graduation examination, and would make it to Vienna and to the university after all. He was very pleased. His father and mother were very pleased and proud too. "Bravo, Rudi, you did it," his father said, giving him a strong hug.

3

LILI, 1905–1931

LILI WAS BORN into a well-established, wealthy business family in Vienna on 16 June 1905. Her father, Alfred Gruen, was part of the business elite, the members of which focused mainly on the development of businesses for the purpose of the accumulation of wealth and status. They lived in a large, elegant, two-story house on the Ringstrasse. The house had an imposing, wide staircase and a dumb waiter. It was expensively furnished with dark-wood-paneled walls and imported antiques, and it was lavishly decorated, including grand chandeliers and exquisite silk blend rugs from the East. Each week abundant fresh flowers were brought in and professionally arranged. Up to ten different arrangements adorned the main rooms at any one time. There was a Boesendorfer piano, which was frequently tuned and which both children learned to play under the tutelage of a piano teacher. A Daimler car occupied the garage and was driven mostly by the family driver. Alfred owned three umbrella factories—one in Vienna, one in Prague, and the other in Budapest. He had inherited the business from his father, Karl, one of thirteen children. Lili's mother, Hedwig, was a stern, somewhat aloof woman who managed the household of up to five servants as well as overseeing, though generally from some distance, the development of Lili and her younger brother, Walter. The household also had a pair of dachshunds, one named Kafka, the other Bela. They were brother and sister, and both had excellent appetites. Kafka was the more mischievous, while Bela was a dreamer. They both liked to run around chasing each other, especially between the legs of the dining table and chairs. They were not quiet dogs. They were known to sometimes sit at the table to dine with their parents.

Although they were Jewish, religion played virtually no role in their lives. Most of their friends and acquaintances were also secular Jews belonging to Vienna's business and cultural elite. They didn't see themselves even as Austrians; they regarded themselves as distinctly Viennese—the Viennese upper class, to be more precise. They had assimilated with Christian Viennese generations earlier.

They attended the opera regularly, select private concerts or dinners with celebrity musicians performing; they received invitations to all opera, ballet, and symphony gala events of Vienna and attended many of them. They often entertained in their own home and played board games and cards frequently after dinner. From time to time they arranged after-dinner recitals by local musicians. In fact, Jewish religious observances and holidays were not part of their lives. Rather, Christmas was celebrated with much conscientiousness and joy. A Christmas tree was always selected with great care and beautifully decorated with dozens of red candles meticulously arranged. Presents were carefully purchased for family and friends, and a series of dinners at the Gruens' residence during the festive season was mainly to exchange gifts. Each year there was also a celebration and gift giving especially for the servants. The dogs didn't miss out either, of course.

During this period there were many visits to A. Gerstner K & K Hofzuckerbaecker to obtain the finest breads, pastries, and confectionaries for the many dining events. In fact, there were nearly weekly visits to this particular bakery. Occasionally Mother would also take Lili and Walter to one of many cafés, which was an essential part of the Viennese Gemuehtlichkeit. Viennese socialites, including the Gruens, frequented the Café Museum in the hope of sighting a celebrity such as Gustav Klimt, Egon Schiele, or Oskar Kokoschka, who were regulars at this establishment. They would often also go to Hotel Sacher to share one of their slices of that rich chocolate cake that bore the name of the hotel.

Both Lili and Walter grew up quite independent from their parents, who gave over much of the caring of the children to servants. A nanny looked after their personal needs, read them stories, looked after their rooms, and washed and ironed their clothes. A cook prepared their meals, which were generally finished before their parents dined—quite regularly with business acquaintances. Lili and Walter wanted for little except for the normal parental attention. They attended school within walking distance and had a private tutor.

Getting little parental love and attention, Lili and Walter grew up very close to each other. They were very good friends from the beginning, providing each other the emotional support their parents and servants failed to provide. From a very early age they became really good pals. They read stories together, played together on the piano, and sang duets. During their school years they took an interest in each other's school experiences and helped each other with homework. One was often in the room while the other took piano lessons, and they took ice-skating lessons together, which soon became ice-dancing lessons. As teenagers and young adults, Lili and Walter were nearly inseparable. On weekend family outings lakeside in the south or to the Italian seaside in summer and to the mountains in winter, Lili and Walter would go off together swimming or skiing. They would often spend whole days away from their parents, only returning to wherever they were staying in the evenings. Frequently on other weekends and occasionally on an evening, they went on long walks within the many beautiful Vienna parks; they visited museums together and listened to concerts, especially in the Stadtpark. Occasionally they would watch the Lipizzaner stallions at the Spanish Riding School. They also spent countless hours in cafés their parents would never patronize. Café Mozart and Café Central were favorites of Walter, who also didn't mind Lili's most frequented ice-cream stop, Café Landtmann. Hotel Sacher also became a regular place for supper for several years during the opera season.

During their late teens and early twenties, Walter and Lili became integral to many of the Vienna opera productions. Their parents got them involved. In any particular opera that required extra people in the production, Walter and Lili had their places secure due to their conscientious attendance at rehearsals and punctuality at performances. Often they just had to sit there, pretend to make conversation, and enjoy a glass of champagne or a mélange. Sometimes they had to saunter across a certain part of the stage, seemingly oblivious to the drama inevitably unfolding. It was a period of considerable change among the leadership of the opera and the Vienna Symphony, and Walter and Lili enjoyed the different conductors and operas, which seem to have been dominated in this period by the productions of Strauss. The two thought about little else other than opera during the season. They were occasionally able to meet the star soloists and sometimes even the conductors, whom Lili and Walter thought were somewhat self-important and pretentious. Characteristically, after each performance they would wander across the way to Hotel Sacher and share a piece of Sachertorte and an Eiskaffee or heisse Schokolade.

One evening Walter asked, "What is your very favorite opera, Lili? I should know after all this time. Do you have one in particular?"

"Oh, hard to say. Let me think now. I think I like grand opera better than comic opera," she replied.

"But you surely must like Rossini's *Barber of Seville* and Mozart's *Marriage of Figaro*," probed her younger brother.

"Yes, I like Bizet's *Carmen* too, but I'd have to say I like the grand operas of Verdi more than any of these lighter pieces. There is no opera grander than *Aida*," she asserted.

Walter interrupted, "Which other Verdi operas do you particularly like?"

"Let me see now…I love *Rigoletto, Il Trovatore*, and *La Traviata*. Didn't he compose these three within a period of a few years?"

"Yes, I think in the early 1850s. You are right," answered Walter, who then began to sing from *La Traviata*.

A waiter quickly asked him not to sing there, as he had asked him on previous occasions. "You could wait until you get home," suggested the waiter.

Walter helped Lili on with her coat, and they left for home. "Oh, I nearly forgot," said Lili. "I really love Puccini too—his *La Boheme, Tosca*, and *Madame Butterfly*."

"I agree," said Walter, and he continued singing from *La Traviata*. Soon, with a little prompt from Walter, Lili began to sing the aria "Semore Libera" sung by Violetta, declaring she loves freedom more than love.

At home they would often spend more time, sometimes hours, in each other's rooms, singing the night away, sometimes singing an entire opera from beginning to end.

This was a period when Lili was no longer at school but still received some lessons from her tutor, who was to prepare her to become a secretary. Her parents were very confident they would be able to place her with a well-respected firm in central Vienna. And so it happened; she was employed with renowned lawyer Herrmann Schwartz, who helped with some of the Gruens' business transactions. She enjoyed working for Mr. Schwartz, as he was a reasonable man and never pressured Lili, although there was always sufficient work to do to keep mentally active: researching articles, composing letters, sorting incoming mail, and filing. At lunchtime she would meet up with a friend or read a book. She was currently reading the novel *Bambi. Eine Lebensgeschichte aus dem Walde*, written by Felix Salten. The best part of work for Lili was that she was rarely bored.

Now in her twenties, she was no longer very happy at home unless she was doing something specifically with Walter. She didn't get on all that well with her parents; her father was constantly worried about his business and appeared to have little time for neither her brother nor her, and her mother always seemed to be preoccupied with one servant or another.

At home Lili was under constant pressure to meet men whom her parents approved of for the purpose of marriage. Lili was often requested to join her parents for dinners at home that just happened to be attended by prospective suitors. Sometimes it was requested that she accompany her parents to dinner parties, where it was hoped she would instantly fall into the arms of a suitor of her parents' dreams. One evening before such a request, Lili asked, "Mama, why do you always insist I meet these boring, unappealing men?"

Her mother, somewhat taken aback, replied, "Lili, you are already in your twenties; it is time you were married, and it is incumbent on your father and me to find you a suitable husband. What was wrong with Joseph?"

"Under no circumstances, Mama," Lili responded.

"And what about Thomas, whom you met the other night?"

"For goodness sake, Mama, he's middle-aged, boring, and only interested in making money…and in impressing you and Papa."

Lili's mother went on: "Thomas is a wonderful man, handsome, intelligent, from a very good home, and already a very successful businessman. And I saw the way he looked at you."

"Ya, bitte, Mama, he is not at all handsome, and he didn't even know that Eduard Strauss was Johannes Strauss's brother. I bet he doesn't know the difference between a waltz and a polka. Mama, I know you want the best for me, but I am really not interested in marrying just for the sake of family appearances and to produce an heir for some boring businessman, however well-to-do he might be. If I meet somebody I really want to be with then maybe…" Lili's voice trailed off as she turned her back on her mother and went to the piano to gain some reprieve. The two dachsies barked, Kafka louder than Bela, as they always did when they detected an argument.

4

VIENNA, JANUARY–JUNE 1932

DURING HIS FIRST few weeks in Vienna, Rudi spent a lot of time walking. He could barely believe his eyes most everywhere he looked. The churches, the government buildings, and the private mansions all seemed beautiful to him. The Stephansdom (St. Stephen's Cathedral) appeared an awesome structure, and by the time he walked around it a couple of times, all while looking up, he had a stiff neck. He was amazed by the palatial building that housed the Museum of Art History on the Ringstrasse. The former imperial palace, Schloss Schoenbrunn, took his breath away, and he vowed he'd be back soon to spend a decent amount of time there. He also admired the Vienna Opera House from the outside and wondered if it was as beautiful inside as the pictures he had seen indicated. *I will certainly have to see one opera in here, even if it breaks the bank,* he mused.

Rudi took a ride on the Ferris wheel, the Wiener Riesenrad, which afforded a wonderful view of the Donaukanal (Danube canal) and of most of Vienna to the southwest. His enjoyment of the experience was somewhat limited, as he felt a little queasy. *Why do I feel uneasy up here?* he reflected. *Perhaps I am not in control here; when I'm up in the mountains and skiing, I feel I'm very much in control. Jesus, I wish Franz were here; he wouldn't be edgy up here.*

Rudi made an effort to get to know Vienna a little bit before university got into full swing. Not being able to ski in Vienna, he thought he'd enjoy an hour or so ice skating. Early one morning he found himself at the Wiener Eislaufverein and wondered why there were so many photographers. He was quickly told that Eva Pawlik, an ice-skating prodigy, was training, and it would not be appreciated if he were to get in the way. Demonstrating single axels and giddying spins, this very young girl—who couldn't have been more than five or six years old, Rudi thought—put on quite a show, a quality of skating he had never seen from adults before. She didn't stay all that long, and Rudi was soon able to do a few jumps and spins of his own.

He had heard of the famous Spanish Riding School, so he wanted to have a look at the specially bred Lipizzaner stallions strut their stuff. And strut they did. He marveled at the carefully orchestrated maneuvers and the unbelievable discipline and training that the horses must endure. *They look in such wonderful condition; hopefully there is no overtraining or maltreatment to bring these animals to perform at such a level,* he reflected. He wandered around the Hofburg complex for a while admiring the various architectural styles and then ambled through the Burggarten and left via the Mozart Memorial to again find himself on the Ringstrasse.

On the way back to his shared apartmenton, he purchased a Wuerstel mit Senf from a street vendor and soon wished he had bought two. Perhaps he would have something else with his flatmate later that day when he was expected to return after a short winter vacation. The apartment was on Salzgasse at street level at the back of a restaurant building, accessible via an alley. A quiet apartment, it had a small kitchen open to the living space with a solid kitchen table also serving as the boys' study desk. There were three wooden chairs. A small window provided light and a view of a dreary narrow street. A table lamp afforded enough light at night. The bathroom was adequate and down a narrow hall, providing access to two small bedrooms. The best part: it was cheap, which was important, as both students came from nonwealthy families. Rudi's flatmate, Joseph, was in his second year studying law. University officials thought it benefi-cial for Rudi to share accommodation with a student who already had some knowledge of Vienna and the university and hence paired him up with Joseph. Joseph's previous flatmate had graduated and moved out in December.

Rudi was lying on his bed, half watching a fly that had taken refuge from the outside cold buzz around the ceiling. His mind wandered from one thing to another, and he was a little anxious about meeting his flatmate. *If things were as they were meant to be,* he thought, *I'd be sharing accommodation with Franz. I miss him so much, and I'm sure we'd just have a wonderful time together here in Vienna. I'd feel much more confident if he were here too. I wonder who this Joseph is, where he comes from, and what sort of a person he is. Will I like him? Will we get on together?*

Rudi would soon discover answers to some of his questions, for the banging of the front door indicated that Joseph had returned from his vacation. "Guten Tag. Ich bin Joseph."

"Pleased to meet you. I am Rudi. Did you have a pleasant trip?"

"Yes, thank you," replied Joseph. "I didn't come very far today, only from Salzburg, where I was for three days. My parents live in Munich. And where are you from?"

"I am from Kaernten, from Annenheim," replied Rudi.

"Oh, yes, I've heard of it; it's on the Ossiachersee, isn't it? I had a girlfriend once who used to go there on vacation," Joseph went on. "Are you hungry, by chance? I haven't eaten since this morning; I'd love to get a bite to eat."

Rudi was happy with that idea and, taking his jacket from the back of a chair, accompanied Joseph for less than a couple of blocks to a small, crowded restaurant. Joseph was a little shorter than Rudi and rather stockily built with a swarthy complexion and thick, dark-brown, wavy hair. He had an open disposition and a twinkle in his dark-brown eyes.

A waitress greeted Joseph by name and both quickly ordered. "Goulash mit extra Brot, bitte," Joseph requested, while Rudi ordered Knoedelsuppe. He thought it might warm him up, as he was feeling a bit cold. "Und zwei achterl rot," Joseph yelled after the waitress, who acknowledged the request with a smile and disappeared into the kitchen.

Rudi ended an awkward silence. "How did you like your first year at law school, Joseph?"

"Not bad…hm, quite good really. Some professors are truly excellent. Unfortunately I was pretty distracted for much of the year."

"How so?" enquired Rudi.

"You haven't heard? You are not Jewish, I suppose? You couldn't be, with that complexion."

"No," replied Rudi matter-of-factly, "I'm not Jewish."

"For us Jews it was really a pretty harrowing…a distressing year."

"I'm sorry to hear that," responded Rudi.

The food and wine arrived. "La Chaim," said Joseph.

"Zum wohl," responded Rudi, as they made eye contact and clinked glasses.

Joseph continued, "There has simply been increasing anti-Semitism in Vienna over recent years and especially so at the university. Nazi gangs have developed, and these thugs have taken to harassing, even beating, Jews on the street, in cafés, and especially within the confines of the university. They must have some organization behind them, as they produce propaganda leaflets and news sheets blaming the Jews for everything."

"What are they blaming them for?"

"These 'Hakenkreuzler,' or 'Brownshirts,' as they are called, are in reality jealous of the accomplishments of Jews, both within the university and within Vienna in general. Jews get blamed for the poor economic conditions, for the high unemployment rate, and anything else the Nazis are unhappy about. They are pretty unhappy about the interpretation of the news in the main Vienna press as well." Joseph paused to finish his goulash and to order two more glasses of wine. Rudi, somewhat astonished at what he was hearing, was keen for Joseph to continue. "You need to know too that a number of the university administrators are themselves Nazis or at least Nazi sympathisers. A couple of years ago, the senate of Vienna University ruled that the German student organization, the main group representing students at the uni, could ban all Jews from their organization. They wanted a pure Aryan race organization and forbade all Jews from belonging. Then in June of 1930, the Constitutional Court of Austria ruled this German student group to be unconstitutional on the grounds that it was against the principle of equal rights of all citizens."

"Ja, natuerlich," Rudi interjected as Joseph paused to take another sip.

Joseph was just getting into his stride as he noticed Rudi was a sympathetic listener. He continued, "The Nazis were outraged and again started harassing and beating up Jews. Matters only got worse. On November thirteenth last year, I'll never forget that date, the minister of education, in a session of the Budget Commission of Parliament, wanted to reintroduce the anti-Semitic rules via some special legislation. The chutzpah! Can you imagine the arrogance? Anyhow, the Social Democratic deputies on the Budget Commission warned the government against any such action to reinstate any anti-Semitic regulations. The reinstatement didn't happen, of course. But what do you think did happen? All hell broke loose in Vienna, all over the city. Anti-Jewish rioting was widespread; Jewish students were beaten on campus and some even thrown through classroom windows. Many were injured. There were demonstrations that condemned the Constitutional Court as a Jewish Constitutional Court."

As Joseph drew breath and had another sip, Rudi asked with a little concern, "Did you yourself get harassed or beaten at the uni, Joseph?"

"No, I kept out of the way, but I will join the Juedische Selbstwehr, the Jewish self-defence organization, if it actually gets set up.

Unbelievable, thought Rudi, thankful that his mother was likely ignorant of these developments in Vienna.

The two flatmates sat quietly for a further couple of minutes as they finished their wine. They shared the bill. "Pretty reasonable, I think," said Joseph. Rudi agreed. "I've been coming here at least once a week, as it's so close to home, and the food is quite good and cheap." Rudi again agreed. "I hope you didn't mind my telling you all this about the Nazis." Joseph went through the door, bidding the waitress "Gute Nacht."

They returned to the apartment, and Joseph immediately disappeared into his room. Less than a minute later he reemerged and placed a half-empty bottle on the table. "Marillenschnaps," he uttered. "Good to help you sleep," he added as he poured a little into two small glasses. "Sorry I haven't got a couple of brandy balloons. My previous flatmate was from Krems, and the speciality of this town is apparently Marillenschnaps," explained Joseph as he took a sip.

"Was he also a Jew?" asked Rudi.

"Yes, he was much like me, a mostly nonpracticing Jew, not particularly interested in religion. My parents are somewhat religious in that they observe basic Jewish traditions, but they only go to temple occasionally. You do not have to be religious to be a Jew. To be Jewish is to be part of a race. We share certain characteristics, such as cultural characteristics and attitudes that make us part of a race. Anyhow, my parents have been made increasingly aware of their Jewishness with the rise of the Nazis in Munich in recent times. Hitler has been making a huge push for power, and my parents know what his views are towards Jews. They are also aware that there has been a marked rise in anti-Semitism in their own community. Hitler has been going around the country giving fiery speeches blaming communists and Jews for the ills of Germany. He's been denouncing the competence of the present German government and claiming that only he, as leader, could return Germany to prosperity and international greatness."

"That sounds pretty scary; what actions against Jews have been actually happening in Munich on a day-to-day basis?" asked Rudi.

"As well as the increased propaganda of the NSDAP, the Nationalsozialistische Deutsche Arbeiterpartei, you can imagine a flood of pamphlets and pro-Nazi newspapers. There has also been an increasing number of attacks on the Jews in Munich. Windows have been broken in Jewish businesses, restaurants, and department stores, while boycotts against businesses owned by Jews are called for on a regular basis. Many citizens are beginning to believe that Jews are to blame for everything."

Rudi emptied the last drop of Schnaps. "Wasn't bad, huh?" responded Joseph as he got up and put his empty glass in the sink. "Goodnight, Rudi; it was nice to meet you today. Tomorrow it's back to uni. Shalom."

"I am pleased I met you too, Joseph. Goodnight."

—◦◦◦—

THERE WAS A buzz of excitement as new law students found their way in unfamiliar surroundings, moving from one lecture room to another, just a little uncertain as to whether they were in the right room at the right time. To be a student at Vienna University was, of course, quite special. It is the oldest university in the German-speaking world; the first university building opened in 1385. The buildings designed by architect Heinrich von Ferstel took their places proudly among the grand buildings of the Ringstrasse, reflecting the status of the capital, Vienna, and the social importance of academia. There was a great deal of positive energy as the new students from many different parts of Austria and beyond politely greeted one another as they commenced their journeys to becoming future members of the law profession.

Along with scores of other freshmen, Rudi heard about the importance of law, though there was not a universally accepted definition of it. He heard about the origin of laws, the distinction between religious laws and secular laws, and the importance of governments, legislatures, and constitutions in the establishment of laws. He heard about the distinction between criminal and civil law. Within civil law there were areas of property, contract, and trust law. There was constitutional, administrative, and international law. It was all beginning to sound somewhat dry, and Rudi's concentration was beginning to fade, when he heard the professor say something about the law raising issues of fairness, equality, and justice. *That's what I thought law was about,* Rudi admitted to himself. It was these concepts that emerged in his mind the previous night as he listened to Joseph describe the attacks to which Jews were being subjected.

The afternoon proved more interesting to Rudi, as new students were introduced to the various extracurricular organizations and clubs. He met a group of students who were part of the wrestling club, some representatives of the chess club, and the editor and a subeditor of the *Wiener Universitaet Zeitung* (*Vienna University Paper*). The editor of the paper seemed a friendly, cheerful fellow. He held out his hand. "Guten Tag. I am Heinrich, the editor of the uni Paper, and this is Thomas, one of the subeditors. Who are you?"

"Guten Tag. Ich bin Rudi."

Heinrich asked, "Do you have any particular interest in journalism, Rudi?" Before Rudi could answer, he continued, "We actually need people who can write about topical issues of substance and of interest to the student body as a whole. We have enough students who can report about the activities of the music club or results of sporting events. Do you write well, Rudi?"

"I'm certainly not a Goethe or Schiller, but I read the newspaper a lot, and I think I write generally in that style."

"That would be perfect. Reading the paper should keep you informed about what's happening in general and to be able to write as a news journalist would be ideal. That's just what we're looking for because two of our serious writers have graduated and have left to start their careers."

"I have a question, Heinrich," asked Rudi. "What sort of time commitment would my writing for the paper require?"

"Oh, you wouldn't have to make too much of a commitment, Rudi, just a few hours a week. We really look forward to you working with us. I realize you are new to Vienna, so you should become really familiar with the *Tagblatt*, the *Wiener Zeitung*, the *Krone*, and any other paper you wish, and we could discuss what sort of subjects you might like to focus on in a week or so. You could look at these and dozens of other newspapers at the Café Central on the Herrengasse, number fourteen, I think. Don't get sucked into a game of chess there unless you are very good. Or you could go to Café Rebhun near the Stephansplatz if you want to eavesdrop on local journalists. Don't know what sort of newspapers you can get hold of there though."

"Sounds good and thanks for the advice," Rudi replied. "Auf Wiedersehen, Heinrich. Auf Wiedersehen, Thomas."

—∞∞∞—

THE FOLLOWING DAY, somewhat tired from the morning lectures, Rudi found his way to Café Central. It was a quiet midafternoon. He hesitated before entering, then selected a table by the windows and near the door so he could observe the comings and goings. He noticed that the café occupied a grand, large space with high, vaulted ceilings supported by imposing stone columns. Large chandeliers overlooked the round, granite-topped tables. A waiter came to receive an order. "Eine Mélange, bitte, Herr Ober," Rudi requested.

"Dankeschoen," the waiter responded and disappeared.

Rudi found the collection of newspapers by the front entrance, took copies of the day's *Tagblatt* and the *Wiener Zeitung*, then returned to his table. The waiter returned with the ordered coffee and a glass of water. Rudi began to read and sip. He read that in recent weeks in Germany, the Nazi Party had organized a nationwide boycott of various companies owned by Jews, and that many restaurants, cafés, and hotels prevented Jews from entering. If Rudi doubted the stories Joseph had told him a couple of evenings earlier, he could no longer doubt them now. He also came across a small reference to the reemergence of anti-Jewish graffiti in various places in Leopoldstadt, the area of greatest concentration of Ostjuden (Eastern Jews) in Vienna.

Rudi so enjoyed his first experience in Café Central, especially the people-watching, that he returned on each of the next three afternoons. On one such afternoon he was curious as to what a group congregating around a table was up to, so he sidled over to observe a very intense game of chess watched by fifteen or so silent onlookers. He would not be drawn into playing against any of those people, he thought. Within the first week or so, Rudi also spent a few hours in the Café Rebhun, just near to the Stephansplatz. He found this café less grand and less international, catering mainly, it seemed, to local journalists. Prices were also less expensive. Over a coffee there he listened in on a conversation about the upcoming local elections throughout Austria. While he could not hear everything, Rudi could discern some snippets of the discussions. There seemed some speculation that the Nazis would likely make considerable electoral gains in April, at least in Vienna. They had expanded their operations and influence during the past couple of years, and Austria had also seen a resurgence in anti-Semitism following a quieter period during the previous decade.

When Rudi got home that evening, he relayed the conversation he had overheard in Café Rebhun to Joseph. "Yes, I'm pretty sure that the Nazis will significantly increase their political influence in the April elections, at least here in Vienna. I am curious as to how widespread their influence will be throughout Austria though," responded Joseph. "And I expect that following the elections, the Nazis and their sympathizers will increase their activities against Jews at the uni. There could be disruptions as there were at the end of last year. I hope it doesn't get any worse than that." After a pause he continued, "And what have you been up to in addition to attending lectures, Rudi?"

"I met with the editor of the uni newspaper, and he wants me to write some substantive pieces that would have a broad appeal to the students."

"Excellent. Have you got any ideas as to what you might write about?" Without Rudi having time to answer, Joseph went on, "You could write about the advertising campaigns the major political parties are engaging in before the elections. Or you could also see what campaigns will be waged at the uni. I could help you with getting information within the school. I know quite a lot of politically active people."

Rudi thought about these and other possibilities. "It would certainly be interesting to follow activities at the uni leading up to the elections, but I wouldn't want to get into any disputes or fights. I wouldn't want to be beaten up by some nasty Hakenkreuzler."

"You should have no concern of that sort," Joseph said, chuckling. "I'd come to your defence. Anyway you would be working as a journalist for the uni paper and just collecting facts and students' views. I think that'd be great. You should do that."

Rudi wasn't so sure; he'd sleep on it and discuss it with the editor in a few days.

———

HE FOUND IT difficult to sleep that night, not sure whether it was the cold or his concerns that kept him awake.

"That's a great idea, Rudi," responded Heinrich when he spoke with his editor the following week. "I can introduce you to a number of politically active students. They would all love to tell you how superior their political viewpoint is over all others. You could write a comparative piece detailing the various support structures and advertising plans that exist for each of the major parties. I think many students and members of the faculty too would be interested in that. Yes, Rudi, that would be excellent!"

Some weeks went by with Heinrich, Thomas, Joseph, and Rudi all promising to keep their ears to the ground to ascertain the best sources of information. Rudi had also developed a liking for the café life and returned, nearly daily, to the cafés where he had previously gone. He also visited Café Louvre. Not far from the Ringstrasse and the university, at the corner of Wipplingerstrasse and Renngasse, it was a small, modest, unpretentious sort of a place with inexpensive and good food. One of the students had recommended it. When Rudi was hungry he would return there for a schnitzel.

On one such evening, walking into the café, he found himself talking with some stranger, who introduced himself as Friedrich and who led him to a large table in a booth overlooking Renngasse.

Both had no sooner finished their schnitzel, with barely an additional word being spoken, when five or six men entered and sat around the table. They all knew each other except Rudi, who was the youngest and a stranger. He certainly felt strange. He introduced himself, stating that he was at the uni, writing for its paper and researching the various political party groups to see what preparations they were making for the upcoming Austrian elections in April. Rudi had no sooner finished when a huge man wearing a large-brimmed Stetson walked over and sat at the head of the table, where a seat had been left vacant. Beers, wine, and some delectable finger foods were soon brought to the table by Herr Ober, whom most people seemed to know.

An animated discussion proceeded for the next several hours. Friedrich leaned over to Rudi and whispered in his ear, "That is Mr. Best, Mr. Robert Best, and we are at his Stammtisch." Rudi nodded a thank-you, well understanding the meaning of "Stammtisch" as a reserved table but not having a clue as to the significance of Mr. Best. Feeling completely out of his depth, Rudi concentrated very hard on looking intelligent and engaged, but he understood very little of the discussions. In varied and with some terrible German accents, they discussed matters regarding the Balkans, Germany, the Catholic Church, business and international currency changes, and the US dollar. Everyone was so involved and animated that Rudi was pretty certain no one would ask him to participate in the discussion. Yet he was still a little nervous that someone might.

A couple of hours after the discussion started, several more people, including women and children, came in, shaking off snow that still remained on their clothes despite having already hung up their coats. Having noticed that Rudi wasn't all that comfortable, Friedrich nudged him, and they left with several "Gute Nachts."

It was snowing heavily as they stepped outside, putting on their coats, when Friedrich asked, "Can you come tomorrow at five? I have a proposition for you. Let's take one of those tables." He pointed in the direction of a number of small, round, marble-topped tables in the middle of the café. "Servus, Rudi, bis Morgen," said Friedrich, and he left.

Rudi pulled his coat collar up as high as it would go and headed towards home. The wind was driving the snow; the roadside gas lamps were swaying. An eerie feeling came over him. He looked over his shoulder. Nobody was to be seen except for a young couple, holding hands and skipping across the snow. He held his head down to shield his face from the snow but found it difficult to walk in the ankle-deep snow, as his were really dry-weather shoes. They were now filled with snow; his feet were wet and cold.

As he trudged homeward, he wondered, *Who were all those people at that table and that American man dominating the conversation? Was he a journalist? Was he possibly the head of an investigation group? I understood so little of the conversation taking place around me for most of the evening that I don't understand the relationships that existed at all. I felt like a fish out of water. And what sort of proposition could Friedrich possibly have for me?*

When Rudi arrived at his apartment, he shook the snow off on the doorstep, kicked his shoes against the doorjamb, and hurried inside. "Shalom, Rudi. There's a bit of a storm out there now. You look cold," said Joseph as he disappeared, only to return nearly instantly with that unfinished bottle of Marillenschnaps and two glasses. Rudi described the events of the evening in detail, ending with Friedrich's forthcoming proposition, while Joseph listened intently and poured the liquor. Joseph looked at Rudi knowingly, a smile appearing on his face, and he took a sip.

"What do you make of it?" asked Rudi impatiently.

"I can't be sure, of course, but I suspect Friedrich wants you to get information for him that he can't get himself. He probably wants insider information about uni political activities. He'd likely want to know what the Deutsche Studentenschaft is planning or perhaps even the Nazi Party. A pamphleteering campaign, distributing terrible lies, would be normal, but what more aggressive tactics might these Aryan, Jew-haters be planning? Would they possibly intimidate citizens on the street? Would they work in collusion to breaking windows of Jewish businesses, setting some buildings on fire, disrupting lectures by Jewish professors, disrupting prayer meetings in Leopoldstadt, or even storming the Social Democrats' headquarters? That sort of information would surely sell copy. And if you'd provided any such information and were found out, you'd be in deep shit...in real deep shit. I'd be in deep shit too; I am your flatmate, and I'm a Jew, and everybody knows I'm a Jew."

Rudi's jaw dropped. "Well, I don't have to tell Friedrich anything. I can tell him I have changed my mind, that my uni workload has become too heavy."

"Sleep on it, Rudi. We can talk about it more tomorrow. It's already very late. Goodnight."

Rudi took the last sip of Schnaps and retired. But he could not sleep. He also couldn't get the whole scenario out of his mind. *Why shouldn't I find out what these right-wing Nazi types are planning?* he began wondering. *What have they all got against Jews like Joseph? He's a very decent human being. And what have they got against Mr. Birnbaum and his family? They also seem like very good, ordinary people. It just isn't right that one group of people should have it in so badly for another group of and wish them harm. Worse—actually want to do them harm or drive them out of their own communities and their own homes. That just isn't right or fair. These thugs need to be exposed. Yes, I should get as much information as to what these Nazis are planning as possible, and it should be made public.*

Rudi found himself tossing and turning. He wasn't sure whether it was because he was cold or because he was still all wound up following the evening's events. He put on a pair of socks and pulled the covers up over his ears. He was determined he would uncover as much as he could about the Nazis' planning and share it with Friedrich. This determination, however, set off another series of worrying thoughts. *What would happen if the Nazis were to suspect or actually find out that I was the informant? They'd probably belt the shit out of me. What would they do to Joseph? I can't have my actions put his safety in jeopardy. God, and if my mother ever found out I was involved in such activity, she'd not only be furious, she could have a heart attack...really she could. And Dad? He'd be furious that I wasn't concentrating on my studies and even more furious that I was causing Mother such grief.*

Rudi nodded off for a while—but only a while. His mind again began to race. *I so wish Franz were still alive. I miss him so much, and his parents must still be in a terrible state. It just isn't fair. One minute you are having a wonderful time, the next you are dead. That's just not fair. I thought God was fair. No wonder I don't believe in God. I couldn't believe in a God that wasn't fair. And these Nazi bastards aren't fair either; they need to be exposed. I'm determined. They need to be exposed.* Rudi finally fell asleep.

———

A CALL OF "Rudi, Fruehstick" woke him up. He put on his coat and joined Joseph in the kitchen. There was a wonderful aroma of freshly brewed coffee and toast.

"Close the door, Rudi; let's keep the warmth in here. Did you sleep well?"

"Ja, for a few minutes," Rudi answered sarcastically. "And you?"

"I slept like a bear," he replied cheerfully. As Joseph plopped a sugar cube in his coffee and began to stir, he asked, "Well, what have you decided?"

Without hesitation Rudi responded, "I have no choice. God is not fair. The world is not fair. The Nazis are not fair. Decent human beings have to do whatever they can to make the world fairer than it is. Those Hakenkreuzler thugs need to be exposed for what they are planning. If some of their dastardly plans can be thwarted, we have to try. Decent people deserve to know who their enemy is, what threats they are under, what danger they might be in."

"You realize you'd be seen as the snitch and likely to be beaten up badly," Joseph cautioned.

"Yes, I realize that," said Rudi. "I had plenty of time to think about it overnight. Perhaps I should move out of this apartment so that you would be left alone. I wouldn't want you to be harassed or beaten, Joseph."

"Don't worry, Rudi, you are doing the right thing, and I'll have all the protection I'll need from the Juedische Selbstwehr. Anyway I'm enjoying the company of a good goy," he said, smiling.

RUDI ARRIVED AT the Café Louvre at about a quarter of an hour before the proposed meeting. He had wondered all night what the proposition might be that Friedrich had for him. He was still wondering now. Rudi hung up his coat and noticed that it was rather quiet. He selected a table in the middle as had been requested. Herr Ober, whom Rudi recognized from the previous evening, came quickly and took Rudi's order for a beer. When he returned, Rudi engaged the ober in conversation. "Excuse me, can you please tell me who Mr. Robert Best is whom you served last night? I was sitting at his table but..."

The waiter, cutting Rudi off with a chuckle, explained, "Ja, Mr. Best is the most well-known person in here at this time, and he has been so for many years. He is an American journalist with a big body and a big persona and with a terrible German accent, and you sat at his Stammtisch. He occupies this table, reserved for him, many afternoons but definitely every night. Journalists from all over the world come to this table. They share news and gossip with one another for many hours each day. Often in the evenings the wives and children of some journalists come to have dinner or just some snacks after dinner. He is well known here."

Just then Friedrich arrived at the table and ordered a beer as the waiter was about to leave. "Ja, guten Abend, Rudi. How are you?"

"Guten Abend, Friedrich. You are right on time," responded Rudi.

Both took a deep draught of beer, and Friedrich asked, "What did you make of yesterday evening?"

"Not much. I was pretty much lost," replied Rudi. "How do you know Mr. Best?"

Friedrich said much the same as the waiter had moments earlier. "I work as a freelancer, selling my stories to whoever is willing to pay for them, the British or the American press. I come to Mr. Best's Stammtisch quite regularly to get news and ideas for stories. When you said what you were doing at the uni, I immediately thought you might like to earn a few extra schillings for providing me with information I cannot get myself."

"What sort of information, Friedrich?"

"With elections about to take place in April, there will be the various political parties at the uni developing campaigns to help get their person elected. You could find out what the main ideas are that each party is putting forward, you could discover the accusations that parties wish to use against their opposition, and you may even be able to find out who is funding them. That sort of information could be valuable to me…and I'd be willing to pay for it. What do you think, Rudi?"

Rudi was trying to size up Friedrich and wondered what he might be getting himself into. He didn't know Friedrich, only met him yesterday evening, and shared little else other than a big appetite when it comes to schnitzel. Rudi replied, "That sort of information is what I want to write about for the uni paper, and I will start next week meeting student officials to find out as much as I can regarding their work in preparation for the elections. If I find the sort of information you might like, I can pass it on to you. I know where to find you."

"Sounds good, Rudi. I'm looking for information you can only get from the inside. Till I hear from you, then. I must away. I'm in a hurry. Guten Abend."

Rudi returned the greeting, sat back in his chair, and thought about the task he was contemplating for himself: *I am definitely going through with this. I can do this, though I've never done this sort of thing before. It is actually important to establish what the political groups are planning, and the people ought to know. They actually have a right to know. I especially want to know what the Deutsche Studentenschaft and the Nazis are planning. One thing is certain—they are up to no good. I hope I'll be taken seriously; the students I'll be speaking with are mainly from Vienna, and I'm from the country. What questions could I ask them? They'll probably laugh at me. I guess we'll see.*

IT WAS EARLY in March 1932, and Heinrich, the uni paper editor, took Rudi around to introduce him to leaders of the university's political groups. He introduced Rudi to Paul and Guenther from the Christian Socialist Party then unexpectedly excused himself and said he'd return in an hour and a half. Rudi felt very nervous and ill at ease for a moment. Paul and Guenther were curious as to what he wanted to write. "Well," said Rudi, "I want to write a piece that informs the students, and possibly even some faculty, how the different political groups at the uni are involved in the lead-up to the elections in April, how they think their candidates will fare, and what their thinking is regarding other political parties." Rudi was relieved; he'd actually got out what he'd wanted to say without stammering or stuttering. With eagerness and a little apprehension, he awaited their response.

Paul looked across at Guenther, who nodded to indicate Paul should respond. "Ja, of course our Christian Socialist Party is very strong here in Vienna, and the party machine is very active in promoting our candidates. We will be distributing leaflets in all the neighbourhoods to inform the Viennese of their best choice."

Guenther took over: "We are their only choice, really. I mean the Social Democrats are godless and Jewish Bolshevists; they are dominated by Marxists."

"Who is their leader?" Rudi asked.

"Can't think of his name, but he's a Jew," continued Paul. "Austrians are a Christian people—they are Catholics; they are sensible people. You will see, after the elections, the Christian Socialist Party will form the government, and Engelbert Dollfuss will be chancellor. You will see, Rudi."

Just then Heinrich returned and said, "Come, Rudi, we need to meet with the Social Democrat leadership in five minutes."

Paul asked Rudi whether he had obtained the information he wanted and wished him well for his writing project. "Ja, dankeschoen, Paul, dankeschoen, Guenther. Auf Wiedersehen."

They went down the corridor, took a left turn then a right turn, and Heinrich knocked on the door of the small room occupied by the Social Democratic Party leadership. "Herrein." Heinrich and Rudi were invited inside a cluttered office; there were dozens of boxes on the desk, chairs, and floor. There was a map of Vienna on the back wall with posters covering up a window to prevent inquisitive people on the outside from looking in. Two chairs were quickly emptied of boxes, and Rudi and Heinrich were beckoned to sit down.

"Servus, Heinrich, how are you? So this is the Rudi you told me about. Hello, Rudi, good to meet you. I am Jeremy; Adam will join us shortly. You want to know what preparations we are making for the elections in April, ja?" Jeremy made eye contact with Rudi for the first time.

"Yes, that's right, Jeremy."

"Well, we have a problem on our hands in that the comparative number of our supporters is shrinking. There are fewer Jews in Vienna now than there were a few years ago. On the other hand, the Jews have no other party to vote for. There is also a rise in anti-Semitism as the pro-Nazi groups are gaining support here, especially following the growth of anti-Semitism in Germany. Ja, what to do? There is a problem. We have to prove to the people that we have everybody's interests at heart."

"And how will you do that?" interrupted Heinrich, getting a little impatient while Rudi was content to just listen.

"We need to have a clear message and to get it out to as many people as possible. We need to show all the working people that we are the only party for them. The Christian Social Party is dominated by Catholics. We will have a very strong representation in the news-papers. Jews, of course, dominate the newspapers, so we have a clear advantage we must make use of."

Just then Adam came in, introduced himself, and, having heard some of the conversation, added, "The Nazi Party is gaining strength and will likely use scare tactics and intimidation. Ja, Rudi, you weren't here last year when the Deutsche Studentenschaft and Nazi thugs from outside rioted against Jewish students and Jewish professors. And there were a lot of Nazis intimidating people in shops, in cafés, and on the streets."

"This seems to have settled down quite a lot, has it not?" asked Rudi.

He wanted to ask if they feared Nazi intimidation leading up to the elections, when Adam continued, "You wait and see, Rudi; there will likely be a great deal of intimidation and coercion leading up to the elections." Adam glanced at Jeremy and asked Rudi if he had any more questions. Rudi hesitated long enough for Adam to continue, "I found something for you, Rudi, some advice from my sage, Karl Marx. Marx said, 'The writer must earn money in order to be able to live and to write, but he must by no means live and write for the purpose of making money.' Not sure what it means, but I thought you would like it."

"Thank you," responded Rudi. "You have been very helpful." The four men stood up and shook hands, then Heinrich and Rudi departed and parted, as Heinrich needed to get back to his office.

What nice people Jeremy and Adam are, thought Rudi. *I wonder if there is any special meaning for me in Marx's words.* He unfolded the piece of paper on which Adam had written the quote. Rudi wanted to reflect on what he had heard and take some notes. He wandered out of the uni grounds and took a leisurely stroll to Café Central, where he knew he could find a quiet corner. He would have preferred to have sat in a desserted area of a park, but the weather was rather cold, although it was not raining or snowing at the moment.

He ordered ein Kaffee mit Schlagobers and took out his notebook and pencil. The cold, sweet, luscious cream contrasted wonderfully with the strong, hot, aromatic coffee. The first sip left Rudi with a white moustache. He used his tongue a little like a windscreen wiper and wiped his mouth with a linen napkin. He began to write. Rudi sat for more than an hour, reflecting and writing. When he looked up, he noticed that the café had filled up quite a lot from when he had come in, mainly young people coming in for a drink and chat on their way from work. Rudi felt satisfied with his meetings that day but was beginning to feel uneasy about meeting representatives of the uni's Deutsche Studentenschaft in the morning.

RUDI HAD A decidedly restless night, including a really disturbing dream in which he was thrown through a lecture room window by a couple of burly thugs shouting obscenities at him and others.

At 10:00 a.m. precisely, he arrived at the door, slightly ajar and clearly marked "Deutsche Studentenschaft." There was yelling on the inside. He heard, "We must create a lot of disturbance in Leopoldstadt."

"No, that will only backfire."

"Yes, we must beat the shit…they have to be discouraged to vote."

"No."

"Yes."

"Yes, intimidation works."

Rudi was having second thoughts about this meeting and considering making a hasty retreat, when a young, tall, blond man, with his hair slicked back and wearing a brown shirt, arrived from down the corridor, pushed the door open, and said, "You must be Rudi; we are expecting you. Come and meet Otto and Manfred. I am from the Nazi Party, and it was not easy for me to get here. I had to do a lot of fast talking and bribe a guard to make it in."

Inside, Otto and Manfred, both tall and light-skinned, were red in the face and wearing brown shirts. Rudi noticed that Manfred wore large, lace-up boots.

The office was well lit with little room to move, as there were many boxes stacked on the floor. The window was pasted over with posters. Rudi had seen this much before. A quick glance told a different story. There were cartoons on the window, a wall lampooning Jews, and a prominent poster of Hitler. A dagger was stuck in a cartoon on a wall. There was another framed photo of Hitler on the desk along with several swastika armbands and rubber truncheons on top of what appeared to be a German flag.

"Sit, Rudi. This is Otto, and I am Manfred. And Klaus brought you in. He is from the Partei. You look like a perfect Aryan specimen, Rudi. We could have you working for us." Rudi smiled nervously. "Well, what do you want from us? We hear you will write an article for the uni paper, ja?"

"Ja," replied Rudi. "I think the students and some of the faculty will be very interested in the candidates, platforms, and plans that the various political parties have in the lead-up to the elections."

Otto looked at Manfred, and they both looked at Klaus. There was a long pause. Klaus began, "You realize we are all ultimately working toward Austrian integration with Germany, an expanded Lebensraum for the superior German people, including most Austrians. Hitler said, 'Our objective must be to bring our territory into harmony with the numbers of our population.' We are working very hard to make this happen much sooner than people think. Hitler has inspired us to bring this to fruition. He is the only person with real leadership qualities."

Rudi raised his hand a little and asked a question: "What are the Fuehrer's leadership qualities, Klaus?"

"Oh, there are so many fine qualities our Fuehrer has," Klaus swooned. "He has a wonderful intellect; he's a visionary, so wise and with a special understanding of what Germans want and deserve. We will expand the Lebensraum for the Aryan peoples of the world—a world for people like you and us, Rudi. There is no place for any inferior beings." Rudi began to feel a lump forming in his throat and was not yet game to ask another question.

"Yes, we must get rid of all that scum who are living in Leopoldstadt. These vermin make lots of children and lots of garbage. If we got rid of all these Ostjuden, there'd be enough housing for the real Austrians, and we would go a long way to solving the poverty problem. All we would then have to do is to get rid of the wealthy capitalist Jew pigs who are thieves and swindlers, depriving the real Germans of what they deserve. We will achieve both these objectives."

Rudi raised his finger again, indicating another query. "There are so many Jews in Leopoldstadt; how will you get them to leave?"

Klaus glanced across at Manfred. "You are the expert in these matters, Manfred. You can share your plans with Rudi."

"Ja, selbstverstaendlich! We must make it very clear to these pigs from the East that they are not welcome in Leopoldtadt or anywhere else in Vienna or in Austria for that matter."

"Or anywhere else in the world?" probed Rudi.

"Ja, or anywhere else in the world! These Ostjuden are the scum of the earth and drag down the living standards and dignity of all good people. We must encourage them to leave, nicht wahr, Otto?"

"Of course we must," Otto confirmed emphatically.

"How do you plan to do that exactly?" asked Rudi quietly, again trying to remain calm and to gain greater details.

"They make our lives very uncomfortable, so we must fight fire with fire."

"Ja, fire is a very good word," added Manfred. "If our pamphlets and newspapers cannot convince them, if some broken windows cannot convince them, if some broken skulls cannot convince them, then we have to apply real heat. Ha, ha, ha."

Otto took over again enthusiastically: "The best way to get rats out of their burrows is to smoke them out. We will light some fires, smoke them out. They will end up squealing and running in all directions. They will tumble over each other to get out. So!"

Rudi, recognizing a pause and a chance to glean still more information, turned the conversation to the well-established, well-assimilated professional Jews who came from the West and now largely dominated the arts, the newspapers, and the medical and law professions. How would those people be encouraged to leave?

Klaus moved a little forward in his chair and crossed one hand over the other on the desk. "This is a more difficult problem," he began quietly. "While these Jews have been here a long time, that just means that they've been cheats, liars, and scoundrels for a longer period of time. This must be made clear to the Austrian people through means of superior argument in well-distributed pamphlets. They will understand; they are an intelligent people. If we are mistaken, and it is possible for us, on a rare occasion, to be mistaken, and they prove to be not more intelligent than the Ostjuden, then we must use the same strategies appropriate for the Ostjuden. Simple."

At that moment Rudi wished he could disappear into the cracks between the floorboards, when he was suddenly put on the spot: "What do you think of these Jews, Rudi? You have said nothing."

Rudi's heart began to pound so heavily he was sure all could hear it. It was in danger of bursting through his chest, he thought. An inner voice suggested some caution: *I could agree with these extreme right-wing sentiments and just act out a lie,* he thought. *That would not cause any difficulties…No, I cannot do that; it is not within me. I believe in the inherent goodness of man; all men are created equal, and there is a funda-mental need for society to be egalitarian.* Rudi noticed three pairs of eyes burning into him. He turned bright red in the face, gulped to clear his throat, and replied slowly, quietly, and deliberately, "All human beings deserve to have a roof over their—"

"Ha, ha, ha, are you—" came an interjection.

"Quiet, please, and let me answer," Rudi said, raising his voice for just a moment. He sat bolt upright, glared, and paused. At that very moment he feared he might get one of those truncheons lying on the table smashed across his head. He looked directly into three sets of eyes.

"You asked me a question, and I want to answer. You deserve the truth. All people deserve the truth. You and I deserve a roof over our heads, and all other human beings do too. None of us is perfect."

Rudi stopped short as the other three all stood up in unison as if on command. They looked at one another. "Jew lover," someone hissed.

"Jew lover!" someone yelled.

"Raus, raus, sofort raus," was blurted out with ascending volume and pitch.

"Be very careful what you write in that paper!"

There was a three-part chorus of "Heil Hitler" as three arms shot in the air in a salute. Rudi needed no further encouragement to leave, and he marched out, on the double, looking over his shoulder, his heart pounding even more furiously. He could hear "asshole, asshole" several times as he disappeared around the nearest corner.

Phew, I've never wanted to get out of a situation so badly. How can such people operate inside a university? How much support for such an element could there be here within the administration?

———

IT WAS NOT yet lunchtime, and Rudi was exhausted. What an ordeal. He walked past the Rathauspark and the Volksgarten around the Ringstrasse and looked up at the Mozart Memorial after entering the Burggarten. He sat on a bench just to the left of the large statue. It was cold and very quiet; only a few people wandered about and a young couple, fifty metres or so away, canoodled. *I can't believe what happened this morning. How can people think of themselves as so superior and have such disregard for other people? Were they born like that, or did their parents give them such a warped sense of values?* After a long pause, during which he might even have nodded off for a moment, he thought.

Rudi fell asleep on the bench despite the cold. He woke up cold with a parched throat, a slight headache, and some hunger. He looked around; a couple of tourists were examining a map, but all the locals would have returned to work by then. He left the park the same way as he entered and bought a Wuerstel mit Senf at the very popular Wuerstelstand. Rudi took one bite and walked back to the same bench he had occupied only minutes earlier. One Wuerstel wasn't really enough; perhaps he'd have another one later. He opened his notebook and wrote for half an hour or so, reliving the events of the morning. He began to feel cold again. It was now approaching midafternoon; the sun was behind the trees in the park, and a breeze added to the chill in the air.

Rudi left the park, looking over his shoulder and wondering whether anyone had followed him that afternoon or would do so in the coming days. He wound his way home through relatively quiet streets, threw his notebook and pencil on the table, fell on his bed, and fell asleep.

RUDI WOKE FROM the sound of the door closing and someone whistling an unfamiliar melody. A rather joyous Joseph met him in the kitchen, picked up a pencil that had rolled onto the floor, and asked excitedly, "Well, how was it?"

Understanding perfectly what he was asking about, Rudi rubbed his eyes, smiled, and gave a bit of a shrug. "You know, if these three I met today were pillars of the Aryan race, I'd rather be a bloody Jew."

They both laughed. Joseph pulled up a chair while Rudi opened the window momentarily and took two beers from the sill. Joseph reached behind him and put two glasses on the table. They poured their beers, looked at each other, and both burst out laughing. "You know, Rudi, you're a real Mensch."

"You're a good bloke too, Joseph, especially if you can get me to join the Juedische Selbstwehr. After today I think I might need it."

Rudi gave Joseph a blow-by-blow account of what had transpired at the meeting. "Oy vey, you know, Rudi, I don't think they'll want to mess with you, not by their response when you told them to be quiet and listen. You were really strong. I think they'll keep out of your way. They don't know your political leanings except that you're a humanist. You will, of course, have to be careful what you write in your article. As long as you write a well-balanced piece, no one will love you, and no one will hate you. I wouldn't write about any threat to Leopoldstadt that you overheard the discussion about, but I will warn my sources, and they will take precautions."

"Thank you for your feedback and confidence, Joseph, but I wouldn't want to find myself alone in a dark alley with those three thugs."

RUDI HAD BEEN attending his lectures but had fallen behind with his reading somewhat. This day he'd be doing some catching up. He attended two lectures in the morning and spent all the afternoon in the library, where he chose a quiet table so that he would have good light and be able to look out the window directly ahead.

He was making quite good headway with his research when he suddenly felt a chill at his back, convinced someone was watching him. He swiveled around quickly. There was no one. After another hour or so he had the same uneasy feeling of someone being behind him. He could feel a set of eyes boring into the back of his skull. His heart jumped into his mouth. He swiveled around so abruptly that he knocked a book onto the floor and hit his knee against the table on the way around. There was nobody. Rudi took a couple of deep breaths, pushed some books across to the window side of the table, picked up his book on the floor, and sat down with his back to the window. His body cast a shadow across what he was reading, but he would now notice if anyone were to approach him.

He had finished with one book and found another one boring, so he walked to the shelves to find a more relevant reference. He was reading from the table of contents of the book *Main Problems in Theory of Public Law* by Hans Kelsen when he became aware of a conversation at the back of the shelves. He was out of sight but not out of earshot. A reference to Leopoldstadt got Rudi's attention.

Voice one said, "Do you really think we should smash all those windows?"

Voice two replied, "Of course…scare the shit out of them. We'll go at three in the morning. The seven of us could do quite well. Five windows each in two minutes then get out o' there—fast. We don't want to have to smash anyone's head in."

"We need to coordinate our time of strike and which buildings to attack."

"Jawohl, and do this at least two weeks before, so those scum Jews will make the right decision and not vote."

"Should we target possible polling places?"

There was no answer to this question, as a librarian ordered, "Kein Sprechen, bitte."

The voices disappeared. Rudi cleared his throat, which he had delayed doing for some minutes, and headed back to his table. Just ahead of him two students turned right as Rudi was about to turn left to his table. He got a glimpse of one of them. *That is Manfred,* he thought. *Pretty sure. I recognize his high lace-up boots. Why did I not recognize his voice? Perhaps because he was whispering in here. What anti-Semitic bastards, planning to harass, to intimidate these people, to break property. I am glad I'm not a Jew. I hope Joseph knows the right people to inform about these plans.*

SEVERAL WEEKS WENT by with lectures, library work, and assignments to complete. There were a further couple of informative conversations overheard about plans leading up to the elections. One conversation was obviously among some Catholic religious types sitting at the back of a lecture theatre a couple of rows behind Rudi. In hushed tones, it related to developing some strong letters and articles for the press depicting the Social Democrats as godless Bolshevists dominated by Marxists and led by Jews—a concoction not to be trusted.

There was another partial conversation that Rudi heard just a couple of days before among three people with a reference to Jews at prayer being surprised. There had been acts of violence against Jews at prayer in the past, so he knew that this sort of even vague threat needed to be taken seriously, for a number of riots had occurred at synagogues, including one on Schmelzhof Street.

Rudi also read the daily newspapers extensively to help with the construction of his article. He had been thinking about it quite a lot and would write it in the next couple of days. Rudi was now also ready to meet with Friedrich, whom he had met at Café Louvre, to share with him what he knew of the major political groups' plans prior to the elections, now about three weeks away.

THOUGH IT WAS already the end of March, the soft warmth of spring had not yet arrived, and Rudi was feeling rather hungry, although it was several hours before his normal dinner time. He decided to get to Café Louvre an hour or so prior to finding Friedrich to allow himself time to eat. As he approached the corner of Renngasse and Wipplingerstrasse, he was beginning to feel somewhat cold and hoping the weather would not turn as nasty as it was when he was last there, caught with his summer shoes trudging through snow on the way home. As he entered Café Louvre, he did a 360-degree pivot and noted that no one was following as far as he could tell. He hung up his coat on the coat stand and sat at a table that allowed him to see people entering the café. Herr Ober came over and asked, "Sie sind, Rudi, Ja?"

"Ja, ich bin Rudi."

Herr Ober continued, "Friedrich left a message a few days ago that he was going away to Germany and would not be back here in Vienna until tomorrow. He expects to be here at the café from six o'clock. He wanted me to let you know if you were to come here to see him."

"Oh, thank you, Herr Ober. I had wanted to meet Friedrich, but I'll stay and have something to eat anyway." Herr Ober returned with a menu and two minutes later with a beer. Rudi ordered ein Schnitzel, took a sip of beer, opened his notebook, and began to write. *I may as well make a start with the article now*, he thought. He wrote a sentence, crossed it out, and wrote another. He wasn't in the mood for writing; he had prepared himself for a discussion with Friedrich. The schnitzel arrived, and Rudi ordered another beer. They must have intuited the extent of his hunger because his Schnitzel overlapped his plate, and the potato salad resembled a mountain. *The Grossglockner,* he mused as he began to make inroads into this more-than-ample meal. He thoroughly enjoyed dinner and left before the evening rush.

Rudi was pleased to find Joseph home. Neither of them felt like doing any uni work that evening, so they decided to go to the cinema. They had hoped to see Charlie Chaplin's *City Lights*, which had been released recently and received excellent reviews. It was unfortunately not showing that day, so they opted to see *Keine Feier ohne Meyer* (*Without Meyer, No Celebration Is Complete*), a German comedy directed by Carl Boese. It is about a Jewish man who presents himself as a successful businessman in order to marry a girl from an upper-class family. Her father is impressed but she loves somebody else. Meyer "cocks-up" a number of situations, yet ends up happily with his secretary who has always loved him.

———

THE NEXT DAY at 6:30 p.m. Rudi found himself back at Café Louvre. He recognized Friedrich immediately at a table where they had met previously. They shook hands, sat down, and each ordered a glass of beer. "Sorry I was not here when you came to see me yesterday; Herr Ober told me you had been here. I was in Munich, meeting with some journalists to see what they could tell me about any plans to influence the elections here in Vienna."

"Did you get any valuable information?" asked Rudi.

"I heard very little except that the Nazi Party will be sending reinforcements to support their comrades here in Vienna. It was not worth my trip to Munich, really. And what were you able to learn from your activities within the uni?"

Rudi paused for a moment, wondering how much he should divulge and what assurance Friedrich would give him that he would not be identified as a source. Friedrich detected that Rudi was ill at ease. "Rudi, I give you my word that no one will know the source of the information you will share with me. You can have Mr. Best vouch for my integrity. He's at his table right now. I saw him come in just a couple of minutes ago."

Rudi responded, "All right, but if I get beaten up by those Hakenkreuzler thugs—"

"Don't worry, Rudi. No one knows me, and no one has seen us together or overheard any of our conversations."

Rudi looked slowly around the café; Friedrich then felt obliged to do the same. They nodded to Herr Ober to bring another couple of beers. He did after a minute or so of silence. Rudi then recounted each of the conversations he overheard and the conversations he was a part of with the Christian Social Party, the Social Democrats, and the Deutsche Studentenschaft with a Nazi Party representative participating.

"How did the Nazi Party guy gain entry into the uni?" asked Friedrich.

"No idea, except he said something about it having been difficult," replied Rudi. Friedrich asked many other questions, especially ones requiring Rudi to repeat himself because Friedrich was more than a little surprised at how much incriminating information he had gained, especially from the Nazi three. Friedrich empathized with Rudi being somewhat wary and nervous about being followed by Nazi hooligans, and they exchanged smiles.

"The plans against the Jews, especially the Ostjuden, should, of course, be made known to them," Rudi emphasized. "Any decent human being who becomes aware of such plans has the moral responsibility, if not the duty, to divulge them to the group in danger, don't you think?"

"Yes," Friedrich agreed after a brief pause.

Rudi went on, "Then there is a timing issue for when your article is published in relation to the time the Jewish authorities are warned of the plans against them."

"Ja, natuerlich," Friedrich agreed.

"I have already given this matter some thought and have discussed it with a Jewish friend who is well connected with the appropriate authorities in Leopoldstadt. The authorities must be warned and have sufficient time to put preventive measures into action before your article hits the streets. Agreed?"

"Yes, then you will let me know when the article can be published, right?" asked Friedrich.

"Of course," replied Rudi, as he and Friedrich both finished their beers, pushed in their chairs, and retrieved their coats.

They were still buttoning up as they left the café, when Friedrich whispered to Rudi, "I think we are being watched; keep looking at me, Rudi. There are two guys behind a column. When I look in their direction, they withdraw behind the column; when I commence to look away, I notice they reemerge. Take your time buttoning up your coat; I'll try to get a better look at them. They are both rather tall, and both are wearing dark clothes. Oh, and one is wearing large lace-up boots."

"Look my way, Friedrich, not at them," Rudi implored with some anxiety.

"Let's split. I'll see you in three days, same time but at Central." Without shaking hands, both walked briskly away, Friedrich down Renngasse and Rudi down Wipplingerstrasse.

Rudi could feel himself breathing heavily as he pulled his collar up as high as it could go. He stopped by the next cross street, pulled a packet of cigarettes from his coat pocket, and slowly lit up, shielding the lighted match inside the collar of his coat and sending a plume of smoke into the dark sky, all the while looking around to see if he was being watched. He hadn't smoked for months but generally carried a pack with him.

Rudi couldn't help but smile inwardly as he thought of himself as James Cagney in a gangster movie. Satisfied that no one was watching, he stepped off the curb, crossed the street, and backtracked on Wipplingerstrasse. He wanted to make doubly sure. He dropped his cigarette, stepped on it firmly, and hurried back into Café Louvre, where he took off his coat. Quietly looking around, he selected a seat that faced the door and allowed him a view to the other side of the street where he and Friedrich had been spied on from behind the columns. He ordered ein Kaffee mit Schlag and sipped it for the next ten minutes or so, his eyes constantly vigilant. Nothing—no suspicious activity as far as he could tell. He left a coin by the coffee cup and raised his hand to gesture goodnight to Herr Ober. He put on his coat and slipped out into the Renngasse. If there was anybody following earlier, Rudi had now lost him.

Not long after, he entered his apartment and turned the key behind him. "Shalom, Rudi. What gives? We never lock the door; are you scared of something?"

Rudi recounted the events of the evening to Joseph, and they both had a laugh as Rudi described his imitation of James Cagney earlier in the evening.

"You were clever to return to the café before coming home," commented Joseph.

"I just wanted to make doubly sure that nobody would follow me home and put you in danger of being beaten over the head by some Nazi thugs. I am just a bit concerned that the man with the high lace-up boots I saw in the library and the man wearing high lace-up boots tonight is the same person as—"

"Yes, Manfred from the Studentenschaft," interrupted Joseph.

"Exactly."

Joseph and Rudi discussed the timing issue of Friedrich's article hitting the streets and the Jewish authorities of Leopoldstadt being briefed regarding the Nazis' intentions prior to the elections. "We wouldn't want a repeat of the attacks on the Jews in Leopoldstadt of the last couple of years," stressed Joseph. "I will go tomorrow morning to inform the leadership of the Juedische Selbstwehr of the danger."

"Good, and you should also relay to them the information Friedrich obtained from Munich," added Rudi.

Serious conversation waned, and Joseph fetched the bottle of Marillenschnaps and emptied it into two glasses. "Pity this is the last of it," he exclaimed with a pout.

"Zum Wohl," they exchanged as they raised their glasses.

"I enjoyed the film we saw the other night," continued Joseph, making light conversation. "Perhaps we should go and see a gangster movie with James Cagney next."

They both laughed while Rudi responded, "That certainly beats reading law textbooks. They really couldn't make them any more boring if they tried. Why on earth would I have any interest in a person by the name of Hermodorus organizing a group of men and sending them to Greece to study the laws of Athens, Crete, and Sparta? What relevance could the laws of Athens and Sparta possibly have to the institutions of Austria today?"

Joseph shook his head in apparent agreement and went off to clean his teeth. "Goodnight, Rudi. Are you sure the front door is secure?" he asked slightly mockingly and not really expecting an answer. "Shalom. Sleep well."

"Thank you. You too."

THREE DAYS LATER, as arranged, Rudi met Friedrich in Café Central, beer in hand. In response to a nod, Herr Ober brought Rudi a Pilsner. They shared pleasantries about the improving weather then together reflected on the incident of being spied on as they were leaving Café Louvre a few days before. Rudi suggested that the man wearing high boots was quite probably the Studentenschaft leader, who had accused him of being a "Jew lover." He was likely concerned that too much information had been divulged during their meeting.

"Manfred, Otto, and Klaus could also want to make sure that their plans do not become known to the university administration and especially to the Jewish authorities. Perhaps they are looking for me to warn me to keep my mouth shut," suggested Rudi. "I fear they may consider that words may not be persuasive enough. Who knows what these thugs might be thinking? When details of some of their plans hit the street, they will most likely see me as the informant, the snitch. Shit, I don't want to be a snitch in a ditch."

Friedrich broke in, "I wouldn't worry, Rudi; it is more likely that journalists like myself will become the object of their wrath. Anyway, after tonight we need not meet again until after the elections."

Rudi and Friedrich silently reflected on their respective situations. "The problem of course, Rudi, is your good looks."

"Ja, ja, ja, my good looks…"

"Yes, seriously," Friedrich continued. "I am sure that Manfred, Otto, and Klaus were taken in with your 'Germanic looks,' and hence told you more than they intended to. Now they regret that, but they could not possibly imagine you were a supporter of those filthy, stinking Jews. No, Rudi, not with those looks."

Rudi was not convinced and turned his thoughts to the article he would submit for the uni paper. He couldn't afford to divulge too much, and he needed to be moderate and fair with what he would write. He thought it better for his article to be published prior to Friedrich's work hitting the streets. Friedrich's article would surely wallop a much bigger punch and would, of course, reach a much larger audience. They agreed that Friedrich's article should be published exactly one week prior the election and Rudi's a few days earlier.

Friedrich thanked Rudi for the information he had shared with him three days before. He took out his wallet and offered to pay for the information, but Rudi quickly responded, "No. Under no circumstances would I want to accept any money for the information I was able to give you. If your article, with even some of the information I provided, thwarts some harassment or even violence in Vienna, I will feel amply rewarded."

Freidrick responded, "I hope you'll allow me to buy dinner when this election is all over."

"Sure. But for now I'll stay on here awhile and work on a draft of my article."

Both stood up and shook hands. Rudi beckoned the waiter as he resumed his seat, while Friedrich disappeared out the door. Rudi was in no frame of mind to do any writing; however, he thought it unwise for both to depart together. He also wanted to be alone to reflect on his situation, and there was no better way of doing that right then than in the company of a goulash soup, ample bread, and a glass of red.

The waiter soon came and set the items on the table. Rudi leaned forward a little to inhale the aromas from the steaming bowl. He broke off a piece of bread and dunked it. The flavor of paprika in the sauce was splendid. A sip of red, and he was now ready to reflect on the situation he was in and how to move forward with his article. He felt pleased with the arrangements he had made with Friedrich and was pretty confident that his friend was trustworthy.

I really need to catch up with my studies though, he thought, *however boring they are in comparison with the political issues I seem to have involved myself with. I am determined to catch up with my uni work, but I am pleased to be involved in combatting prejudice, human rights abuses, racism, intimidation, and thuggery. I know that Mother would prefer me to just focus on my studies, but I am sure Father would be pleased with my decision to become involved with the other issues as well. I'm sure Mr. Birnbaum would be happy with me too. I still miss Franz a lot; he would be such a good colleague at this time, and we'd have such a splendid time in Vienna. I really can't complain though. I have an excellent flatmate in Joseph, and a nicer person one would never meet.*

Rudi mopped up the remaining goulash, drained his glass then roughly folded his napkin and used it to flick a few crumbs onto the floor. He pushed in his chair, waved to Herr Ober, and left Café Central while buttoning his coat. He casually glanced over his shoulder a couple of times and wended his way home, occasionally turning around just to make sure no one was following him.

⸺

RUDI SPENT THE next few days catching up with his research and writing his article. He was very careful to confine himself to aspects of the political parties' processes that would not be seen as inflammatory. He wrote about the political parties developing leaflets and newspaper articles and representatives canvassing on the streets. He wrote about the parties' perceived strengths and their optimism and fears about other parties' advantages. The Social Democrats feared the power of the pulpit, the Nazis feared the "unfair dominance" of the Jewish-dominated press, and the Christian Social Party feared the rise of the Nazis in Germany. He included the university administration's statement that university classes would continue as usual during the election period and the request for students to respect one another and to refrain from any violence. Rudi omitted writing about any possible uses of violence, sabotage, or intimidation. He did not wish to incur the wrath of any particular political group but to avoid any negative actions against himself—and he certainly didn't want to be beaten up by any thugs.

He was certain that the information about intimidation and worse that he gained from the Nazis would emerge when Friedrich's writings hit the streets several days after his own article was published at the university. Rudi was confident that his approach would spare him any trouble. He was also determined to spare his mother from anything she might have cause to worry about; she'd be anxious enough with her boy being in the big city and away from her direct influence.

Only a few minor modifications were made to Rudi's article by the editor, Heinrich, and then it was published as planned ten days prior the election. Over the next couple of days, there were no strongly worded responses. A handful of people complimented Rudi on his article, including a professor, while another professor, either being pompous or paternal, pointed out a punctuation error. Rudi was pleased that the project had been completed, and he looked forward to reading what Friedrich's piece would reveal the following day. But he also had a slightly uneasy feeling that one or more revelations might be linked to him, whether correctly or not, for he had received and shared far more information than the Deutsche Studentenschaft had intended.

At home Rudi wondered, *Will Friedrich's article detail the plans of intimidation and harassment against the Jews by the Nazis? Has he found out more information than I provided about the Nazis' intended activities? Have the folks in Leopoldstadt taken appropriate precautions? Could they perhaps fight back and give the attackers a hiding? That would be good.*

He dozed off for a while but not for long. *Would it be possible to trace any information back to me? Does Friedrich write under an alias? Were we really followed that evening as we left Café Louvre? Was the man with boots really Manfred? Was he the same person I overheard in the library? Will I be seen as a snitch? Jesus, I would then be in big trouble; I could be beaten up at any time in any place: at the uni, in a café, on the street, even at home. Would it be worse to be stabbed with the dagger I saw stuck in the wall or clubbed like a helpless baby seal with one of those truncheons? I guess I'll have to be super careful going anywhere, especially going home. Perhaps I should lie low for a while and not go anywhere.* All this thinking and his concern for the worst made Rudi very anxious and tired. He put his head on his arms on the table and waited for Joseph to come home, thinking he might be able to assuage his fears.

When Joseph came in, Rudi was suddenly awakened. "What time is it? I was just thinking about Friedrich's article coming out tomorrow. I could be identified as the informant, and the Brownshirts would be after me."

"Ach was! Rudi, let's see what's in the article tomorrow and then make an assessment as to whether you should escape to Greenland," Joseph said with a smile.

———

EARLY THE NEXT morning, Joseph went to get the paper, while Rudi put on the water for coffee. The coffee was still brewing when Joseph came in with the *Wiener Zeitung* and some Semmel that were still warm. Rudi put the butter and confiture on the table and poured the coffee as Joseph began to read: "Anxiety for Jews increases as election nears. Buoyed by Nazi gains in Germany, Vienna's Nazis plan broad campaign of intimidation against Jews, who are considered as not worthy of having a vote...Leopoldstadt and the university are seen as the Nazis' likeliest targets. Jews are blamed for all economic difficulties in Vienna, and the Jewish press is charged with spreading nothing but lies..." Joseph kept reading about the Nazis possibly eclipsing the impact of all their previous acts of intimidation and harassment, as they would have armed German thugs to support the Austrian Nazis leading up to the election.

"What do you make of all that, Joseph?" Rudi was a little anxious.

"I warned the appropriate people in Leopoldstadt a short time ago, and they are confident that they will be able to repel any Nazi thuggery in their community. Those Hakenkreuzler could wreak havoc anywhere in the city of course, picketing Jewish stores and other businesses, breaking windows, setting buildings on fire, harassing, and even beating people on the street. Harassing and beating people is very likely to occur at the uni if they think they can get away with it there."

"Do you think I could be blamed for—"

Rudi was in the process of asking his question when Joseph interrupted him. "I think the Nazis have got many other things on their minds rather than going after you. I wouldn't cross the path of Manfred and company if I didn't have to though. It will be interesting to see if there is any Nazi intimidation or violence in the coming days before the elections."

⁓

THERE WAS INDEED very little Nazi intimidation in Vienna leading up to the elections at the end of April 1932, when Austria was at the height of the depression and when unemployment in the country had reached 25 percent. Incidents were heard of following the appointment of Engelbert Dollfuss as Bundeskanzler (chancellor). He became head of a coalition government consisting of the Christian Social Party, the Landbund (a right-wing agrarian party), and Heimatblock (the parliamentary wing of the Heimwehr, a paramilitary ultranationalist group).

The Nazis had not made the gains in Vienna that they had hoped. At the same time, the Nazis in Germany had some setbacks in their program of Nazification. However, they did make some significant electoral gains in local elections. They must have been somewhat emboldened by this, because they attacked Jews in various parts of the city on 24 May.

Joseph overheared a conversation that detailed an incident of Nazis bashing some people on the trams, and Rudi read an article on 25 May that stated:

> On 24 May, crowds of Nazis attacked Jews in the principal streets, on the tram cars, and in cafés on the occasion of the opening meetings of the Vienna City Council and the Vienna State Parliament.
>
> The cry "Jews, go to Palestine!" was raised repeatedly by the Nazis in the vicinity of the Parliament building. Many Jews have been injured.
>
> The police were slow at first in taking action against the Nazis, but afterwards they adopted a vigorous attitude in putting a stop to the disorders and dispersing the rioters.

Rudi and Joseph had by then become very good friends and were attending university regularly. Rudi had nearly caught up with his work, though he still found many of his courses lacking in interest. Despite still being in the habit of looking over his shoulder occasionally, he found a certain calm and regularity about everyday life: attendance at lectures, research in the library, cooking simply at home, occasionally going out for dinner, going to see films, and sitting in cafés and reading the papers, often from other counties or countries.

Joseph sometimes spent evenings with his girlfriend in Leopoldstadt. Rudi exchanged letters with his parents every couple of weeks, and they were looking forward to him coming home to Annenheim for the summer holidays.

IT WAS IN late May, on a particularly beautiful spring morning, that Rudi made his way to an 11:00 a.m. lecture that he was actually looking forward to. As he approached the lecture room door, he heard some commotion and quickly observed three students being shoved out by five or six young men. These men were all wearing brown shirts and wielding truncheons, which Rudi had seen before. His heart began to race. Several more students were bundled out amid shouting and truncheon blows. "Raus, Arschloecher, Rattendreck, raus…" could be heard.

Behind him Rudi first heard then saw a dozen more brown-shirted figures in boots and with truncheons in hand, thundering down the corridor on the double toward him. Several of them wore yellow-and-black swastika armbands. Rudi pressed himself hard against a wall and breathed in as they ran past him and into the lecture room. He had half expected a truncheon blow across the body.

There was more screaming and yelling and more people running every which way. Soon a dozen or so police, whistles blowing and with swords or truncheons in hand, ran from the opposite direction into the lecture room. Truncheons were flying as police weighed into the Hakenkreuzler. Some backed off, but some fought back with truncheons. Other students were supporting the police. Soon several students ran from the lecture theatre with Nazi thugs in pursuit and police close behind. A melee developed very quickly.

A Brownshirt was wielding his truncheon at a student as he ran passed Rudi. The student was about to be struck. This had to be prevented. Instinctively Rudi thrust out a foot to save the student from a certain blow. The Nazi went flying. Several Brownshirts pounced on Rudi. He got up and fended off attackers as he never had before. Nazi thugs, police, and students were in a real brawl. There was much shouting, many threats, and truncheons being viciously wielded. Some hit their marks. There was screaming as some people hit the deck. There was also squirming, kicking, and bleeding. Several policemen drew their swords.

Rudi was in the thick of it all, pushing and shoving and trying to avoid blows. Whack! He went down, having been hit under the chin. He put his hand to his chin and saw blood everywhere. It was the last thing he saw before he passed out.

Rudi awoke with his head on somebody's lap and a towel or some other material being held under his chin to reduce the bleeding. "Bleib still," was all he was told.

There was no longer any screaming, just groaning and sobbing as half a dozen bodies writhed on the floor. Police could be seen escorting five or six people from the building. One by one the injured got to their feet. "Can you stand?" Rudi was asked. He got to his feet and was led outside. "I'm taking you to the hospital. Keep holding on to my arm. I don't want you crumpling to the ground. It isn't far."

A couple of others were all walking in the same direction. A policeman, without saying a word, accompanied them to the hospital.

Rudi was quickly brought in to a doctor, who smiled and shook his head from side to side. "You are lucky the blow was not with the sharp side of the blade. They'd be putting you in a box. Instead, I've got to sew you up."

The doctor kept talking while he stitched Rudi up, all the while wiping blood away. "The cut is about eight centimetres and nicely symmetrical He did a good job really. Why can't you boys just concentrate on your studies? You could make something of yourselves. You could even make your parents proud. Things have changed, ja? When we were young, we didn't have all the opportunities you young people have today. You don't know how lucky you are. OK, I am finished with you, young man; keep yourself quiet to let the wound heal and come back here in fourteen days. Stay out of trouble."

As Rudi was led out, Joseph came running toward him. "What the hell happened to you?"

Before Rudi could get a word out, the policeman explained, "He was involved in a brawl at the uni with some Hakenkreuzler, and he must come to the station to answer some questions. He is forbidden to talk with anybody until we have spoken with him. Be on your way."

WITHIN THE SPACE of ten minutes, Rudi was led into a small room with one table and three chairs. "Sit down, stay seated, and wait," he was instructed. His whole head hurt, and he could feel his heart beating in his chin. He waited and waited and waited. It was becoming dark.

An officer came in with a bowl, some bread, a glass of water, and a spoon on a tray. "This is your dinner. You will stay here overnight. As soon as you have finished eating, we will take you to another room."

Rudi was trying to think of what he wanted to ask as the door was closed and locked. He was not confused; what was happening was clear. He was locked up and had to wait to be interrogated, and there were others before him. But he was still a bit stunned, and his head still hurt. He ate his goulash and bread, carefully opening and closing his mouth so as not to increase the pain. Although a bit too cool, the goulash was quite good, he thought, and the bread was not bad either. He drank his water then waited for more than an hour before desperately needing to go to the toilet. *I shouldn't have drunk all the water,* he thought.

Soon the door opened, and Rudi was led a few paces down the corridor to another room. It was small with a bed, a toilet, and a wash basin. The only light was through a small, barred window near the ceiling. A light bulb hanging from the ceiling was not illuminated. Rudi couldn't concentrate on anything other than going to the toilet, so he did not really hear what the officer said as he slipped out and locked the door. Passing urine had never provided such relief before.

There were two grey blankets folded at the end of the bed, but there was no pillow. Rudi took off his shoes and lay down, pulling both blankets up to cover his shoulders. He rested his head carefully on his arms. *Hm, not all that different from being in a ski hut,* he thought. He moved his head and arms a bit this way and that, but his chin still throbbed. Rudi knew he hadn't done anything wrong, but he thought, *How stupid of me to get involved in this. I should have just walked away when I saw those first three being bundled out by those Brownshirts. Perhaps it was worth it though, because I was able to prevent that innocent Jewish student from an almighty whack from a truncheon. I hope Joseph knows what's going on and isn't too upset. We had actually planned to go to the cinema tonight.*

Rudi was beginning to feel drowsy. *How I wish this were really a ski hut and Franz were with me. Waiting to fall asleep, we would chat away, hear the snow falling, and imagine waking to a blue sky and taking those first runs on untracked snow.* With those comforting thoughts, Rudi finally fell asleep.

THE NEXT MORNING, he was awoken by the door opening. He was thrown a towel and told to be ready in five minutes. His chin was still throbbing as he carefully washed the sleep from his eyes and got ready to be taken to be interrogated. He was quickly led back to the room where he had spent several hours the day before. There was no interrogation yet. Instead, a tray arrived with a plate of scrambled eggs, one semmel, and a glass of water. As the officer set these items on the table, he explained, "We wouldn't want you to run out of strength while answering questions. Sorry there's no coffee."

Better food than we'd have in a ski hut, Rudi mused as he finished all but the Semmel, which hurt his jaw when he chewed. He took only a sip of water lest he be kept waiting again.

Two officers arrived. "Good morning. Boy, you were hungry," one said.

"Good morning," answered Rudi.

An officer then asked a whole series of questions, while the other took notes. "Why were you at the lecture theatre yesterday? What was the name of the subject? What was the name of the professor? Why did you stay and not walk away? What political group are you a member of? Do you belong to the Deutsche Studentenschaft? Are you Jewish? Do you have any Jewish friends? Are you a communist? Why were you fighting? Why were…Why…? Why…? Why…?"

It seemed to go on forever. Rudi answered all questions honestly. The officers left the room and locked the door. Rudi's head still hurt, and he could feel a bruise on his left arm. In fact, much of his body felt bruised.

I wonder what's next, he thought as the door swung open. "You're ready to go, young man. Off with you. Stay out of trouble."

Rudi was led outside. It was a beautiful, clear, sunny day with just a slight breeze. There, leaning against the wall just a few feet away, was Joseph with a smile on his face. Rudi, a little sheepish, had a big bandage on his.

"Shalom. Rudi, do you want some nosh, something to eat? Want a coffee?"

"Servus, Joseph. A coffee would be great."

A modest Viennese coffee house sat on the opposite corner, and in less than three minutes they were sitting at a table.

Joseph glanced at Rudi. "Oy vey, Rudi, you look like a loser from the Colosseum. All those bruises. What's under the bandage?"

In the meantime two coffees arrived. "Twenty-seven stiches holding my head together," replied Rudi.

"Oy vey. Who did that to you, a Brownshirt?"

"Well, actually, no. It was an officer defending himself against four or five Hakenkreuzler, using the back of his sword, and I got in the way. Actually I was pushed into the middle of the skirmish and was hit. Went down like a sack of potatoes. Ah, the coffee is good. That was a great idea. It was very nice of you to be waiting for me, Joseph."

"No problem, Rudi. I put off meeting Ester today, but she was more worried about you than interested in seeing me."

DURING THE NEXT few weeks there were several incidents of Jews being harassed, especially in Leopoldstadt, where there was some picketing in front of Jewish-owned shops. There were also a few random beatings reported.

University life was continuing as normal, as though no skirmish at all had occurred. A rumour was about that several students had been arrested for attacking police officers and that these students would not be returning to the university.

Summer was now fast approaching, and students were generally busy completing their obligations before the summer holidays. Rudi's bruises were disappearing, and his stitches were taken out as had been planned. The scar beneath his chin would still take a while to heal completely.

One evening when Rudi had nothing planned, he went to Café Louvre, where he and Friedrich, over a Schnitzel and beer, congratulated each other on their articles. They chatted away for some time over a second beer and parted with the hope that they would come across each other again at the café.

Still looking over his shoulder occasionally, Rudi wandered home on this beautiful, springlike evening, knowing that there'd be no more university work for some weeks. He was ready for the holidays. He and Joseph were both quite tired from the rush of getting all their university commitments fulfilled, and both were looking forward to their summer vacations. Joseph and his girl-friend, Ester, were going to spend some time in Munich with his parents, who had never met her. Rudi would be taking the train to Annenheim to be with his parents and to spend a great deal of time on or near the Ossiachersee.

5

ANNENHEIM AM OSSIACHERSEE, SUMMER 1932

RUDI HAD NOT seen his parents for several months and was excited to be home with them. His mother gave him the longest hug he'd ever had and his father the strongest. His first few months in Vienna had been most exciting, though his studies had not been a big part of that. He felt really fortunate that he was matched with Joseph as a flatmate.

Rudi was now looking forward to pleasant days around the Ossiachersee when he was not helping his father at the Annenheim railway station. He might also do some hiking in the mountains if he felt that he could cope with the memory of Franz's death, still so vivid. He was looking forward to a quiet summer with a lot of time to do some swimming or to just dangle his feet in the water and reflect.

On a beautifully balmy summer evening, a particularly crowded train disgorged hundreds of holiday makers. The stationmaster was greeting passengers as they were handing in their tickets— "Habidiere, Frau…, Habidiere, Herr So-and-So"—and several groups were particularly warmly greeted with an extra "es freut mich" as they were recognized as repeat vacationers.

"Rudi," called the stationmaster, "would you please help carry Familie Gruen's luggage to Haus Stein?"

"Natuerlich," replied Rudi as he took two cases and headed down the road just a few metres in front of the Gruen party of two middle-aged women, who looked like sisters, and a young woman. Rudi did not remember the group of three, but his father remembered the Gruens well because they had been coming to stay with Frau Stein for a number of years. The stationmaster did notice that Mr. Gruen and the son were not there this time.

At the front entrance of the Stein residence, one of the women gave the youngest of the three a couple of coins and said, "Lili, give this to the young man."

For a couple of hundred metres, Lili had been watching Rudi from behind. She noticed he was well tanned, athletically built, and strong, as the suitcases he was easily carrying had been difficult to lift onto the train at the Wiener Hauptbahnhof by a porter. As she pressed the coins into Rudi's hand, giving it an extra squeeze, she noticed that he was also very handsome. She gave him a discreet smile, and her heart began to pound as he returned the favor.

Rudi ran back toward the station and recognized another family struggling with luggage. He took a suitcase and a large bag and left it at the front door of a Pension just a few doors past Haus Stein. As he passed Haus Stein on the way back to the station, he noticed a first-floor window being opened and recognized the young lady who had, just minutes before, given him a tip and a very nice smile. He wandered back to the station, certain he would meet her again soon. *She did smile at me after all and squeeze my hand unlike anybody else giving me a tip.* He'd noticed that she was good looking with very dark, shiny hair and prob-ably a little older than him. *I don't mind being alone,* he thought, *but if I had someone to spend a little time with here on vacation, that'd be nice too.*

After dinner Rudi took a stroll through Annenheim, watched a beautiful sunset disappearing behind the gabled roofs and trees of the picturesque village, and returned to walk back. As he was about to pass Haus Stein, he noticed the light go on in the first-floor room behind some curtains. He stared up at the window for a while to see if there was any movement or if the light would go out again. He wanted this young lady's attention—exactly what for, he wasn't really sure…some impulse. He threw some small pebbles up against the window, hoping she would open it. When a second pebble hit its mark, the curtains were slightly pulled apart. The young lady appeared at the window, saw Rudi, gave a slight smile, and closed the curtains again. Rudi repeated his pebble throwing, and the curtain was again pulled apart. The young lady appeared at the window, opened it a little, and waved her right arm with a gesture, suggesting he should go away.

What to do? he thought. *I can't be put off that easily. I'm just not going to be put off.* Rudi saw a ladder propped up against the side of the building. He quickly retrieved it and carried it to the front. He looked around but saw nobody about. He quickly pulled the rope to hoist the ladder to a height just above the windowsill. He set the ladder down quietly, climbed up it with ease, took a deep breath, and quietly knocked on the window. No response. He quietly knocked again. The young lady opened the window and, with an expression of disbelief, recognized the porter from earlier that day.

"Go away. Go away. Are you crazy?" she asked.

"No, I just want to see you tomorrow."

"Are you really crazy, playing some Romeo-and-Juliet game?" chuckled the young lady, who was very familiar with the opera and ballet interpretations of the famous William Shakespeare play.

"No, but please meet me tomorrow at the ice-cream stand by the lake at two o'clock. Have your swim costume with you."

The young lady closed the window and drew the curtains as Rudi descended the ladder and returned it as quietly as he had retrieved it.

THE FOLLOWING DAY was picture perfect, and Rudi could barely wait until two o'clock. He strolled up and down the lake shore, skimming a few stones across the surface of the lake, kicking the water with a bare foot, talking to the fish swimming aimlessly by, whistling or humming a tune, and imitating some birds singing. He was just whiling some time away, feeling a little nervous. Well, very nervous, but he was also feeling extremely happy. He was glad to be away from uni and happy that he didn't need to look over his shoulder everywhere he went, and he loved it there on the shore of the lake, with which he was so familiar.

As two o'clock approached, Rudi sat on a log at the lake's shore facing toward the ice-cream stand. He was getting edgy, all the while gazing in one direction. Suddenly he heard, "Hello. Are you waiting for me?"

The voice absolutely startled him, and he shot up to his feet. "Yes, hello. Where did you come from? You surprised me," he answered, his heart in his mouth.

"I can see that. I came from that direction," the young lady answered while pointing.

She sat on the log, and Rudi sat beside her—close but not too close. "I am Rudi, Rudi Auer."

"I am Lili, Lili Gruen," she mimmicked.

"How are you?" enquired Rudi politely.

"I am well. And you?" she responded with a smile and a mischievous air. "Will we have an ice cream now?"

They both got up and walked twenty or so metres to the ice-cream stand. "Bitte," Rudi beckoned for Lili to order, and he followed suit. Rudi paid, and they both strolled back to the log without a word. They ate their ice cream, sharing an occasional glance and a smile...not shy but a little reticent. Rudi noticed Lili's dark, shiny hair and very dark eyes. She was wearing an expensive dirndl and sandals not usually worn by locals there in Annenheim.

He broke the short silence. "Are you from Vienna, Lili?"

"Yes, I've been there all my life except for holidays here and in the mountains—and, oh, also in Trieste."

"I've just started to live in Vienna. I am at the university."

"What are you studying?"

"Law."

"So you want to be a lawyer, Rudi?"

"I'm not sure. It's pretty boring so far," he explained reluctantly.

"Surely you don't find Vienna boring though?" queried Lili.

"No, Vienna is a wonderful city. I really love it there."

They talked a lot about Vienna—its architecture, its cultural richness, its cafés. The more they talked, the easier their conversation became. They enjoyed being with one another, sitting on a log looking out over the lake.

"It's getting rather hot this afternoon," Lili commented.

"Do you want to go for a swim?" invited Rudi.

"Not today, but if you want to go, I'll wait for you."

Rudi stood and quickly took off his shirt and shorts, revealing swimming trunks. He threw Lili a glance, dived into the water, and swam strongly into the distance. She confirmed her initial view that Rudi was a strong, athletic young man. He powered through the water effortlessly yet elegantly until he was but a speck in the distance. Soon the speck became larger again as he swam back to shore and sat on the log a good distance from Lili so that she would not get wet. "You should come too sometime. The water is quite warm."

Lili answered with a smile, "Must go. Mother and Auntie will be expecting me. Will you be here again tomorrow, Rudi?"

"Yes, I'll be here from midday."

"Good. I might bring my bathing suit. Auf Wiedersehen," she said as she did a little pirouette and skipped away.

What a nice young lady. I hope she comes again and brings her swimsuit. I bet she won't swim. Yes, she will. No, she won't. Yes, she will. No, she won't, he toyed with himself. He felt really good in Lili's presence, and he felt that she too was very comfortable with him. She wouldn't have had enough time to have made it back to Haus Stein, but Rudi was already missing her and wishing tomorrow would arrive.

—∞—

IT WAS AGAIN a picture-perfect day as Rudi arrived at the lake just before midday. It was already very hot, and under normal circumstances he would have dived straight into the water. But he wanted to wait for Lili, to make sure he'd not miss her if she came. He was pretty sure she'd come; perhaps it was just wishful thinking.

He sat on the log on which he and Lili had introduced themselves, and he frequently looked at his watch, becoming a little more anxious as each minute passed. He waited and waited. An hour went by, and he was beginning to think Lili might not show up. Trying to relax, he wandered up and down a bit, skimmed a couple of stones across the lake, and sat back down on the log. He began to whistle a tune he was very familiar with. By the second or third time, he was interrupted by Lili singing, "In einem Bächlein helle, Da schoß in froher Eil Die launische Forelle…'Die Forelle' by Schubert, Franz Schubert," she declared.

"Hello, Lili, I notice you sneak up on people. How are you? Nice to see you."

"Hello, Rudi. How are you? It's hot today." Fanning herself with a hand, Lili sat beside him and placed a bag at her feet. "You were whistling about a trout. Does that mean you are ready to swim?"

"Of course," replied Rudi.

He slipped off his shorts and watched Lili carefully unbutton her dress down the front and kick off her sandals. She turned, ran a few metres to the water's edge, dunked a foot in, and said, "This is not as warm as I thought it would be."

Rudi watched as she slowly started to wade out from the shore, stopping occasionally to splash water on herself. She eased into the water and swam out from the shore. Rudi dived in and was soon beside her, both swimming sidestroke and facing one another. They swam for a good ten minutes without saying a word, when Lili turned around and beckoned to go back.

"Is the water still cold?" Rudi asked, swimming beside her.

"No, it's nice now. Beat you to the shore," she said jokingly.

Rudi flipped onto his back and swam backstroke, all the while staying beside her. "Better to stay with you just in case you need to be rescued," he returned the banter. They both smiled and swam to the shore. Lili went to her bag, took out two towels, and threw one to Rudi.

"Thank you. You swim very nicely," he complimented her.

"So do you," she replied, "but I already noticed that yesterday." Lili partly dried herself in her one-piece black swimsuit while Rudi just sat on the towel. They felt very close. *Swimming together is quite an intimate activity,* Lili thought to herself. She bent over her bag and took out a purse. "Rudi, why don't you get us a little lunch from the kiosk? I'd really like a Wuerstel mit Senf—lamb, if possible."

Rudi refused to take any money and asked, "Would you like anything to drink, Lili?"

"No, thanks. I drank enough of the lake." They exchanged smiles and Rudi left but was back in about five minutes. Lili had dried herself a little more and put her dress back on. When Rudi returned, she was brushing her hair.

Lili took a bite of the Wuerstel. "Very good but not quite as good as you get in Vienna," she said with a twinkle in her eye.

"Well, you'll just have to show me where you can buy the best in Vienna," responded Rudi. Lili did not take the bait and kept eating.

After lunch, Lili took a towel, shook it once, and laid it half on the sand and half on the log they had been sitting on. She sat on the towel with her back leaning against the log. As Rudi was a bit slow on the uptake, she looked up at him and beckoned for him to sit beside her. "How did you get that cut under your chin, Rudi? I just noticed it."

His mother or father hadn't asked about it yet, and he was not sure whether they had noticed it. After a short pause, Rudi answered, "I had a midnight duel behind the university chapel for the love of a woman, and I lost."

"You what?" she asked in disbelief. "I thought they only did that in tragic operas."

"No, it had nothing to do with a woman," Rudi corrected himself. "Do you really want to know?"

"Well, of course. Otherwise I wouldn't have asked."

"In a nutshell, I tripped up a Nazi thug about to thump a Jewish student, and I got caught up in a nasty fight involving some students, Brownshirts, and police. I ran into the blunt side of a sword. Well, I was pushed actually. I went down like a sack of potatoes and got a few stitches before they threw me in a cell for the night."

Lili stared at him with her big black eyes, a frown, and her mouth half open. "You're kidding me. That's a better tragic opera plot than your first story."

"Yes, it is, isn't it? But it's true."

After some silence, Lili asked impatiently, "Well, aren't you going to tell me?"

"I have. That's what happened."

"Who are these Brownshirts you mentioned?"

"They are Hitler youth, thugs who harass people, especially Jews."

Lili was flabbergasted. Rudi then relayed the whole story of becoming a writer for the uni paper, having interviewed several political groups, being thrown out of a meeting with the Deutsche Studenschaft, having met with Friedrich, being followed, getting involved in the brawl at the university, visiting the the hospital, and being interrogated.

"We didn't read any of this in the paper in Vienna."

"Well, it was covered but only in a small article hidden in the middle of the paper somewhere. The uni administration works very hard to keep such incidents quiet," Rudi explained.

"Did you tell your parents?" asked Lili.

"No, I'll only tell them if they mention my scar, and even then I'll tell them a story that will upset Mother as little as possible."

Lili did not pursue this any further, but she was questioning the wisdom of spending so much time with Rudi. She really liked him, and he seemed to like her, but he must have only been about nineteen, if that.

Breaking the silence, Rudi suggested, "Tomorrow we could take a boat and do a little exploring; would you like that, Lili?"

"I'd probably fall out," she jested. "Would I have to do any rowing? The last time I tried, the boat kept wanting to go in circles."

Rudi smiled. "I think it would be nice on the water tomorrow because it's supposed to be even hotter than today. Bring your swimsuit just in case you do fall in…or get pushed in," he whispered to himself.

Lili was quick. "What did you say? I heard that." She smiled.

"I'll bring some lunch. See you tomorrow at eleven."

Lili picked up her bag, blew Rudi a kiss, and skipped away. Rudi sat on the log, happier than he'd been at any time since Franz's death. He had missed him a lot over recent months, while still at school, then in Vienna, and now back in Annenheim. He'd missed him less since he met Lili. *Is that fair to Franz? Would he be so interested in spending time with another person if he were alive and I were dead? What would Franz think of her?*

Walking home, Rudi was wondering about Lili. He felt really fond of her. Not only did she seem to be a good mate to spend time with doing all sorts of things, but she was so easy to talk with about almost anything, he thought. He also felt romantically attracted to her. He couldn't get her out of his mind. *Is it really possible for us to have an intimate relationship with me so much younger than her? I am just a country boy, while she is far more experienced and a sophisticated woman from Vienna.*

———

HE LAY AWAKE looking at the ceiling much of the night, thinking about Lili. He planned the next day's boating trip with her at least ten times in his head before he finally fell asleep.

Straight after breakfast, he grabbed a couple of apples, put them in his pocket, and went to hire a flat-bottomed, sturdy rowboat. He rowed it around to a spot opposite their meeting place and pulled it up onto the shore, where he sat on the usual log and stared into the distance. It was at least an hour before Lili would arrive. He took an apple from his pocket, polished it on his shirt, and began to eat it. A couple of cheeky sparrows hopped toward him, and he bit off some little pieces and watched the birds fight over them. Within seconds there were more than half a dozen at his feet waiting for their morsels. He finished the apple and threw the core towards the water, knowing that it would all be eaten in no time. It was. He still had some time to kill, so he decided he'd go for a swim. He left his sandals on the sand and his shorts and shirt on the log. He dived into the lake, as flat as a mill pond, and swam out into the distance.

He was a long way from shore when Lili arrived, also early. She had been thinking half the night about Rudi and questioned how sensible she really was to continue spending time with him. She was not only attracted to him, but she liked him a lot and thought he was a lot of fun to be around. She decided she was just going to enjoy being with him and let fate do its thing. *What will be will be*, she mused.

Feeling in a mischievous frame of mind, she took Rudi's clothes, including his sandals, put them in her bag, which was already quite heavy, and retreated to behind the trees at the edge of the sand. While she waited for him, the thought came to her, *With this man I feel so joyous, so young. I was never allowed to be young, to be a teenager. And now I'm behaving like one. I think I have a lot of catching up to do.* She didn't have to wait long before Rudi came more clearly into view, swimming strongly and then jumping up in knee-high water and running to shore. He immediately noticed that his clothes were missing. He hadn't expected Lili yet, but no one else would take his clothes, he thought. He was convinced it was Lili as he scoured the trees behind the sand.

"Hello!" Lilli came running toward him so fast she nearly flew into his arms. She dropped her bag at her feet and grabbed Rudi by both hands as he pulled her towards him in a big, spontaneous embrace. They both surprised themselves and pulled apart. "I'm all wet now," she exclaimed.

"Does that matter?" asked Rudi, still panting as much from running out onto the sand as from the embrace. He put his hands out. She accepted them, and they fell into a second warm embrace.

"I missed you so much," they said to each other nearly in unison. They both felt a little embarrassed and a little shy.

Lili put her hand in her bag and declared, "I'll get you a towel, Rudi."

"Oh, Lili, I don't need one, thanks." He sat on the log to drip dry in the sun, while Lili retrieved his clothes and laid them out on the log, sandals on the sand. "You've got quite small feet for a man," she observed.

"Yes, but a big heart." He threw Lili a warm smile.

"That I know already, and that's what worries me," she said, her voice trailing off. Rudi heard but neither he nor she was really in the mood for a deep discussion. They were aware of the unlikeliness of this relationship being sustainable, but both hoped against the odds that this one would be the exception.

Rudi didn't wait to be completely dry before he put on his shirt and shorts and slipped into his sandals. He took the apple from his pocket, threw it towards Lili, and requested she put it in her bag. "Come help me with the boat," Rudi said as she followed him to the water's edge. "Throw your sandals in the boat and put your bag in as well. Pull, Lili, pull," commanded Rudi as they pulled the boat into the water.

Rudi gave Lili his hand, and he helped her into the boat as he steadied it with the other hand. She sat on the bench in the stern. Rudi pushed the boat into the water and jumped in. He sat on the bench, picked up an oar, and locked it into the starboard oarlock. He secured the second oar and shuffled to the center of his seat, facing Lili. He picked up a bucket at his feet and threw it behind him. "Hope we won't need this," he said. "These boats are notorious for springing a leak when you are in the middle of the lake and a storm is brewing."

Lili looked aghast for only a moment then responded, "Is that a Kaerntner sense of humor, Rudi?"

He responded with a smile as he picked up both oar handles simultaneously, glanced over his shoulder, and pulled on the oars. With his symmetrical movements, clean blade entries, and powerful stroking, the boat headed directly out to the middle of the lake, its wake remaining perfectly straight. "Where to, Lili? Where should we go?"

"How about across to the other side? I haven't been there. Will it take long? I'm hungry." Lili was not really hungry, but it was something to say.

"Do I make you hungry?" Rudi asked, hoping he would not get a reply because he probably wouldn't know how to respond to it. "Take the apple out of the bag and eat that while you are waiting."

Lili ate about half of it. "I've had enough."

"Throw it to me. Thanks." Rudi ate the rest of the apple, including the core.

"Why do you eat the core?"

"Better than throwing it into the water or into your bag. It's good anyway," he responded.

As they approached the opposite side of the lake, Rudi turned the boat to run parallel to the shore. He wanted to look for a little, quiet cove where he and Lili could enjoy lunch. Soon they found a small, secluded cove in shallow water with a sandy beach leading to a grassy patch and overhanging trees. Rudi faced the boat towards the shore, unhooked the oars, laid them inside the boat, jumped overboard, and pushed the boat onto the sand, where it ground to a stop. He gave Lili his hand, helped her from the boat, and gave it another shove up the beach. He leaned into the boat and retrieved the bag for Lili.

"Dankeschoen," she said with a smile.

"Bittesehr."

They walked across the sand, paused, and looked at each other for a moment, then stopped a few metres further on the grass and in the shade. "Help me with the blanket, please, Rudi," Lili said as she pulled it from her bag.

Together they spread the blue blanket, brushing out the wrinkles. Rudi pulled her onto the blanket beside him and held her hand. They glanced at each other and looked up at the overhanging tree branches; they observed the boat, safely up on the sand, and the blue-green, still water beyond with barely a ripple. There was an ever-so-slight breeze in the air and the faint fragrance of a flower that neither could recognize.

Sitting up, Rudi asked, "Do we have time for a swim, Lili?"

"You go, Rudi, and I'll just watch," Lili said with a twinkle in her eye. Rudi took off his shirt and shorts, threw them on the end of the blanket, and, adjusting the back of his swim trunks, ran to the water, dived in, and swam out.

Lili watched Rudi for a few moments then proceeded to get lunch set up. She opened and spread a small blue-and-white-checkered tablecloth on the middle of the blanket and unloaded the food items from her bag. She set a breadboard in the middle and placed three different cheeses, some salami, and bread, all still wrapped, on the board. She placed a paper bag of strawberries and a bag of cherries beside it and took out two silver knives, which she set down, tips on the breadboard. Then she took out a flask, ran it down to the water's edge, and half buried it in the sand to ensure that the water remained cold. She returned to the rug and shooed away a couple of inquisitive and possibly hungry sparrows. Lili sat, waiting for Rudi's return, and thought, *I really like this man. I really love to take care of him, and I truly think he likes me too and equally wants to take care of me. Why shouldn't this relationship work? I realize he is very young, but he seems to be a very responsible and caring young man...and lots of fun. In three more years he will be a lawyer and...*Her reflecting was interrupted as she glanced up to see that Rudi was only a few strokes from the shore.

She ran toward him with a towel and wrapped it—and her arms—automatically around him. "You can't drip dry sitting on the blanket."

He put his arms around her to reciprocate. Moments later they were on the blanket, one sitting on each side of the spread. "What have you got here, Lili? It looks beautiful."

"I hope you'll like it. There are some cheeses, salami, and bread."

"Very nice. Shall I get my pocketknife to cut the bread?" he enquired, leaning towards his shorts.

"No, thanks. I cut it this morning; I didn't want to bring a bread knife this long," she said as she demonstrated with her hands.

"And what's in these paper bags?" he asked, not able to curb his curiosity.

"Some strawberries and cherries."

"Oh, very special."

"Rudi, would you please run down to the water, just to the left of the boat? There's a flask I half buried," she said.

Rudi fetched the flask and brought it back, drying the bottom of it on his shirt. He sat and unwrapped the bread, while Lili did the same with the cheeses and salami. "That salami smells good," Rudi said. She asked him to cut some cheese, which she promptly put on some dark rye bread and began to eat. Rudi started with some salami on a lighter piece of bread, probably wheat, he thought, and made some approving noises, looking wide-eyed at Lili.

After the first few bites, they ate quite slowly, happy in each other's presence in this idyllic location, the slight breeze fanning them ever so gently and the silence broken only by occasional chirping from the branches above. "Are you finished with the salami and cheese?" Lili asked, prompted by the arrival of a wasp or bee.

Rudi nodded with a smile and flicked his hand at the wasp. He lay down, hands behind his head, looking at the branches above, and turned his head to give Lili a smile. This had the desired effect, as she came and sat beside him. She leaned over him, retrieved a paper bag, and handed it to him as he sat back up. Rudi opened the bag, smiled, took out a pair of cherries, and placed them over Lili's ear then did the same for the other ear. She smiled, moving her head to and fro, showing off her earrings. They both ate a few, all the while looking at each other adoringly. Rudi lay down, and Lili took off her cherry earrings and passed them to Rudi. He dangled them teasingly just out of reach of her mouth for a moment before she ate them.

She soon lay beside him, snuggling into him while holding his head in her hand. "You know, Rudi, I hope this is more than a summer romance, and that we can see one another in Vienna. I really like being with you."

Without hesitation, Rudi confirmed he felt the same. They held each other very tightly and kissed passionately, both wishing they were somewhere softer and darker. They lay together with that continuing thought for a long time until the shade had disappeared and the sun was adding to the heat. It was now the hottest part of the day and time to be on the water, where there might be some relief because of an afternoon breeze that was expected. They packed up all their items and took them to the boat.

"How about a quick swim before we head back?" requested Lili. She was unbuttoning her dress before Rudi could answer, and soon they swam out together for a short distance just to reduce the body heat. Treading water, they briefly held each other tightly, shared a kiss—just averting going under—and, facing each other, swam side-stroke back to the shore.

Together they pushed the boat off the sand, and Lili climbed in. Rudi gave the boat another shove and jumped on board. Within moments they were on their way out of their little cove and heading back across the lake from where they came. The sun was shining brightly, and a light breeze helped reduce the heat on that perfect summer day. As Lili and Rudi were quietly enjoying each other's company, she mentioned how tanned they were becoming after spending so much time in the sun.

This prompted Rudi to sing, "Schwartzbraun ist die Haselnuß, Schwartzbraun bin auch ich, ja bin auch ich. Schwartzbraun muß mein Madel sein, gerade so wie ich!"

"Very nice. Thank you, Rudi. You have such a beautiful voice; did you get that from your mother or father?"

"Mother, I think."

"Where did that song come from?" enquired Lili.

"It's a tune from Salzburg; I happen to like it."

They were a hundred metres or so from the beach when Rudi suggested they stop for some water and strawberries. Lili nodded approval, so Rudi pulled up the oars, allowed the boat to drift to a halt, and threw the anchor overboard. He pulled on the rope to ensure that the anchor took hold. Lili threw Rudi a towel, which he laid on the floor of the boat, while she took the bag, and both sat with their backs against the center seat. Lili took out the water, and they both quenched their thirst. She opened the paper bag to release a strong strawberry aroma. "They smell wonderful, don't they?" she said as she gave the bag to Rudi, which he passed beneath his nose.

He took a strawberry by the stalk, and Lili bit off most of it; Rudi ate the rest. This procedure was repeated three or four times while Lili snuggled up to Rudi, who put his left arm around her. She looked up at him adoringly, which led to some passionate kissing. "Where can we go tomorrow, Rudi? I love the days we spend together, and we will not have many more during my vacation here before I have to get back to work."

"What work do you do in Vienna?"

"I work as a secretary; I'll have plenty of time to tell you later. Let's just plan tomorrow," Lili said eagerly.

"We should do a little hiking tomorrow; it's cooler in the mountains."

"That would be very good."

Rudi took charge. "Let's go to the Gerlitzen. We will need to leave before the heat of the day; you'll need some sturdy walking shoes and bring something to wear on top, as it might be cooler up there. I will get Mother to make us some lunch. How does that sound, Lili?"

"Prima, Rudi. Should we meet at ten o'clock on our log?"

Rudi answered in the affirmative, and they consummated their plan with a kiss. Hugging and kissing had become very easy and natural for them, responding to each other's moves with warmth, complete trust, increasing emotion, and a desire for more.

Rudi pulled up the anchor, dropped it in the bow, and coiled the rope neatly on top, while Lili repacked her bag and sat back in her spot. They smiled at each other as Rudi, having replaced the oars, began to row the short distance to shore. Rudi helped Lili out of the boat, and, holding hands, they waded a few metres to shore. Rudi retrieved their sandals and pulled the boat a few further metres up the sand to prevent it from floating away. He sat beside her on their log, and they revised their plans for the next day.

"Servus, Rudi, bis Morgen. Thank you for a lovely day."

They both stood up. Lili brushed some sand from her legs, slipped on her sandals, and picked up her bag. She dropped it again to embrace Rudi, which led to a short but passionate kiss, and she was on her way. Rudi was transfixed, observing every step until Lili disappeared from view. He was extremely happy, though a little worried about possibly being hurt should their relationship come to an end. He took another swim before returning the boat from where he had picked it up in the morning.

THEY BOTH HAD some questions thrown at them that evening. "You look so very happy, Lili. What did you do today?" asked Lili's auntie, having forgotten what Lili had told her that morning.

"I met this very nice man a few days ago, and today we went boating. Tomorrow we're going hiking. Did I bring my boots, Mother? Do you know?"

"You shouldn't go hiking with a man you have only just met. I was worried enough today, you going on the boat with this young man."

"Walter is not here, so I'm going hiking with Rudi. He's a very nice young man, very competent, knows these mountains very well, and he is very caring. I understand your concern, Mother, but I have very good instincts, and I have made up my mind," Lili said emphatically.

"Your father would not have approved."

"Walter is not here. Father is not here, and for me, he was never really here."

"How can you say that, Lili?" asked her mother sternly.

"Because it's true, Mother. He never cared about the things that I wanted. For years now you've both just wanted me to marry a well-connected Jewish businessman of your choosing, all for the sake of family appearances. Everyone you introduced me to was self-important and boring, oh, so boring. Not once did you consider what I might want. Well, I want to have a nice relationship with a man I choose. If I make a mistake with a choice I make, I can live with that," Lili said earnestly as she walked away.

Auntie chimed in, "You know, Hedwig, Lili is probably right. She has not been at all interested in any of the men you have introduced her to. She needs to find the right man for her, and the sooner, the better, as she's now closer to thirty than to twenty. You never know, Hedwig. This one might just be the man for her. I haven't seen Lili so happy for a long time. And as she said, she does have good instincts."

Rudi's mother and father didn't have any concerns about him going hiking on the Gerlitzen with a young lady. He was very responsible and had been hiking in that area for a very long time with both young men and women, even before they were referred to as men and women. Rudi was absolutely at home in those mountains, knowing every trail, every shortcut, and every peak. The only questions about this outing were: "Where did you meet this young lady...at the lake? Is she nice?" and, "Do you want cheese and ham separately or together with gherkins on the sandwiches? Is by nine o'clock early enough?"

"Yes, thank you, Mama. And could you put in a couple of napkins as well, please?" Rudi requested.

"Napkins to take with you into the mountains? She must be very fancy," was his mother's reply.

6

CONSOLIDATION OF A FRIENDSHIP

RUDI SLEPT SOUNDLY, with romantic dreams and fantasies bordering the possible. In the morning, he packed his rucksack carefully with the sandwiches his mother had lovingly made, the napkins, a flask of water, his trusted penknife, and some matches. He included a couple of apples from the fruit bowl and took a bar of Italian chocolate he had received as a tip a couple of days before. He threw in a pullover just in case and tied up his pack. On second thought, he decided to take a tarpaulin and some rope just in case the weather turned bad, so he repacked.

He arrived at their log early and was thinking about some alternate routes they could take, depending on what footwear Lili was wearing. If she had ordinary street shoes, they would need to take an easy route; if she had proper hiking boots, they had a couple of options for more difficult climbs. As was normal for Rudi, he was whistling, not even aware of the lyrics or the name of the melody.

"I have been to the Gerlitzen a few times with Walter so I know I need decent boots. I'm really looking forward to our hike," Lili said as she stood and held her hand out. Rudi took her hand, and, without letting go, they walked along the Ossiachersee shore towards its northern perimeter, from where access to the Gerlitzen is most common.

"Do you want to take the shorter, steeper route up here or the longer, gentler one?" aked Rudi.

"I've never been on the steeper route so let's do that. I promise you won't have to carry me."

Rudi took the lead up the relatively steep, uneven track winding through the fir forest. "Tell me if I'm going too fast," he said, turning his head back a little. He started at a quite slow pace and looked behind him regularly to ensure Lili was keeping up. After a short time, he no longer needed to look back because he could hear her breathing, and they had settled into a good, comfortable rhythm.

Without being aware of it, Rudi began to sing: "Tirol, Tirol, Tirol, Du bist mein Heimatland. Weit ueber Berg und Tal, das Alphorn schallt. Die Wolken ziehn dahin, sie ziehn auch wieder her…"

They were making good time, and Rudi was surprised that Lili was keeping up so well. "Would you like to stop for a drink?" he asked.

"No, thanks. Let's keep going."

They kept making good progress until they reached a steep, rocky outcrop. Rudi stopped and waited a few moments for Lili. He put his rucksack on a rock, took out the flask, and unscrewed the top that doubled for a cup. He half filled the cup with water and offered Lili his hand as she sat on the rock beside the rucksack. She was panting quite heavily, so Rudi just quietly waited to allow her to get her breath back.

All was hushed except for the gentle movement and noise of the swaying canopy when there was a sudden crashing through the trees just above them. Rudi looked to see, partly camouflaged between some trees, a brownish-grey Gemsbok, a wild goat, staring down at them. He knew that those Alpine ibex were in danger of extinction and generally lived above the snowline.

"Look, Lili," he whispered. "We must have woken him from a sleep. Isn't he beautiful? What an excellent specimen of a mountain goat with those long, curved horns. They are quite rare, and it's most unusual to see them so low down. I haven't seen one for years."

A minute later the Gemsbok was gone, and Rudi and Lili were again on their way. Rudi offered Lili his hand with a few difficult steps until they reached some flatter ground, and they were soon on the grassy plateau. The grass was only about fifteen centimetres high, and there were patches of wild flowers, mostly yellow and moving in waves with the breeze, attracting lots of bees and other insects. "Do you want to stop for lunch before we say hello to the summit or afterwards?"

"Let's go to the summit first," replied Lili as she took Rudi's hand; it was now easy to walk side by side. They walked comfortably together nearly in unison, occasionally looking at each other with warm smiles.

Rudi began to whistle a melody Lili had never heard, and she asked, "What's that you're whistling?"

He smiled and started to sing: "Ein Tiroler wollte jagen einen Gemsbok, Gemsbok silbergrau. Doch es wolt ihm nicht gelingen, den das Tierlein, Tierlein war zu schlau. hol la ri a ho, hol la ri a ho, hol a ri a ri a hol a ri o ho…"

"I know I've told you before, but you have a wonderful voice, Rudi," Lili said as she squeezed his hand just a little. "Where did that song come from?"

"It is a local Tirolean song that's very popular among many people who spend time in the mountains."

They soon reached the summit; it was not really special, as it consisted of little more than a collection of rocks in the form of a cairn. The view, however, was splendid in every direction with many snow-covered peaks to be seen in the distance. "Do you know we're one thousand, nine hundred, and eleven metres above sea level here, Lili?"

"Are you sure it's not nine hundred and twelve?" she queried cheekily.

Rudi smiled and pointed out several of the major peaks in the distance. "There are the Karawanken; there is Nockberb. All that area over there is referred to as the Hohe Tauern, and that peak is Hochalmspitze." He let out a brief yodel. "Listen," he said, cupping his left hand over his left ear. Within about a second and a half, the echo of a yodel came back—a second, third, and fourth time. Lili smiled.

Rudi dragged Lili off to the side of the summit, let go of her hand, and said, "Wait there." He ran a few metres to a rock outcrop, where he looked around a little. *Ah, there you are.* He ran back to Lili and gave her an Edelweiss as he sang to her, "Edelweiss, Edelweis, bist so schoen weiss." Lili was most appreciative and gave him a peck on the cheek.

She was now beginning to develop a different interest. "Can we have lunch soon, Rudi?" she asked as she dragged him away. Tightening the hold on each other's hands, they headed downhill.

Rudi knew the exact spot where he thought they should stop for lunch. At the edge of the plateau, there was a little stream cascading down from a rocky area and a short grassy slope to calmer water only a metre or so across. In among the rocks by the stream, Rudi recognized the blue bell-shaped flower of the Enzian growing in a couple of clumps. Across the stream there was forest, mainly of fir, behind them mostly the open meadow where, in winter, skiers would come before taking their descent. Rudi set down his pack and opened it. He unrolled the small tarpaulin, laid it flat, and threw his pullover on to it to keep it in place. He took out the wrapped-up sandwiches and two apples and sat them beside his pack, which he also put on the edge of the tarp. Running to the water's edge, he vigorously washed his hands and face in the icy stream. He shook the excess water from his hands, which he then partially dried on the front of his shirt. Lili was now sitting on the grass, shooing away an inquisitive bee, and Rudi joined her on the grass beside the pack and the food. He took the flask from the pack and offered her some water. She shook her head and gestured towards the sandwiches. "Cheese, ham, or cheese and ham?" asked Rudi.

"Just cheese, please."

Rudi handed her the sandwich. He leaned over to his pack and pulled out two embroidered napkins. He flicked one open and flipped it onto Lili's lap. She gave him a big smile and took another bite of the sandwich. "I can see you are hungry, Lili. Is it good?"

"Very good, thank you," she said while still chewing.

He took a ham sandwich, leaving another ham, the second cheese, and two mixed ham-and-cheese sandwiches. He too ate voraciously. Lili ate the second cheese sandwich, while Rudi demolished a third. He ran to the water's edge with the two apples, washed them, and returned, shaking them of excess moisture. He laid them down, took out his penknife, and proceeded to cut an apple into quarters and remove the core. He handed two quarters to Lili, and it wasn't long before the second apple was cut and eaten. "Excellent apple, Rudi."

"Yes, apples are always good at this time of year; they're locally grown in the valley." Rudi wrapped up the remaining sandwich and put in the pack, from which he took a block of chocolate.

"Oh, you know the way to a woman's heart, Rudi." Lili gave him a cheeky smile and accepted a piece of chocolate.

After some more chocolate, Rudi smiled back and placed some remaining things in the rucksack. He got up and said, "Lili, I need to look at something just above the waterfall. I'll be back in a minute." Rudi walked briskly up the hill. He had been planning this since they decided to come to the Gerlitzen.

The day before, he had wondered whether he really wanted to be on the mountain with someone else when he returned to the place where Franz had lost his life. He wondered whether he could cope with it emotionally. He wondered whether it would be fair to Lili.

Still somewhat uncertain, Rudi walked up to where the trees gave way to a cleared, undulating slope. He leaned against a tree and peered down the slope then began to sob as he recalled the last time he had been there. It was the day Franz died. He bobbed down on his haunches, head between his hands as his sobbing turned to uncontrollable crying.

Lili, observing this, became very concerned and ran to his side. She bobbed down beside him. "Was ist los? Rudi, was ist los?" She got no answer.

Rudi stood up and, continuing to cry nearly as heavily, stumbled his way back to their picnic spot, where he sat on the grass, head between his hands and elbows on his knees. Lili, quite shaken by this outburst, sat beside him and put an arm around him. She just quietly tried to be of comfort without saying anything.

"Sorry," Rudi sobbed. "I'm sorry, I'm so sorry," he repeated as he tried to compose himself. "This is where I lost my best friend." Rudi again burst into near-convulsive crying. "Franz," he blurted out. "He was my best friend." The crying continued. "He and I were doing some ski jumping when it happened."

"What happened, Rudi? What happened?" Lili stuttered.

"He got too much air, far too much air."

"So what happened?"

"He got too much air; he fell. He had a big fall. Put the point of his stock through his heart." Rudi lost it again and sobbed bitterly. He rolled over, putting his head on Lili's lap. It took nearly half an hour before Rudi could compose himself and tell Lili all that happened on that day. They hugged each other very tightly and packed up to leave. Rudi filled the thermos from the stream, where he also washed his face.

They took the easier route down, Lili leading the way. Though it was already well into the afternoon, it became distinctly warmer as they descended. They stopped about halfway down for a drink. They also shared the remainder of the chocolate. Rudi crumpled up the Gianduitto wrapping and put it in his pocket. Lili gave him a big hug, and they continued their descent, single file down the mountain, the temperature increasing as they descended.

As they reached the lake, both quite drained emotionally, they held hands and slowly made their way back to what had become known as their log. "Do you still have some time?" Rudi asked as they sat on the log, swishing away a few flies that had been basking in the sun.

"Yes, Rudi, of course."

Rudi undressed to his underpants, walked to the water's edge, and dived in. He rolled over onto his back and beckoned Lili to join him. She smiled and shook her head. Rudi rolled back over and swam strongly into the distance then back again. Lili watched every stroke, and, as he neared the shore, she strolled out to where the water was just above her ankles, took Rudi's hand, and led him back to their log. Rudi sat to drip dry in the sun and smiled at Lili. She returned his smile, gazed into his eyes, and began, "Rudi, I don't know whether I can continue with you. I am becoming very fond of you, and I can't see how this can work. I am eight or nine years older than you, and I am Jewish, not really religious but I am a Jew."

Rudi interrupted what he was afraid might continue as a justification for her not wanting to see him again. "Ja, Lili, liebe, Lili. It would make no difference to me if you were Buddhist, Confuctionist, or atheist." Lili smiled. "And, anyway, age is only a state of mind. I can see that in the mountains, where you can be as young as me, and in Vienna…"

Lili cut him short and went on. "I fear you will not want to see me in Vienna—that this, for you, is just a summer holiday romance. I don't want to become all involved with you and then not see you after next week."

Rudi was a bit taken aback, because he was also quite smitten. He pulled on his shorts, buttoned up his shirt, and began to try to reassure her. "Lili, I am at least as fond of you as you are of me. I have never felt for anyone as I feel for you. I have never been so close to anyone before. I will want us to continue seeing each other in Vienna."

There was a pause, Lili taking in what she just heard. "My mother would be aghast if she thought I was falling in love with you, Rudi. She wants me to marry a well-connected, successful Jewish man from Vienna."

"That's well and good for your mother, but this is your life, and you must make choices that you want to make."

"I'm sure I'll be getting the third degree tonight and tomorrow from Mother and Auntie, wanting to know all about you. I can't see you tomorrow anyway because I have to go with them to the Woerthersee."

"That's fine. I don't want to take you away from them. I'll be here every day, Lili, and I'll be here for you."

They stood tightly together, their arms wrapped around each other and with tears streaming down Lili's face. "Sorry," she said.

"That's fine," said Rudi. "I ran out of tears a few hours ago, and I thank you for being so understanding."

"I must go now. I'm sure they'll have been worried for some time already," declared Lili.

After a long, passionate kiss and several sighs, Lili turned and walked away.

SHE ARRIVED HOME, called out a hello, and went straight to the bathroom to wash the remainder of tears from her face. Lili joined her auntie and mother in the sitting room, where they had been playing cards. "It's high time you were home. It's nearly dark, and you've been away with this man alone for a long time. What on earth could you do with him for so long?" her mother asked.

Lili wanted to answer, "A whole lot, Mother," but instead just said, "It's not dark for several hours yet, and in any event, we had a very full day hiking. We climbed to the top of the Gerlitzen, had a very nice picnic lunch, and came back. Rudi then went for a swim, and then we talked."

"You had all day to talk, and we were here sitting at home worrying."

"You can't do much talking while climbing with Rudi. We went the steep route, not the easier one that Walter and I took several times. And we saw a Gemsbock on the way up, and he was quite close. Rudi and I had a very nice time, and we plan to see each other again the day after tomorrow before we leave here."

——⚬——

At 10:00 a.m., a well-dressed man in an expensive car came to pick up Lili, her mother, and Tante Mizzi to spend a day at the Woerthersee, the largest of the Kaerntner lakes, very beautiful with several islands and mountain peaks all around. The resort area there was favored by the wealthy.

It was a pleasant day that involved a luncheon, playing bridge, Spazieren, and afternoon tea. Auntie excused herself from a second game of bridge and went for a walk with Lili along the lake. The water was as flat as a mill pond and a deep blue, with the sun shimmering off the surface. It was again very hot, only the seagulls flying about, providing a lightness in the air. Tante Mizzi understood both Lili's desire to find a man she wanted to spend time with and her mother's desire to have Lili marry a young Jewish man who would provide for her daughter to the standard to which she had become accustomed.

"Well," Auntie began, "who is this young man who seems to make you so happy? I see it in your face."

Lili, taking her auntie's arm, began with a sigh. "His name is Rudi. He comes from this area and is now studying law in Vienna. He is just back here during the vacation. He is a very caring, unselfish, charming, exciting, and really warm person."

"And he likes you a lot too, I guess, Lili," interrupted Auntie, smiling in response to her niece's characterization of Rudi.

"Yes, I believe he does. He even sings to me and has a beautiful voice. And Auntie," she said, stopping momentarily and looking into her eyes, "it doesn't hurt that he is exceptionally handsome and very athletic."

"Are you sure you are not dreaming about a Roman god?" After a pause, she asked, "And what do you want to do with him, Lili? No, don't answer that," Auntie added quickly.

"Well, we promised each other that we would meet in Vienna," declared Lili.

"Mama mia, you are serious about this young man, then. Is he Jewish?" Lili shook her head. "You realize your mother is quite determined that you marry a Jewish businessman who is part of the same cultural community she is a part of." Lili understood and did not respond.

A couple of children skipped in front of them as her auntie continued. "It is all well and good to have fallen in love with Rudi, but you must be practical about such things. You are nearly thirty, and most women already have children at this age. Do you want to have children with this man?" Lili looked at her auntie, who went on. "Yes, that must be the major question for you, Lili."

The two children ran in front of them again, chasing seagulls, and Lili clung to her auntie's arm, deep in thought. *Rudi will still be at uni for several more years and not earning any money. If I leave work to have babies, I will not earn any money either. We'd have to put off having children for at least three years. What would Rudi think about being a father?*

Lili and her auntie just kept walking, with Lili trying to make sense of her situation. She stopped and looked at Auntie, giving her arm a bit of a squeeze. "We'd make beautiful babies, Auntie, because he is so handsome...and he's very intelligent too," she said lightheartedly.

"You must be serious, Lili. You'd have beautiful babies with whatever man you married. Do you really want to disappoint your mother so much? She and your father, who worked so very hard to develop a reputation within the Vienna community, only want the best for you. They just want to make sure that you are happy and well taken care of."

Lili didn't want to offend Tante Mizzi, so she said nothing but thought a great deal. *I don't really want to be part of their Vienna community with the pretense that all is well. Father was not a happy man. All he ever wanted was to make money, build the business his father had left him, and to show off... to have an impressive house at the best address, own an expensive car, and keep a house full of servants so that Mother could boss them about. And they would often go to the Musikverein and the opera when they didn't even feel like it or not particularly like the program. They just went for the sake of appearances. My father even told me what I should wear when we went to visit some of his business friends. He wanted to control everybody. Walter was told what to wear and what to say and not say. And all their friends, if one can call them that, were similarly into appearances. My mother and father cared about Walter to some extent because he was expected to take over the business and to build it further. What if Walter didn't want to do that? They didn't care what he wanted.*

They cared even less about what I wanted. I had to take piano lessons, which I didn't like because I was not any good at it. My piano teacher knew that and never pushed me or was ever demanding. She cared more about what I wanted than my mother and father did. If I had to perform for them, she would always choose a simple but very nice piece that I could learn to play and that everybody liked. Walter always knew and gave me a knowing and approving wink. My father cared so little about his wife, Walter, and me that he killed himself. His ego, all tied up with being successful in business, was more important than being a husband and father.

I want to live my life as I want to live it. I have a job; it is a respectable position, and I don't want to rely on my mother for anything anymore. I will not just run away from home; I don't want to hurt Mother at all, but I do want to make decisions about how I live my life and with whom I want to live it. I will talk this through with Walter. He has been my best friend for a very long time, and he will give me good advice.

Lili then very carefully responded to her auntie, hoping that these sentiments would indeed be relayed to her mother. "I certainly do not want to offend Mother or to disappoint her. I appreciate what she and father built up in Vienna and the advantages that resulted for me. I never wanted for anything materially…no, nothing. But I am a different person than Mother. While I love the opera and the music of Vienna and certain coffee houses, I do not feel compelled to go to be seen. I don't want to go just for the sake of appearances. I am very fortunate I have a respectable job and can be independent from my parents and any man. And isn't that how it should be, Auntie?"

"Yes, of course."

Lili continued, "I do not feel a need to marry a Jew. There are other nice people in the world, and many Jewish people have married Christians or people who do not believe in any religion. I will get Walter's advice, and I will not marry Rudi in a hurry. I only know him in his environment, and we will soon get to know one another in Vienna. I am really looking forward to that, Auntie. There you have it. That's how I feel," she concluded confidently and emphatically.

"I understand you well, Lili," said her auntie resignedly. "I'm sure you will make the best decision for you. I trust your intelligence and instincts. And it is a good idea for you to talk it over with Walter—the sooner, the better." They left the discussion at that and soon returned for some lovingly prepared afternoon tea.

—⊗⊗⊗—

WHILE LILI WAS at the Woerthersee, Rudi spent the morning with his mother and the afternoon with his father at the Bahnhof, helping with some platform sweeping and downpipe cleaning. Neither his father nor mother had any inkling of the seriousness of the relationship developing between him and Lili. They were just happy that Rudi was home for a while, having breakfast and dinner with them each day and apparently enjoying himself by the lake or in the mountains as he had done since he was a young boy. They were pleased that Rudi hardly mentioned Franz, suggesting that he had managed to at least deal with the tragic loss. They were proud to have a son at university, the first in their family to be educated beyond high school, and that he seemed to be managing his life pretty well in Vienna. They were pleased that he and Joseph had become good friends and that there was basically nothing to worry unduly about.

Over dinner the day before, his mother asked Rudi, "How did you get that cut under your chin?"

Rudi didn't completely lie when he said, "I ducked into a sword while sword fighting at uni. The other guy was more shocked than I was." His mother didn't pursue it, but Rudi's father gave him a look of doubt, suggesting he realized that not all had been told.

After dinner the three of them walked to a Gasthaus, to which they had been many times, for some wine and to listen to a quartet playing Kaerntner melodies. The proprietor greeted the Auers warmly and asked, "Ja, Rudi, why did you not bring that lovely young lady I saw you with at the Ossiachersee the other day? She'd like it here."

Rudi, somewhat taken aback, answered, "Next time, maybe."

Rudi's mother and father just looked at one another and at their son, who wondered whether he'd been observed in an intimate embrace.

THE NEXT DAY there was indeed an intimate embrace as Lili and Rudi found one another at their log. It was again a wonderful summer day but even hotter than on previous days and quite humid, with developing clouds that could possibly bring some afternoon showers. The water was a deep blue and as calm as could be. The atmosphere was heavy.

"How was your day?" Rudi enquired.

"We had a very nice day, and I had a particularly good talk with Tante Mizzi about us. I emphasized that we would continue seeing one another in Vienna whether Mother approved or not."

Rudi was relieved. "Where and when should we meet in Vienna, Lili?"

"I don't care, as long as it is soon. You say, Rudi."

He thought for a moment: "Let's meet at the Mozart Memorial in the Burggarten."

"Near the Ringstrasse, yes. And when?"

"Hm, at noon next Monday," suggested Rudi.

"Sounds good. That will brighten up my day." She gave his arm a squeeze. "Let's go for a swim, Rudi," she suggested as she began to unbutton her dress.

"Do you need any help with that?" asked Rudi cheekily.

"Not today, thank you, but maybe—"

Just then there was a loud thunder roll they had not expected. Lili held her hand out to Rudi as he was taking off his shorts. "Come, let's get into the water before the rain starts."

Hand in hand, they ran into the lake until they fell into the water and into each other's arms. "I love you, Rudi."

"I love you, Lili," he declared as they ever-so-gently embraced one another, realizing they both meant what they had just said. Tears welled up in their eyes as their embrace became tighter and it began to rain.

Rudi kissed Lili on the forehead and said, "Come" as they both swam out away from the shore. Soon it began to pour cats and dogs, and, treading water, they held hands. The raindrops stung as they hit their faces, so they looked down and watched the drops create little craters as they hit the surface of the lake. It was fun being in the water during this downpour, and they felt very close as they waited for it to subside. Indeed the rain didn't last long, and they soon swam back to shore. It was very steamy as Rudi sat on their log, watching Lili dry herself. The sun shone brightly again as she folded her towel and sat beside Rudi.

"Shall we go for a little walk?" Rudi suggested.

Lili stood up and took his hand as they strolled along the water's edge, Rudi's feet in the water, disturbing a few minnows. Though the earlier rain had reduced the humidity a little, it was still quite hot as they wandered and wondered. As they wandered along the shore, they wondered whether they would enjoy each other as much in Vienna as they were enjoying each other there in Annenheim. Neither could imagine their relationship in Vienna being as joyous, as free, and as uncomplicated. Each intended to try, and each knew the other would try also. So, very contented, comfortable with, and confident in each other, they continued to walk hand in hand away from and then back toward their log.

As they approached the log, they noticed a couple sitting on it facing the other way. When Rudi and Lili arrived at the spot, a young man asked, "Could we leave our things here while we go for a swim? Do you mind?"

"Not at all," said Rudi as the young couple headed to the water. Turning to Lili, he asked, "Shall we get something to eat? I'm hungry."

"Sure. Wuerstel mit Senf again, please, Rudi. I'll get the sand off my feet and make myself more acceptable for lunch in the meantime."

Rudi went off to get lunch, while Lili took her sandals and walked to the water's edge, where she washed off as much sand as she could from her legs and slipped into her sandals. She returned to the log and had just finished brushing her hair when Rudi arrived with lunch. They were quietly and happily eating when the couple returned from the water unobtrusively and collected their bag. "Thank you for watching it for us. Au revoir," they said as they slipped away.

"The next Wuerstel I'll have will be with you in Vienna." Rudi smiled at Lili.

"I can't wait. Silly, isn't it? I am still eating this one, and I'm already looking forward to the next. I'm so looking forward to spending time with you in Vienna, Rudi."

"I'm looking forward to it as well, Lili."

It was so hot that day, they took their bag into the shade just a few metres away, spread two towels beside each other, lay down, and dozed off. A little while later Rudi rose with a thirst, so he sneaked away to fetch some fruit juice and two ice creams. He hurried back to Lili, licking both on the way to prevent spillage. Sitting up, Lili happily accepted an ice cream as she smiled adoringly up at him. Rudi sat down beside her, and they fed each other. The ice cream didn't last long, but they were both confident that their love for one another would.

After another snooze, they again found themselves in the water, embracing more than swimming. They were delaying the inevitable—a goodbye for now. Lili would return to Vienna the following day, driven by friends from the Woerthersee, and Rudi would return to Vienna by train on Sunday. They had not been apart for more than one day since they had met, so three days seemed like an eternity.

They lingered in the water then lingered getting dried and dressed. As they were about to part, Lili said, "I feel so sad to leave you now, Rudi," and she wiped away some tears.

"Oh, Lili, Lili, I am so happy, so pleased we met, that we had such a good time together, that we like each other a lot, and that we'll meet in Vienna."

There were several big hugs, several tears, and several goodbyes, and then they went their separate ways. Monday could not come fast enough for either of them.

———

LILI AND HER mother and auntie were picked up as arranged and driven to Vienna on Friday. Lili was pleased that she was not alone in the car with just her mother and auntie, for she didn't want to hear from her mother, likely for several hours, how inappropriate it would be for her to see Rudi in Vienna. She would get enough of that when back in Vienna, she thought.

It turned out that the weekend was free of any mention of Rudi by her mother. Her auntie had counseled her against that, and her counsel had obviously been heeded. Lili mentioned Rudi to Walter, who was at home for just a couple of days before returning to Paris, where he was currently working. While they were together in the Stadtpark for an afternoon concert, Walter was curious. "Tell me about this man, Lili…Rudi, right? Auntie briefly mentioned to me that you were more than a little interested."

Lili stopped, stepped in front of Walter, looked into his eyes, and declared, "I love Rudi."

Walter had never before heard her say that she loved someone. He smiled and gave her a brotherly hug. "Congratulations, Lili. I am so pleased for you. Come, sit over here and tell me everything you want to tell me."

While she relayed to Walter most everything she knew about Rudi, she noticed the color drain from his face and a deep grimace develop as if he were in pain. After a considerable pause, Walter inwardly questioned Lili's sanity while having a number of things reconfirmed: "Rudi is a Gentile, a Catholic, and he is from Kärnten…

in the country. He is nineteen years old and unsophisticated, still a first-year university student."

There was a long pause as Walter began to breathe heavily and deeply. "Ey vey!" he gasped. "But he is gallant, intelligent, very caring, very practical, has a beautiful voice, and is athletic and very handsome," he emphasised.

"Yes, Walter, and he loves me. He told me but he didn't have to. I already know," she said.

"Ei-yei-yei, Lili! If Father were still alive, you realize he would not allow such a relationship to continue."

"Yes, I realize, but Father is not alive. Furthermore, Father never cared about me, our mother, or you. Did he think about us when he killed himself?" she asked rhetorically while becoming visibly angry.

Walter put his arm around her and quietly asked, "What do you think it would do to Mother if you continued this relationship with Rudi? He is neither Jewish nor well connected."

"I realize she would be very upset, and I would do a great deal to avoid having her upset. But I am twenty-eight years old, have my own job with a good firm, and want to build my life with someone I love and not be married off to some boring old fart." Lili and Walter both laughed. "It's true, Walter—all those self-important, smug, boring men that Mother and Father introduced me to over the years."

"Do you intend to marry Rudi and have children with him?"

"Maybe," she said with a hint of a smile. "I first want us to get to know one another, enjoy each other's company in Vienna, go ice dancing together, attend some concerts, go to museums, and do some skiing with him in winter. I bet he's a fabulous skier. Who knows? Maybe," she repeated.

"I really am very pleased for you, Lili; I hope the two of you can make it work, and I'd love to meet him as soon as you are comfortable with that. You realize Rudi would have to be very, very special for me to give my approval."

———

IN THE MEANTIME Rudi spent the rest of his vacation with his mother and father, doing nothing special, just helping out where he could and thinking about Lili a great deal. On Saturday afternoon, they visited with Tante Marianne, and in the evening Rudi went for dinner with his mother and father to the same Gasthaus they were at only a few days earlier. This would be the last dinner they would have together for several months. They enjoyed the food, a few too many drinks, and the music from the same Kapelle. Rudi danced with his mother and assured her that he would continue to be a conscientious student and would not be too distracted by Lili, whom his parents knew little about. But they knew that Rudi hadn't been that happy for a long time, certainly not since Franz was killed. *Is he in love perhaps?* they wondered.

———

THE TRAIN JOURNEY to Vienna was uneventful. Rudi arrived at his apartment and pushed the front door open to be greeted by Joseph. "Shalom, my friend."

"Servus, Joseph. Good to see you. Have you been back long?"

"No, just arrived a little while ago. How was your vacation, Rudi? How are your parents? I bet they were pleased to have you back home with them for a while."

"Yes, we had a good time together. Mother and Father are both well, and they seemed pleased that I spent most of the time there with a young lady I met who was on vacation from Vienna. And how did Ester get on with your parents, Joseph? Did you have a good time?"

"Yes, thank you, Rudi. All went well. But tell me about this woman you spent so much time with. How did you meet her? Where does she live in Vienna?"

Rudi shared the details of his holiday getting to know Lili, and Joseph was very pleased that she was a Jew. "She's one of us, Rudi, and soon you'll be related to us. But then I guess you already have empathy with our situation, our predicament, having saved a Jewish student from a certain crack on the skull. And if you were to make babies together, your children would be Jewish, of course."

"We've only known each other for a very short time, so the idea of making babies hasn't come up yet. I certainly wouldn't want to make Jewish babies here in Vienna. The future here, with Hitler just across the border and the rise of anti-Semitism in Austria, has become very problematic, Joseph, don't you think? Why is it that most people here don't understand the threat?"

7

VIENNA, AUTUMN 1932

ON A WARM, balmy day, Rudi strolled through the Burggarten and observed that summer would soon be coming to an end. The foliage was changing from bright green to golden with tinges of red, some birch trees already beginning to lose a few leaves. It was just before noon on the Monday he and Lili had arranged to meet for the first time in Vienna after their whirlwind romance by the Ossiachersee. It was only three days since they were together so happily, so joyously, so confident that their feelings for one another would be sustained wherever they were to meet next. Yet Rudi felt anxious. Though he had now lived in Vienna for several months and settled in well at the university and with his flatmate, this was not where he felt most comfortable, most at home.

As he wandered along through the Burggarten, occasionally kicking a fallen acorn in front of him, he asked himself, *Why would Lili, who seemingly has everything going for her—a good home, a good job, a close cultural network—want to get entangled with me? She is a Jew from a well-established family with prospective suitors in abundance. She is nine years older than I am and so very much at home in Vienna. I am making out quite well here but am still a bit at sea. I am still a bit like a fish out of water. And her family, what will they...*Rudi's thought was interrupted as he saw Lili walk quickly towards him, a paper bag in her hand and the Mozart Memorial just behind her. She was elegantly dressed in a calf-length summer frock and midhigh shoes.

She had a big smile and sparkling eyes as she and Rudi hurried towards one another and embraced as if they hadn't seen each other for a year or more. "Now we are together in Vienna," said Lili, stating the obvious. "How are you, Rudi? Did you have a good trip?"

"Yes, thank you, Lili. How are you? How was your trip back by car?" They took each other by the hand and walked further along a path to their left. Rudi flicked a few leaves from a bench, and they sat down to answer each other's questions.

"I brought us a couple of Wuerstel because this is my lunch hour. They should still be hot, as I just got them. I knew you'd be on time."

"Thank you, Lili. Very thoughtful. And how was your trip back home?" Rudi repeated.

"It was very pleasant because Mother didn't dare complain to her friends, in front of me, that I had fallen head over heels for a non-Jew. I got the third degree from my brother over the weekend though."

"This is a better Wuerstel than the ones we had at the Ossiachersee. You were right, Lili. What did Walter have to say?" Rudi asked anxiously.

"Well, I think he is worried for all the reasons we have discussed and especially concerned that Mother will find it difficult going forwards, explaining my liaison with a non-Viennese and non-Jew. Walter is a very caring person and very protective of me, of course. He looks forward to meeting you. He wished us luck, and he meant it, Rudi," explained Lili as she gave his hand a reassuring squeeze. "He will remain in Vienna for a few more days before he goes back to France, so I will need to go home straight after work. We could meet again on Wednesday at the same time but closer to my work—at the Rathausplatz perhaps. I need to do some shopping at lunchtime tomorrow."

Rudi put his arm around Lili, and she nestled her head on his shoulder. They chatted on quietly about nothing of consequence, each feeling very comfortable with the other. Lili looked at her watch. "Oh, Rudi, I'm sorry. I must away. I mustn't be late on my first day back." They both stood up, and after a short, passionate embrace, Lili hurried away.

———

WEDNESDAY CAME AND went, and Rudi and Lili arranged to meet at Café Landtmann on Friday at 4:45 p.m. Over the next couple of weeks they met there and at other locations several times while they got back into the rhythm of their daily routines. Most of Lili's days were spent at work, where her boss, Herrmann Schwartz, had become very appreciative of her conscientious attitude and professional work. He was a quiet man and did not speak of professional matters that concerned her parents. He gave Lili minimal instructions, and days would often go by when there was little exchange between them.

On Lili's second day back after her vacation, his inquisitiveness got the better of him: "Lili, what happened to you during the holidays? You not only have a healthy tan, but you seem to be beaming, have some extra spring in your step, and have a real sparkle in your eyes. Did you meet someone special?"

"As a matter of fact I did, Mr. Schwartz," Lili said, beaming even more.

"Would you like to tell me about him, Lili?"

"Well, he is tall, in comparison to me anyway; he is very athletic and extremely handsome. He is intelligent, has a beautiful singing voice, and is very caring."

"That's very nice. Go on. I'm happy for you and curious. How old is he, where's he from, what's his profession, and where does he live?"

"I wish you had not asked these questions because to deal with that reality will likely be very difficult."

Mr. Schwartz paused for a moment. "If you love each other then all obstacles that at first seem insurmountable can be overcome."

"Oh, thank you, Mr. Schwartz. Rudi will be pleased when I tell him what you said. But how will I handle the reality, really? Rudi is not Jewish, and he is not from an established Viennese family."

Mr. Schwartz looked down, rubbed his hands together, grimaced, and paused. "Where is he from? What are his professional connections?"

"Rudi is a law student here in Vienna, and he is eight years younger than I am."

"Why do you make it so hard for yourself, Lili? What does your mother say? No, no, you don't have to tell me; I know exactly what she'd think and say." There was a long pause. "Lili, if you want to talk things through with me as the weeks and months go by, do not hesitate. But in any event, you should not be like Violetta in Verdi's *La Traviata* and sacrifice your love to preserve the family's good name. Good luck, Lili. You'll make it work. I believe you have good instincts. Bring Rudi in sometime. I'd like to meet him."

Lili returned to her work, pleased to have had the conversation with her boss.

FOR THE FIRST couple of weeks after his vacation, Rudi was busy with lectures and catching up on some reading at Café Louvre. He enjoyed returning to his now familiar haunt, ordering his favorite Wiener Schnitzel, and browsing through newspapers from far and wide. He came across an article by Thomas Mann in the *Berliner Tageblatt* that aroused his curiosity. It was in the aftermath of the Nazis running riot in Koenigsberg, which witnessed much vandalism, arson, and even some killings. In the article titled "What We Must Demand," Thomas Mann denounced Nazism as a "national disease," a "hodge-podge of hysteria and moldy romanticism, megaphone Germanism that is a caricature and vulgarization of everything German." Rudi wondered what sort of reprisal the *Berliner Tageblatt* might receive for publishing such an article. *Good for Thomas Mann to call Nazism as he sees it,* thought Rudi.

Rudi had several meetings with Heinrich, the editor of the uni paper, to discuss future research and articles he might focus on. Heinrich thought that the rise of Hitler in Germany and the concomi-tant rise in anti-Semitism would be of interest to students and faculty alike as a disproportionate number of people at the university were Jewish. Regular discussions with Joseph also included the increasing difficulties Jews were experiencing in certain parts of Vienna. His girl-friend, Ester, had come over recently and described how she witnessed some four or five Nazi types attempting to boycott some Jewish stores in Leopoldstadt. "Some Jewish shopkeepers banded together, sur-rounded them, and gave them a hiding for their chutzpah," explained Joseph. "They shouldn't be back for a little while."

Ester continued, "You should come over and see where we live, Rudi. You have probably never been to this part of Vienna. You could come and enjoy some real Jewish food you don't find here, like matzo ball soup, stuffed cabbage leaves, Latkes, and Hamantaschen."

"Sounds good to me. Thank you, Ester. I would enjoy that," responded Rudi.

RUDI THOUGHT A little about Franz and a great deal of each day about Lili. They continued to enjoy being together several times a week, and Rudi was really looking forward to having her show him around the opera house that coming Saturday. Lili was looking forward to the day too, because they would have a long time together, but she was not looking forward to telling him about her father's death.

While Lili was still preparing for their picnic lunch, Rudi was wandering around the Stadtpark whistling a tune he had heard a couple of times in recent days and was trying to remember the lyrics: *Mein Herz und mein Sinn/Schwärmt stets nur für Wien/Für Wien, wie es weint, wie es lacht!/Da kenn ich mich aus/Da bin i halt z'Haus/Bei Tag und noch mehr bei der Nacht.*

Und keiner bleibt kalt/ Ob jung oder alt/ Der Wien, wie es wirklich ist, kennt/ Müßt' ich einmal fort/ Von dem schönen Ort/Da nähm' meine Sehnsucht kein End./Dann hört' ich aus weiter Ferne ein Lied/ Das klingt und singt, das lockt und zieht.

It was an early autumn day; a slight breeze helped some colored leaves drift to the ground, while the occasional squirrel was seen trying to bury some nuts for a rainy day. Rudi was admiring the park in general and stopping regularly to look at the many statues of musicians and artists, including Franz Schubert and Franz Lehar. The most famous of all the statues, the Johann Strauss Memorial, was created in 1921 by the Austrian sculptor Edmund Hellmer. Rudi didn't like this statue as much as some others; he thought it was too bright and garish, and Johann Strauss had a rather pompous disposition. He was gazing up at the back of the statue, which he preferred to the view from the front, and was still whistling the tune that seemed to have become transfixed in his mind when he heard Lili behind him singing the refrain: "Wien, Wien, nur du allein/Sollst stets die Stadt meiner Träume sein."

"It's becoming a habit, you sneaking up on me," Rudi said as he turned around and embraced Lili, who was carrying a basket. They continued looking into each other's eyes and continued with the refrain: "Dort, wo die alten Häuser stehn/ Dort, wo die lieblichen Mädchen gehn!/Wien, Wien, nur du allein /Sollst stets die Stadt meiner Träume sein!"

"I wish I could sing like you, Rudi," Lili said as she took his hand.

"At least you know the words, Lili," he replied. "How are you? Did your mother warn you against meeting this mere boy who speaks a lot of Quatsch?"

"Don't be silly, Rudi. She didn't even mention your name. I had a long talk with my boss, Mr. Schwartz, about you though."

"And did he advise you to find someone more suitable?"

"No, he said something like 'if you love one another then all obstacles that at first seem insurmountable can be overcome.' He wants to meet you."

"Gut," said Rudi. "We should meet sometime. I would also be interested in his views about the threat that rising anti-Semitism has to the Jews of Vienna."

Rudi took Lili's basket from her, and, hand in hand, they wandered up and down a few paths of the park. There were a few other couples doing much the same. A few beautifully dressed children were running about, kicking leaves in front of them as they chased a pair of pigeons from one place to another; three teenage boys were throwing a ball, careful not to aggravate an elderly couple shuffling along arm in arm, he with a cane. Rudi and Lili spied a vacant bench just ahead of them in the shade, and they soon sat together as Lili beckoned Rudi to pass her the basket. She rubbed her hands together as if to suggest the beginning of proceedings and placed red-rimmed napkins on Rudi's and her lap and one between them on the bench. She handed Rudi a drinking glass and carefully placed one beside her on her left, on the third and flattest slat of the bench. She glanced up at Rudi, handed him a bottle of apple juice, and began to unpack an assortment of sandwiches on the bench between them. A pair of hopeful sparrows scratched nervously around in front of them as they began to enjoy their picnic of cheeses and cornichons on dark rye, ham and mustard on light rye, and meatloaf with chutney on wheat bread. A couple of reticent pigeons observed from a distance.

"Thank you, Lili. This is very nice." Rudi helped himself to seconds. "Shall I pour you some?" Lili handed him her glass.

They lingered over the remainder of lunch, shook the few crumbs from their napkins, to the delight of the sparrows, and wrapped everything up in them, then placed them in the basket.

Lili shuffled over to Rudi, who put his arm around her, and they both sat quietly. After a little while Lili's breathing became heavier. She sat back and looked up at Rudi. "I have to tell you something," she began. "I wanted to tell you while we were in Annenheim. You noticed that neither Walter nor my father was with us in Annenheim, and we had all been coming there together over summers for years. Walter just recently started working in France."

"So where was your father? Papa noticed he was missing this year."

Lili paused for a moment. "Father committed suicide; he killed himself."

"Oh, I'm so sorry, Lili. Was he sick?"

Lili wiped a few tears away. "No, it was this year…on March fifteenth. His business had been going from bad to worse, and he was convinced it would go kaput. The business had not been going well for years following the depression. I guess people were not buying that second or third umbrella, or preferred to get wet rather than buy another if they'd left theirs at home," Lili said with an awkward smile; she wiped away some more tears and snuggled closer to Rudi. With some anger, she continued: "Intelligent and yet so stupid. He cared more about making money and what people thought of him than caring about Walter and me and his wife. I can't remember when he ever cared about Walter and me really. Yes, he was proud of us when we were little, and he could show us off to his colleagues. Not very different to showing off a new piece of imported furniture. That's why he wasn't with us this summer." They sat quietly for quite a while when Lili said, "I feel all right now. We should leave, as we have quite a walk to the opera house."

They exited the park on Johannesgasse, turned left at Schubertring, and turned right into Kaerntnerring. Before long they were there, it having been a shorter walk than they had anticipated.

As they walked in, Lili greeted a guide, who gave her a set of keys for the back rooms, including the dressing rooms, the library, prop rooms, costume rooms, and various other storage areas not normally accessible to the public. Rudi was most impressed by the grandeur of the interior, especially the staircases, and the opulence of the paintings and fittings, notably the main chandelier. As they entered the "haus," Lili pointed out the box her parents normally occupied as well as the standing-room area that students generally dominated.

"You must take me here one day, Lili; it would be fascinating for me to see a production. We could go when one of your favorite operas or ballets is being staged."

"Yes, I would like that a lot. I should take you when Gusti Pichler is dancing. She is our prima ballerina, and the productions with her are always wonderful. Let's have a look at some of the dressing rooms behind here," Lili invited.

"These rooms are so opulent; the stars who get ready here must think they are really something."

"Well, of course, Johann Strauss is like a king here. If he wanted a throne, he would get one, no doubt." Lili took Rudi's hand and led him to various more rooms, including a music library and a costume library. They wandered onto the stage, where tour party members were attentively listening to a guide. They walked to the front of the stage, admired the half-drawn curtains, and gazed up at the circular rows of boxes. They returned to the back of the stage, where Rudi quickly twirled Lili towards him, held her tightly, and gave her a quick kiss on the mouth.

"Naughty boy!" she exclaimed. They both smiled as she led him to some more rooms housing production props. "Had enough yet, Rudi? One could spend a whole day here, of course." She could tell by his facial expression that it was time to depart, so she led him down the grand stairway, pausing momentarily on a landing to observe a sculpture.

"Do they have weddings here?" queried Rudi.

"It would surely be pretty special." She smiled adoringly up at Rudi. Lili returned the keys to an office and led Rudi outside. "I'm a little hungry now," she said as she led him across the street, dodging a tramcar that seemed to be epitomizing Vienna Gemuetlichkeit.

"Come, this is where Walter and I spent many evenings after perfor-mances before we went back home."

A waiter approached as they entered. "Gruess Gott, Lili, how are you? How was your summer? How is Walter?"

Finding a table by the window and delaying answers, she finally replied, "Herr Ober, this is my friend Rudi."

"Welcome to Café Sacher, Rudi."

Lili continued, "Walter is working in France, and he is well, thank you. Rudi and I spent some time together over summer, and we are both a little peckish. Zweimal Sachertorte und zwei Melange, bitte, Herr Ober." That sent the waiter from the table. "It is obligatory to have Sachertorte here on your first visit."

Rudi noticed the elegant interior of this coffee house and the matching demeanor of the waiter in formal black-and-white attire. Café Sacher, a classy Viennese coffee house, was part of the Sacher Hotel, which specialized in catering to the aristocracy, the wealthy, and the famous. As Rudi was gazing around this grand café, Lili got to thinking, *This would be the perfect place for Rudi and me to spend our first night together. I'm just so looking forward to that but can't think of how I can stay out for the night without Mother being highly suspicious. I should say I'm staying the night with Hanna and her husband. My deception would be safe with them.*

The rich chocolate cake with apricot filling and chocolate icing came served on a gold-rimmed white plate; the hot black coffee with foamed milk and Schlagobers (whipped cream) arrived on an oval silver platter with a glass of water, a spoon balanced on top of the glass. Rudi picked up his fork, waited for Lili to start, and nervously took a piece, taking great care to prevent it from tumbling back onto the plate. If that were to happen most anywhere else, he would sim-ply pick it up with his fingers—not appropriate for here.

"Wunderbar," pronounced Rudi as he gained confidence with his fork. He wanted to feed Lili a piece but had second thoughts, as a second waiter came to the table to greet her.

"Servus, Lili, so nice to see you. How was your summer?"

"Hello. This is my friend Rudi."

"Servus, Rudi, pleased to meet you." Rudi offered his hand.

"Summer was fine, thank you, Herr Ober." She threw a smile at Rudi, which was noticed by the waiter.

"I hear Walter is in France. I guess we won't have to ask him to stop singing then for a while." There were smiles all around, and the waiter left.

Rudi and Lili ate and talked for a while about music and ballet and opera, and Rudi became increasingly aware that there was a big part of Lili's life he had little familiarity with. He again began to doubt how sensible it really was to be committed to her. Though he was strongly attracted to her, he realized they weren't all that compatible. He was much more outdoorsy than she, and Lili really was steeped in Viennese culture. She clearly was from different economic and social strata in society, and he was pretty sure he wouldn't fit in well with her people at all. Her mother, and probably most of their circle, would likely not approve of him either, he thought. It also dawned on him that, being close to thirty years of age, Lili would probably want to have children soon. *I'm not ready to have children. I won't want to have children for a long time. I need to finish my studies and get a job first. With the rise of anti-Semitism, perhaps I'm really foolish to be involved with a Jew. It has been prevalent for a long time, but it is clearly on the rise, and I have no doubt that it's going to become very bad over the next few years. Why is it that most people don't seem to see the wave of anti-Semitism becoming stronger? Don't they read the newspapers? Don't they follow the dramatic events in Germany? Don't they hear about the picketing of Jewish stores, the smashing of windows, and Hakenkreuzer or swastikas being painted on doors here in Vienna? There is even a strong anti-Semitic faction at the university, for God's sake. I am sure this is only the beginning. If Hitler comes to power in Germany, it will not be long before it's no longer tenable to be a Jew in Vienna, perhaps even to be related to one. Perhaps I should meet a nice young Christian girl; life would be much less complicated for me.*

Noticing that Rudi was deep in thought—and feeling somewhat constrained in showing her affection for him in that place—Lili suggested they go for a little walk in the Burggarten. They beckoned the waiter to their table, paid the bill, left a little Trinkgeld, and departed, Lili taking Rudi's arm. They returned to the Operngasse, turned into the Opernring, and crossed Goethegasse, entering the Burggarten with the Goethe statue lauding over the entrance. They strolled along with arms around each other and with similar thoughts as to how nice it would be to take a room at the Sacher and stay there the night.

Disregarding his thoughts of a little while earlier, Rudi said, "You know, Lili, this coming Saturday we should go out and have a nice dinner, and you should stay the night with me. Joseph will be with Ester at her Leopoldstadt apartment."

"I would love that, Rudi." She initiated a passionate embrace.

"How will you be able to escape for the night?"

"I've already thought about that. I'll pretend I'm spending the night with Hanna, an old school friend. She and her husband understand the situation well."

"I rather like it at Café Louvre. The food is certainly good," Rudi said, remembering the oversized Schnitzel he had eaten there several times. "And it has a very pleasant atmosphere."

"Sounds perfect, Rudi. That's where all the journalists meet, isn't it? And where you met with Friedrich a couple of times?"

"Yes, that's right."

"It is also unlikely that anyone there would recognize me, so that'll be perfect, Rudi. I don't think Mother would have even heard of Café Louvre. She'd think it's in Paris."

———

DESPITE BOTH RUDI and Lili having a very busy week, the time dragged as both were really looking forward to, and at the same time a little anxious about, spending Saturday night with each other. Lili had already made arrangements to meet Hanna for dinner on Tuesday evening, at which time she'd invite herself over to her place Saturday night. Lili also acceded to her mother's wishes that she attend bridge classes on Wednesday. In the meantime, Rudi had to catch up with some reading he had been putting off because of its boring subject matter, and he had to keep up with his research regarding political developments in Germany in preparation for his next article. He also needed Friday to clean the apartment.

On Saturday morning at breakfast, Joseph noticed that Rudi was a bit edgy. "Are you worried about having Lili over tonight?"

"I guess I am a bit anxious; I've never been with a woman before and—"

"Oh, have no fear," interrupted Joseph. "Let nature take its course; it'll all be fine. Where are you going for dinner, somewhere close?"

"Yes, Café Louvre. The times I've been there the food has always been good, and none of Lili's acquaintances would ever go there, so we'll not be anxious about being spotted at least."

"Just relax, Rudi. Everything will be fine." Joseph finished his Semmel and coffee. "Can I leave the dishes to you? I'm running a bit late. Mazel Tov."

Rudi smiled. "Of course. Servus, Joseph," he called as his flatmate disappeared out the door.

Rudi spent the next couple of hours washing a few dishes, dusting, wiping, cleaning, and rearranging the living room a little. He shook the curtains out the window and replaced them. He changed the bed linen in his room and produced a second pillow. He replaced a small black candle stub with a new red candle in his candle holder—a familiar schnaps bottle. He returned to the kitchen to see if there was a suitable vase for some flowers he was planning to buy. *What should I have at home for after dinner? Some chocolates, some biscuits perhaps? Will Lili want coffee, wine…red or white? Champagne? Fruit? Why don't I know these things?*

Soon Rudi found himself on the street going from one shop to another. First he bought a square white tablecloth with a red edge. It cost about the same as a month's food, he lamented. Next he purchased a bottle of Piper-Heidsieck champagne and two champagne glasses, then he went to the Hofzuckerbäckerei, the Demel where he purchased a selection of chocolates and some mini pastries. On the way back to the apartment he picked up some red and white carnations, which he knew Lili liked.

Back at the apartment he replaced the old tablecloth with the new one and now remembered he needed a vase. He looked everywhere; there was no vase, but he found an appropriately shaped jar.

It still had a confiture label glued to it: Staud's Donautal Marille. *Never tasted that, he thought. Must have been from a previous era.* He soaked the jar in water, and it still took at least half an hour to scrub the label off. *Amazing what one does for the love of a woman, he pondered. What if I'm no good at this? What if I become too nervous? I might disappoint Lili. Then what? Relax, remember what Joseph said…just relax, as difficult as that might be.*

Rudi arranged the flowers, which were quite aromatic, and set the vase on the table with the two champagne glasses. He left the Demel products in their boxes, placed them on the table, and set the two best matching dessert plates he could find beside them after wiping them clean of all marks. Rudi stepped back, looked at the room as a whole and at the table in particular, and, quite satisfied with his efforts, concluded, *This is as good as it's going to get.* A while later, Rudi polished his shoes, spent more time than normal in the bathroom, and took his recently ironed trousers from the chair they were hanging over. He required three attempts to get his tie properly tied and put on his jacket, adjusting his pocket handkerchief three times.

It was a beautiful, warm, balmy autumn evening with barely a breeze as Rudi locked the door and left the apartment. There were quite a few people about in small groups and couples going to wherever they were going in a most unhurried way. It was for most Viennese, after all, the commencement of the weekend. As he walked along Wipplingerstrasse, Rudi felt quite anxious, his heart pounding as if he had just finished a five-kilometre race. He tried to reassure himself. *Relax, Rudi. This is not a test. This is not something to fail. Just enjoy a nice dinner and a nice evening. Be calm and confident, as Lili will likely be a little anxious herself. What's the worst thing that could happen?* Before he could answer, he arrived at the corner of the Renngasse. He glanced at his watch; he was a couple of minutes early. He stepped inside and, gaining a waiter's attention and pointing, asked, "Herr Ober, would you please be so kind as to save that table in the corner for Lili and me? We'll only be a few minutes. Oh, and bring two glasses of champagne before we've warmed the seats."

"Sicher," he answered.

Rudi stepped back outside, looked around, and soon noticed Lili, swinging a bag, walking towards him from the opposite side. Looking across, Rudi remembered being spied on by a couple of Brownshirts when he was leaving the café the time before last. What different circumstances that was, he thought.

Lili wanted to be sure to be on time as she had learned that Rudi was a stickler for being punctual.

"Servus, Lili."

"Servus, Rudi."

They embraced, each feeling the other's heart pounding. "How are you, Lili? You look wonderful."

"Just a little anxious, as I feel guilty deceiving my mother. It's worth it though, to be here with you."

Rudi took Lili by the hand. The waiter opened the door for them, winked at Rudi, and led them to the desired table at the far end of the restaurant. He took Lili's coat and pulled out the chair for her then pushed it in again as she sat down, placing her bag on the chair next to her. Rudi sat down. Lili let out a sigh. "My feelings of guilt have gone." She smiled.

The waiter unobtrusively placed two glasses of champagne in front of them and disappeared. "Zum wohl und zu uns," Rudi declared as both clinked glasses. Lili gave a big smile and returned the wish.

Lili gave another big sigh. "So this is where you met with Friedrich and sat at Mr. Best's Stammtish?"

"Yes, he's sure to be here tonight, as he is virtually every night. So how did you spend today, Lili?"

"I helped Mother with some shopping and arranging flowers. I went to the hairdressers…see? It's a little shorter." She made a quick motion with her head.

"You look wonderful, Lili, and I like your dress."

"Thank you, Rudi. I actually wanted to wear something a little nicer, but I had to be careful not to get too tizzied up just to go and stay with Hanna overnight. As it was, Mother queried why I got my hair cut today. And what did you do today, Rudi?"

"I did a little housework and a little less reading than I should have."

They both clinked glasses again and took another sip. "Nice champagne. Thank you, Rudi," she said as the waiter appeared with two menus.

Rudi knew what he was going to order before he even came there, but Lili, not having been there before and wanting to guard against any unwanted after-dinner consequences, took another sip and took her time to peruse the Speisekarte. She would have something light and leave room for dessert. She shared her desires with Rudi and closed the menu.

A waiter appeared. "Bitteschoen?"

"Eine Gulasch Suppe fuer madam und ein Wiener Schnitzel, bitte. Ja, und zwei achterl Rot." As the waiter disappeared, Lili and Rudi placed their hands on top of each other's in the middle of the table.

"It's so nice to be here for dinner with you, Lili."

"I feel the same."

They leaned across the table for a quick kiss then finished their champagne, set their glasses down together as if it were orchestrated, and leaned back in their chairs. The café was now beginning to fill up, mostly with couples. A family took their places a few tables away as two excited children briefly fought over their preferred chair. Rudi and Lili exchanged smiles, but there were still some feelings of uncertainty in the air as they both had private thoughts as to the progression the evening might take. Their thoughts were soon interrupted as the waiter arrived with their meal. The rich aroma of paprika wafted from the steaming soup, and Lili gave out a little chuckle as she observed the Schnitzel overlapping Rudi's plate. They clinked glasses, and Rudi cut off a piece and fed Lili across the table.

"Don't worry; I won't do that when we are at the Sacher."

"Sehr gut," said Lili, Rudi not knowing whether she referred to the Schnitzel or his understanding of appropriate behavior at the Sacher. He didn't query it and began to eat his Schnitzel with some gusto. Lili ate more tentatively but said that hers was also very good. They had expended so much nervous energy during the time leading up to then that they actually felt hungry, and they ate their main courses, interrupted little by conversation. Rudi ordered a second glass of red and noticed Lili pushing her plate forward, indicating she had had enough.

"Must leave room for a little dessert." She smiled.

"You can have as much dessert as you wish," Rudi teased.

They could hear quite loud laughter emanating from the direction of Mr. Best's Stammtisch as the waiter cleared their table. "Hatt's g'schmekt?" he asked.

"Ja, Danke."

They were beginning to feel more relaxed as they chatted away about all sorts of matters and drank their wine. Their waiter arrived again and, without a word, placed a dessert menu in front of them. Lili studied it carefully, while Rudi didn't open his at all. "Aren't you having dessert, Rudi?"

"Yes, I am; I know what I'm going to have. Take your time, Lili."

"I can't decide between a piece of Esterhazytorte (almond-butter cream cake) and Vanillecremeschnitte (mille feuille and vanilla ice cream). OK, I'm ready," she announced as the waiter came to the table.

"Ja, meine Lieben?"

Rudi ordered. "Einmal Esterhazytorte und einmal Strudel mit extra Schlag. Auch zwei Melange, bitte."

The waiter returned in less than five minutes. Rudi and Lili fed each other their first piece, and both made appreciative noises. They lingered over their Mehlspeisen and coffee, which they enjoyed. They also enjoyed each other, played some footsies under the table, and held hands above it. After a trip to the bathroom, it was time to go. The waiter helped Lili on with her coat and handed her her bag. Rudi left a little extra Trinkgeld to acknowledge the waiter's sensitivity. He led them to the door and opened it with, "Noch eine schoene Nacht. Danke und Wiederschaun." Rudi and the waiter exchanged smiles as Lili handed Rudi her bag and took him by the arm.

It was a beautiful, clear night, stars twinkling above and a number of couples finding their way home, some with more difficulty than others. Down Wipplingerstrasse, a turn right, and one left, and they stood in front of the apartment door. An instant mini attack of the nerves had Rudi fumbling with the key. He led Lili inside to be greeted by the clear aroma of carnations and placed her bag on a chair. They fell into a brief but passionate embrace. Lili checked herself and looked around the living room.

"It really is very small, Rudi," she said, catching her breath.

"Yes, but it's sufficient for a couple of students," Rudi responded as he took her coat and hung it behind the door. He found the champagne bottle and was soon opening it. Lili took a closer smell of the carnations and sank into the couch behind her. Rudi sat beside her with two glasses in hand. They linked arms with glasses somewhat awkwardly and took a sip.
"Zu uns, Lili."

"Zu uns, Rudi."

Rudi got up, took a napkin and a dessert plate, and passed them to Lili. He produced the box of Demel delights, at the same time taking a plate and napkin for himself. Lili untied the bow and opened the box. "Fabelhaft, Rudi. I see you did very little reading today," she said as she threw him an approving smile. There was an assortment of mini pastries, one more delightful than the next. "What's in the other box, Rudi?" asked Lili inquisitively, and he produced the second, smaller Demel box. It revealed an assortment of chocolates, including orange straws, almond bark, chocolate-dipped strawberries, and rum balls. "Are you going to try to get me drunk with these rum balls?" she asked cheekily as Rudi took a chocolate-dipped strawberry and put it to her mouth. She took a bite, and he ate the rest. They fed each other and drank champagne until the bottle was all but empty. That took a while, as there was much kissing and canoodling in between.

While the temperature was dropping outside, it was getting hotter inside, and they soon found themselves in Rudi's room, under the covers, with only the light of a candle. Rudi and Lili experienced one another as neither had experienced anyone else before.

———⊗⊗⊗———

THEY LINGERED OVER a breakfast of Semmel with Marrillen confiture and multiple coffees until late in the morning, when Lili looked at her watch. "Gott im Himmel, Mother would have expected me home already. I hope she hasn't phoned Hanna."

She took her coat and bag and gave Rudi a long embrace. "Last night was wonderful. Thank you for everything, Rudi. We must do it again soon."

"Thank you, Lili. You are wonderful. Have you got everything?"

Lili struggled on with her coat as she skipped out of the apartment and threw Rudi a farewell kiss. Rudi watched as she disappeared, closed the door, and sat back at the table. He put a little confiture on a half-eaten Semmel, poured a little more half-cold coffee, and breakfast turned into lunch. He leaned on one arm; he had a thumping headache, but that did not prevent him from grinning from ear to ear like a Cheshire cat. He got up as he decided some water and aspirin might help. He took his coffee and his Cheshire-cat grin and plopped onto the couch, reflecting on the night before and remembering all the times he and Lili were together. He felt very fortunate. He fell asleep and had a terrible dream.

He was coming out of the Café Louvre late one evening after having been with Friedrich, when he was thumped over the head from behind and strong-armed by two men into an alley, a third man following close behind. The alley was particularly narrow, unlit, and cobblestoned, and there was a distinct stench of a dead animal. There he was thrown against a stone wall and beaten about the head and chest. "Juden-Lieber, Arschloch, Schwein. Raus von unsere uni. Piss off with your Jewish girlfriend and your newspaper articles. Piss off, arsehole." As he crumpled to the ground, he noticed one of his attackers leaving. He was wearing high boots.

Rudi woke in a cold sweat and took himself into the bathroom to wash his face. He was not sore, nor was he bruised or bloodied. He only had bloodshot eyes. He was no longer wearing a Cheshire-cat grin, however.

Rudi felt a foreboding. He felt alone. Vulnerable. He moped around as he tidied up and did the dishes. He opened the window to let some air in. There was no appreciable wind that entered, just the chirping of young people returning from lunch or wherever. He stuck his head out the window to confirm that the apartment was not being watched. He plopped back on the couch, but, feeling edgy, he bobbed up again to make a coffee. He was greeted by a strong, slightly bitter aroma of an Arabia blend and was about to sit down when he was also greeted by Joseph, who burst through the door.

"Shalom, my friend."

"Servus, Joseph. You are a little earlier than I expected."

"Great timing for the coffee. I'll get it, Rudi. Put your Tuchus down. You look spent."

"Too much champagne," said Rudi.

"Probably a little too much Lili as well. How was it?"

Rudi's Cheshire-cat grin returned just a little. "We had a very nice time, thank you. Have a chocolate."

"Thanks. From Demel, very swish," he observed as he chomped on a chocolate straw. "Did you leave the Piper-Heidsieck bottle to impress or—"

"We need it for another candle, you Klots."

"Better a klots than a goy."

"This goy was just thinking when you came home what it's like to be a Jew in Vienna now. Is there no concern about the rise in anti-Semitism that is clearly occurring? When I spoke with Lili about it some time ago, she expressed no concern at all, and when she told her mother about my observations, her mother thought I was 'narrish'- off my head."

"To be a Jew in Leopoldstadt is quite different to being a Jew in the Altstadt of Vienna. The Jews in Leopoldstadt witness anti-Semitism on a regular basis. Most incidents are pretty minor shop break-ins, swastikas painted on doors, the occasional beatings, but it is omnipresent, and it is like a cloud hanging above. In the Old Center the Jews are far fewer in number, are far more integrated, and are not really subject to any harassment at all...at least for the present."

"I had this dream," began Rudi.

"How about telling me over dinner? You look as if you could do with some fresh air, Rudi."

"Sounds good."

As they stepped outside, Rudi could indeed feel the fresh air doing some good. Less than a couple of blocks later, they were at their usual establishment. Rudi ordered Knoedelsuppe and a glass of water, Joseph stuffed cabbage leaves and a glass of red. "What's this with your dream, Rudi?"

Rudi recounted the dream. "Do you think the man with the boots was one of the Hakenkreuzler?"

"It was Otto, Klaus, and Manfred, whom you interviewed at the uni, wasn't it?"

"I couldn't recognize a voice, but those boots…In any event, it was just a dream. I just hope it isn't predictive."

A waiter brought the meals, a wonderful aroma rising from the soup. The conversation waned somewhat as it took a backseat to eating. Joseph ordered another glass of wine, and Rudi ordered his first. "You should come to Leopoldstadt this coming Thursday and have dinner with Ester and me," Joseph invited. "You've never been there, have you? Though it's just over the Donaukanal, you will see a very different neighbourhood and maybe understand why it would be targeted by the Nazis."

"That's very nice of you. I'd be delighted. Are you sure Ester wouldn't mind?"

"It was Ester's idea in the first place, remember? We'd enjoy your company. If you have time, Rudi, I could show you around the neighbourhood before we meet Ester for dinner."

"That'd be good, Joseph, if you don't mind taking the extra time."

"Ah, my friend, beats studying. Let's leave here at four thirty, and that'll give us enough time to see a little of Leopoldstadt before we meet up with Ester."

8

Troubles in the Second District, Ignorance in the First

Leopoldstadt occupies the second district (Bezirk), adjacent to the first district. During the time of the Austro-Hungarian Empire, Leopoldstadt attracted many Jews from the eastern part of the empire, who generally arrived at the Nordbahnhof (railway station). This forceful expulsion during the Roman Empire had largely been due to the hatred towards Jews of Holy Roman Emperor Leopold I, with the support of the local non-Jewish population. As a way of giving thanks to the emperor, the inhabitants of the community renamed the area Leopoldstadt (City of Leopold). It was not long before Jews, along with other immigrants, were again attracted to the area, and Leopoldstadt again became a very cosmopolitan neighbourhood, indicated by several important synagogues of different congregations. As well as a variety of yeshivas, there was the Leopoldstaedter Tempel (which was often referred to as Der Grosse Leopoldstaedter Tempel because it was the largest temple in Austria), the Schiff Schul, the Polnische Schul, the Tuerkischer Tempel, and the Pazmanitentempel. Indicative of the cosmopolitan nature of the second district is the existence of the Karmeliterkirche (Carmelite Church), with its long and checkered history.

ON THAT PARTICULAR Thursday the weather was a little more inclement than it had been for a week or more, but rain didn't seem imminent. It took Rudi and Joseph only about half an hour to walk to the Nordbahnhof. A huge, grand structure, the train station was designed to double as an exhibition hall. It was one of Vienna's main train stations, linking major cities, including Prague and Warsaw. It was still the main entry point for the many immigrants, including eastern Jews, who settled in large numbers close by in Leopoldstadt.

"Come, let's survey the neighbourhood from on high, Rudi. I'm not too good with heights, but a mountain goat like you will love it... and it's a great view," Joseph suggested as they headed a couple of hundred metres southeast.

It was not very busy, and they were soon on the Riesenrad. Constructed in 1887, this giant Ferris wheel could be seen from many parts of Vienna. It was constructed to celebrate the Golden Jubilee of Emperor Franz Joseph I and had been one of Vienna's most famous tourist attractions from the beginning.

Despite the weather not being as clear as it had been recently, the view from the top was really special, the main buildings of the Innerestadt being visible, as, of course, was the area of Leopoldstadt to the west. Coming down, Rudi commented, "You can certainly see a long way, can't you? I hadn't realized how expansive the city of Vienna really is, and the vast areas of meadow and woodland there to the south and east really surprised me. I hadn't noticed the first time I was here."

"That's where the aristocracy used to take delight in killing such beautiful creatures as pheasants and deer. You don't go hunting, do you?" Rudi shook his head.

They headed west, following the Donaukanal to their left, and found their way into Tempelgasse, where the Leopoldstaedter Tempel dominated its surroundings. Also known as the Israelitische Bethaus in der Wiener Vorstadt Leopoldstadt, it was built in 1858 in a Moorish revival style. The tripartite façade of the Leopoldstädter Tempel, with its tall central section, became the model for many Moorish revival synagogues in various parts of Europe. There was quite a lot of activity as Rudi and Joseph approached. There were many groups, clearly both locals and tourists, congregating. There were no particularly strict protocols as Rudi followed Joseph inside. Joseph quickly looked around to check if men were wearing Kippahs (skullcaps) as Rudi looked around and up to admire the architecture. They did not stay long, as neither Rudi nor Joseph was particularly fond of any religion's structures.

"How are you holding out, Rudi?"

"Just fine, thank you, Joseph."

They crossed Praeterstrasse, turned right into Taborstrasse, and then left into Karmeliter Gasse, opening to an attractive square at the end of which stood the Karmeliterkirche. It was first built as a monastery in 1627 and endured many destructive events over the centuries. Rudi found the early baroque structure very attractive. The area was now the center of Jewish culture, which quickly became evident. There were throngs of Jews, particularly men, congregating in groups, standing, or sitting at café tables. Their dress was indicative of their allegiance. Most of the men were in all black, including hats, and were mostly bearded. Many were returning from errands with shopping bags filled with items from the market stalls all around. There were also several women, mostly covered from head to toe, and some pushing prams with infants. There were food smells waft-ing about with onion and roasted meat aromas inviting people into cafés.

Rudi and Joseph found their way to Grosse Sperlgasse, just past Kleine Pfarrgasse, where Café Sperlhof had been warming the neigh-bourhood for generations. The two arrived with quite a thirst just at the right time to meet Ester, who was in the process of sitting at a table by the window. She bobbed up again. "Shalom, Joseph. Shalom, Rudi."

"Servus, Ester," said Rudi as they sat themselves down and looked up at a waitress on the ready.

Joseph looked at Ester and at Rudi. "Ein Apfelsafft und zwei Bier, bitte," he requested.

"Pilsner?"

"Ja, bitte."

"Danke, kommt sofort."

The drinks were on the table before any conversation could really begin. "La Chaim. Zum wohl," they said as they clinked glasses.

"Well, what do you think of Leopoldstadt, Rudi?" enquired Ester.

"It's more crowded than I expected and more cosmopolitan than the Innere Stadt," he replied, without mentioning that it was clearly a poorer area with fewer grand buildings and less-interesting architecture.

The waitress arrived with menus and was about to turn around and depart when Rudi, looking at Joseph, ordered, "Noch zwei

Pilsner, bitte." Then, opening a menu and looking at Ester, he asked, "What are your suggestions?"

"Everything is really good here." Some Challahs (twists of bread) were brought to the table with the two Pilsners, and Ester continued, "I really like the Holishkes Huluptzes and the matzo ball soup and..."

"What are the Holishkes...?"

"Holishkes Huluptzes are cabbage leaves stuffed with rice and meat and baked with tomatoes. It's really delicious, Rudi. That's what I'm having," reassured Ester.

Rudi and Ester ordered the same while Joseph ordered goulash, which he had had there before. Three glasses of red completed the order with a request for more challah. "I love the seeds they put on this bread," commented Rudi. They sat back, sipped on their drinks, and observed people coming into the café. They were mostly regulars who came there to enjoy not only the high-quality, inexpensive food but also the cameraderie as people read the newspapers available and the many books stacked on tables. Patrons played cards and board games, often into the morning hours.

"I've been sucked into playing cards and chess with complete strangers here at times," explained Joseph. There was also a prayer room, where Jews, often in groups of ten or more, prayed together. It was a place that exuded warmth and hospitality.

At just after eight o'clock, there was a warm and convivial atmosphere, when a group of four young men, all in brown shirts and wearing high boots, entered the café and sat at a table near the entrance. They looked completely out of place and conspicuous by their seemingly confident, if not arrogant, demeanor. Many eyes turned toward them. "Nazi louts," declared Joseph quietly. "Aufpassen," he warned as one thumped a fist on the table and demanded, "Vier Bier!"

The waitress, recognizing the situation for what it was, went to get the manager. There was a whack as a fist hit the table again with a loud, "Vier Bier hier!" This attracted more attention, as it now became obvious that those men were not well intentioned. There was some nervous shuffling at some tables; a threesome walked to the back of the café, while a group of four quietly packed up their board game and closed the box. Four beers were put on the table. "That's what we have to put up with a lot here in the second district," whispered Ester.

"Watch this, Rudi," alerted Joseph as the four men downed their beer and stood up as to leave, seemingly without wanting to pay. Without a word being spoken, they were quickly surrounded by six mature men. Two were large and burly, in their forties or early fifties; two were considerably older and somewhat slighter; and two, both with red hair, were of the short and dumpy variety. All eyes within the restaurant now quickly turned to the group of ten. One of the brown-shirted youths glared, grunted, and groped for some coins then thumped them on the table, a couple of coins rolling onto the floor. A large, imposing man grabbed the offender by the arm and twisted it behind his back, which caused a shriek of pain. "Geh mah," he said as he frogmarched the swearing, struggling young man, arms flailing, out the door. The three other Brownshirts were also forcefully dragged out, two screeching as half nelsons were tightened around their necks, causing very high-pitched squawks, and the other lifted off the ground with a gigantic bear hug that left him momentarily breathless. He was thumped to the ground outside the door with a decided thud and was obviously winded.

"Get out of here before you get a mighty kick up the arse." He was picked up by the scruff of the neck and given one almighty shove.

The Nazi thugs ran down the street, yelling, "Juden, Schweine, verdammte Schweine! You'll pay for this. We'll be back. You'll see." Most of this could be heard from inside the café.

The six men waited a few moments to reassure themselves that the young men would, at least for the moment, not return for another beer. As the six members of the Juedische Selbstwehr reentered the café, there was quiet applause from every corner. Ester was visibly upset. "You know, coming here tonight, I saw several swastikas painted on some shop walls. And a colleague of mine recently witnessed a couple of covered women pushing prams being accosted by a group of Brownshirts. I wonder how this will all end."

The convivial atmosphere quickly returned. The meal was barely delayed as it now arrived at the table preceded only by the wafting aroma of the stuffed cabbage and matzo. "Prost," offered Rudi as all clinked glasses and took a sip of red. Eating irons in hand, all three were focused on the meals before them. Some extra bread arrived just in time for cleaning the plates. "Sehr gut," declared Rudi.

"Sehr gut," declared the waitress, having noticed the uniformly clean plates. "Noch a Glasserl, 'twas suesses vielleicht?" she enquired.

Ester, Rudi, and Joseph all looked at one another. "Just bring us some Rugelach, Mandelbrot, and Hamantaschen with three coffees, please," requested Joseph to approving nods of the other two. Rudi's favorite was the Mandelbrot, Ester's was the Hamantaschen, and Joseph loved them all. Not a crumb was left thanks to Rudi and Joseph's persistence, and the coffees were all finished. They lingered and chatted about nothing in particular until the conversation seemed to run out, as had the food and coffee.

Ester broke the silence. "I think I need to go. I'm tired, and I can't be late for work tomorrow."

"Rudi and I will escort you home, and then we'll decide how we'll get home ourselves." Rudi and Joseph paid the bill and left a little Trinkgeld. The waitress smiled and passed Ester her coat, which she folded over her arm as she led the group out. They walked up Grosse Sperlgasse a block, turned left and walked half a block, and then Ester was at her front door. After appropriate goodnight wishes, Joseph and Rudi were headed west. It was after 11:00 p.m.

"Do you have lectures in the morning, Joseph?"

"No, I don't."

"I don't either. Then let's walk. It shouldn't take us long. Too short a distance to take a taxi."

The weather seemed to have cleared up; there were only a few clouds remaining, and a considerable number of stars were shining brightly in a dark sky. There was just a slight breeze, which made it a pleasant night for walking. Rudi began to quietly whistle a tune that had been in his head since the late afternoon. "What's that you're whistling, Rudi? I haven't heard that before."

Rudi began to sing, "Lustig ist das Zigeunerleben, faria faria ho. Brauch dem Kaiser kein Zins zu geben." He stopped singing in mid-phrase. "I've got this funny feeling we are being followed. Don't look back now but to your left, just behind you, there are a couple of men who I think have been following us."

Instinctively Joseph looked back, and he did indeed see at least two characters, half hidden and peering out from an alley. "Shit, I think you are right. Let's just increase our pace a bit and see if we leave them behind." They sped up a little and after a minute or so, Joseph glanced over his left shoulder. "I'm sure we are being followed, and I think both men are wearing knee-high boots." Rudi and Joseph were both beginning to feel worried and a little scared.

"Do you think they could be two of the group from the Sperlhof? I don't want to get into another skirmish with some Nazi thugs," Rudi told Joseph as their pace quickened. "My father once gave me advice that if you can't avoid a fight, it's best to win it by a hundred metres. I'm beginning to think he was right. Around the next bend, we should run as fast as we can and turn off this road to our right at our first chance."

"Ja, gute Idee," agreed Joseph, who wanted to avoid getting into any altercation at all costs. Hearts began to beat faster, and as soon as they rounded the bend, Joseph and Rudi took off and ran like hares. Joseph went over on an ankle, and Rudi quickly dragged him up. *Shit, will we get caught?* went through both their minds as they continued to run as fast as they could for thirty or so metres, Joseph in quite some pain. They turned into a sidestreet and jumped into a doorway, their hearts pounding fiercly. Next was the pounding of boots on the pavement as two men flew past—both in brown shirts and wearing high boots.

"That was close," gasped Joseph, catching his breath and rubbing his ankle at the same time. "Let's continue down here for a block, and if we turn left we should be heading directly across the canal and end up at Schottenring." Rudi agreed, and both remained super vigilant until they got to Schottenring, where they let down their guards just a smidgen. They agreed to walk home, despite Joseph still feeling his ankle hurt a little.

"It's good to walk it out," suggested Rudi. There were some people about, so their feelings of safety and well-being quickly returned. "Do you know, Joseph, most people here in the first district wouldn't believe us if we told them about the incident in the café or of us basically being chased from the second district? Lili wouldn't believe it either, and her mother would think I was crazy to make up such a tale. I bet people here aren't even aware of the existence of the Juedische Selbstwehr. They couldn't imagine there'd be the need for such a group." Joseph agreed.

A clock struck midnight as they approached their front door. Joseph pushed it open with a foot, and from behind, out of the dark, came a question: "Why have you been so long?" It was Lili's voice.

Startled, Rudi responded, "What are you doing here? Is everything all right?"

"I've been here for about an hour, and I was about to go away," she said as she and Rudi met in a clinch.

"Come in, come in," beckoned Rudi as he took a bag from her and led her by the hand into the living room. "Joseph, I'd like you to meet Lili; Lili, this is Joseph."

"Pleased to meet you, Lili."

"Pleased to meet you too, Joseph; I've heard so much about you from Rudi, I feel I know you quite well already."

"Well, what happened, Lili?" asked Rudi. "Did you and your mother begin World War Two?"

"Nearly."

"Tell us what happened."

"My mother became objectionable, very objectionable. I got angry, packed a bag, and stormed out, slamming the door so hard the whole building shook."

"Eie yei yei," exclaimed Rudi.

"Oy veh," said Joseph. "Come and sit down. Can we get you something to drink?"

"I would like a glass of red wine if you have a bottle open. My mother went into a rage about how irresponsible it was of me to be involved with you, Rudi, being so young and a non-Jew."

"That's nothing new."

"I know," continued Lili, taking more than a sip of wine. "But Mother began to tell me about how irresponsible it would be if I were to sleep with you and possibly get pregnant. That really hit a nerve."

"Why would that be unusual?" asked Rudi. "Most mothers would have that as their greatest fear."

"Yes, but she was so sanctimonious, so…I know that Mother and Father were married on the ninth of October 1904. I was born on the sixteenth of June the next year. I weighed five kilos, a big baby and not premature. My arithmetic skills, as poor as they are, tell me that I was conceived before they were married. She's a hypocrite to lecture me about such matters. I told her so. I'm twenty-eight years old. I told her I loved you, and that I was not practicing to become a nun." Lili took several sips. Rudi laughed, and Joseph nearly choked on a piece of cheese he deemed unsuitable to put on some biscuits he was preparing for the three of them. Lili took several more sips until her glass was empty as Joseph came to the table with a platter of cheese and biscuits with some cornichons on the side.

"Here's a little nosh for you." He topped up three glasses, picked up one and a biscuit, and was about to leave.

"Stay, Joseph, I have nothing I wish to hide from you," exclaimed Lili. "Anyway I went to Hanna's place, and we had a long talk. Hanna is a long-time friend of mine, Joseph; we've known one another for more than ten years. I intended to stay with her and her husband for the night. I am always welcome there. They asked me straight out whether I preferred to stay with them or wanted to come stay with you, Rudi." Lili took another sip. "I'm here," she said as she smiled at Rudi. "Do you mind if I stay the night, Joseph?"

"Not at all, Lili. Beware though; he snores something fierce. Sounds like a sawmill. Ester stays here sometimes, and I sometimes stay at her place."

It was now close to two in the morning, and all three were wide awake. Lili asked, "And how was your day?"

They told her about the incidents with the Brownshirts in detail.

"But that's terrible," exclaimed Lili, with eyes larger than normal and somewhat flabbergasted. "What's this Selbstwehr thing?"

Joseph explained the origins, the need, and the practices of the group. "I am a member of the university Selbstwehr myself, Lili. Have you not believed Rudi when he has detailed some of the harassment that we encounter on a regular basis?"

"Well, of course I believe what Rudi tells me, but it's unbelievable."

"Unfortunately it's a fact of life for many of us Jews. Only a few hours ago, Ester told us there were swastikas painted on walls near her work, and people have noticed groups of Brownshirts harassing young covered women. The disdain, hatred, and harassment of Jews are quite common in the second district. You haven't heard it all yet, Lili. Why don't you tell her about us being chased, Rudi?"

"You were what?" questioned Lili. "Were you in danger?" When Rudi was finished explaining. Lili exclaimed, "Meine Guete, that's terrible. And then you walked all the way home? No wonder you were as late as you were. I'm so glad I didn't leave."

"You see, Lili," began Joseph, "Jews from the east really are targeted more than the Jews of the west who established themselves in the first district. The Jews of Leopoldstadt are less assimilated than Jews like yourself whose families have been here for generations."

Lili interjected, "None of our circle sees themselves as Jews. We see ourselves as Viennese. While not rejecting their Jewish roots, many are not very religious, and some have even converted to Catholicism to help be accepted and become assimilated. We even reject being lumped in together with Austrians in general. I guess we are snobs, if you look at it like that."

Joseph chimed in, "I don't wish to be rude, Lili, but many Jews from well-established families here behave like snobs. They have nothing to do with newly arrived Jews, most of whom are from the east and who have also made Vienna their home. Most recently arrived Jews gravitate to Leopoldstadt, of course, where rent is cheaper and where they feel more quickly at home."

Lili volunteered, "My mother and father were married in Leopoldstadt, but I don't think they've been back much since."

"Good for them, Lili. Probably got married at Der Grosse Leopoldstaedter Tempel."

"Yes, I think so."

Rudi was pleased that another Jew was explaining matters to Lili. He pulled the cork from another bottle of red and topped up glasses all around as Joseph went on. "You see, Lili, while the anti-Semitism is currently being directed mainly at eastern Jews, Hitler and his followers make no distinction between eastern Jew or western Jew, rich Jew or poor Jew, religious Jew or secular Jew, well-established Jew or new arrival. Nazis want to get rid of all Jews. They see us as contaminating the German people, the German race, the Vaterland, and that of course includes Austria and all lands occupied by German speakers."

Lili was still skeptical. "How could this be? If the Jews were run out of Vienna, most of the Viennese culture would disappear; most of the intellectuals and thinkers of Vienna would be gone, as would most of the doctors and lawyers. Jews are an integral part of the community."

"You make perfect sense, Lili, but the facts are clear: The Nazis want to get rid of all of us Jews. Hitler is gaining more power in Germany each month, and he wants to take over Austria to include it into a greater German Vaterland; he wants more Lebensraum for the superior Aryans of this earth," Joseph concluded with some frustration, if not anger, in his voice. He ate a leftover biscuit, drank the remainder in his glass, and refilled it. Rudi, listening intently and agreeing with every sentiment, was pleased to have had Joseph dominate the previous discussion. Hopefully Lili would finally be able to perceive the threat against Jews as he and Joseph did.

Neither Rudi nor Joseph had lectures in the morning, but Lili was expected to show up for work as normal. "Unglaublich, what a day it has been," she declared.

"Yes, for all of us," added Joseph.

"I must get a little sleep. I have to get up again in a few hours," said Lili.

Rudi stood up. "Gute Nacht, Joseph," he said as he took Lili's bag and offered her his hand.

"Gute Nacht, Joseph."

"Gute Nacht, Lili, Schlaf' gut."

Sunrise was only a couple of hours away.

—⊰⊱—

THE SUN WAS indeed already shining before any of the three got to sleep; they had been all wound up from the previous evening's events and discussions. Lili managed to get to work on time, and Mr. Schwartz, noticing that she was not at her best, left her completely alone for some hours. In the afternoon he asked, "Alles in ordnung, Lili?"

"Not really," she confessed. "I was extremely angry with Mother yesterday, and I stormed out of the house and stayed with Rudi last night. Rudi and his flatmate, Joseph, were at dinner when they witnessed an incident that led to Nazi hooligans being thrown out, and then on the way home they were followed, also by Nazis. We talked till very late."

"I see you are not making this up, Lili. Do you want to talk with me about some of this?" Lili hesitated. "Come, Lili, let's have a coffee; you look as if you could do with that, and if you want to share anything with me, you'll have my full attention away from the office."

Mr. Schwartz had been realizing for some time that Lili and her mother were not getting on well and that she was still angry that her father had committed suicide. Walter's having left Vienna after the death of their father also left a big gap in Lili's life. She missed him dearly, but she also realized he had to leave Vienna to fashion a life for himself and not be forever associated with his father and the business. *Rudi has come along just at the right time,* Mr. Schwartz thought.

Just around the corner in a coffee house, they sat by the window at the far end of the room, where they would not be heard. Mr. Schwartz ordered two coffees and a few macaroons and patiently sat, looking out the window and occasionally glancing at Lili. So much was going on in her head that she didn't know where to begin. Mr. Schwartz, who had good intuition, could tell that Lili, while hesitant, had lots to share. Lili slowly took a sip of coffee and, again slowly and carefully, set the white cup back in its saucer. She picked up a pink macaroon, took a bite, and put the remainder on the saucer with the cup. She then explained all that she had discussed with Rudi and Joseph

"Aber was." That's terrible.

Lili and Mr. Schwartz both took another sip and Lili was beginning to feel guilty about doing so little work today. She was ready to leave when Mr. Schwartz asked: "And what's this with your mother, Lili?"

She took a deep breath and described the encounter with her mother, including her storming out. "I don't know what will happen when I go home tonight," she said with some real concern. She waited so long for a response that she began to shift in her chair.

"Let's look at the reality. Your mother's home is also your home. While she does not approve of you having a relationship with Rudi, she cannot stop you. You are old enough to make your own decisions." After another long pause, he added, "Mothers and daughters do not have to be best friends. They are often not." Mr. Schwartz stood, picked up his cup, drank the last drop of cold coffee, and pushed his chair back. While Lili got up and was getting ready to leave, Mr. Schwartz continued, "Always tell your mother where you are. You know all that. Spend some time with her; she hasn't gotten over the death of your father either. Rudi needs some time for his school work too."

They walked quietly back to the office. Just as Mr. Schwartz was about to walk through his door, he looked over his shoulder. "Lili, go home. Get some sleep. Have dinner with your mother tonight. Bis Morgen."

Lili took her bag and was about to leave when she had a thought. She sat down, took a sheet of paper, and wrote the following: "R., Lunch tomorrow Burggarten 1:00. L." She folded the paper in half and put it in her bag. She would put it under Rudi's door on her way home.

IT WAS A nice Friday afternoon but definitely no longer summer. There was a crispness in the air, considerably cooler than it had been just a couple of weeks before. As she pushed the folded paper under the door, Lili had the strange feeling that the apartment was not empty, and it seemed foolish to leave a note if someone were home. On the off chance, she knocked. The response was Rudi's voice, "Who is it?" as he went to open the door.

"Ja, hallo, servus."

There was a big embrace. "What are you doing here at this time, Lili? Why aren't you—"

"Aren't you pleased to see me?"

"Well, of course. I was at home reading in preparation for a lecture on Monday, and Joseph is at the library." He ushered her inside. "Would you like a coffee?"

"No, I'd like to go to bed. I want to be a little less tired when I go home and have dinner with Mother."

"What a good idea." Rudi took her by the hand and closed the bedroom door behind him.

"Please set the alarm for six-thirty p.m."

———

LILI INDEED HAD dinner with her mother that night, though there was little conversation. As she went to her room at about 10:00 p.m., she told her mother that she would be spending the weekend with Rudi and would be home again on Monday evening. She did not wait for a response and closed her door.

Just after midmorning, the next day, Lili arrived at Rudi's apartment. Joseph was staying the weekend with Ester, and Rudi was reading the *Wiener Zeitung* and finishing a coffee. The window was wide open, the curtains blowing in and allowing crisp air to freshen the apartment. Lili knocked on the door, and Rudi opened it. "Hallo, Schatzerl. How are you?" He gave Lili a hug and twirled her around, her feet scraping a side wall.

"Why did you have the door locked?" asked Lili.

"I live here with a Jew, and I'm a Jew lover, and some Jew haters would love to hit a Jew and a Jew lover over the head—that would not be so lovely. How is your mother?"

"We're not talking much, and I don't want to talk about her either. What are we doing today?" Lili asked with excitement.

"Whatever you want, Lili; I'm just happy that you're here."

"I'd like to go on a nice long walk in the park and then cook something together this evening."

"Cook something together?"

"Yes, why not? That would be fun. Let's leave soon; we will not have decent weather for many more weekends. We can go to the Stadtpark, get a Wuerstel from the Wuerstelstand there, and just wander about. On the way back we can stop at a market, buy a few items, and nestle in for a nice evening."

"That's a good plan." And so it was.

Just before they entered the Stadtpark, they bought two Wuerstel. "Mit Senf oder Kren?" came the question from a man craning over the counter.

"Lili?" prompted Rudi.

"Mit Senf, bitte."

"Und Sie?"

"Kren, bitte."

"Dankeschoen. Here is a big one for you. Auf Wiederschaun!"

Rudi took a bite immediately. They only had to walk a few steps, and they sat on a bench to enjoy their Wuerstel. Hand in hand, they walked and walked for a couple of hours, Rudi occasionally kicking an acorn before him, Lili occasionally putting her head on Rudi's shoulder. The sun was shining through a partly cloudy sky, and a breeze was helping a few golden leaves drift to ground. Rudi picked up a perfectly shaped leaf as Lili took a cardigan from her bag and draped it over her shoulders. They were wandering along with other couples and small groups of people quietly enjoying an autumn afternoon when Rudi stopped. "Is that music I hear from a concert, Lili?"

"Yes, that's why people are all heading in that direction. We could go and listen for a little while too."

"Is that Strauss they're playing?"

"Mm-hmm. That's actually the 'Jugend Traume (Dreams of Youth) Walzer.'"

"How clever. They must have known we were coming." They both smiled and kept walking towards where the orchestra was playing. Instead of joining the throng of people close to the orchestra, they sat on a bench where they could hear but not see the orchestra. They listened to at least half a dozen pieces, each of which Lili could name. Among them were the "Kaiser Walzer," "Tales from the Vienna Woods," and part of the operetta *Die Fledermaus*. Rudi hummed along, as he was familiar with the tunes. The "Tritsch-Tratsch Polka" brought them to their feet, and they headed back home via the market.

Lili really enjoyed going from stall to stall as she had shopped very little for food; it had always been done by her mother and the family cook. "Some tomatoes, Rudi?" she asked. "Do you like cabbage? Do you have any rice at home? What about peppers? Onions?" Rudi just smiled and nodded a lot. "Do you have any flour at home, Rudi?"

"Yes, we do."

"Eggs and milk?"

"Yes. What on earth are we going to have tonight?"

"You'll see." Lili cheerfully continued on between stalls, carefully making selections. "That's all," she declared as she asked for three green apples.

A round-faced, smiling merchant in an apron, who had been watching Lili skipping from one stall to another, asked, "Do you want them for eating or for cooking?"

"We want them for cooking," she said as she smiled at Rudi.

"Aha, that's good. You'll need a lot of sugar with these."

Rudi gave Lili his purse and took the bag. "Heiliger Strohsack! We have enough food here to feed an army." Lili just smiled and took Rudi's arm. She couldn't remember having ever been happier than she was right then. Rudi was glad that she was in such a good mood. He wasn't giving the evening meal any thought at all, while Lili was enjoying planning ahead in some detail.

"I don't suppose you have any cinnamon at home," she queried.

"As a matter of fact, we do. Ester and Joseph sometimes put it in their eastern dishes."

Lili smiled. "Good." They were nearly home when Lili recognized some familiar smells. "Wait a minute; I won't be long." She ducked into a delicatessen and emerged with a paper bag.

"That smells good. What is it?"

"Wait and see," she said as she took Rudi's hand.

Upon entering the apartment, Rudi swung the bag onto the kitchen counter and gave Lili a gentle bear hug. She gave him a big squeeze. She put the four quite warm Knishes onto a plate, and Rudi asked, "Are you thirsty?"

"I was just about to ask you the same; I'll have a beer, please."

Rudi carefully poured two and handed a glass to Lili. "Prost."

"Prost," she responded as two glasses were clinked together and their eyes met.

"That was an excellent idea to get some Knishes."

"Thank you. I thought you might need some strength to make the dough for the Kaiserschmarrn, Rudi."

He was quite happy about the thought of making it. He had made Palachinken many times before, and Kaiserschmarrn was really just a variation. Lili and Rudi sat together on the couch, drank their beer, and made short work of their potato and onion Knishes. "The Knishes go really well with beer. Shall I make the Apfelmus (stewed apple) now so it will cool in time?"

Rudi took the three apples, rinsed them under the tap, and, sitting at the table, began to peel them with a short vegetable knife.

"Haven't you got a peeler, Rudi?"

"No, this is just fine," he responded as he kept on peeling. Three long, spiraled apple peel strips marked the end of that exercise. Rudi got up and put a saucepan with a little water on the stove. He took a jar of sugar from a cupboard and sat it on the table. Steam was just rising from the pot as he finished coring and dicing the apples. He tasted a piece and screwed up his face as the acidity got him. He emptied the apples into the pot and added a couple of heaping tablespoons of sugar then gave a quick stir. He added two pieces of lemon rind and gave an additional stir before returning the lid, not completely closing the pot. The aroma of apple quickly filled the room as Lili took her position at the sink. She took the cabbage and began to carefully cut off about twenty outer leaves, put them in a colander, and washed them thoroughly. Next a steamer rack went in the bottom of a large saucepan, a little water was added, and it was placed on the stove, just as Rudi gave the apples a stir. "Careful…two in the kitchen is dangerous," said Lili with a smile. She gave him a quick kiss and presented him with two onions and instructions to dice them into half-centimetre pieces. At the table, Rudi did as instructed and scraped the onion into a bowl. "Can you cut this green pepper into pieces the same size, please?"

"Natuerlich, Schatzerl."

"The Apfelmus is finished," declared Lili as she set it to one side.

The larger pot began to steam, so Lili dropped the cabbage leaves into it and returned the lid, only to notice the kitchen becoming filled with more complex aromas. "Would you open the window a little more, please, Rudl?" Lili was obviously becoming very comfortable in the relationship; she had even begun to call him "Rudl" instead of "Rudi." She turned the stove off for a while and allowed the cabbage leaves to cool. Upon request, Rudi spooned the Apfelmus into a bowl.

Noticing that there were only two pots, Lili returned to the sink with the pot, wanting to wash it out. Rudi jumped up and said, "Let me. It's not your fault this kitchen is a little inadequate." They did a little tug of war with the pot until Rudi pinched Lili on the backside. That elicited a giggle and a smile, and Rudi washed the pot. He refilled it with water for the rice. Soon there was rice boiling in the back and a shallow pan in the front with onions and pepper gently cooking in olive oil.

"Can I see what spices are in here?" Lili stretched to open the cupboard above the sink.

"Of course. Make yourself at home."

I wouldn't be allowed to do this at home, she thought to herself. "I can't reach."

Rudi came from behind and with a reverse bear hug, so to speak, and lifted Lili a few inches higher so she could reach several spice jars. Then he put her down.

"You rather enjoyed that, Rudi."

"Didn't you?"

Lili glanced back at Rudi with a smile then added the rice to the pan and stirred for a few minutes. She added salt and pepper and several spices that Rudi had never used. She did a little more stirring. "This is beginning to smell like the Karmeliterkirche Quartier that Joseph and I were in the other evening."

"Good. I must have the proportions right, then," responded Lili as she turned the stove off.

"Can I get you something to drink?" asked Rudi as he stood up.

"I'll have just a little beer, please, Rudl."

He poured two glasses and handed one to Lili. Rudi took a sip and pulled a cork from a bottle of red. "Should breathe a little," he said as much to himself as to Lili. Another sip and he noticed Lili clearing as much from the table as she could. She put both the rice mix and the cabbage leaves on the table. Lili prepared each leaf by cutting the hard center piece away and piled one on top of the other. Laying a leaf on a plate, she spooned a couple of tablespoons of rice mix onto it and carefully rolled it up, tucking in the ends as she went. Rudi was watching very closely because he knew he'd be doing that very soon. He had seen his mother make cabbage rolls at home but had never observed the process with such a keen eye. The cabbage rolls were carefully placed in a casserole dish in such a way so that they would not unravel. Rudi got the hang of it pretty quickly and scored several looks as he licked his fingers. "OK, you lick them," he teased. As punishment, he soon found himself roughly dicing three tomatoes and cooking them in a pan for a few minutes, while Lili got up and turned on the oven. The tomatoes were poured over the cabbage rolls and the dish put in the oven. Lili and Rudi smiled at one another. This was the first meal they had prepared together. Well, not quite—for Rudi took flour, a sieve, three eggs, a bottle of milk, and a bowl and, adding a pinch of salt, painstakingly produced a perfect Kaiserschmarrn mix that he covered with a fresh cloth and set to one side. While performing this task, which he could do without thinking, it occurred to him that Lili was very competent at these wifely chores of shopping and cooking, and she appeared to enjoy such activities as well. *Promising,* he thought.

Rudi cleared the table, gave it quick wipe, unfolded a tablecloth he had used only once before, and threw it over the table, centering it and smushing out the creases. A familiar schnaps bottle with a candle was produced at the same time that Lili set out plates and cutlery. Fresh napkins were found, and Rudi cut some rye bread in readiness. Some smooching on the couch allowed the oven to do its part, and soon the casserole sat on a mat on the table. "Viola," said Lili as both smiled. Lights were turned off, the window closed, curtains drawn, and a candle lit. The rich aroma and steam wafting from the casserole added to the homely and romantic atmosphere. "It is so nice to be able to have dinner together like this, Rudi."

"Yes, it is."

They thoroughly enjoyed the meal and each other. "Do they taste any different than the ones you had at the Sperlhof the other night, Rudl?"

"Just as good, if not better. The Sperlhof ones had some meat too, I think."

There was a lot of handholding, and Rudi fed Lili a cabbage roll by hand, which caused a bit of a giggle. Lili had to lick several of Rudi's fingers before he could withdraw them. Only three cabbage rolls remained. It had been a big day, and they had not yet fully recovered from Thursday evening. They didn't make it to the Kaiserschmarrn, not even to the bottom of the bottle of red. But they made it to bed.

9

TENSIONS BUILD

THE RINGING OF church bells heralded in Sunday morning. While Lili was still dreaming, Rudi went to make a pot of coffee and found the kitchen area resembled a hurricane zone. He washed and dried what seemed to be an extraordinary number of dishes. He was deep in thought and drying his hands when he was given a big hug from behind.

"Hallo, Liebling."

"Hallo, Schatzerl. You gave me a fright, sneaking up on me again. Your hair's wet."

"I snuck into the bathroom while you were preoccupied at the sink and whistling."

"What was I whistling? Would you like a coffee?"

"Ya, bitte. You were whistling a part of 'The Blue Danube.'"

"Oh, I guess I was. Shall I make some Kaiserschmarrn to go with the coffee?"

"That would be wonderful." Lili didn't hesitate to put the Apfelmus on the table.

"Come here first; I need some inspiration before I toil over the stove," declared Rudi as he took Lili in his arms for a passionate embrace. "I think that made me weak in the knees rather than inspired." Lili smiled as Rudi put a blob of butter in the pan, gave the bowl a stir, and filled the bottom of the pan with a ladle of mixture made the previous evening.

"Would you please pass me the cinnamon and sugar, Rudl?" Lili mixed a little cinnamon with sugar in a bowl and put it next to the Apfelmus. She poured two coffees while Rudi flipped the thick pancake. "Bravo, Rudi; I'd have it on the floor if I did that."

"Oh, I've done this hundreds of times." Rudi took a couple of spatulas and shredded the pan's contents into Schmarrn. This process was repeated until there was a mountain of Schmarrn. Served with Apfelmus or other fruit compote, often plum, Kaiserschmarrn, which was generally dusted with a little powdered sugar, became a popular dessert after it was, according to legend, prepared for Austrian Emperor (Kaiser) Franz Joseph, who lived from 1830–1916.

Their Kaiserschmarrn soon disappeared from the plate, with just a few crumbs left. Rudi licked his right forefinger, dabbed it onto the plate to pick up a few crumbs, and fed it to Lili. She pretended to bite him but didn't. She smiled and momentarily closed her eyes. They finished their coffees and together collapsed contentedly onto the couch for a smooch and a snooze.

It was just after midday on a grey sort of a Sunday that was overcast and cooler than it had been for quite some time. Lili woke with some lingering questions in her mind that were rekindled by the events that Joseph and Rudi witnessed just a couple of days before and by previous discussions she had had with Rudi. "Rudi?"

"Yes, Lili?"

"Do you really think that anti-Semitism in Vienna is increasing and becoming serious?"

"That's a serious question for a Sunday afternoon, Lili. But, yes, I do. I think it is becoming a very serious issue."

"But there's been jealousy of Jews from non-Jews for a long time, and there have on occasion been reports of harassment and minor skirmishes, but this has never been taken very seriously."

"No, it has not, yet it seems that people know about Jews being harassed, gangs of thugs molesting helpless covered women, shopkeepers being threatened, some stores being picketed, and propaganda leaflets being distributed. Even Jewish uni students are being targeted. Some of the administration is anti-Semitic. Imagine—at the university! These are human rights being violated. You see, Lili, the well-off, cultured Viennese believe they are all immune from such thuggery. People do not understand that Hitler's a thug, his followers are thugs, and together they believe that the only worthy people on earth are the Aryans: white-skinned, blond, tall, blue-eyed German speakers."

"Sounds like you, Rudi."

"I have brown eyes. And they want to increase their Lebensraum and rid their communities of any impurities. You are an impurity, and they use much more offensive language than that. In their eyes, your mother is, your brother is, and all Jewish people that you and she know are impurities. Hitler and his National Socialist German Workers Party, the NSDAP, have been gaining power steadily in

Germany, and anti-Semitism has become worse there over recent years. It will become very bad. Soon. I'm convinced. You wait and see." Rudi took a breath and continued. "As Hitler increases power and lots of Germans are taken in by his oratory, Jews will cop it. People with anti-Semitic leanings in Austria will begin to feel empowered to give Jews, even their neighbours, a very hard time."

After a considerable pause, she asked, "Why do we Jews not see this?"

"Most of the Jews of Vienna are comfortable in their own little world; they reinforce each other's views. They, for the most part, read only Viennese mainstream newspapers, listen to Jewish-dominated radio programs, and do a lot of waltzing."

"Do you know that the king of the waltz, Johann Strauss, was a Jew? Well, his grandfather was a Jew," interrupted Lili.

"That would make him impure. Any person with relatives who are Jewish is regarded as impure. The Nazis want to drive all impurities out of their neighbourhoods. That's how it is, Lili. You've heard this before from me."

"Yes, I know, Rudi."

Lili was in a pensive mood for the next several hours, weighing in her mind all that Rudi had said. However, she put on a good front and outwardly appeared happy and cheerful. Rudi asked, "Can we do something that'd be out of the ordinary this afternoon?"

"Of course, Rudi. What do you have in mind?"

"You'll probably think I'm childish."

"No, go on. Whatever you'd like."

"Would you take me to the Tiergarten (zoo)?"

"At Schoenbrunn?"

"Yes, I've never been, and I think it would be fun. Mind you, I have mixed feelings; I'd prefer to see animals in their native habitat and not within enclosures...Remember the Gemsbock on the Gerlitzen?"

Lili glanced at her watch. "Then, let's leave now. We can take the streetcar down to Hietzing, and we can get there in time to still have a few hours before they close. Take a jacket or pullover, Rudl; it might be cool by the time we get back," she suggested as she took a cardigan. Lili then took Rudi's hand, and they were out the door.

It was not at all long, and they were on the tram. "I'm really looking forward to this. I'm sorry if you think it'll be boring, because I'm sure you've been there many times before."

"I have been there many times before, but I've never found it boring," Lili reassured him. She squeezed Rudi's arm warmly while still reflecting on the serious conversation she had with him earlier that day. The question crossed her mind as to whether Rudi would end their relationship should Jews become undesirable citizens in Vienna as he could foresee happening. *He could find any number of good Catholic girls who would love to have a relationship with him,* she thought. She still felt pretty confident in their relationship and turned her thoughts to which animals they might see that afternoon.

Rudi took Lili's arm as they alighted the tram and walked toward the Schoenbrunn Palace. Lili explained, "The zoo is actually not within the palace grounds but next to them. We should come and spend another whole day here in the palace grounds sometime, Rudl. Both the Schloss Schoenbrunn and the zoo have been very popular and highly regarded Vienna landmarks. The palace's origins go back to Holy Roman Emperor Maximilian II, when this area was mainly for hunting by royalty and the rich and famous."

"The Wiener Tiergarten is the oldest zoo in the world, isn't it, Lili?"

"Yes, its origins go back to 1540. The zoo was constructed in 1752 next to Schloss Schönbrunn at the order of Holy Roman Emperor Francis I, husband of Maria Theresa. It was built to serve as an imperial menagerie and was centered around a pavilion meant for imperial breakfasts. Thirteen animal enclosures in the form of cake segments were established around this central pavilion."

As they wandered hand in hand around the various enclosures with many fellow visitors, Lili couldn't get the earlier conversation out of her mind, while Rudi kept wondering what the animals thought about being confined within such small spaces. *Many of them are used to running freely in very large areas, playing, mating, and hunting,* he contemplated. *They look healthy enough and seem not to be under any stress, but how would we humans know anyway? They certainly don't have smiles on their faces.* "Lili, do animals ever smile? These animals seem well enough behaved and aren't tearing down any fences or screeching, bellowing, trumpeting, or doing anything untoward. But they are not free. Do we, as one animal species, have the right to act on other animal species like this, to incarcerate them?"

"If you look at it like that, we are not being fair to the animals; you are right. I think some of them do smile though, Rudi; look at that giraffe."

"It's not smiling, Lili; it's got that expression on its face because it's chewing."

They walked around many enclosures and saw hundreds of different animals found in most zoos, and they noticed the joy that so many children got from them.

"Lili, we haven't eaten since breakfast. Are you not hungry?"

"I wasn't till you just asked."

"I'm quite hungry," declared Rudi. "Should we have a snack before we take the tram back or wait till we get home?" Lili shrugged her shoulders. "OK, then let's go home, and I'll concoct something to satisfy your desires."

"And what will that be, Rudl?" asked Lili with a mischievous smile."

As they turned toward the train, Lili dragged Rudi off to an ice-cream stand. "This will keep us going…maybe," she said as they fed each other in between eating by themselves. Lili continued, "We must come back here soon, Rudl, to visit Schoenbrunn, maybe to hear a concert. Walter and I were here a number of times, and the concerts were always excellent."

"That's a good idea," agreed Rudi.

———

ON THIS SAME Sunday in Leopoldstadt, while Ester was having a coffee at home with her friend Sarah, Joseph attended a meeting of the Juedische Selbstwehr. There were twelve men sitting around a large, wooden table on unupholstered chairs in a poorly lit room of a corner café. The windows were open, the curtains were billowing, and the smell of Eastern spices was filling the room. Some of the men had known each other for years, while others, like Joseph, had joined the group only recently. Joseph learned of this group through Ester. First they discussed the recent actions against the community. One member reported seeing swastikas painted on doors and on a pavement. A number of other members had also seen them, but nobody had any idea as to who might have been responsible. There were a number of reports of mothers pushing prams, being yelled at and jostled by three youths. "They were rather young, definitely all teenagers, and all wearing brown shirts, according to a couple of the mothers," a member reported.

The picketing of a clothing store the previous Wednesday was reported by another member. "There were four of them. They were carrying signs that said something like, 'Don't buy from Jews; they're cheats,' and 'Jews are dirty.'"

"Were you able to do anything about this?" someone enquired.

"Yes, I went to get reinforcements; five workmen having their lunch at a café a few doors away came to assist. We approached the picketers. A really small man said, 'Come here' as he waved a finger at them all. He then said, 'See this klots here?' pointing to a big, burly man who was folding his arms and standing menacingly tall. 'He'll break every bone in your body if you aren't out of here within thirty seconds.' They dropped their signs and took off like scared rabbits." Everybody laughed.

"We need this klots in our group," someone said, adding to the mirth.

"We had this incident in Café Sperlhof last Thursday," Joseph volunteered, beginning to provide a detailed description of the event.

"Ja, I was there," one of the members interjected.

"Yes, of course, sorry. I remember you now; you had that Brownshirt in such a great headlock his eyes nearly jumped out of their sockets. Two Brownshirts then followed my friend Rudi and me for several blocks south towards the canal till we were able to get away."

"Rudi? That's not a Jewish name."

"No, but he's a good goy—tall, blond, and athletic looking. He's my flatmate and has a Jewish girlfriend."

Some smiled. "We should recruit him; with those looks, he'd be a perfect foil." There were more smiles.

One of the members, very tall and holding his head in his hand, asked, "What should we do given the increase in such incidents in recent months, the Brownshirts seemingly becoming quite emboldened?"

"I think we need to make sure we all have good defensive skills," someone said.

Another suggested, "We need good offensive skills as well to actually make an impact, because the police do nothing."

Several other opinions were offered: "Many police are scared of the Brownshirts." "Yes, some police are in their pockets." "Some police may even be Nazi sympathizers."

"What do we need, then?" asked the tall man a second time. Before anyone could respond, he went on: "Let's begin with a training session here, this time next week. Each one of us should recruit another person and bring them along. Agreed?"

RUDI AND LILI had no sooner arrived home before Rudi suggested he was hungry and should start preparing dinner. Lili poured two beers, while Rudi fetched an onion, three potatoes, and three eggs. "Can I help?" asked Lili.

"You could set the table, cut some rye bread, and put the butter on the table, please."

Lili did as she was asked and took the candle in the schnaps bottle from the bedroom and set it in the middle. Soon there was a distinct smell of onions as they browned in a pan; potato slices were added, and Rudi paused to drink a little beer. The potato slices were individually turned, and Rudi had another sip as Lili was observing from the side. He picked up a slice in his fingers, blew on it three times, and put it in his mouth.

"Careful you don't burn yourself," Lili advised.

Rudi smiled. "Perfect," he said as he broke in three eggs and began to mix the contents with a wooden spoon, covering the potatoes and onions with egg. A pinch of salt and a generous grinding of pepper led to one more stir. "There you have it, Schatzerl: Kartoffelschmarrn. It's a very simple and hearty dish that is very popular in the ski huts."

"It smells wonderful, and it tastes very good too," Lili said as she took her first bite.

"We did it in reverse order here, of course," said Rudi knowingly. "In the mountains one often has a breakfast of Kartoffelschmarrn, to which you can add all sorts of different ingredients, and in the evening you have Palachinken or Kaiserschmarrn." They finished the little red wine left over from the night before, and Rudi took no time to pull a cork from another bottle.

"Wunderbar," said Lili as she pushed her empty plate a little forward and finished her second piece of bread. As they drank another glass of red, Rudi noticed that she was beginning to look a little forlorn.

"Something bothering you, Lili?"

"I think I might have eaten too quickly."

While Rudi realized that might have been the case, he knew it was not responsible for her mood changing to somber. "Lili, I detect that something is bothering you, and if it is, you should just say."

"Oh, it's nothing. I'm probably just being silly."

"Silly or not, out with it; I promise I won't laugh."

"Rudi, will you leave me if Jews become ostracized here in Vienna?"

The question was completely unexpected and caused Rudi to gulp. "No, Lili, of course I wouldn't. What on earth made you think of that?"

"Are you sure, Rudi?"

"Yes, I'm sure. And in any case, Vienna is so dominated by Jews... every aspect of Vienna is so dominated by Jews that it would take a long time for Jews to become ostracized here in their own city. We'd be out of here a long time before that were to happen. Perhaps we'll end up in New Zealand or Canada."

Lili didn't mention the subject again that evening, and color returned to her face. She went to the sink and washed some dishes. Rudi dried them and put them away. "I'll go to the bedroom and pack some things for the morning, Rudi. Is that OK?"

"Of course, Schatzerl. I'll just finish cleaning up a bit."

Lili was taking some items from the wardrobe when she noticed a violin case on the top. "Rudi," she called from the bedroom, "what's this violin doing on top of the wardrobe? Is it yours?"

"Yes, Schatzerl, it's mine. Haven't played it in nearly a year." Rudi went in to get it down. "Phew, it's dusty, and it's probably got a broken string or two." He put it down on the bed, opened the case, and was surprised that there were no broken strings. He sat on the bed, picked it up, and held it with his chin. He took the bow and turned the bow screw three times to tighten the bow, ripping a couple of long, loose hairs and letting them drop on the bed. Rudi rubbed the length of the bow hairs with resin, and Lili watched with considerable interest as he tuned the violin with utmost concentration, turning one tuning peg at a time; this process took several minutes. He turned towards the wall to help him concentrate, paused for a moment then quietly began to play.

Lili immediately recognized the melody and knew the lyrics well: *"Mei Muatterl war a Weanerin, drum hab' i' Wearn so gern..."*

"Ja, Rudi, you never told me you played violin. Why didn't you tell me? Play that again from the beginning." This time Lili sang the lyrics but didn't get far before she started to cry. Rudi played the song to the end and, after a momentary pause, began to play "The Blue Danube Waltz." When Rudi stopped, Lili asked, "How can you play without music, Rudi? Perhaps you are related to the famous violinist Leopold Auer."

Rudi smiled and shook his head. "I prefer to play without sheet music, but for more complicated works I need it. Don't ever expect me to play Paganini without sheet music. Impossible. In fact I don't think I could ever play it, even if I practiced eight hours a day. To be a good violinist, you have to practice many hours every day." Rudi released the tension of his bow, ready to put it away. "One of the greatest violinists, Jascha Heifetz, was quoted as saying, 'If I don't practice one day, I know it; two days, the critics know it; three days, the public knows it.'"

"Play something else, Rudi," Lili requested.

"Are you sure?" He tightened the bow again, stood up, and began to play some Strauss polkas that led into some lively Gypsy music for a few minutes and finished with a vigorous climax.

———

WHILE LILI WAS in the bathroom the following morning, Rudi ducked out to get some Krapfen and the *Wiener Zeitung*. As he entered the apartment, he was greeted by the aroma of coffee from inside and a voice from behind him. "Shalom, my friend."

Rudi held the door for his flatmate. "Servus, Joseph."

"Shalom, Lili," Joseph said as he stepped into the kitchen and slid a bag across the floor.

"Servus, Joseph. Would you like a coffee? I've just made it." Lili poured three coffees as Rudi set three dessert plates and six Krapfen on a dinner plate.

"Thank you, Lili. No Krapfen for me; I had breakfast with Ester. Ja, that's a fancy tablecloth we have here. Did you have a good weekend?"

"Yes, very nice, thank you. And you with Ester?"

"Yes we had a very pleasant weekend too, although Ester was still somewhat upset about what happened at the Sperlhof on Thursday night and Rudi and I being stalked and run out of the second district."

Lili finished her Krapfen and coffee, gave Rudi a big kiss, expressed a hearty thank-you, and with a "Shalom" and a "Servus," rushed out the door. Both Joseph and Rudi had lectures to attend, and they soon left, one after the other, Rudi finishing an article he was reading before he went.

THERE WERE TWO days of nearly back-to-back lectures and tutorials for both Joseph and Rudi, who also had an article to write for the uni paper. He couldn't quite make up his mind for some time as to what focus the article should take; then after some consideration, he decided to write about the increase in Nazi hooliganism against Jews in Vienna. He thought that that should be of some interest to students and faculty alike, as Jews proportionately far outnumbered other ethnic and religious groups in the institution. He passed the idea by the editor, who agreed that such an article should indeed be of considerable interest.

A smile slowly began to develop across Heinrich's face. "You understand, Rudi, it would likely also elicit some opposition, as Nazi sympathizers within the student body and the administration are apparently increasing in number and are still smarting over recent setbacks at the campus, especially the ruling against the Deutsche Studentenschaft."

"I understand," said Rudi, beginning to think he might have made a foolish decision; after all, he didn't really want to be harassed or beaten up by any of the Studentenschaft types.

"You may also want to begin to follow developments regarding elections in Germany, as the outcomes there will likely have some effect here in Vienna. Servus, Rudi. I must away."

Rudi would be quite busy for the rest of the week with lectures and research but would try to fit in some time each day to write the article. On Thursday he also had a lunch arranged with Lili's boss, Mr. Schwartz.

10

Rudi Meets with
Mr. Schwartz

At 12:30 p.m. Rudi walked into the same café where Mr. Schwartz and Lili had their long conversation the previous week. As he did, a gentleman dressed in a grey suit with a colorful bow tie and overflowing pocket handkerchief stood up at the far end of the café, smiled, and, hand outstretched, said, "I'm Herrmann Schwartz. You must be Rudi."

"Yes, I'm Rudi. Pleased to meet you, Mr. Schwartz."

They both sat, Mr. Schwartz a little away from the table, his legs crossed and leaning back. "Herr Ober," he called and asked Rudi, "Something to drink? Lunch is on me today."

"A small beer, please."

"Lili speaks so highly of you; I just had to meet you." The waiter arrived within a minute and a half. "Zwei Bier, liebe Herren."

"Dankeschoen."

Mr. Schwartz continued, "I hear you met in Annenheim and that you are studying law." They clinked glasses. "Cheers, Rudi. What aspect of law do you wish to concentrate on?"

"I'm not sure yet; it is only my first year, and it's all still pretty new to me."

"Yes, you have till nearly the end of your second year to decide what you want to specialize in. Sehr gut, and Lili tells me you are very musical; you sing and play the violin. Who is your favorite composer, and do you get to practice a lot?"

Rudi was beginning to feel he was being interrogated. "I love Paganini, but he is too difficult to play well. I play some Strauss and Schubert; they are less difficult. I don't have time to practice much; professors all think students are speed readers."

Mr. Schwartz smiled. "We should order something. Their Schnitzel is excellent, and so is their Schweinebraten (roast pork) und Tafelspitz (boiled beef)," he declared as he beckoned the waiter. Mr. Schwartz ordered the Schweinebraten and Rudi the Tafelspitz, as he had not had that dish for a long time and remembered liking it a lot. "Red wine, of course?" Rudi nodded in agreement, and Mr. Schwartz ordered a bottle of Bordeaux. "I prefer French reds and Austrian whites," he declared. The waiter arrived, presented the bottle to Mr. Schwartz, hesitated, waiting for a nod of approval, and, without looking, quickly unscrewed the cork. He placed it on a saucer on the table, wiped the bottle opening with a napkin, and gently poured a sample for Mr. Schwartz to taste. Mr. Schwartz tilted the glass against the white tablecloth, swirled the glass three times then raised it to his nose to sniff for the aroma. *Good berry nose,* he thought. He took a sip, allowed the wine to sit in his mouth for a moment, and then swallowed. *The middle and back palates are well balanced,* he concluded. "Danke," he said, and the waiter gently poured two glasses and set the bottle on Mr. Schwartz's side of the table.

"Zum wohl, Rudi. I wish you and Lili all the best. She deserves the best; she is a fine woman." There was a considerable pause in conversation as Mr. Schwartz contemplated how he would broach the next subject. "I realize that you love Lili very much, and that you are concerned for her safety because she is a Jew. That is correct, yes?"

"Yes, that is correct, Mr. Schwartz, but I am also aware of the increasing incidents of many actions against Jews here in Vienna."

"What sort of action are you referring to?" Rudi cited several examples.

"The behaviors you refer to have been common against Jews for decades, if not centuries. And there are many more incidents in Leopoldstadt, because that is where the greatest number of Jews live. These Ostjuden are not integrated into Vienna society; they are conspicuous, and that is why they are targeted, Rudi."

"No group of people should be harassed, bullied, and prevented from going about their daily business by another group, Mr. Schwartz."

"You are perfectly correct, but the people who are engaging in such negative behavior are just hooligans, and all societies have such people."

The food arrived on the table piping hot, with tantalizing aromas of burnt onion and vinegary red cabbage particularly discernible. "Bon appetit."

"Bon appetit."

The food tasted as good as the aromas promised, and the wine, now having breathed a little, complemented it perfectly. "They are often young men," continued Mr. Schwartz, "who come from poor homes, who are unemployed and jealous of other people who have more than they have."

"What about the brown-shirted hooligans at the university who attacked Jewish students not that long ago and even threw some of them out of the lecture room window? These people are not from poor—"

"Yes, Rudi, these young men are not from poor homes; they are probably frustrated with their professors and seeking an outlet for their creativity. Of course, I do not condone their behavior, but there will always be a few ruffians within a group of hundreds, if not thousands, of students at a place of higher learning. In the total scheme of things, they are pretty harmless."

"With all due respect, Mr. Schwartz, it was not all that harmless when a group of these Brownshirts were railing against the Jews and actually rioting in the lecture room, swinging batons at other students and at police who were called in. I was caught in the middle of this, trying to prevent a Jew from being clubbed over the head, and I copped one right here," said Rudi, pointing under his chin. "Got me to hospital and more than twenty stitches."

"Oh, I am so sorry, Rudi."

"The Brownshirts," continued Rudi, "had reinforcements from outside, maybe eight or ten Nazis, also with clubs, attacking Jewish students and the police."

"I didn't realize it was so bad. As long as you are all right, Rudi."

"I am all right now, thank you, Mr. Schwartz. The problem, however, is that hatred and actions against Jews are on the increase and will get much worse as the Nazi types become increasingly emboldened all over Austria and particularly here in Vienna."

"Why do you think they are becoming emboldened, Rudi?"

"The Nazis in Germany are gaining increasingly more power. Already in April this year, in Prussia, the Nazi Party became the largest single party in the state parliament and won more than two hundred seats in the Reichstag just this July, a couple of months ago; I think it was two hundred and thirty seats."

"But this is in Germany and will not have any effect here in Vienna."

"But of course it will have an effect here in Vienna, Mr. Schwartz. Hitler hates Jews, wherever they are. He wants to throw them out of Germany."

"That's a crazy idea; there are hundreds of thousands of Jews in Germany, and they are leaders in every aspect of society. Crazy to think like that." Mr. Schwartz took several sips of wine as the plates were taken from the table, then went on. "And how do you think this can affect Vienna?"

"Hitler believes that the German race—pure Germans, Aryans—needs more Lebensraum, and he has been advocating for the annexation of Austria."

"Maybe that's not such a bad idea. Austria's economy has been bad for a long time, and Austria may benefit from being joined to Germany."

"But with all due respect, Mr. Schwartz," Rudi said, beginning to get somewhat impatient, "Hitler hates the Jews, thinks they are vermin." The word made Mr. Schwartz cringe. "He wants to rid all German lands of them. He would want to get rid of all Jews in Vienna also if he had his way. Such ideas are increasing in Germany and here also."

"Do you know how absurd an idea that is, Rudi?" Mr. Schwartz was really making a statement more than asking a question. He poured the remainder of the wine equally into two glasses, taking time to formulate a continuing rebuff of Rudi's assertions. "You know, most of us Jews in Vienna are nonreligious, nonpracticing; we are not really regarded as Jews by the non-Jews of Vienna. We do not see ourselves as Jews. We are Viennese and very proud of that. We are thoroughly integrated into the Viennese society. It is nearly correct to say we *are* the Viennese society. We dominate the intelligentsia, we dominate the main professions—legal, medical, and media, both newspapers and radio—and we dominate the culture, especially the culture—the music, the opera, the theatre. We do not even see ourselves as Austrian, Rudi." Mr. Schwartz took a breath and a sip. "Yes, many Austrians outside of Vienna probably see us as snobs. That's bad luck. We are who we are. We are Viennese."

And you are a klotz, as Joseph would say, thought Rudi. "Hitler doesn't care how upstanding citizens might be," Rudi began with renewed patience. "Hitler doesn't care whether people are religious or not. He only cares that they are a pure German species. They must be pure Aryans. They cannot have an ounce of Jewish blood in them; they must not be contaminated. They must not have any Gypsy in them; they must not be homosexual; they cannot be physically or mentally impaired in any way. Anyone who is imperfect is seen as a blight on the German people. The German people must not be subject to contamination. The German people are superior. They must rule over all others. That is Hitler's view and the Nazis' view. They are becoming emboldened here in Vienna because they are becoming increasingly empowered in Germany."

"How can you be so convinced, Rudi? Such ideas are completely narrish (crazy)."

Rudi had tried his utmost to be convincing; he felt he had gotten nowhere. He drank half a glass of water and tried another tack. "My roommate is a Jew, as you probably know; he's a second-year law student, and he understands the situation much as I do. His girlfriend is also a Jew, and his parents are in Germany. Would you be willing to have a conversation with him and me sometime?"

"Of course, Rudi. You are obviously very bright, and you care about Lili. How about here again, one week from now? If that time does not suit, just let Lili know and suggest another time. Why don't we invite her for dessert now? She would like that, wouldn't she?" He called the waiter over. "Would you please call Lili on the house phone and say that her presence is requested for some dessert and that she might want to bring her bag with her?" The waiter returned with three menus and reset the table.

Barely three minutes went by when Lili, smiling, walked towards her boss and her lover. They both stood. Lili gave Rudi a kiss directly on the lips. "Thank you, Mr. Schwartz, for inviting me," she said as she placed her bag on the fourth chair and Rudi helped her into hers.

"Did Mrs. Rosenkranz call to confirm our meeting time, Lili?" She nodded. "We will not mention work again, Rudi," Mr. Schwartz promised as he led by looking at the dessert menu. The waiter arrived, took the order, and left with a slight nod of the head and ein "Dankeschoen." "Have you found a concert you want to take Rudi to?" Looking at Rudi, Mr. Schwartz continued, "I thought she should take you to a concert, as you've just resumed with your violin playing. It might provide you with some incentive."

"That would be nice," Rudi said as his eyes met Lili's. At that time they were also met by the waiter, who placed three cups of coffee before them and a bowl with extra cream. Three sets of eyes watched as Lili's Gugelhupf was placed in front of her, Kaiserschmarrn set before Mr. Schwartz, and Salzburger Nockerln (fluffy egg soufflé) placed in front of Rudi.

"They make the best Kaiserschmarrn here," volunteered Mr. Schwartz as Lili and Rudi smiled at one another, and they all took a sip of coffee through the ample cream. Mr. Schwartz got some on the tip of his nose and discreetly wiped it off with a serviette.

Everyone enjoyed their desserts, barely a crumb being left on a plate as the waiter arrived to take them away. Rudi folded his serviette and thanked Mr. Schwartz very much for his hospitality. Lili nodded in agreement, and Mr. Schwartz said, "So very nice to have met you, Rudi."

Hand in hand, Rudi and Lili had barely left the building when she remembered that Tante Rosa would be at home for dinner. Her mother wouldn't care if Lili was there or not. "Rudl, can I have dinner with you? I'll just call Mother to let her know," she said as she dragged him towards her office building. Lili skipped inside and made the call, while Rudi waited outside.

When she returned, Rudi said, "It will be very nice to have dinner together. You will be able to stay for a while, of course?"

"Of course. I would just want to be home by ten-thirty or something like that. You seemed to get on well with Mr. Schwartz, Rudi. How did he respond to your understanding of the increasing threats towards Jews here in Vienna?"

"Firstly, he has his blinders on; he believes what he wants to believe but seems to have little knowledge of the developments in Germany politically. He really has his head in the sand. He basically said I was 'narrisch.' He has, however, agreed to meet Joseph and me next week for more discussion. Perhaps he will believe more of what Joseph has to say. We'll see."

"That's nice that he'll meet with you and Joseph together. I can imagine that could be interesting: a middle-aged western Jew, a young eastern Jew, and a goy."

RUDI AND LILI enjoyed the evening together; they also enjoyed the weekend together, spent much the same way as the previous week-end, mostly cooking and canoodling. They also went to a concert. Lili spent weekdays at work, while Rudi kept busy with research, reading, and writing. He actually began to write his article for the uni newspaper, the contents helped by the recent events at Café Sperlhof and discussions with Mr. Schwartz and Joseph. But Rudi needed an additional discussion with Joseph in preparation for their joint meeting with Lili's boss.

Monday evenings for both Joseph and Rudi were becoming a time for recuperation following weekends spent with their respec-tive girlfriends, some essential uni reading, quiet conversation, and an early night. It was now Tuesday evening, and while Rudi prepared a meal of Bratwurst and Kartoffelschmarrn, Joseph ducked out to fetch some bottles of beer. On his return, he put the beers on the table and opened the window to let out some smoke. "Meine Guete, Rudi, how can four sausages make so much smoke?"

"Easily, as you can see."

"Smartarse! Are you ready for a beer?"

"Yes, please." Rudi served up the Bratwurst and Kartoffelschmarrn.

"Smells good," observed Joseph as onion-dominating aromas swirled around them, the open window not yet having much effect. "La Chaim, Rudi."

"Prost, Joseph. Bon appettit. Are you ready to help remove the blinders from Mr. Schwartz? I thought I had reasonably good persuasive skills, but I had no success at all with him."

"Does he not read any German newspapers or beyond page three of the Vienna papers?"

"He probably doesn't, but the main issue is that because he hasn't experienced any negative behaviors towards himself personally, he thinks they don't exist."

"And what was his response when you told him about the riots at the uni just a few months ago? He must surely have heard about that incident." Rudi and Joseph finished their dinner and looked at each other as if to ask "where's the rest?" when Joseph suggested they'd have to just have more beer.

Rudi said, "Yes, he was aware that thugs beat up Jewish students. He dismissively put that down to some expression of frustration on the part of the uni students."

"Did you tell him about the Deutsche Studentenschaft, Rudi, what their goals are and about their grab for influence?"

"No, I unfortunately didn't think of that at the time. I will certainly make a big point of that when we meet Mr. Schwartz this Thursday. Oh, and another real problem with him is that he doesn't see himself as Jewish. He doesn't see anyone within his circle as Jewish."

"They are though, aren't they?"

"Yes, they all are, but they see themselves as having been so integrated that they regard themselves only as Viennese. If they were asked whether they were Austrian, they would probably say, 'No, we are Viennese.'"

There was a pause, then Joseph, becoming a little angry, was curious. "Do they not understand that in Hitler's eyes they are just as Jewish as I am, as Ester is, and as all the Jews in Leopoldstadt? They are Dreck (dirt) like we are. They are vermin like we are. They need to be eradicated as we do."

"When I made a similar point, Mr. Schwartz just said I was narrisch."

After a brief silence, Joseph continued, "Of course, Rudi, the western Jews here in the first district see themselves as superior to us eastern Jews in the second."

"Yes, Mr. Schwartz himself admitted that the established Viennese were regarded by many as snobs," interrupted Rudi.

"Their forebearers may have come to Vienna poor, but they have done well and are now thoroughly ensconced within the business class. They have suitably forgotten about their beginnings in Vienna. Well, they need to be careful; all Jews need to be careful, or we'll all have Vienna taken away from us."

"We will clearly have our work cut out for us on Thursday, Joseph. Mr. Schwartz is an intelligent man. He is a successful lawyer; he has lived in Vienna all his life."

"I know, I know, Rudi. We are novices and he's a klotz.

11

RUDI AND JOSEPH MEET WITH MR. SCHWARTZ

ON THURSDAY RUDI and Joseph rushed home after morning lectures and upgraded their dress for the afternoon to jackets and ties. It was now clearly autumn, as midday temperatures saw few people in just shirtsleeves; many men in suits headed off to lunch. Trees were beginning to lose their leaves. Joseph and Rudi were each just a little anxious and aware of the other being so as well. Rudi recalled, "At a lecture this morning, the professor shared a quote from Plato. If I remember it correctly, it went something like 'Nothing in the affairs of men is worthy of great anxiety.'"

"What subject was he talking about, Rudi?"

"No idea. I was thinking about this afternoon, but I thought Plato was correct."

An impeccably dressed Mr. Schwartz stood up as Rudi and Joseph walked towards the same table where Rudi had found himself before. "Servus, Rudi, nice to see you again. You must be Joseph. Very nice to meet you. Why don't you both sit down, please?"

Joseph was a little taken aback by the presence of Mr. Schwartz: good-looking, elegant, perfectly groomed, beautifully dressed, and charming—at least so far. "Lunch is on me. What would you like to drink, liebe Leut?"

"Ein kleines Bier," requested Rudi, and Joseph nodded.

The waiter was now standing beside them. "Drei Bier, bitte, Herr Ober."

"Sofort, Herr Schwartz."

Mr. Schwartz had a way of making people in his company immediately at ease. "So you are a law student too, Joseph, I hear, and some help to Rudi as you are in your second year, yes? That's very nice."

"Second year, that's right."

"And your parents, they are not in Vienna?"

"No, they have never been to Vienna; they live in Munich."

"Oh, that's a pity; you should bring them to Vienna if only for a short time. Some time is better than no time, yes?" Three beers arrived, as did three menus. Joseph noticed the clean, elegant décor, tables generously spaced, with 1920s bentwood chairs, white tablecloths, and white serviettes pristinely folded. "Gesundheit (here's to your health) and to your parents' too, with the wish that they can visit Vienna soon. What do they do in Munich, Joseph?"

Joseph put down his beer and licked his upper lip with his tongue to capture the froth. "My parents work in a clothing store, and at night my father is also a cleaner to help pay for my stay here in Vienna."

"That must make him tired. I trust you appreciate his efforts, Joseph?"

"Yes, I do; things have not been easy for them in Munich."

The waiter arrived to take the order. "Yes, we should order now. I'm sure you are getting hungry as I am. Their Schnitzel is excellent, and so is their Schweinebraten und Tafelspitz." Rudi had heard the exact same comment before. Mr. Schwartz ordered the Schweinebraten, which caused Joseph to flinch as he and Rudi took a final look at the menu. Rudi ordered Wiener Schnitzel and Joseph the Tafelspitz.

"You said it was very good, Rudi, didn't you?" Rudi nodded.

"Why have things not been easy for your parents, Joseph?" queried Mr. Schwartz.

"It may be a strange thing to say, but my parents have been made increasingly aware of their Jewishness with the rise of the Nazis in Munich in recent times."

"Oh, how so?"

"Hitler has been making a huge push for power, and my parents know what his views are towards Jews. They are also aware that there has been a marked rise in anti-Semitism in their own community. Hitler has been going around the country giving fiery speeches, blaming Communists and Jews for the ills of Germany. He's been denouncing the competence of the present German government and claiming that only he, as leader, could return Germany to prosperity and international greatness."

"That does not sound good," interrupted Mr. Schwartz. "And what actions against Jews have actually been happening in Munich, Joseph, on a day-to-day basis?"

"Not only is there increased propaganda of the NSDAP, the Nationalsozialistische Deutsche Arbeiterpartei, there has been a flood of pamphlets and pro-Nazi newspapers. There have been increasing attacks on the Jews in Munich, windows being broken in Jewish businesses, restaurants, and department stores. The shop where my parents work was recently broken into; clothes were stolen, and graffiti was written everywhere."

"That's terrible. What did some of this graffiti say?"

"Things like 'Jews out—you are not welcome here,' 'Jews are thieves,' 'Jews are responsible for others' poverty,' lots of things like that." Joseph looked down with a rather sad expression.

The food arrived piping hot; napkins were unfolded and took their lap positions as the waiter arrived with a bottle of Bordeaux. "Would you prefer beer or wine, gentlemen?" Wine was the unanimous response, and the waiter presented the bottle to Mr. Schwartz, hesitated a moment for for a nod of approval, and, humming ever so quietly to himself, quickly unscrewed the cork, sniffed it, and placed it on a saucer on the table. *What a pretentious rigmarole*, thought Joseph as the waiter did his thing with the wine. "Ausgezeichnet," declared Mr Schwartz, and the waiter gently poured three glasses to a third full and set the bottle on Mr. Schwartz's side of the table. "Zum wohl, Joseph; zum Wohl, Rudi. Bon appetite. I wish you both much success at uni. Let's eat before it gets cold." There was a considerable pause in conversation as the three all enjoyed their first mouthfuls.

"You know, Mr. Schwartz," Joseph began, wiping his mouth with his serviette, "boycotts against businesses owned by Jews are called for on a regular basis now in Munich, and many citizens are beginning to believe that Jews are to blame for everything. Many newspapers there have adopted this nearly as a slogan: 'Jews are to blame for everything.' Another version is 'Jews and Communists are to blame for everything.'"

Rudi chimed in, "I was telling Mr. Schwartz that it seemed to me that the Nazis were becoming increasingly emboldened here in Vienna too, and that anti-Semitism was on the rise here and would likely get much worse."

Before Mr. Schwartz could get a word in, Joseph followed. "Yes, that is true. I have...well, Ester and I have witnessed an increase in incidents against Jews just this year."

"What have these incidents been, Joseph?" asked Mr. Schwartz, still with a degree of disbelief.

"There has been an increase in threatening pamphlets, threatening boycotts, threatening destruction of shops, even threatening violence against people. Hoodlums have taunted children and women, even spitting on them." Mr. Schwartz flinched. "Ester and I have seen swastikas painted on shop windows belonging to Jews; we've read graffit such as 'Jews out,' 'Jews can't be trusted,' 'Jews are filth,' 'Jews are vermin.' Some windows were broken. It has become so bad in several parts of the city that we have been forced to set up our own Juedische Selbstwehr." Joseph paused as he ate the remaining morsels and wiped his lips. "Sehr gut; sehr, sehr gut. Rudi may have told you. It was exactly two weeks ago in Café Sperlhof."

"Yes, Rudi may have told me. I'm not sure. Go on, Joseph."

Joseph recounted the events that occurred and concluded, "When the six members of the Juedische Selbstwehr reentered the café, there was quiet applause from every corner."

"Ja, of course," commented Mr. Schwartz. "These men are quite brave and quite well skilled. Bravo."

"Did I get that pretty right, Rudi?"

"Yes, perfectly."

"And then there was this incident I learned about at our Selbstwehr meeting. It took place in front of a clothing store two weeks ago." Joseph related the events in detail. "Incidents such as these, Mr. Schwartz, occur against Jews every week, maybe not here in the first district, but there are many more incidents now than in the past." The main courses were nearly gone.

Rudi remembered the increasingly insidious developments of the Deutsche Studentenschaft at the university and decided this would be a good time to talk about it. "You know, Mr. Schwartz, at our university, not in Leopoldstadt, but here in the first district, there has developed a very worrying phenomenon. I don't know how long this has existed. Both Jewish students and Jewish professors are being discriminated against by the Gentiles of the university."

"How is that possible, Rudi?"

"The Deutsche Studentenschaft was give permission by the university administration to exclude Jews. I think it was last year sometime."

"Yes, that's correct, Rudi," contributed Joseph.

"Then the government in Vienna declared that to be unconstitutional."

"On human rights grounds," interjected Joseph again.

"Yes, then there were three days of ugly riots perpetrated by uni Nazi sympathizers with help from a Nazi contingent from outside. Half a dozen or so Jews were injured, a number of facilities were closed for three days—"

"No, Rudi, they were closed for the remainder of the year," interjected Joseph. "The administration refused to call the police to help; in fact they had them stopped at the gates. They wanted to hush it all up and keep it an internal matter." Joseph took a breath and a sip. "And, of course, everybody knows that Jewish professors are now being targeted as well. Highly qualified Jewish professors are no longer getting tenured positions, while more junior, Gentile teachers are being given tenure."

"I'm sure that was not the case when I was there," declared Mr. Schwartz.

"We believe you, Mr. Schwartz, but anti-Semitism is now rife at the uni, including within the administration."

Rudi interjected, "A couple of Jewish students in my class, who are the brightest and write brilliant papers, are getting low grades from certain professors who are non-Jews."

"Yes," Joseph continued, "it is becoming well recognized that certain goy professors are giving Jews poor grades just because they are Jews."

"You know, Joseph, anti-Jewish sentiments have existed in Vienna for a long time. There is jealousy against us Jews because we are so successful as a people. But we, in my circle, do not actually see ourselves as Jews. Jews constitute less than ten percent of the total population, but fifty-two percent of doctors in Vienna are Jewish, and eighty-five percent of the lawyers here are Jewish." Mr. Schwartz finished his glass as the waiter, standing to just one side and out of earshot, noticed, walked to the table, and emptied the bottle into the three glasses. "Seventy-five percent of the banks are owned by Jews." There was another pause. "But the people in my circle do not see themselves as Jews," he repeated. "We don't even see ourselves as Austrian. We are Viennese." There was a pause as Mr. Schwartz took his glass, swirled it around a little, held it to his nose, and took a sip. "We are not the ones targeted by the Nazi hooligans."

Joseph grimaced and began to get somewhat agitated with Mr. Schwartz, feeling that he really was a self-interested snob and couldn't care less about other Jews, especially about less-well-established Jews in Vienna. "That may be well and good, but the non-Jews are increasingly showing their opposition to all Jews in many differen spheres of society," Joseph said, raising his voice to the level that people at several tables looked over at him.

"Not so loud, Joseph, please. What spheres of society?"

"Many private organizations that have tended toward anti-Semitism for a long time are now becoming overtly and increasingly so."

"Oh?"

"The Turnerbund, for example, which does not allow Jewish membership, has seventy thousand adult members and forty-five thousand children as members."

"Oh, Joseph, Jews are not interested in gymnastics."

"That's not the point. Just in one club, so many people go along with anti-Semitic policies. Is that OK? Then there's the Austrian Tourist Club and the Austrian Skiing Association, which also exclude Jews from membership."

"Oh, let them have their private clubs; that will not do us Jews any harm."

"But that is discrimination, Mr. Schwartz," protested Rudi.

"Correct," affirmed Joseph. "Even within professional organizations for doctors and lawyers, such discrimination is getting worse. You must have read or heard what recently happened within your own professional organization, Mr. Schwartz."

"And what was that, Joseph?"

"You know that Dr. Siegfried Kantor was recently elected president of the Chamber of Lawyers."

"Yes, I heard that."

"Well, this was not tolerable for many non-Jewish members; the previous president had been a Gentile."

"Really? And?"

"They formed their own League of German-Aryan Lawyers of Austria." Joseph emphasized the term "Aryan," turning red in the face and raising his voice even more. "What the shit is this display of anti-Semitism?"

"Shush, ruhig, not so loud, please, Joseph," responded Mr. Schwartz. Joseph noticed a number of people looking his way and one man shaking his head. Mr. Schwartz was apparently not able to acknowledge the severity of the rise of anti-Semitism in Vienna. Joseph felt very frustrated and slighted. Rudi couldn't believe Mr. Schwartz's intransigence and was most disappointed at his apparent lack of understanding. Did he not comprehend what was clearly becoming a trend? Did he not want to acknowledge this development? Could he not see the wood for the trees? Or did he just have his head in the sand?

This conversation had exhausted their train of thought, and all three were relieved when the waiter presented them with a dessert menu. "Another glass perhaps to help you make up your mind?" asked the waiter.

"Bitte," responded Mr. Schwartz quickly, and the waiter returned momentarily with three glasses of the same wine. Mr. Schwartz looked at the students.

"Apfelstrudel for me, please," requested Rudi, and Joseph decided on the same. They sipped their wine with quite a lull in the conversation, Joseph's facial color and heartbeat slowly returning to normal. Pleasantries were passed about such things as the weather, the traffic, and favorite cafés.

The waiter returned. "Dreimal Apfelstrudel, drei Kaffee, und extra Schlag, bitte," requested Mr. Schwartz.

"Sofort, Herr Schwartz." The waiter disappeared.

Each was hoping that the Apfelstrudel would come soon so that they didn't feel obliged to make any more conversation. As if the waiter understood the situation, the strudel and coffees arrived as if they had been already prepared, along with a mountain of whipped cream in a bowl. Rudi was not sure whether the mountain of cream was a better representation of the Schafberg near Salzburg or the Großglockner. Joseph, in the meantime, was wondering to himself whether Mr.Schwartz was a better representation of an ostrich or a mule. The meal was finished very quietly, all references to Jews and anti-Semitism avoided. It was as if the conversation had never taken place.

As soon as the coffee was finished, Rudi and Joseph thanked Mr. Schwartz very much for lunch and his company. Mr. Schwartz graciously bid the two students adieu, and they both left as depleted as their coffee cups.

"UNBELIEVABLE, RUDI, UNBELIEVABLE," declared Joseph as they both left the café. The two young men had done their darndest to have a sensible conversation, not really with the intention of convincing Mr. Schwartz of the escalation of anti-Semitism in Vienna but rather of discussing the likely consequences if this phenomenon were to continue. "Is he blind and cannot see, or can he see but refuses to understand?"

"I have no idea, Joseph; I am as flummoxed as you. I understand Lili's mother also believes that she and her entire circle are immune to anti-Semitism. In their world, there is no anti-Semitism."

"I wouldn't really wish this on anyone, but it seems to me it would benefit their comprehension if they were jumped by a couple of Hakenkreuzler one night on their way home from the opera," suggested Joseph. "Did you get any sense that Mr. Schwartz had any empathy for the newly arrived Jews, most of them living in Leopoldstadt?"

"No, I did not," declared Rudi. "Neither did I get the feeling that he was offended by what has been happening at the university."

"Some of the students would have to be children of his friends and colleagues," postulated Joseph. "Enough! Let's talk about something else."

12

ROSH HASHANAH, FRIDAY, 30 SEPTEMBER 1932

RUDI BURST THROUGH the door at about four-thirty that Friday afternoon laden with food items, when Joseph was just about to leave. "I'm running late; I promised I'd help Ester clean her apartment this afternoon. I must rush off so have a great weekend, Rudi. Shalom aleikhem."

"Don't forget to take the letter that arrived yesterday, Joseph," reminded Rudi.

"Mazel Tov."

As soon as Joseph walked out the door, he opened the letter from his parents, which he had expected and would certainly contain wishes for Rosh Hashanah.

Muenchen, 1 September 1932

Lieber Joseph und liebe Ester,

We wish you both a wonderful Rosh Hashanah and a Happy and Successful New Year.

We are very worried about our new year, as the shop has again had windows broken, and all around our neighbourhood there has been picketing and the appearance of the Hakenkreuz in many locations. At least four or five shops on our street have been vandalized in the last two weeks. The whole neighbourhood is very worried.

Unfortunately, President Hindenburg has become an old man and seems too tired to deal with the political intrigue and backstabbing that is going on. Hitler is in the middle of it all and has been crisscrossing the country giving fiery speeches. In the meantime Germany is suffering very badly with the highest level of unemployment, and there are many people with not enough to eat. Everything is now being blamed on the Jews, and many people are being threatened and beaten. Nazi Brownshirts can now often be seen in groups, roaming the streets and singing Nazi songs. These songs are scandalous and adding to our being frightened. I heard them singing a song several times, so I was able to write the words down: "Blut muss fliessen, Blut muss fliessen! Blut muss fliessen Knuppelhageldick! Haut'se doch zusammen, haut'se doch zusammen! Diese gotverdammte Juden Republik!"
("Blood must flow, blood must flow! Blood must flow as cudgel thick as hail! Let's smash it up, let's smash it up! That goddamned Jewish republic!")

Terrible, terrible. They want to bring down the republic and chase all of us Jews out of Germany.

We are sorry to bring you such news. We will be all right somehow.

L'shanah tovah tikatev v'taihatemt.

Hilda und Johan

It took Joseph just fifteen minutes to reach Ester's apartment. Ester, who was given the day off from work, was at the stove, checking on the brisket in between cleaning house. Not appreciating that Joseph was hours later than he'd promised, she was at the moment only civil. "Shalom; would you please set the table for six? The new cutlery is in the drawer. You will need soup spoons and dessert knives and forks. Make sure the cutlery is nice and straight."

"What else can I do, Ester?"

"Not much left to do. At seven o'clock you can open two Rote Veltliner and just before eight the Gruener Veltliner; it doesn't need any time to breathe." Joseph felt guilty about not having arrived several hours ealier; he could have done some dusting and swept and mopped the floors to give Ester more time to arrange the flowers and rest up a bit. He turned the radio on, rearranged the antenna wire a little, and the crackling stopped. *Gut.* Joseph lit a pair of candles on the table.

"Before our guests come, I must show you the letter we got from my mother and father yesterday."

Ester bit her bottom lip as she read the letter. "That's terrible to have such worries at Rosh Hashanah. I have been worried for them for months. And that song. That is really scary. I have also been worried about my parents and sisters in Poland. There has always been some anti-Semitism there, and I wonder whether it will get worse there too."

Within five minutes after eight, two couples, no one yet in their thirties and all colleagues of Ester's, arrived. They were all in good spirits. "Shalom." "L'Shanah Tovah Tikatevu." "Shanah Tovah." "Shalom."

Joseph poured six glasses of kosher Gruener Veltliner as they all sat around the dining room table. "La Chaim." "Mazel Tov." The wine did not last long, and a second bottle was soon opened. Some small talk was exchanged among the six, and Ester, being conscious of timing at a dinner party, nodded at Joseph. He quietly slipped into the kitchen and brought out a big round of challah on a board and a bread knife, which he set before Benjamin. He handed him the knife and smiled. Benjamin cut nice, even slices, eight or ten of them. In the meantime Joseph transferred the matzo ball soup into a large terrine, placed a ladle in the bowl, and carried it to the table. As soon as the bowls were filled, there were several choruses of "Es gezunterheyt," and a silence fell over the table for only a moment. "Very good, Ester" was heard several times as the chicken aroma from the broth pervaded the room, and dinner conversation resumed. Joseph shared with the group the substance of his conversation with Mr. Schwartz and Rudi, and the small talk quickly changed to serious conversation.

"Yes, it's amazing how some people in the first district seem to be oblivious to what's happening around them."

"I can understand people not being at all religious, but I can't understand how they can deny being a Jew."

"I guess if they don't see themselves as Jewish, then they don't see themselves being under threat."

"Most of them don't see there's a threat because they have been so used to some bullying behavior ever since they were children. And what's happening is nothing new, just normal thuggery."

"Yes!"

"Some can't even comprehend the Nazi behavior as being discriminatory."

"That's right—human rights violations."
This concluded the matzo ball soup chapter, with the exception that serious conversation continued. Soon plates and bowls were replaced with a new set of plates, and six fresh glasses were brought to the table. Joseph did the honors with the red wine, while Ester

slipped out to the kitchen. She cut the brisket into thin slices and transferred them to a large platter. She then transferred potatoes, onions, and chunks of carrot and ladeled some sauce carefully over the brisket. *Perfect,* she thought as she carried the platter to the dining room table. Some rye bread was brought and butter replenished. Chicken aromas were now replaced by stronger and more complex aromas of slowly cooked beef and onions. Guests admired the platter and compleminted Ester. "How long did you cook the beef, Ester? It is so beautifully tender."

"Here's cheers to the new year." Joseph raised his glass, and people stretched across the table to clink glasses. "Let's hope that our little community is safer this coming year. It's awful that young mothers pushing prams have been harassed and long-established stores picketed."

"Has the shop that was vandalized recently been reopened?"

"I was just thinking that the likes of Mr. Schwartz will not understand what's been happening until their businesses are ransacked and vandalized with Hakencreuzer painted everywhere," Joseph continued. "I suggested to Rudi yesterday that it would benefit their comprehension if they were jumped by a couple of Hakenkreuzler one night on their way home from the opera."

"Yes, that might wake them up."

"What did Rudi think of that idea?"

"He thought it a good idea."

"Really?"

"Yes, he's a good Gentile. Actually he's a heathen and a good goy with a Jewish girlfriend. Lili is a posh, well-connected Jew, and her mother thinks just like Mr. Schwartz, Lili's boss."

"Ignorant woman."

"Rudi agreed. More wine, anyone?"

They lingered over their brisket for a while longer and continued to enjoy the Rote Veltliner. Ester noticed one of her guests close to nodding off, so she turned the radio volume up a little and cleared the table with the help of another guest. They soon returned with a round fruity challah loaf and a bowl of honey, while Joseph was struggling to dislodge a cork from a bottle of dessert wine. "Give it here," asked Benjamin, stretching a hand towards Joseph. "Very nice, from the Neusiedlersee too," he observed. A little was poured in each of six glasses. "Shalom" was said a number of times as glasses clinked. A competition soon commenced, everyone trying to avoid honey drips on the tablecloth as challah was dipped into the honey bowl. This became a little more precarious as couples fed each other with honey-dripping challah. There was quite a bit of laughter with assistance from the dessert wine.

Four people didn't feel much going home, with just a little swaying and fortunately no stumbling. There would be enough time for recuperation before attendance at synagogue from noon. The same sextette had arranged to meet for dinner at Benjamin and Rivka's place the next night. Joseph dragged Ester off to bed with a thank-you, well-deserved congratulations as dinner was a startling success, and another apology. He promised he'd do the cleaning up in the morning.

And so he did. Ester woke and found the kitchen and dining room pristine. Joseph was resting at the table with a coffee. He poured Ester a cup. She smiled and thanked him for his work. "Sorry I was grumpy with you yesterday. Some breakfast?"

"Just a little challah. Slices from last night are fine and another coffee. That's all I want." Ester brought in the challah, the bowl of honey, and an apple. Joseph quartered the apple and passed two pieces to her. He turned on the radio and fetched another apple. It was a quiet sort of Sabbath day—cool but not too cool, a slight breeze but not sufficient to affect the window curtains. The window was open to get rid of any lingering food smells from the previous night. The usual frenetic twittering of birds was missing; there was only the sound of two crows talking to one another in the distance. Ester headed for the bathroom to get herself ready for temple; she would take considerably longer than Joseph. Joseph was listening to the radio while finishing his coffee and hoping his headache would go somewhere else. His turn in the bathroom didn't take long, and they were ready for temple in their least faded and elegant best.

They hadn't taken three steps when they could hear the sound of a distant march beat. Curious, they walked towards the noise, Joseph feeling wary and worried.

Around the next bend the sound became more distinct: a marching song and the stomping of boots. They could hear the stomping get louder and louder as the lyrics soon became clear as well. This was the Sabbath; it was Rosh Hashanah. This was on their turf; this was in Leopoldstadt. This was a provocation. *Purposeful intimidation,* Joseph was sure. He was furious and fuming, and Ester grabbed him tight by the arm as they marched past in the middle of the road, probably a hundred or more in perfect formation, four abreast, the first rows all in brown shirts, the last rows in black shirts, many wearing swastika insignias on armbands. Links, rechts, links, rechts, left, right, left, right, right. They could certainly march with robotic precision. And they could sing in perfect unison and pitch. *Bastards! The chutzpah, the bastards.*

"Deutschland, Deutschland, über alles, Über alles in der Welt, Wenn es stets zu Schutz und Trutze Brüderlich zusammenhält. Von der Maas bis an die Memel, Von der Etsch bis an den Belt, Deutschland, Deutschland über alles, Über alles in der Welt!"

This was the German National Anthem and had been so since 1922. The music was written by Austrian composer Joseph Haydn in 1797 as an anthem for the birthday of Emperor Francis II of the Holy Roman Empire. The German poet August Heinrich Hoffmann von Fallersleben wrote the lyrics in 1841. The Nazis adopted this as one of their propoganda songs.

"Those bastards! How dare they? How dare they?" Joseph used swear words Ester had never heard before and in multilingual combinations of Yiddish, Heberew, German, and Italian, He didn't think he had it in him himself. He had never been so angry before in his life. He was trembling.

Ester tightened the grip on has arm and said, "Let's go home, Joseph. We can't go to temple like this."

"Scheissdreck!"

"Joseph, please."

"We must go to temple as we planned and not be so intimidated by these arseholes."

"Please, Joseph, please, your language; you'd prefer not to go to temple anyway."

Joseph took several deep breaths to compose himself. "I have never been more determined to go to temple; let's go." He unclasped Ester's grip from his arm and took her hand. They marched off to temple. Around the next corner and one block from the temple, they suddenly stopped. They could hear it again, pounding feet—links, rechts, links, rechts, left, right, left, right. "Deutschland, Deutschland, über alles, Über alles in der Welt!" It now seemed clear the Nazi brigade was marching around Leopoldstadt when many of its inhabitants were on the way to synagogue.

They undoubtedly chose this time to send a message and were now marching right towards them. They were all young men, athletic, mostly with short blond hair. At the head of the march there were three flags held high—one was the German flag, one was the Nazi flag, and the third they didn't recognize. The color red returned to Joseph's face. Beads of sweat covered his head; even his thick shock of hair was wet. His nostrils began to twitch. Ester worried he might have a heart attack. He wanted to scream—what, exactly, he did not know. He wanted to do something, but he did not know what. "Shit, I wish Rudi were here. He's a practical guy; he'd think of something."

The Nazis were quite loud now as the formation passed, boots pounding, voices forceful and in harmony. They were perfectly orderly, marching and singing. There was something very nerve-racking, very troubling, foreboding as their actual presence faded in the distance while the streets emptied and the synagogues filled.

Few people in the synagogue could concentrate on the activities they had planned. The mood was somber. No one talked openly about the disruption on this Sabbath, on the second day of Rosh Hashanah. There was some whispering but about what—parents giving thanks, lovers sharing dreams, or what might the meaning of that march be, that perfect march? Time dragged really badly as most congregants tried to ignore the earlier intrusion in their neighbourhood, probably pretending it didn't happen. There was a grey sky, not of storm clouds, just an even grey sky, an eeriness on the streets as Ester and Joseph walked home, wondering how they would get to Benjamin and Rivka's. *Perhaps it will not be safe,* they thought.

Joseph was exhausted from anger, fury, and the loss of liquid. Ester was exhausted from worrying about Joseph. When they got home, they were too tired to undress and have a nap. They slumped on the couch. Ester brought Joseph a glass of water. He got up and returned to the couch with a glass of the Neusiedlersee dessert wine, now leaving the bottle less than half empty and with too little to bring to the dinner that evening. Ester was not happy on two counts.

Joseph and Ester made it to Benjamin and Rivka's just after 8:00 p.m., literally following the other couple in the door. "Shalom." "Shanah Tovah." "Shalom." "Shalom."

"Why didn't anyone stop them? Why didn't the police stop them?"

"Look at it from their point of view; it's not against the law to march and sing."

"Yes, marching perfectly, singing very well. What's against the law about that?"

"They were happy; they were joyous."

"We all know you can do anything you like in Vienna except drink poor wine."

"Ha, ha, because there isn't any."

"Come in. I think we can all do with some more Veltliner right now."

Benjamin and Rivka's apartment was much like Ester's, with a separate dining room beside the kitchen. Benjamin suggested where people should sit, and everybody sat. The Shabat candles were lit, wine was poured, and Benjamin recited Kiddush. The conversation continued. "What was the purpose of this march, do you think? Was it to demonstrate the power, the strength, of the Nazi movement?"

"Yes, and not just in Germany but here in Austria too. It was to intimidate us, to rile us. No coincidence, the day they selected."

"No, no coincidence. Do you think the march was locally arranged?"

"Don't think so."

"No, nor do I; I think the German NSADP organized it. And very well it seemed too. We Jews couldn't march like that if we practiced for a month of Sundays." Everyone smiled. "Somebody would be sure to get their lefts and rights mixed up."

"Anybody know what the third flag was?" asked Joseph.

"There was the German flag, the Nazi flag...I didn't recognize the other one."

"I think it was an old Weimar Republic flag."

The aromas of stuffed cabbage began to waft in from the kitchen as rye bread and chopped liver with chopped hard-boiled egg were put on the table and a Rote Veltliner served. Joseph could not get the incident out of his mind. "What could this hatred towards us mean for the coming year? Increased intimidation, increased harassment, more vandalism?"

"Yes, probably" was a common response.

"We can't let the bastards get away with that, treating us all like Shmuks."

"What do you suggest, Joseph?"

"We must build up our Juedische Selbstwehr, that's for sure."

"Do you belong, Moshe?" asked Benjamin, who joined recently.

"Oy vey! Not possible, I'd only get my head bashed in. I'm afraid of my own shadow." He cowered.

"Don't be so silly, Moshe," said his wife, Rachel.

"Moshe, be a Mensch. I'll take you to a meeting next Thursday. You'll see there are many there smaller than you. You will be trained and issued with a metal truncheon rather than a wooden one."

I'd be lucky to lift it, he thought as he agreed to go.

A pot of stuffed cabbage rolls was placed on the table and wine glasses refilled. Ester, who made this dish quite often herself, asked Rivka, "What spices did you put in here? This is delicious."

"Actually, it's due to a mistake…well, not a mistake really. I was shaking in some paprika, and the lid flew off, and so I had a lot more paprika on the rolls than normal."

Moshe was deep in thought. *I'm a pacifist, physically small, and weak. I have trouble lifting the big chess pieces. No one could imagine me wielding a truncheon. I'd probably hit myself in the hip if I didn't fall over first.*

Benjamin noticed something was up with him. "Hey, Moshe, we'll turn you into a feared gladiator." Moshe nearly choked. "Have no fear. Those Hackencreuzler will run away like hares when they see you." Moshe managed a forced smile for the others and drained his glass, motioning for a refill.

Joseph told the story of how a diminutive man frightened several picketers recently with just the use of his voice and sent them scurrying. "You'll have your stick as well, Moshe."

There were several smiles as the table was partly cleared, and Benjamn, who had ducked out, came in blowing a Shofar. This bugle made of a ram's horn is very difficult to play, and Benjamin did not play it well. As he tried to incorporate traditional sounds into the Rosh Hashanah ritual, everybody burst out in laughter, Rivka cupping her hands over her mouth. "As you can see," said Benjamin, "I'm no Ba'al T'qiah (master of the blast)."

"Pass it here," requested Joseph. He wiped the mouthpiece with his serviette and, with all eyes on him, put it to his mouth. He strained to produce a note, his cheeks puffed out, face red, and eyes bulging.

"You look like a pregnant toad about to fart," suggested Benjamin.

"Really," complained Rivka as everybody else broke into hearty laughter.

Joseph strained again to produce a note, but he couldn't focus, not being able to contain himself. "Your turn, Moshe."

"You'd have to be kidding. Only if you play chess first...for one hundred Schilling." No one took Moshe up on the offer, and the Shofar was put to rest.

By then all the cabbage rolls had also been put to rest, and Benjamin took three empty bottles of red back to the kitchen, where Rivka was putting the finishing touches on her simple dessert. She was carefully spooning pomegranate seeds in the middle of dessert plates, each with a circle of apple slices carefully arranged in the shape of a flower. Benjamin had just poured six glasses of Stift Klosterneuburg Eiswein, a fresh dessert wine, when Rivka and Ester carefully carried Rivka's creation to the table. "Oh, Rivka, that looks lovely. You are so creative." "La Chaim." "La Chaim." Rivka did a little curtsy and sat with her guests. Honey was passed around to provide the finishing touch.

The evening drew to a close with some coffee, some thanks to Rivka and Benjamin, and some expressed hope that the coming year would ensure good health, be hassle free, and be free of any Nazi activity. "Anyone like this Shofar?" asked Benjamin. "I'm never going to learn to play this thing." Joseph took it with a thank-you and a smile.

"Moshe, don't forget our rendezvous on Thursday night." Now everybody smiled as Benjamin and Rivka waved from their doorway. "Shalom. Goodnight."

⚬

JOSEPH AND ESTER had a quiet Sunday with some reading and leftovers from Friday night. Joseph could find no reference in the *Wiener Zeitung* to the Nazi march, and he wondered why that might be so. He came to the conclusion that providing no publicity was the best response. He was satisfied with that and returned to the rest of the paper. Actually, he read little, as his mind was elsewhere. *Where might this Nazi activity all lead? I wonder what sort of Rosh Hashanah they were having in Munich? Dad wrote that things were pretty bad. I wonder what my parents were doing yesterday. Will next year's Rosh Hashanah be any different? What would happen if Hitler came into power before then? Oh, shit, that doesn't bear thinking about.* A smile developed on Joseph's face.

"What are you smiling about?" asked Ester.

"I was just envisaging Rudi trying to squeeze a note out of that Shofar."

13

SCARY NAZI DISPLAY

WHILE THE GROUP of six was spending their Rosh Hashanah weekend in Leopoldstadt in the second district, Rudi and Lili were spending a quiet weekend in Rudi and Joseph's pad in the first district. Joseph had no sooner rushed out the door than Rudi unpacked a heavy bag of groceries. He had been to the delicatessen, the greengrocer, the butcher, the baker, the wine shop, and the flower shop. He looked at the bottle of red that had been suggested to him and pulled the cork. It was French and cheap. It had no label. He was advised it would need at least a couple of hours to breathe. But it was good. He took a sniff. *It smells terrible,* he thought. *Hope the air does it some good.* He found the only vase to be found and arranged the red roses with care and attention, picking up a ladybug carefully from a leaf and allowing it to take off from the open door. He thought he'd prepare as much as he could for the evening's meal so that when Lili came, he could give her some attention; she had, after all, had a very busy week at work.

Rudi put a pot of water on the stove and washed some potatoes, which he then halved. Waiting for the water to boil, he unwrapped the five pieces of thinly cut veal and pounded them even thinner with the knuckles of his clenched right fist. *Have to tenderize them some way, and this household didn't come equipped with any special tenderizing hammer or mallet. Glad Lili isn't here yet,* he thought. Potatoes were put in the boiling water with a pinch of salt. The veal then got the rest of the treatment: salted, peppered, floured, egged, and crumbed. He set them aside and wiped the bench. *Test the potatoes. Two more minutes. Check the wine. Smell not terrific but not bad; tastes better than expected. Potatoes drained in colander.* There was a knock at the door.

"Coming! Servus, Schatzerl," Rudi said as he swept Lili up into his arms.

"Servus, Rudl. I can smell potatoes."

"I can smell you. Nice perfume. You're early."

"Mr. Schwartz left early because of Rosh Hashanah."

"He doesn't celebrate."

"Didn't stop him from using it as an excuse! Actually, he just wanted to leave early to fetch some flowers for his wife." Lili put down her bag. "Oh, look at the roses; they're lovely. Thank you, Rudi."

"I got them for Joseph," said Rudi with a smile.

Lili just made a face and gave him another big hug. She also gave him a bottle. "This is from Mr. Schwartz. He said you had really enjoyed this wine, and we should enjoy it together at the weekend."

"That's very nice of him; please thank him for me. I could never afford to buy such a bottle—a really good Bordeaux."

"I see you have some schnitzel ready."

"Yes, and you can decide what you want to do with the potatoes."

"Let's make a potato salad. You can slice them, while I make the dressing. I notice some fresh dill. Do you have some paprika?"

Rudi's task was quickly finished, so he decided to taste the wine again. "Oh, quite good now. Very good really! Would you like a glass now, Schatzerl?" Lili nodded, and Rudi poured two glasses. She interrupted the making of the dressing. Clink, clink. "Prost." "Zum Wohl."

"Should be good with the schnitzel. Not too big."

Rudi opened the window as smoke accumulated from Schnitzel in the pan. Lili was at the stove. "Sorry, Rudl, they need to be burnt just a little." She waved a hand in front of her. "They'll be ready soon. Can you set the table?" Moments later, that was done, and Rudi was wiping an imperfectly clean knife with a napkin. He lit the candle, turned off the lamp, and topped up the wine glasses, adding two glasses of water from the tap. Viennese water, after all, had a fine reputation. Lili brought the schnitzel, piping hot, to the table on a very nice but slightly chipped platter as Rudi fetched the bowl of potato salad.

"Cheers, Schatzerl. Schnitzel fit for a king."

"Hope they're done to your liking."

"Hm, sehr gut." Rudi got up again to close the window.

He had planned for the fifth schnitzel to be eaten cold, probably on rye on Monday. That would not happen. "Too good not to be eaten now," he said as he took the last one, Lili having already suggested that she'd eaten too much.

Rudi and Lili took their freshly topped-up glasses to the couch, where they spent the rest of the evening. There was a fair share of canoodling and chatting, and Rudi took out his violin and played a few pieces. "Think my scales sound better than my waltzes," he said in between playing excerpts from the "Fledermaus Waltzer" and "Wo die Citronen blüeh'n."

"Don't be silly, Rudi. You play beautifully." When Rudi began to play "Wiener Blut," Lili sang along: "Wiener Blut/Wiener Blut!/ Was die Stadt /Schönes hat/In dir ruht!/Wiener Blut/Heiße Flut!/ Allerort/Gilt das Wort/Wiener Blut!"

He stopped playing, pulled Lili up from the couch, and, singing, they waltzed around the room and around the furniture until cuddling seemed more desirable than bashing into the furniture. One thing led to another, and it was soon morning.

As HAD BECOME a bit of a custom, while Lili yawned, stretched, and went to the bathroom, Rudi went to fetch some breakfast. He returned with Schnecken, Krapfen, and the *Wiener Zeitung* then quickly put on water for the coffee. Lili's timing could not have been better, for no sooner had milk, sugar, and coffee been set on the table beside the food than she bounced into the room. "Busserl, bitte." Rudi obliged with a smile, hug, and kiss. "Hm, schoen," swooned Lili as she sat and unfolded her napkin. "Can I pour the coffee?" she volunteered. There were a lot of noises of approval as they ate their Schnecken, licking fingers in between bites and avoiding jam dripping as they ate their Krapfen. "Wunderbar," they agreed.

They soon found themselves on the sofa with their coffee and newspaper. They swapped pages and snoozed from time to time. "Do you think we could still get tickets for the three o'clock concert at the Musikverein, Lili? There are some very nice pieces being played today."

"We could try; if we are there an hour before the performance, we could well get a couple of tickets, I think. Let's try."

"I might get some pointers for my Strauss pieces," suggested Rudi.

They arrived at Boesendorferstrasse Twelve, just around the corner from Karlsplatz, at two o'clock on the button and were lucky enough to get two tickets. Rather than just wander around for a while and come back, they were able to enter the hall early. Their seats were upstairs at the back of the Großer Saal but with a good view all the way to the stage. Lili had been there many times with her parents and Walter; Rudi had been only once before.

The hall had an architectural beauty and a stylish splendor, making it one of a kind. It was built in the style of an ancient Greek temple, beautifully proportioned, and resplendent in ivory and gold, with "Apollo and the Muses" as the focal points on the ceiling of the main concert hall. Rudi was entranced as he examined the details all the way to the organ pipes, not noticing that the hall was filling up.

The lights soon dimmed, the conductor raised his baton, bows were poised, final coughs were heard, and the audience of der Großer Saal fell completely silent. With the conducor's gentle nod and the downward movement of his baton, Johann Sebastian Strauss filled the auditorium. Lili slid her left hand under Rudi's right arm. Sounds of Strauss, Mozart, and Schubert took turns to occupy der Großer Saal, all pieces played to perfection, Rudi thought. At the end, when the applause died down for the last time and people wandered out the same way as they came in, Rudi and Lili remained seated. Rudi wanted another minute or two to take in the splendor of this music hall and imagine how it must have been when Strauss himself occupied the stage. They were nearly the last to leave.

They happily hummed their way home. There was some conversation about whether to stop for a late-afternoon coffee. They decided against it. Instead they picked up some knishes from the same deli they'd picked them up from before, and they could open their Bordeaux for sipping while making dinner. Rudi's mind drifted elsewhere.

"I was just thinking before of Joseph and Ester and hoping they were having a good Rosh Hashanah.

"Are you concerned about them, Rudi?"

"No, not really. Just had a premonition that something wasn't quite right."

They dined on goulash...as good as a goulash could be, the Knoedel were perfect, and the wine exceptional. And the company...what more could one ask for? Rudi and Lili felt very content.

—∞∞∞—

SUNDAY MORNING WAS nearly the mirror image of Saturday morning. Schnecken were replaced by Semmel and the Krapfen by Kipferl (vanilla-flavored crescent-shaped biscuits). The coffee aromas and flavor were as good as the day before. The day's paper had little news of interest. Rudi was about to set it aside when a two-sentence article, hidden away as if it were not meant to be seen, caught his attention. "Lili, look at this: 'NSDAP march took place in Leopoldstadt on Saturday. Police are investigating.' These Nazis, these Jew-haters, these arseholes have no shame. I wish we had a radio; there might be more news we could get."

"Yes, you and Joseph should really have a radio, both of you being so interested in current affairs. You could have good music to listen to as well. Radio Vienna (**Radio Verkehrs AG**) broadcasts lots of concerts and Vienna Opera productions."

Rudi was upset and became visibly angry. "They can't even leave them alone on their Sabbath, not even on Rosh Hashanah."

"You did have a premonition, Rudi. Do you think it could be anything serious?"

"I'm afraid so. I have known quite a lot of Germans, some at school, some who were taking holidays in Annenheim, and some I met skiing. Too many of them have been arrogant. They think they are superior, better than other people. Living in Kaernten, I have also met lots of Italians and Yugoslavs. They have never been arrogant like those Germans. Some are bullies too."

"Do you think the NSDAP—"

"Exactly. The Nazis are arrogant bastards and believe all other human beings are inferior. They are thugs."

Lili interrupted as she took Rudi's hand. "Rudl, let's not worry about this now; we'll see what Joseph knows about this march. He'll be here soon."

Rudi and Lili took a long walk, taking in one of their favorite spots, the Burggarten. They sat on the same bench they had sat on that afternoon when they were first together in Vienna. Now, as then, they enjoyed a Wuerstel mit Senf. *What a difference a season can make,* Rudi thought.

We fell in love by the Ossiachersee, but we are a couple now. Her mother knows we are a couple and resents it; her brother knows, and he is happy for Lili; her boss knows, and he is happy for both of us; and Joseph is happy for both of us. We actually understand each other well. Lili now has some understanding of present-day anti-Semitism in Vienna. Her boss and so many others, however, are in the dark; they have their heads in the sand like ostriches with their precious posteriors poking toward the sky. It will not be long before they'll get such a kick up the behind that their heads will spring up, and they will see the light. There will no longer be darkness. Aberwas! I'm just kidding myself!

"Are you OK, Rudl? You were away with the pixies."

"Sorry. Yes, I'm OK. I was just watching those two doves making whoopee and wondering whether they will still make babies before winter."

"I was watching them too, Rudl. Do you think we could go home now?" They walked with arms around each other for some time then held hands for the rest of the way, Rudi humming or whistling as he so often did.

JOSEPH CAME HOME at about nine o'clock and thrust the Shofar into Rudi's hand. "L'Shana tova, Rudi. Happy New Year, Lili." Lili and Rudi both returned the greeting.

"What do you expect me to do with this, Joseph?"

"You could try to serenade Lili with a tune."

Rudi smiled and was always up to a challenge. He had blown an alpine horn before, but never a ram's horn that the poor beast might have lost trying to prove his manliness during the rutting season. Rudi contorted his lips in a variety of ways and buzzed and trilled into the mouthpiece until he got a shriek from the horn. He flinched, Lili smiled, and Joseph applauded. "Better than anyone else during the weekend!" Rudi smiled and tried again and managed a couple of different squeaks and grunts, which gained some more applause. As for serenading Lili, well, he wasn't sure about that.

"Joseph, what was the NSDAP up to yesterday? There was a two-sentence reference to a march in the paper this morning."

"Shit, Rudi...oops, sorry, Lili. Did you have to spoil my evening with your question?"

"Sorry I asked."

Joseph's face became taut. "There was a well-organized march by maybe a hundred of them."

"A hundred?"

"Maybe only ninety. Anyway..." Joseph described the whole event in detail, sighed, and shrugged his shoulders. The atmosphere was now much more somber than it had been. "It was eerie; they were basically so well behaved, they were scary. They marched up the middle of the road, but it was the Sabbath, so no traffic. They marched in perfect unison and sang impeccably like a well-trained choir. But those bastards wore uniforms, Nazi uniforms. The front rows in brown, the back rows in black shirts. All with swastika armbands. I didn't see the end. I heard they finished with a stop, a halt so perfect it sent shivers down people's spines. I think the Americans say 'stopped on a dime.' And then, all in perfect unison, they said, 'Heil Hitler.' Scary, so bloody scary! Then they just quietly went away."

Still quite emotional, Joseph took three beers and poured two, Lili putting a hand over her glass. Joseph's beer barely touched the sides. Rudi refilled Joseph's glass and took a sip himself. He had rarely seen Joseph so emotional and currently had no response. Joseph stated again, "On the Sabbath, on Rosh Hashanah! What chutzpah, the bastards! The chutzpah! They knew exactly what they were doing. I bet I know exactly what they were doing too. You know,

Rudi," Joseph lowered his voice momentarily, "no one mentioned it in temple; it was as if none of us had noticed." Joseph, sounding very frustrated, was becoming louder and louder. "What is wrong with us? If we ignore it, how the hell can we ever do anything about it? Are we such weak Schmucks? Yes, we're just weak Schmucks, damned weak Schmucks, that's what we are!"

"Calm down, Joseph. Finish your beer. Don't be so hard on yourself."

All the while Lili sat quietly, yet becoming agitated and ever more aware that anti-Semitism was a far greater problem than she had believed even a few weeks before. She was now also sure that her mother, boss, and their acquaintenances were so very ignorant of the looming threat. Lili had become tired and needed to go home. She didn't want to have her mother angry, though they were barely speaking those days. Lili packed her bag, wished Joseph goodnight, and left with Rudi.

Rudi had become quite upset to see Joseph so emotional. He too was tired and escorted Lili, hand in hand, with some reflection and mutual thanks for a lovely weekend together.

When Rudi arrived back home, Joseph emerged from the bathroom. "Sorry I was so angry before."

"You have every right to be angry, Joseph; I am really angry with those bastards too. Lili is now getting more worried by the day."

"Rudi, I was thinking…I think we should have a radio."

"I was just thinking the same. Lili and I mentioned it this morning."

"I know a guy in Leopoldstadt whose father has second-hand radios. I think he repairs them. I'll see what we could buy one for."

"I'm tired, Joseph; I'm off to bed. Tomorrow I've got to try to finish my article, and I have a couple of lectures as well. Goodnight."

14

WRITINGS AND RESPONSES

As RUDI SAT in front of the Remington typewriter in the uni newspaper office, his problem was not what to write but how he should frame what he wanted to say. He was aware that his article would likely receive far more flak than his previous ones. He opened his notes beside him, put a sheet of paper into the machine, and began to type:

Nazi Thuggery to Change Vienna for Ever
There has been an increase in recent months of Nazi thuggery against the Jews of our beloved Vienna. Citizens have been harassed and beaten while some Jewish establishments have also been vandalized. Our esteemed university has seen outbursts of anti-Semitism with some members of the administration in cohouts with Nazis. Even some police have cooperated with the Nazis. There is evidence that the Nationalsozialistische Deutsche Arbeiterpartei (NSDAP) from Germany has been behind this development. It is clear that Nazis are gaining power in Germany and here in Austria. This is to be feared by all decent human beings because the Nazis have no regard for human rights and want to drive all the Jews out of German-speaking lands, Austria included. Hitler is not well-intentioned. He is only interested in power and the ability to implement his repugnant views. It is time for all decent citizens to repel the Nazi encroachment in our city.

RUDI WAS LOOKING forward to sharing the draft with Joseph over dinner. *Joseph must be held up somewhere; he was expected home more than an hour ago.* Rudi opened a beer to keep him company while waiting for his flatmate. *I hope he's OK. I hope he hasn't been harassed or beaten up. After all, the city is becoming less safe.* He thought he might need to open a second bottle, when the door opened and Joseph appeared, puffing and carrying a largish box. "Shalom, Rudi."

"Servus, Joseph. You're late. I nearly drank your beer as well as mine. What have you got in the box?"

"You open it, Rudi, you'll get a surprise; I'll get a beer." Rudi opened the box bound together with twine. "A radio. How did you get that?"

"I went to see Menachem, who took me to his father, and voila!"

"I'll pay you half. What do I owe you?"

"He gave it to me for nothing, because it was not in good enough shape to sell without a major overhaul, and he was appreciative of what we do in the Juedische Selbstwehr."

"Excellent. I was not looking forward to a month of just Huehnerschmalz (chicken fat) and no beer. Looks all right to me; we basically just want to be able to hear the news, right?"

"It's a Radiola, Rudi; that's a well-known make, isn't it?"

"Now that we've got one, it is."

Joseph proceeded to hook up the Radiola, and there was soon some music with crackling to be heard. While he fiddled with the antenna to get a clearer sound, Rudi put on the Saturday night's leftovers. "Gulasch and Knoedl OK for you, Joseph?"

"Sure, especially if Lili made it."

"She did. Are you ready to listen to the article I finished today?"

Rudi read the article from beginning to end, interrupted only to take a sip of beer. "Shit, I'm glad I joined the Selbstwehr. You'll certainly get some reactions to this, Rudi."

"I know, but to write this is necessary."

"The Nazis at uni will not be pleased. They'll likely want to give you a hard time."

"You are right. I had that dream some weeks ago, remember?"

"You will also certainly hear it from some of the uni administration. They hate to be critized and accused of complicity with Hakenkreutzler…phew, you'll get some reaction from there for sure. This goulash is wonderful; I hope Lili will make it again soon. Want a refill?" he asked, pointing to the beer.

"Bitte. Yes, Joseph, but I feel an obligation to expose these developments for the readership."

"In any event, Rudi, I would from now on select courses where the professors are Jewish."

"Comprendi!"

RUDI SUBMITTED THE article to his editor, who was interested only in the number of words. "The paper must come out in a few days," he told Rudi.

Looking forward, Joseph and Rudi had a heavy work schedule with self-imposed research deadlines and lectures galore to attend. They enjoyed their evenings listening to Radio Wien with their "new" Radiola while limiting themselves, for a number of days, to just one beer and Huehnerschmalz on rye as they had both spent more than their weekly allocation over the Rosh Hashanah weekend.

They both also wrote letters to their parents, and on this particular Thursday Rudi received an unexpected letter from his high-school science teacher, Herr Birnbaum. It read:

Sattendorf
September, 1932

Lieber Rudi,

Your father kindly gave me your address, as I have been wondering about you and wanted to write to you. I hope you are doing well at the university and enjoying your stay in Vienna. There was a brief reference in the paper earlier in the year of some fighting involving Brownshirts and NSDAP supporters against Jewish students and faculty. You would be well advised not to get involved with any matters political, Rudi, as this would distract you from your studies. This is terrible for a university.

I heard that you had enquired about me from one of the staff at the school. It was very nice of you to have taken an interest. I have become increasingly concerned for my relations in Munich and in several parts of Prussia. Life in Germany has become increasingly uncomfortable for Jews during this last year. Ever since April this year, when the Nazi Party *in Prussia became the largest single party in the Prussian Parliament, the arrogance and aggression of the Nazis has become very worrying. When the ban on the Sturm Abteilung (SA) was lifted by Franz von Papen in June, Hitler had a private army of c. four hundred thousand\ men to storm around the country with to support him and others of the NSDAP as they gave fiery speeches, winning over the desperate population. What Hitler would say depends on his audience. In rural areas he promises tax cuts for farmers and government action to protect food prices; in working-class areas he promises redistribution of wealth and attacks the high profits made by the large businesses. When he speaks to industrialists, Hitler concentrates on his plans to destroy communism and to reduce the power of the trade union movement. Everywhere he goes with large bands of SA there are demonstrations, but these are quickly put down. Because he is such a powerful and emotional orator, he has been able to get a great number of people to follow him. His efforts have led to huge success, of course, all over the country, and since July the Nazi Party now holds 230 seats in the Reichstag. My direct relations, in different parts of Prussia, have not been individually affected; they still have work, but they are extremely fearful.*

Where my other relations are in Munich, the situation is not much better. There are intimidating marches by the SA, which invariably lead to fiery speeches by Hitler that seem to be getting increasingly larger followings by the week. There is ongoing intimidation against the Jews there—shops picketed, windows broken, some shops set on fire, and some harassment and beatings as well.

Even musicians are now being driven from their teaching positions or positions with orchestras because they are Jews. We hear that Franz Schreker was forced to resign from his directorship with the academy of music.

I wish I could share more positive news with you. I cannot decide whether to stay here or to help my parents in Germany. Please look after yourself, Rudi. It would be very nice to receive a few lines from you.

With very best wishes,

M. Birnbaum

Rudi slowly folded the letter, using the existing creases, placed it down ever so slowly in front of him, and put his hand to a worried face.

"What's up, Rudi?"

Without looking up, he slid the letter across to Joseph. "Read it for yourself, Joseph. Unnbelievable," said Rudi angrily.

Just then Lili knocked on the door; she was on her way home from work. "Servus, Rudl. Why do you look so down?"

Rudi gave Lili a tight hug. "Shhh…Joseph is reading. It's a letter from one of my high-school teachers," he whispered. "It's rather worrying."

Joseph looked up briefly. "Shalom, Lili," he said and kept reading.

Lili put down her bag. "Have you been eating chicken?" she asked Rudi, having detected certain aromas and spied a stack of dishes from the day before.

"Yes, excuse me." Rudi began to do the dishes. "How was your day, Lili? I missed you today."

"Ja, terrible, terrible!" Joseph looked up.

"Can I read it, Rudi?" asked Lili.

"Yes, please do."

"Just dreadful," proclaimed Joseph.

"Frightening," added Lili after reading it. "We in Vienna seem to be largely oblivious to these developments happening just over the border. My mother has no idea of them, and if she read about it or heard it over the radio, she wouldn't believe it anyway."

There was an eerie quiet as the three reflected individually on the contents of the letter from Rudi's old high-school teacher. Lili broke the ice. "I wonder how many SA marchers there are typically as they march into German towns."

"Sometimes hundreds, other times thousands, I think," answered Joseph.

"I wonder whether there'll be another march by Brownshirts over Yom Kippur as there was last weekend during Rosh Hashanah," queried Rudi, knowing that Yom Kippur, or the Day of Atonement, is the holiest day of the year for Jews. The holiday's themes are reconciliation and atonement. Its purpose is to bring about reconciliation between people, and between individuals and God. According to Jewish tradition, it is also the day when God decides the fate of each human being.

"They wouldn't have the gall to demonstrate twice in just over two weeks, would they?" asked Lili.

"I'd put nothing past them, Lili. They are becoming more and more brazen. I just hope they don't use the fact that most Jews will be in synagogue next Monday to vandalize Jewish property," said Rudi.

"They'd get a nasty shock if they tried. Our rabbi in Leopoldstadt has allowed a large group of our Selbstwehr to be on patrol on Sunday night and all day Monday. They'd get a fight they hadn't bargained for. I won't be here Friday night to Monday, of course. Ester and I will be in temple most of the day Monday."

"Is that to make sure you don't weaken and break your twenty-five-hour fast?" questioned Rudi cheekily.

"Something like that. We'll need a bit of extra time to pray for you, of course, Rudi. Our fast will start Sunday, an hour before sundown and an hour before Yom Kippur begins. It doesn't end until after nightfall on Monday. In addition to food, we are also forbidden from having sex, bathing, or wearing leather shoes. The prohibition against wearing leather comes from a reluctance to wear the skin of a slaughtered animal while asking God for mercy."

"And how do you break the fast, Joseph?" asked Lili.

"I'm happy to go along with what Ester wants, of course. Her family has always started with tea and cake. Then they put on a more serious spread of bagels, cream cheese, smoked fish, cucumbers, capers, red onion, things like that. Have you shown Lili the article you just finished, Rudi?"

"No, I will give her a copy though." He gave Lili a smile.

Joseph stated, "I think it would be good to have her mother and Mr. Schwartz read it as well."

"I was just thinking that I should also have them read the letter from Mr. Birnbaum."

"Yes, that would be excellent. Then they couldn't think you're just making all this up, Rudi."

———

ON FRIDAY, 7 October, at 4:25 in the afternoon, Joseph left in time to pick Ester up from work. At about the same time, Lili went home from her work with a bunch of flowers for her mother. Sunday, 9 October, Lili remembered was her parents' wedding anniversary; they'd wed in 1904. Lili also gave her mother a copy of Rudi's article and the letter from his teacher. Then she changed her shoes, repacked a larger bag, and hurried off to be with Rudi. On the way, she did a little shopping for items she thought Rudi would be less likely to buy.

As Lili wandered around the shops, she reflected on how nice her life was here in Vienna. *I am in the most wonderful city in the world. I am so happy here. Vienna is at a cultural zenith with its splendid architecture, its music and ballet and opera, museums, and many cinema options, better than anywhere else. There is excellent food to be had from many parts of the world: wine from Italy, Hungary, and France, dates and figs from Turkey, and all the wonderful pastries here, the envy of the rest of the world probably. And the cafés—yes, the cafés—Sacher and Demel and Mozart, Landtmann and Central and hundreds of others. Could all this be in danger, in jeopardy with the rise of the Nazis in Germany and the anti-Semitic behaviors on the rise here in Vienna? Oh, that would be terrible,* she thought, becoming quite melancholy.

When she arrived, Rudi was whistling some tune being played on the radio while unpacking from a comprehensive shopping expedition. "Servus, Schatzerl."

"Servus, Rudl. Can I help you unpack?"

"You could deal with these flowers." He gave her a smile and a vase.

"Thank you, Rudi; they are lovely." Lili quietly rearranged the autumnal bouquet held together with a white bow. The static on the radio had worsened, and she then began to fiddle with the antenna wire to try to reduce it. There was little improvement, so Rudi had another look and tugged at the wire, noticing it was somewhat loose where it exited from the radio box. He rummaged around the kitchen drawer for a screwdriver, and with a little effort the antenna was again tight and the sound better, though not static free. As was often the case, Strauss waltzes filled the air.

Rudi took Lili into his arms, and they waltzed around the apartment a couple of times before they fell into an embrace. Over the next few days, they dined, danced, and drank at home and wandered about Vienna, wending their way between shops, museums, and cafés, all the while wondering how Joseph and Ester were doing.

JOSEPH AND ESTER were faring well. On Saturday morning they went food shopping for two feasts: the prefast feast to be enjoyed late Sunday afternoon and the feast to break the fast on Monday after sunset. They went to temple briefly and then listened to music for much of the afternoon prior to dinner at home on Saturday night. Ester spent some of Sunday morning repairing the dress for Monday temple, replacing a couple of buttons that had fallen off and sowing up part of the hem that had gone adrift. Joseph cleaned house. Following a large late-afternoon meal on Sunday, Ester and Joseph listened to music and both hoped their holiest day would not see any Nazi presence. They listened to the radio news then had an early night.

Monday was spent mostly in temple, and Ester and Joseph, who had looked over their shoulders more than usual going to and from temple, were indeed pleased to have arrived home without incident. Tea and cake broke their fast, and a full meal then returned their strength. Tuesday would again be a normal workday for Ester, and Joseph would be back at university.

LILI WAS ALSO back at work on Tuesday and spent the whole day curious as to what Mr. Schwartz's response would be to Rudi's article and to the letter he'd received from Mr. Birnbaum. The response came just as Lili was packing up for the evening. "Rudi writes very well, Lili. If what he writes is true, he'll get it in the neck, and if it is untrue, he will also get it in the neck. He would be better served if he just concentrated on his studies. I am sorry to hear of the troubles Mr.

Birnbaum's family is having in Germany. That is not here, of course. Goodnight, Lili."

Lili worried about what Mr. Schwartz had in mind when he forecast that Rudi would "get it in the neck." But she was about to get it in the neck herself.

No sooner had Lili stepped inside than her mother started. "Um Gottes Willen, Lili; are you out of your mind to spend so much time as you do with Rudi, who is just setting himself up as a troublemaker?"

"Excuse me, Mama?"

"Have you read the article yourself, Lili? Is he crazy or something? How foolish can you be to criticize the university? And to suggest that the police are in cahoots with uni administration? Really."

"Are you finished, Mother?"

"No, I am not, Lili. You should seriously think about ending your relationship with this man; he is clearly immature and not of the appropriate status. He's just not right for you." After a pause, as Lili turned away, Hedwig continued quietly, "I could arrange for you and Thomas to meet up again." Lili exhaled noisily with disbelief. "Thomas is a wonderful man: handsome, intelligent, and already a very successful businessman."

"Yes, Mother, and boring, self-centered, calculating, and ignorant as well. Mother, please don't interrupt! Rudi is exciting, very intelligent, honest, and practical. And you know something else? He cares more about the way Jews are being mistreated than Jews themselves. Think about that, Mother."

"Lili, Lili," Hedwig called as Lili walked to the front door.

Lili turned and said, "I'm going to see Hanna. I will be home late tonight."

———

"SERVUS, LILI, WHAT a nice surprise."

"Servus, Hanna, am I disturbing you?"

"No, come in, Lili, I have all the time in the world." Hanna and Lili chatted about family matters, about some shopping they had done, and some winter clothes they had recently purchased in readiness for the coming colder weather. They discussed their work and concerts each had been to recently.

"You know, Hanna, I just found out that Rudi plays violin, and he plays very well and mostly without music."

"That's very nice. Did you get to the concert at the Musikverein recently, a mainly Strauss program?"

"Yes. Rudi loved it, as did I." Lili all of a sudden became quite downcast and sullen.

"Is something wrong, Lili?"

"I guess so. Mother does not approve of Rudi at all, and I'm finding it quite upsetting."

"For goodness' sake, what are her objections?"

Lili went into detail about her mother's view of Rudi: how he was a country boy, very young and immature, and not an appropriate suitor. She explained his job as a writer for the university paper and the subject of the articles he has been writing. And she relayed her mother's attitude to those writings.

Hanna thought for a while then put her glass down to speak, thought better of it, and took another sip. "You know, Lili, perhaps your mother is right."

"But—"

"Wait a minute. Perhaps Rudi makes poor judgements, poor decisions. To write negatively about the university administration seems most unwise. It also seems to show poor judgement to imply that the police aren't doing a good job, though we, of course, know that they often don't."

"But he is such a well-intentioned man, Hanna, and he loves me; he really does."

"You know, Lili, there'd be many men in Vienna who would love you just as much." Lili began to feel sad as she heard Hanna continue. "And to expose the Brownshirts as he did is to just invite retribution. He does seem to make poor decisions. Perhaps you should listen to your mother."

Lili walked home with a heavy heart and a few sobs. She had known Hanna for a very long time and had always valued her opinion as she was always so sensible. Rudi had become so much a part of her life, how could she possibly cut herself loose from him? *Hanna and her mother don't even know Rudi, so they do not understand what a wonderful person he is. And I love him.*

LILI TOSSED AND turned and hoped that sleep would free her from her anguish. It did, but anguish was replaced by fear. She had a terrible dream: Rudi was coming out of the Café Louvre late one evening after having been with Friedrich to discuss another article, when he was thumped over the head from behind and strong-armed by two men into an alley, a third man following close behind. The alley was particularly narrow, unlit, and cobblestoned, and there was a distinct stench of a dead animal. Here he was thrown against a stone wall and beaten about the head and chest. "Juden-Lieber, Arschloch, Schwein. Raus von unsere uni. Verschwind mit deiner Juedin und deiner Zeitung. Verschwind Arschloch." As he crumpled to the ground, Rudi noticed one of his attackers leaving. He was wearing high boots. Rudi was badly beaten and bleeding from various places as he crawled from the alley like a bludgeoned rat.

Lili woke startled and in a lather of perspiration. She was so wet she thought she may be covered in blood herself. She felt sore and bruised. Had she been beaten? Had she even been there? Was she going crazy? She turned on the bedside light. There was no blood, just perspiration. Her head fell back onto the pillow, and partial reality returned. *"Juden-Lieber" he was called. He must have been beaten up because of me, because he loves me. It must be the Hakenkreuzler who did this, who want to teach him a lesson not to support the Jews. They must have been following him; they must have been following us. Otherwise, how would they know he had a Jewish girlfriend? Perhaps they don't. I guess they must.* Lili felt exhausted and wanted to sleep, but sleep would not come. She tossed and turned and turned off the alarm. Sleep finally came, and several hours had passed when her mother came in, as she had expected Lili for a conversation-free breakfast hours earlier. Lili got herself ready for work and hurried out the door.

Hours late, she was greeted fortuitously at her workplace front door by Mr. Schwartz. "Guten Morgen, Lili. Looks like you need a coffee." Lili nodded her head, and she followed Mr. Schwartz to their café.

"Guten Morgen, Herr Schwartz. Guten Morgen, Lili." The waiter took them to the table they had sat at before.

"This will become my Stammtisch soon," Mr. Schwartz said as he pulled the chair out for Lili and pushed it in behind her. "Kaffee?" Lili nodded. "Krapfen oder Schnecke?" Lili nodded again. Wanting to entice a word from her, Mr. Schwartz repeated, "Krapfen order Schnecke?"

"Eine Schnecke, bitte."

Mr. Schwartz ordered two coffees and two Schnecken, and they were soon before them. He was halfway through his coffee when he was able to fleetingly make eye contact with Lili.

"Hanna agrees with Mother that I should leave Rudi."

"Oh?"

"They both think he's immature."

"Oh, I don't think he's immature; I found him to actually be mature beyond his years."

"Hanna and Mother both think he has poor judgement and makes poor decisions. They say that his article proves that. They cannot believe he made derogatory comments about the university administration, and they thought it highly naïve and foolish to implicate the police as being somehow in the pockets of the uni administration."

Mr. Schwartz ordered another two coffees, having noticed Lili's cup empty and her eyes welling up. "Yes, probably naïve. He will certainly suffer some consequences as a result of what he wrote. When does the article come out?"

"Thursday."

Mr. Schwartz was about to take another sip, thought the better of it, and set his cup down again. "You know, Lili…his writing did not show good judgement. It would really be better if Rudi were to just concentrate on his studies and become a good lawyer here in Vienna or wherever he wanted to practice in Austria. His behavior at uni could affect his later employment opportunities too, of course."

Lili wiped tears from her eyes and wanted to ask Mr. Schwartz for his advice, but she couldn't cope with the possibility, maybe the likelihood, of him agreeing with Hanna and her mother. Mr. Schwartz did not want to give advice either. "He is a principled man, Lili. Yes, Rudi has strong principles." Mr. Schwartz folded his napkin. They walked back to the office and did not speak with each other for the rest of the day.

Lili felt herself to be at a threshold, in a quandary, somewhat conflicted, and needing clarity regarding her own thinking. She decided to phone her brother. Mr. Schwartz had never objected to her using the phone, so she decided to call him after lunch when her thoughts might also be clearer. Though it was a little cool, Lili took herself to the Burggarten, bought a Wuerstel mit Senf at the same Wuerstelstand where she had been most recently with Rudi, and sat at the same bench where theyhad first rendezvoused in Vienna and which had become known to them as "our bench." Lili shed more than a few quiet tears, some even falling on her food. She pulled herself together and dusted off some crumbs as she stood up.

On the way out of the park she kicked a couple of acorns away as Rudi would do and pulled up the collar of her coat around her ears. She had no memory of her walk back and wiped her face as she entered the office doorway. She headed past Mr. Schwartz's office to the bathroom. Mr. Schwartz glanced up as she walked back on her return, and he was pleased with his last words to Lili earlier that day.

Lili took some deep breaths and rang her brother. The voice at the other end was unusually clear. It was not her brother; it was the voice of a coworker. Walter was away from the office on business and would not be back until the following Monday. She should call again then.

Lili felt the blood drain from her face as she readied herself to do some work. She couldn't concentrate on drafting a letter, and she couldn't make sense of reading a passage she needed to understand for a research project. She decided to do some filing. Lili was sure that she'd file documents in the wrong place. She felt depleted. *Perhaps Rudi is not good for me,* she mused. *For several months now I have not been able to do my work as well as before; I sometimes come to work very tired. I have not always been able to focus. I must be honest: I think a lot about him during the day, and the quality of my work has deteriorated. This is not fair to Mr. Schwartz. It's not fair to me.*

<hr />

LILI KEPT AWAY from Rudi for days. She knew he was busy with his university work, and she knew that if she went to see him she would just fall into his arms and fall in a heap. She needed to keep her head. She desperately wanted to speak with Walter to gain his perspective. She had trusted his judgement more than anybody else's as long as she could remember. *I must speak with Walter before I meet Rudi again. The weekend will be miserable, I'm sure. Rudi won't know what's up; he'll probably think I've found another man.*

15

LILI IN A QUANDRY AND RUDI IN THE WARS

ON THURSDAY AFTERNOON Rudi was enjoying a lecture when a young man walked in and interrupted the professor. The professor looked up and saw Rudi. "Herr Auer, bitte. You are excused from class; you must report to the main administration office at once." Dozens of eyes followed Rudi out the door.

As Rudi made his way, he tried to think what might be so urgent for him to be called from a lecture. *I hope my mother and father are OK. Could something have happened to Joseph? Has my scholarship been rescinded? They surely haven't read my article yet,* he thought.

"Herrein…what is your name?"

"Rudi Auer."

"Rudolf Auer?"

"Ja."

"Sit down, please." Three stern-faced men, all grey at the temples and beyond their middle age, sat at the table opposite Rudi. The one seated in the middle carefully and slowly opened a folder in front of him and took out the latest edition of *Die Universitaet's Zeitung*. He picked it up, turned the page, and creased it down the middle then held it up and handed it to the person on his right. He walked it around to the other side of the table and placed it front of Rudi. "Did you write this?"

"Ja."

"Did anyone help you write it or contribute to it?"

"Nein."

"You wrote this by yourself?"

"Ja."

"Did you have a Nervenzusammenbruch (mental breakdown)?"

"Nein."

"You realize these allegations are very serious?"

"Yes."

"Where is the evidence for these allegations?"

"I have evidence. I have firsthand evidence. See this?" Rudi said, pointing to the scar under his chin. "I received this during a fight here at our beloved university. Members of the Deutsche Studentenschaft attacked Jewish students, and I inadvertently got in the way."

"How did you know they were members of the Deutsche Studentenschaft?"

"I recognized some of them."

"This body is no longer operating in our university. No members of the administration would allow such behavior."

"There were also a dozen or so Nazis from outside who took part in this action against Jews."

"Quatsch! No outsiders could get in."

Rudi was beginning to feel that he was not going to successfully defend his position with these men; he thought he should just get out of there as unscathed as possible.

"Do you wish to make trouble?"

"No, I do not."

"You must promise not to write anything that reflects poorly on members of the university."

"Of course."

"Do you understand?"

"Yes"

"If there were another infraction, you would be summoned to appear before the UDB, the University Disciplinary Board. Do you understand?"

"Yes."

"That would be very serious. Dou you understand?"

"Yes, I do."

"You are dismissed. Use the door on your left."

Rudi did not breathe until he was outside, for he felt quite out of breath and gave such a heavy sigh that a person who had just passed him spun around. *Phew, let me get out of here before they call me back.*

RUDI LEFT THE university grounds via the main entrance on the Ringstrasse and nervously looked back. He soon calmed down and found his way to Café Louvre, where he always felt at home because of the relaxed atmosphere, the serious readers, and the abundant newspapers available. He took a *Fankfurter Zeitung* from a rattan rack and sat at a round, marble-topped table. He empied the coins from his Portmonee into his left hand to see what he could afford. The waiter arrived as he slipped his purse into his pocket. "Ein Huehnerschmalzbrot mit Zwiebel und ein Bier, bitte."

Rudi read several articles and came across one that covered a recent NSDAP rally with a thousand SA and tens of thousands of followers. The writer reported that some protesters were beaten and others dragged away. He thought about Joseph's parents and Mr. Birnbaum's relations and promised himself that he would write to Mr. Birnbaum early the next week. Rudi was mentally exhausted following his "meeting" with university administration officials. He was looking forward to the next evening, as he would see Lili again, and they would spend the weekend together, as had become the custom.

He wandered home; it was only barely dark, and he decided to go to bed to be well rested for the next day.

———

LILI'S LAST COUPLE of days had been miserable. Her mother had become increasingly opposed to Rudi, and now Hanna seemed to think that Lili should look elsewhere for a companion. Yet Lili was convinced that Rudi was a good choice for her; they loved one another and got on very well together. Lili sat at work, wishing the weekend were over, wishing that Rudi had to skip off for the weekend for a good reason so she could speak with Walter before she saw him next. She still couldn't concentrate on drafting that letter that needed to be written, nor could she make heads or tails of the passage she needed to read and understand for a research project. She continued with her filing, focusing very hard to ensure that documents found their rightful places. She desperately wanted to speak with Walter before she saw Rudi next, but he was expecting her straight after work that evening. *What to do? I can't just not show up. That wouldn't be fair to him. I know he will be looking forward to seeing me all day. Will he? Yes, I know him. He will be cleaning the apartment; he'll do some washing or ironing and do some shopping. He will buy some flowers. He likes to give me flowers. He will be anxious to see me. I must contact him some way. But what excuse can I give him? I hate to lie to him; he would never lie to me. Oh, why was Walter not in the office? Walter, Walter, please, can't you call me? Perhaps I should write a note and put it under Rudi's door at lunchtime before he is home from uni. What on earth can I write? I should be strong; I should be brief.* Lili took out a piece of paper and wrote:

> *Dear Rudi,*
> *It is not possible for me to spend this weekend with you.*
> *Sorry. I will contact you next week.*

Lili She folded the paper carefully in half, creasing it on the desk with the back of her thumbnail. She put it in an envelope and returned to the task of filing, but she couldn't concentrate. She looked at her watch frequently, wanting lunchtime to hurry up. She tried filing again, but concentrate she could not. The minutes went by ever so slowly. Eventually the churchbell chimes heralded midday. Lili hurriedly put on her coat and disappeared out the door, note in hand.

The closer she got to Rudi's flat, the harder her heartbeats became. She slipped the envelope under the door as silently as possible lest Joseph or Rudi was inside and would hence open the door. She tiptoed away a few steps, glanced behind her, then marched toward work, her heart still pounding.

Lili ducked into a cosy café to have a little lunch before heading back to the office. She was determined to complete some tasks that had eluded her in recent days, but she found it very difficult. She plodded away without making much progress, becoming quite self-conscious about her poor work performance. *At any other place I would certainly be reprimanded,* she thought, *if not dismissed. I couldn't blame them. My work has become very substandard. Some days I actually do very little; other days I am not in a good mood. I am really very lucky to have Mr. Schwartz as my boss, especially since Father died and since Walter left Vienna to work in France. I so wish Walter were still in Vienna. I really need to talk with him. Can't he feel that I need to talk with him? Can't he just ring?*

Just then Mr. Schwartz came to the door. "Is that letter ready yet, Lili?"

"I'll bring it to you momentarily." Lili scrambled to finish the letter she had put down half a dozen times. She gritted her teeth and, with considerable guilt and focus, finished it in minutes. She took it to Mr. Schwartz, aware that it was not her best work.

He popped his head into her office a few minutes later. "Very nice letter, Lili, thank you." Lili let out a sigh of relief and attacked that article she had been having so much difficulty with. She was doing better with it than she had done for days, and her heart rate was nearly back to normal. Not for long. The phone rang, and it was from France. She knew it must be Walter.

"Servus, liebe Lili. How are you?"

"Oh, lieber Walter, how wonderful of you to call! How nice to hear you. How are you enjoying Paris?"

"It's OK; it's not Vienna. Have you been to any nice concerts lately, Lili?"

"Yes, Rudi and I have been to several."

"What's the matter, Lili? I hear it in your voice." She began to sob and was momentarilty unable to speak. "Lili, are you there?"

She pulled herself together. "Walter?"

"Ja, Lili, what is it?"

"Mother wants me to leave Rudi."

"Why, Lili? Lili, are you there?"

After some more sobbing, she managed, "Hanna does too."

"What has Rudi done? Why have they become to disapprove of him so?"

"Oh, Walter, Rudi is a journalist for the uni Paper, and he wrote this article."

"So he wrote a paper. Good for him. Most students are too selfish with their time to do anything other than their course work." Lili told Walter of the article's contents and of their mother's and Hanna's responses. "Ei yei yei, Lili. Have there been any repercussions?"

— 254 —

"Not that I know of; the paper only came out yesterday. I haven't spoken with Rudi since."

"He could certainly write less provocatively, Lili. He's obviously made lots of assertions he cannot prove."

"But, yes, he can; everything is verifiable. I know. Everything he writes is true, but most people do not believe him. Is there similar anti-Semitism in France, Walter?"

"There are the occasional attacks by hoodlums against Jewish shopkeepers. Not very different to the incidents we've read about in Vienna from time to time."

"It is definitely getting worse here in Vienna, even since you left."

"Come to think of it, I did read about increased incidents against Jews in Germany. A violent incident happened in Königsberg, I think."

"Is that in East Prussia?"

"Yes, apparently shop windows were broken, gasoline stations were burned to the ground, and I think there were some murders too."

"You see, Walter, things are getting worse for Jews."

"I should read the papers more to keep in touch with what is happening, but Rudi cannot be right about some of the things he wrote."

"Yes, Walter, believe me, he is."

"I don't believe everything you said he wrote either. But, Lili, getting back to what Mother and Hanna think of Rudi, they have their opinions, and they may be right that he makes some poor decisions. I'm sure he does; we all make poor decisions from time to time. They do not know him, but you do."

"Yes, I know him. I really do know him, Walter. They disapprove of him because they say he is not of the right class."

"Lili, Lili, listen to me. What is important is what you think. I know you love him. Is he a responsible person?"

"Yes."

"Is he trustworthy?"

"Oh, yes."

"Does he respect you? Respect is very important."

"More than Father ever did; more than Mother does."

"I have always thought that you have good instincts, Lili. What do your instincts tell you? Do you want to build your life with Rudi? It is your life, Lili, and you must make decisions that you believe are good for you. Mother can advise you, and Hanna can advise you, but you must make decisions for yourself. Lili, I must run. I will always support the decisions you make."

"Thank you, Walter. I always appreciate—"

"Lili, I must away. I'm running late."

"When are you coming to Vienna?"

"Soon, I promise. I will write soon. Servus, Lili. Servus."

Lili reluctantly replaced the receiver and sighed two big sighs. She tried to return to her article and was trying very hard to focus, when Mr. Schwartz came into her office. "Is everything all right, Lili? You were on the phone much longer than is usual for you. I was just a little concerned."

"It was my brother, Walter. I wanted his advice about what my mother and Hanna said, which made me very upset."

"Of course, Lili. Is there anything you are doing right now that can't wait till Monday?" Before Lili had time to think and to answer, he said, "Go, Lili. It's nearly time to leave. Have a lovely weekend. Servus, Lili." She quietly cleaned her desktop while she wondered whether to go straight to Rudi or to go home first and get some things she had not brought with her that morning. Still wondering, she looked at Mr. Schwartz on the way out with a smile and a thank-you. *Will I go home first? Will I not? Yes. No. No.*

It was barely four in the afternoon; the door opened, and Lili flew into Rudi's arms. "I love you. I love you. Did you get the note?"

"Yes," said Rudi, a little perplexed.

"What are you doing with a broom in your hand?"

"Just in case I need to protect myself."

"From what?"

"From a flying woman. I was sweeping. I always sweep on Friday afternoons; it's become part of my routine. What's with the note?"

"Oh, please don't ask; it was a mistake."

"But—"

"Please don't."

"You look washed out, Lili. Are you OK?"

"Yes, I am now."

"Oh, well, that's good, Schatzerl. Would you like to put these roses in a vase?" He quickly took Lili's bag and handed her the roses, still in paper wrapping. Lili's eyes welled up, and she couldn't look at Rudi. She put down the flowers and disappeared into the bathroom, where she had a big cry that relieved the tension in her whole being. She wiped her face, rearranged her hair a little with her hands then came out and gave Rudi an extended hug. She returned to the flowers, and she knew she had made the right decision. She would want to be with Rudi as long as he wanted to be with her.

Lili went home to tell her mother to get lost…well, not really. Rudi went to escort her; they were holding hands all the way and feeling as close as they ever had. Rudi sat on the front step while Lili went inside. She said nothing except that she'd be back on Monday night. Lili filled her bag with what she'd need for the weekend and went to the door.

Her mother was looking out the window and asked, "Is that Rudi waiting for you?"

"Yes, Mother."

"Why did you not ask him in?"

"You shudder at hearing his name, Mother. You would hardly want him in your house, this second-class person," Lili said with a smidgeon of venom. "Bye, Mother."

Lili went outside, handed Rudi a bag, and skipped away holding his hand, her mother unhappily peering down at them from between the curtains with Kafka and Bela, who were not being all that quiet.

"Got everything, Lili? You know, your mother living in this neighbourhood…it is little wonder that she doesn't know how the other half lives and what goes on in most of Vienna." Rudi and Lili strolled back to the apartment, Lili sometimes putting her head on his shoulder as they walked. They were in no hurry. There was nothing to be

in a hurry for really. They were together, and that was all that mat-
tered right then.

RUDI AND LILI had a romantic weekend, wining and dining at home
and out, sleeping in, wandering and wondering, sharing the week's
happenings, including Rudi's meeting with the uni administration,
and reading to themselves and to each other. Rudi played the violin,
and both sang a little. They listened to the crackling Radiola and
danced to the music of Strauss. Lili left half the items she brought
in the wadrobe. The weekend was over all too soon; Lili returned to
work with a clear head and Rudi to university for a week of lectures.

Rudi told Joseph of his meeting with the uni administration, and
Joseph invited him to join the Juedische Selbstwehr. Monday and
Tuesday proved to be regular workdays. Leftover dinners were excellent but were soon depleted, so Joseph suggested to Rudi that he
invite Lili over Wednesday for dinner. They both smiled; Joseph did
the dishes, and Rudi went to bed.

Rudi did not invite Lili for dinner on Wednesday. They tossed a
coin to see who would cook. Joseph called heads as the coin landed on
the floor and rolled under the stove. That was enough of an excuse to
go out for dinner. They couldn't really afford to go out, so they settled
for the cheapest. "Huehnerschmalz auf Brot und ein Bier, bitte."

"Fuer Beide?" asked the waitress.

"Ja, bitte." They both nodded. Two beers came quickly and
overflowing.

Joseph and Rudi both noticed three men staring at them. Rudi
thought the three had come in after them but wasn't sure. Neither
Joseph nor Rudi recognized any of them. Whenever Rudi or Joseph
looked at them, they looked away.

The food arrived. "Quite large portions tonight," commented
Joseph as the waitress came with two fresh beers, a sympathetic smile,
and an "auf mich."

"Ja, that's very nice." They finished their first beers and did a cheers with their second. They looked up; the three men had gone. Soon their food was gone as well. They quietly finished their beer and left with an especially appreciative thank-you.

On their way home, Rudi and Joseph took turns looking behind them. Nothing. They looked out from their doorway. Nothing. They went to bed. Joseph was planning to work at home on Thursday, and Rudi had lectures in the morning.

LILI HAD HAD an exceptionally good three days. Her head was clear; she knew what she wanted in her life. She had been able to concentrate at work and deal with the backlog, including that elusive article she had been required to understand. Mr. Schwartz noticed that she was upbeat but aked no questions. He was just happy for her. She was happy for herself, but not for long.

The phone rang.

"Lili?"

"Ja."

"This is Joseph. I thought I needed to tell you. Rudi was beaten up, and I just brought him home from the hospital."

"Um Gottes Willen. What happened? How bad is he?" Lili began to sob.

"He was apparently going to get some lunch when he was jumped, dragged into an alley, and beaten up."

"Is he OK now?"

"Not really."

Lili began to sob so loudly that Mr. Schwartz came into the office.

"What did they do to him?"

"He can't remember anything. He woke up in hospital. He was obviously beaten quite badly. His clothes were badly torn, he is heavily bruised, and he had to have stitches. The doctor thought he'd been beaten with a truncheon and kicked."

Lili burst into tears, and Mr. Schwartz took the phone. "Joseph, this is Schwartz. I'll send Lili there by taxi as soon as possible." Mr. Schwartz helped Lili compose herself and assured her that Rudi would be OK. He sat her in a taxi, gave the driver the apartment address, and handed him some coins. "Dankeschoen. Lili, don't hug Rudi too tightly," he suggested as he closed the door.

When she arrived, Joseph let Lili in; she was still teary-eyed. "Shalom, Lili. Rudi is asleep. Beware, he doesn't look so good."

Lili went into the bedroom and immediately came out again with her hands cupped over her mouth in an attempt to muffle her loud sobs. She fell into Joseph's arms, screaming uncontrollably. He didn't really know what to do except to hold her and try not to fall over with her. He had her in a bearhug for minutes, which seemed much longer, before Lili released her hold. He sat her down then poured them each a cognac he had saved for a rainy day. Lili nearly choked, but she had another sip. She sat with her head between her hands, elbows on the table, for quite a while. She took another sip. "He looks terrible, Joseph."

"He does."

Lili threw down the rest of her cognac in a large gulp. "Sorry, but he looks like that dog with a big bandage in the dentist's ad." They both managed a glimmer of a smile. Rudi indeed had a large bandage from under the chin to over his head, another over an ear, and a third across his chest. Both eyes were bruised, and stitches were hiding in one eyebrow. "The doctor said he had several cracked ribs, so it is important that he doesn't catch a cold and doesn't cough."

"Do you know what alleyway he was in when he was attacked, Joseph?"

"No."

"Do you know who would have done this?"

"No, but probably some Hakenkreuzler."

There was a groan from the bedroom, and Lili rushed in, closely followed by Joseph. Rudi half opened one eye, groaned as he turned over, and fell back to sleep. Lili threw some clothes from a chair onto the floor and sat beside the bed with a very grim face. She sat there for a long time, certainly more than two hours. Joseph came in a couple of times and brought her some tea. "I guess your mother is expecting you home, Lili. Do you want me to call her to tell her you'll be staying here the night?"

"Oh, how thoughtful. That would be very nice of you. What will you tell her?"

"I could just say that Rudi was in an accident and that you wanted to be with him. I could, of course, tell the truth and say that he was beaten up by some anti-Semites."

"Yes, tell Mother the truth; that truth could be good for her."

"I'll go, and you should lock the door behind me. I'll just go to our café; I won't be long, Lili."

"Thank you very much, Joseph." Lili didn't move.

Joseph came back shortly with some dinner items for later and walked into the bedroom. "Thank you so much, Joseph; what did Mother say?"

"She just said, 'Make sure Lili is all right.'"

Just then Rudi woke, groaned, and looked around, barely with it. "What happened?"

"You got beaten up."

"Oh, really? At uni?"

"No, in a lane."

"Oh, hello, Lili. Sorry." Lili gave a half smile. Rudi managed to turn to face Lili and groaned, grimaced, and grunted in the process. "How did I get home?"

"I brought you home from the hospital by taxi."

"The hospital?"

"Yes, do you think I sewed you up with some kitchen twine?"

"Can't you remember what happened, Rudi?" asked a concerned Lili.

"Huh?"

"Can you remember what happened?" Joseph repeated.

"Huh?"

"Do you remember your name?" asked Joseph with a wry smile.

"Don't make me laugh; it hurts. My chest…it hurts just to breathe. I think I was run over by a car. Ow, my chest…" Rudi closed his eyes and fell back to sleep. Lili was very worried and thought perhaps they did run over him with a car, and that was how he got cracked ribs and all that bruising.

"How did Rudi get to hospital, Joseph?"

"An architect has an office overlooking the lane. He apparently heard Rudi screaming and saw it all happen below his window."

"Why didn't he run to help?"

"I believe he ran down to Rudi when the three attackers ran away and then drove him to the state hospital. He told the doctor he was scared of these hooligans himself. He had seen them before."

"Did he call the police?"

"I don't think so. As you know, Lili, some of the police are scared themselves, some just turn a blind eye, and some don't want to do all the paperwork to write up an incident."

"But this is not just an incident; it is assault. Who is this man?"

"He refused to give his name."

"Terrible that he didn't call the police. Did the doctor call them?"

"No, he said his job was to patch people up, not to speak with police. In any event he also thought the police were themselves frightened, and some were actually complicit in attacks on certain people."

"Poor Rudi."

"They gave him very heavy painkillers, Lili; he might sleep through the night."

"Really? What if he needs to go to the bathroom?"

Joseph got up, went to rummage in a kitchen cupboard, then came back and handed Lili a milk bottle. "The best we can offer." Lili half smiled and put it on the floor beside her. Rudi was now in a deep sleep and began to sound like a sawmill. Lili left his side and went to sit at the table.

Joseph was doing some reading he had planned to do earlier in the afternoon. "Lili, I have some food to heat up. Are you hungry?"

"Not really."

Joseph heated up some Latkes and some cabbage rolls and put them on the table. Lili had a better appetite than she had thought, but she remained worried that Rudi was sleeping for so long. Joseph noticed Lili's discomfort and poured two cognacs. "Good for the nerves, Lili, and the digestion too. Cheers. Why don't you listen to some music? That might distract you." Joseph turned on the radio, and they were both greeted by some operatic warbling. Joseph adjusted the crackling and the volume, and they settled down, one reading, the other ruminating.

There was some movement from the bedroom. "I muss Wischerln." Lili went in and handed Rudi the milk bottle then looked at the wardrobe door.

"Sorry it stinks." Rudi passed the bottle to Lili, who took it to the bathroom and emptied it without breathing. She gulped some fresh air and returned to Rudi. "Come to bed, Schatzerl."

"Of course, Rudi." Lili said a goodnight and thank you many times to Joseph, went briefly to the bathroom, and crawled carefully in beside Rudi, who shuffled over a little. She gave him a kiss on his least bruised cheek and turned over. This was the first time Lili wished the bed were larger than it was. They were soon both fast asleep, Rudi's imitation of a sawmill, however, waking Lili a short while thereafter. She lay there and began to relax, happy to be beside Rudi, who seemed to relax himself. Lili hoped he would have sweet dreams. Her hopes were quickly shattered as Rudi was about to have a terrible nightmare and relive the ordeal.

It began pleasantly enough, Rudi humming a tune that had been on his mind all morning. *Must have heard it on the radio*, he thought. He was heading towards a little café for a bite to eat, when he came to a lane. He looked left to check that it was clear to cross. Seemingly out of the blue, there was *whack, clunk* as he was jumped, thumped, gagged, and dragged into the lane. There were two men. Strong men. Rudi was hit with a hard object, *whack* across the head, *thump* across the chest, *whack* across the head again. He tried to shield his head with his arms, but each time he lifted them, he copped one across the chest. *Whack, thump.* "Du Arschloch, grosses Arschloch!" Rudi sat bolt upright in bed and let out a scream. "Lass mich in Ruh!"

Lili sat bolt upright. "Rudi, Rudi, it's OK." Rudi plopped back onto his pillow. *Whack, bang,* as he felt the pain of another truncheon blow. He saw stars. He began to feel dizzy; he felt blood on his face. He could smell the blood as it flowed past his nose. "Du Arschloch, du Schwein. Judenlieber." The blows rained on him.

Lili was stroking Rudi gently on the arm and speaking not so gently. "Rudi, you are having a dream."

Rudi bobbed bolt upright again in a heavy sweat. "Lass mi' in ruh…hilfe, hilfe," he yelled then fell silent and fell onto the pillow again, writhing and squirming.

"Rudi Rudi…" Lili tried to release him from his nightmare. A cool, moist facecloth on the forehead didn't help. Nothing helped. Joseph stood at the door transfixed as Rudi was writhing and Lili rubbing his arm and talking to him. He was sweating severely, in a high fever, delirious. *Whack, whack, bam* as he was smashed against a stone wall, and *thump, boom, thump* as he was kicked, kicked, and kicked again, finally crumpling to the cobblestones. He felt boots kicking, heavy boots. "Raus, raus von unsere uni. Disappear with your Jewish girlfriend and your uni paper. Du Arschloch, du Rattendreck." Rudi became limp. The beating suddenly stopped, the lane fell silent, but his head throbbed, and everything hurt. Through half-closed eyes, he could see three figures quietly disappearing through the entrance of the lane. He could make out that the alley was particularly narrow, unlit, and there was a distinct stench of a dead animal. He could feel the blood running down his face and suddenly felt very woozy and very cold. Joseph shook Rudi, and he woke, quietly sitting up.

"What's happening? Oh, sorry," as he slid back onto his pillow and fell asleep once more. Joseph returned to his bed, and after a while Lili fell asleep too.

THE SUN WAS halfway to its zenith when Rudi and Lili woke, seemingly together. Lili immediately realized she should have been at work a couple of hours ago and rushed to the bathroom. Joseph stopped her momentarily. "Don't rush. I phoned Mr. Schwartz to tell him you'd likely be late. He was very understanding. He asked after Rudi and you, and he wished Rudi a speedy recovery and both of you as good a weekend as possible. He hoped to see you on Monday, but if he didn't, he would understand. I will stay here for a while and work here, Lili. If you need anything, just say."

"Thank you so much."

Rudi was sitting on the edge of the bed when Lili returned. "Um Gottes willen, Rudi, look at you, all those bruises."

Joseph stuck his head around the corner. "Shalom, Rudi. How are you? You look like a chameleon with a sore head."

Rudi made a face. "Thank you very much, Joseph."

"S'pose you want something to eat." Rudi nodded. "You haven't had anything for more than twenty-four hours. And you used a lot of energy for your nightmare."

"Yes, it was terrible, terrible! Can you help me to the bathroom, please, Lili? Thank you. I'll be fine now." There was some groaning as Rudi tried to make himself respectable. The Eierspeiss (scrambled eggs) was ready, and ample toast was buttered and warm, yet there was no movement from the bathroom.

"Have you fallen in?" yelled Joseph.

"I'll be there in a minute. You start."

Rudi emerged looking not much better than before. He had taken off the major bandage and wiped most of the blood from his face and arms, revealing two black eyes, a collection of cuts and bruises, and a few stitches. Lili slowly looked at Rudi all over and shook her head in disbelief. Rudi was indeed quite battered. Joseph started, "I seem to have seen you like this before, Rudi. I wouldn't make a habit of it though. I hear one heals less well as one gets older." Both Rudi and Lili managed a smile, and all three managed to finish their Eierspeiss.

There was a knock at the door, and a bouquet of flowers arrived via messenger from Mr. Schwartz. "What a nice man," all agreed.

Rudi was recuperating quite well, though he and Lili didn't go dancing that weekend. Joseph might have, as he spent the weekend with Ester. "He's a real Mensch, Joseph," she said. "Fights for the Jews more than most Jews fight for themselves. You should take back some nice fruit to him on Sunday when you return."

———

RUDI RECOVERED QUICKLY. He and Lili even took a long stroll on Sunday. Lili returned to work on Monday, Rudi to university on Tuesday and to the hospital exactly a week later to have his stitches removed.

The same doctor who removed his stitches from under his chin about six months earlier removed these as well. "Greetings, young man; Auer, isn't it? I didn't expect to see you again so soon. I see the scar under you chin has healed very nicely. Try not to cough too hard; we want your ribs to mend well. Keep away from those Hakenkreutzler; they are becoming more numerous by the month. I had to sew someone else up only three days ago. I think he was coming home from temple when he was beaten up. Take care. Servus."

"Auer, what happened to you?" asked Rudi's professor who had excused him from class a week before. "You look as if you were in an accident."

"Actually, Herr Professor, I was beaten and kicked."

"Oh, that's not good. Do you know by whom?"

"I have a pretty good idea, Professor. By members of the Deutsche Gesellschaft here at the uni."

"How do you know that?"

"When they were beating me, they warned me about writing for the uni paper and referred to me as a Jew lover."

"I heard the administration was not happy about your article."

"Yes, they said what I had said was not true."

"Was it?"

"Yes, but they did not like—"

"I read the article, Auer. Let me just say you were quite correct, but the administration is in denial about such things. There are also some in the administration who are sympathetic to the views of the Deutsche Gesellschaft. I just wouldn't write on this topic for a while if I were you, Auer, and just watch your back wherever you are, especially at night."

Rudi decided to go home and write a couple of letters, one to his parents and one to Mr. Birnbaum. He thanked his parents for giving Mr. Birbaum his address and told them he intended to be home for Christmas and that Lili would join him on 28 December.

He'd appreciate it if they'd find a room in a Pension in Villach because they intended to do some skiing, and train and bus service would be best from there. His letter to Mr. Birnbaum would be somewhat different.

Dear Mr. Birnbaum,

Thank you for your letter. It was a pleasant surprise.

I'm afraid your advice not to become involved in matters political came too late. I have been writing articles for the uni newspaper, and they have unfortunately landed me in some trouble with the Deutsche Gesellschaft at the university. I include a copy of my last article. I got myself involved in a brawl. I was beaten up. Please do not tell my parents about these incidents; I would not want them to become worried.

I am sorry to hear that the Nazis are making such inroads in Germany, but I am relieved that none of your relatives has been harmed. I indeed read about a violent incident that happened in Königsberg recently where shop windows were broken and gasoline stations were burned to the ground. There were perhaps some murders too. I am sorry to report that such actions, especially against Jews, are also becoming more frequent in Vienna.

My law studies have been going well, but I am already looking forward to the holidays.

I hope your family continues to stay safe and that you remain teaching in Kaernten, where your students have a great appreciation of all you do for them.

Kind regards,

Rudi Auer

NOVEMBER 1932 CAME and went for Rudi and Lili. Within weeks of his attack, Rudi's wounds had healed, and his bruising shades of blue, black, and yellow had vanished. Rudi was a conscientious uni student, attending all lectures and completing his required reading. He had a tendency of looking over his shoulder rather more frequently than in the past. He and Joseph continued to get on extremely well. Lili remained happy at work, appreciating Mr. Schwartz's qualities and at times wishing her father had been as caring as he. Lili and Rudi had been spending every weekend together, each as romantic as the one before, filled with cafés, concerts, canoodling, and candlelit dinners.

The weather was now generally on the chilly side, and most trees looked rather naked, downed leaves and acorns generally swept up in preparation for the forthcoming snows. Rudi was pleased that, from his reading, it seemed as if the Nazis were on the decline. During November, the NSDAP lost more than thirty seats in the Reichstag, and rumour had it that many of Hitler's industrialist backers were decreasing financial support. Reports also came from Berlin that a common sight there now was Nazis in uniform, with small tin boxes in hand, soliciting contributions for party funds. Rudi and Joseph drank a toast to the projected Nazi decline several times, as they also observed a reduction in the incidents of Nazi hooliganism in Vienna. Perhaps it was because of the approach of winter, they mused.

One evening when neither Rudi nor Joseph felt like studying, Joseph suggested they should go to a film he thought sounded interesting. Rudi didn't need much of an excuse to give studying that evening a miss. The film was showing in a theatre in Leopoldstadt and was billed as a comedy. As they sat and waited for it to start, Joseph pulled out a flyer advertising the film and passed it to Rudi. It read:

Die Stadt ohne Juden (*The City without Jews*)

An Austrian Expressionist film made in 1924 by H. K. Breslauer is based on the book of the same title by Hugo Bettauer. The film was first shown in Vienna in 1924.

The novel, published in 1922, was intended as entertainment and as a satirical response to the primitive anti-Semitism of the 1920s.

Shortly after the premiere of the film, in which Vienna becomes "Utopia," Hugo Bettauer was murdered by a former member of the Nazi Party, Otto Rothstock, who was lionized by the antisemitic Austrian masses and was released from jail shortly after his conviction for murder.

In the plot of the film, which takes place in Austria, the Christian Social Party comes to power, and the new chancellor, Dr. Schwerdtfeger, a fanatical anti-Semite, sees his people as being ruled by the Jews. He, therefore, has a law passed requiring all Jews to emigrate by the end of the year. The law is received with much support by the non-Jewish population, and the Jews leave the country.

After a short while the economy declines as business diminishes and moves to other cities, such as Budapest and Prague. Unemployment runs wild. The cultural life becomes diminished.

The film also dwells on the love relationship between Lotte, a typical Wiener Mädel and the daughter of a member of the National Assembly, who voted for the banishment of the Jews, and the Jewish artist Leo Strakosch.

Toward the end of the film, the National Assembly decides to bring the Jews back again. However, in order to achieve the necessary two-thirds majority, Lotte and Leo, who has already illegally returned to Austria, have to remove the anti-Semitic parliamentary representative Bernard. They do this by getting him drunk. The drama reaches a peak as he is committed to a psychiatric institution.

The action of the film is revealed as a dream of the Anti-Semitic councillor Bernard. Councillor Bernard awakens from his dream, finds himself in the tavern at a very late hour, and remarks, "Thank God that that stupid dream is over. We are all just people, and we don't want hate. We want life. We want to live together in peace."

Rudi and Joseph were both unsettled by the film. They were surprised that it had been written as early as 1922 and that the film had existed since 1924. "Can you imagine," asked Rudi, "that the murderer of the book's author—what was his name?—was released from jail despite his conviction for murder?"

"Yes, I can, actually. I think we often forget that anti-Semitism has been part of Vienna for a long time. We should actually get a hold of a copy of the book, as the storyline is very different from that of the film, I've been told." After a brief pause, Joseph continued, "I must say, Rudi, I am heartened by the apparent decline in Nazi activity in recent weeks here and, according to my parents, in Germany as well."

"Wouldn't that be damned good?" Rudi agreed.

16

VIENNA, NOVEMBER–
DECEMBER 1932

THE FIRST SNOW flurries, the sight and smell of freshly cut firs to serve as Christmas trees, and the newly decorated shop windows were accompanied by the aromas of nutmeg, cinnamon, and Maroni (chestnuts) served by street vendors. It was again the season of Heisse Schokolat and Gluehwein in the countryside and especially in the mountains. Rudi was looking forward to spending some time in the mountains skiing with Lili. Lili was a little fearful that her skiing skills might not live up to Rudi's expectatons, but that was still weeks away.

Friday, 9 December, was an ordinary workday for Lili; of late Rudi had been finishing early at uni in order to do some apartment cleaning and some shopping in readiness for having her stay for the weekend. It was a brisk evening, cold and lightly snowing, when Lili arrived at the apartment. She flung her arms around Rudi, who swirled her around until they were both nearly dizzy. "Servus, Schatzerl. How are you?"

"Servus, Rudl." Rudi took Lili's coat and hung it in the bathroom, as it was still a little wet, then took a towel and wiped the floor near the front door of a little dusting of snow.

"Why are you so dressed up, Lili? Are you going out somewhere special?"

"No, we are. Happy birthday, Rudl, for yesterday." She gave him a big kiss.

Lili was wearing an elegant, ankle-length, drop-waisted black dress, flaring out a little below the knees and with a short, upturned collar. Rudi looked at her adoringly but couldn't help uttering, "But I've bought all—"

"Never mind, it won't go to waste. Here's a little something that you need." She handed him a beautifully wrapped package about the size of a bottle. "You're allowed to open it," she said enthusiastically as Rudi held the parcel in his hands and turned it around several times, trying to think of what it could be.

Rudi gently and slowly unwrapped the parcel without tearing the wrapping paper and smiled. "Thank you, Schatzerl." He carefully smoothed out the creases of the paper, leant over and gave Lili a long, lingering kiss then stood the red candle in a silver holder and lit the candle. "Thank you, Lili; it's far too good for here. You don't like the one we have?" he asked, looking at the multicolored, wax-encrusted Schnaps bottle.

"You can take it with you when we leave," said Lili with a cheeky smile and a twinkle in her eye.

Some canoodling later, Rudi dressed according to Lili's description of their destination as "somewhere nice." He cut a dashing figure in a dark grey suit, white shirt, and his best tie. They didn't have overly far to go, and Rudi was intrigued as Lili steered him towards the entrance of a traditional Viennese café, Café Museum. He had never been there before, it being a place mainly frequented by artists. "This is one of the cafés my mother and father preferred, and the food is excellent," said Lili.

Rudi admired the interior originally designed by renowned architect Adolf Loos. He was very pleased that they were seated in a plush, semicircular leather booth normally reserved for at least four people, though the present crowd suggested that the café might soon be filled to capacity. Lili ordered two glasses of champagne as the waiter offered the menus. Rudi smiled as he looked around and admired the elegant and simple interior, quite different from the ostentatious baroque interiors of a number of Viennese coffee houses, such as the Demel, and the classical grandeur of others, especially that of Café Central. The champagne came, and Lili wished Rudi a happy birthday before they both took their time perusing the menu.

Herr Ober appeared at their table at the closing of the menus. "Bitteschoen, liebe Herrschaften?"

"Baked trout for madam and the roasted duck for me, please, Herr Ober...und ein Gruener Veltliner, bitte."

The waiter came back just as the champagne was finished and poured two glasses of the ordered wine after the appropriate preliminary protocols. Both dishes arrived soon thereafter with gentle aromas and parsleyed potatoes, the trout also with a side salad of delicate greens and the duck with a trio of winter vegetables. "Sehr gut," they both declared as they fed one another a little. The quality of these dishes was really excellent, and both Lili and Rudi enjoyed every mouthful. They lingered to finish their wine before they shared some biscuits with their coffee.

IT WAS TIME for shopping for Christmas and Hanukkah, both of which fell at exactly the same time in 1932, Hanukkah commencing on the twenty-fourth and going through to the thirty-first of December. The less-religious Jews, living mainly in the first district, also did a lot of Christmas shopping, as they had adopted Christmas festivities as well as, or even instead of, Jewish festivities. In the meantime the eastern Jews, mainly living in Leopoldstadt, were serving as an increased labor force, cleaning middle-class homes, making and altering clothes to fit, and baking Christmas cookies for the holiday season.

Lili and Rudi spent hours alone and together, buying presents for family and each other. Window shopping and actual shopping had to be spaced out between times lingering in a café over a hot chocolate and some Lebkuchen and maybe a newspaper. Lili bought her mother a watch she had been admiring for years and hoped she'd be able to part with the one her husband had bought her. For Rudi she bought Italian leather gloves to replace the woollen ones his mother had knitted and now exposed several fingertips to the elements. Lili also bought presents for Walter, Hanna and her two children, and Mr. Schwartz. Rudi bought his mother a tablecloth and serviette set and his father a new winter hat to replace one that had seen better days and likely was more than a decade old. He had a very difficult time looking for what he wanted to give Lili. He went to at least ten jewellers before he settled on a silver and glass-fronted locket and a silver chain. He carefully brought a pressed Edelweiss he had picked when he and Lili were together hiking on the Gerlitzen to be sure it would fit. It did fit, and he was very pleased with the little gift-wrapped box he would give her at the appropriate time. Rudi and Lili spent a weekend afternoon carefully wrapping all the presents and tying them up with ribbons.

They also carefully discussed their plans for the coming week or so. Lili looked forward to Walter coming home and staying in his old room down the hall from hers. She also hoped he'd be in Vienna before Rudi left for Villach so that they could meet. Walter, in a brief letter, had not specified to Lili when exactly he'd be arriving.

A DAY BEFORE Rudi was to take the train to Villach, he and Lili were wandering around Vienna arm in arm in their winter coats, making footprints on the snow-dusted pavement. It was cold. The snow was sparkling and drifting down ever so lightly from a mainly blue sky. The smell of chestnuts faintly filled the air. They were just entering Albertinaplatz, quietly enjoying just being together, when someone called after them from behind: "Lili, Lili." They both looked around, a little startled. It was Walter; he had just arrived that morning.

"Walter! Walter, you are here. How nice. I want you to meet Rudi. Rudi, this is Walter."

"Good to meet you, Walter. Lili has told me so much about you."

"Have you had lunch yet? I was just heading to Café Mozart. Do you have time? Come," Walter said as he put an arm around both Lili and Rudi. "Stay at least for a little while so we can talk." Lili looked across the front of Walter to Rudi and nodded her head vigourously. They chatted as they walked to the café.

"Ja, Herr Gruen, bitte, as a waiter led the three to a very nice, quiet table. Rudi took Lili's coat and gave it and his own to the waiter with outstretched arms. He hung them on a nearby coatstand and returned to the table. Rudi had never been in that particular café, though he'd been in a number similar: elegant décor with mainly round tables covered with ironed linen tablecloths. "Something to drink?" the waiter asked.

"This meeting should start with champagne," Walter suggested, and as there was no speedy reaction, he ordered, "Drei Glasserl Champagne, bitte, Herr Ober." When it arrived, Walter proposed a toast to Lili and Rudi and wished them a wonderful vacation together.

That was a good start, thought Rudi, as he was a little nervous meeting Lili's brother for the first time. Rudi found him to be an elegant, well-mannered man, a younger version of Mr. Schwartz, he thought. Walter ordered ein Huehnerfilet, Lili the Frittatensuppe, and Rudi the Leberknoedelsuppe. Walter suggested a bottle of

Bordeaux, and, there being no obvious objections, a bottle of Walter's choosing was brought to the table. For a short while Walter was the center of attention as Lili asked him many questions about Paris. Then Rudi became the center as Walter was curious to learn about his sister's lover. The lunchtime meeting went very well, though without there being any real chemistry between Walter and Rudi.

Walter excused himself from the table briefly, paid the bill, and returned with two small and beautifully wrapped boxes of biscuits, which he gave to Rudi and Lilli as they said thank you and good-bye and wished each other happy Christmas. "See you tomorrow, Walter," said Lili, giving him the message that she would be staying with Rudi that night.

They arrived at the flat virtually at the same time as did Joseph. They turned on the radio, lit the coalburning heater, and closed the slightly open window to try to heat up the apartment. They shared their plans for the holiday period. Joseph would stay at Ester's for a couple of days from that evening and then together take the train to his parents in Munich. Rudi and Lili wished them a happy and safe holiday with his parents. "Thank you very much," exclaimed Joseph. "In the past people didn't wish each other a 'safe' holiday because we assumed we'd all be safe."

"Exactly," agreed Rudi, "and especially where your parents are; there is every chance of some danger lurking there." Rudi fetched a nicely wrapped bottle and an equally nicely wrapped box of choco-late money, used when playing the dreidel game, both of which they had purchased earlier. "Here is a little gift for Ester, and here's a bottle of cognac to replace the one you fed Lili to keep her from fainting."

"Oh, thank you so much, but we don't celebrate Christmas."

"Of course you don't, but Hanukkah starts on the twenty-fourth, doesn't it? Happy Hanukkah."

"Thank you," he said as everybody smiled.

Lili added, "We so hope that the time you spend with your parents is free of Nazi activity."

Joseph wished Rudi and Lili happy holidays and "Hals und Beinbruch," took a large bag and the presents, and waved to them as he left the apartment.

The next morning, at the conclusion of breakfast, Rudi gave Lili a very small package that was her Christmas present with the clear instructions that it could only be opened on Christmas Eve. Lili reciprocated with a slightly larger package but with the same instructions. He walked her home carrying a large bag, including Christmas gifts they wrapped together. Lili gave him a passionate embrace and disappeared inside. As Rudi turned around to gain a final glimpse of Lili, he noticed her mother and Kafka and Bela. He waved, turned, and left.

Once back home, Rudi packed his own bag and was soon on the train to be with his mother and father, whom he would introduce to Lili in a matter of a few days.

Rudi wondered how his parents would react to her. He was certain that the twinkle in his father's eye would brighten even further, as he genuinely liked all people but especially young, good-looking women. Rudi was not sure what his mother's response to Lili would be. She was, after all, a relatively devout Catholic on the one hand but saw Rudi as the apple of her eye, and if he had chosen Lili then she'd surely like her too.

Rudi the elder was on the platform to greet his son. "Servus, Bua," he greeted him with a big hug. Rudi was very happy to see his dad; he had always liked him a lot. He rarely reprimanded him and seemed to tolerate his missteps and misadventures much more so than his mother was able to. At home, Rudi's mother opened the door, smothered him with kisses, and saturated him with questions before he was even inside. "How are you feeling? Have you been eating enough? Is your apartment warm at night? Have you been getting enough sleep?" She felt her son had still been a boy when she last farewelled him, and now, only months later, he was a young man. She saw him as a strong, good-looking man and with some maturity from attending university and living in the big city. Surely Lili, from a well-to-do Viennese family and considerably older than Rudi, had helped him a great deal as well. Rudi's mother was really looking forward to meeting Lili and was just a little nervous.

Rudi unpacked his bag, placing some presents beneath a beautifully decorated Christmas tree with the same silver star perched on top as had been there each year since Rudi was a baby. The apartment was comfortably warm with aromas of pine, ginger, and chestnuts clearly in the air, which Rudi had always remembered. His mother passed around the hot Maroni until they were gone and then produced some hot chocolate to help wash down the Lebkuchen. The three of them talked through the afternoon and into the night, but there was not enough time to catch up on all there was to share.

"By the way, Rudi, Tante Marianne would love for you and Lili to stay with her for as long as you like. I know she actually bought new sheets and pillowcases in preparation."

"Oh that would be very nice; I've always regarded her as my favourite relation. Lili and I could just walk to the Kanzelbahn to go skiing."

"In that way Lili could also experience real Kaerntner home cooking, quite different than the Viennese kitchen," added Rudi's mother.

RUDI HELPED HIS mom with some shopping and cleaning leading up to Christmas Eve. The afternoon of the twenty-fourth was very busy, especially for his mother, for she was preparing a venison roast to be served with red cabbage and parsleyed potatoes. Kaiserschmarrn mit Zwetchken compote would be dessert. Rudi's mother never seemed to remember her husband's and son's preference for Apfelmus, but there were never any complaints. Hours later the venison roast came out of the oven and was just perfect, the Austrian mountain berries providing a luscious complement. An inexpensive Italian red wine also complemented the venison well; Rudi Senior would venture into Italy several times a year with some friends to purchase wine. Everybody ate too much, but there was always room for some Kaiserschmarrn.

With dinner mostly over, it was time for the giving of presents. The Christmas tree candles were lit, and everybody admired the tree, as was customary. Rudi received some yearly homeknitted woolen socks and this year a Loden jacket that his mother thought he would need in the city. His father was delighted with the new hat, and his mother was very impressed with the tablecloth and set of serviettes. "You are getting used to classy items, I see," his father said as he admired the fine linens.

"What did you get for Lili?" asked his mother.

"I got a silver, glass-fronted locket with a deep burgundy red velvet lining, and I put in a small Edelweiss flower that I picked in summer and pressed."

"Very nice, Rudi. And with a silver chain? Papa, did you hear that?"

"Yes, Mother," Rudi replied. "I'm sure Lili will be wearing it when you meet."

And so she was. Rudi met her on the platform, as had been planned, and escorted her to his parents' place for some afternoon coffee.

"Welcome to Villach, Lili. Very nice to meet you. What lovely hair you have," said Rudi's mother as Rudi's father stroked his very bald head and admired Lili's dark brown eyes. The stationmaster vaguely recognized Lili as part of the family Gruen, whom he'd welcomed many times to Annenheim for their annual vacations.

"Thank you very much. Nice to meet both of you too," replied Lili, who handed Rudi's mother a box of the finest Wiener Feinigkeiten. Rudi recognized the locket around Lili's neck, and so did his mother. She nodded at Rudi approvingly and complimented Lili on her beautiful necklace. Lili was quite nervous, not having met Rudi's parents before, and she didn't take much notice of her surroundings, mainly watching Rudi. Coffee was poured and Lebkuchen passed around on dessert plates.

Rudi Senior picked up the phone and dialed. "Marianne, they are here. They'll be over later this afternoon."

After chatting for another couple of hours, Rudi, with skis over his shoulder and taking hold of Lili's hand, caught the train for a short ride to Annenheim, arriving midafternoon. It was very quiet, with just a few skiers returning from the slopes. Ice was beginning to form on the Ossiachersee, but it was yet nowhere near ready for skating. Rudi and Lili paused in front of Pension Stein and gave each other a knowing hug. Another hundred yards and to the right, and there was Tante Marianne, sweeping the front entrance. Rudi let out an "Uh-huh."

Tante Marianne looked around, leaned her broom against the wall, and wiped her hands on her apron. She gave Rudi a kiss and pinched a cheek as she looked into his eyes. She gave Lili a big hug. "You must stay as long as you like, even if Rudi wants to disappear into the mountains. You know, Lili, he used to do that sometimes when he was bored with school or just because there had been a big snowfall overnight. Come." Tante Marianne, with an arm around Lili, showed her proudly into a modest little room with a small wardrobe, one chair, and fresh bedding. "I'll leave you two to unpack, and Heisse Schokolade will be ready in two minutes.

The kitchen-dining area was a very cosy space with a largish table and built-in benches on three sides. Lili slid in, with Rudi at the other end. A white and green tablecloth with embroidered flowers covered the table, and matching cushions resided on the benches. The large woodburning stove was for cooking and warming the home. Heisse Schokolade was poured, and a mountain of cream placed on each one. Cinamon stars, tiny apricot thumbprints, baby merangues, and the omnipresent Lebkuchen were offered. Rudi was not reticent to try everything, but Lili, already smelling chicken and having an understanding that dinner was likely to follow shortly afterwards, confined herself to a thumbprint.

It was just turning dark, and all of a sudden there was a crashing sound just below the kitchen window. Lili jumped. A deer had jumped into the garden. "They come down to forage on what's left in the vegetable garden; I just wish they wouldn't break the fence all the time," Tante lamented.

"Tante, can I put on the light around the back, and I'll fix the fence?"

"Oh, thank you, Rudi." He took some nails and a hammer and went out. "You know, Lili, he's a very practical boy. He'd make a good husband; he's very handy and reliable." She picked up a photo on a cabinet. "This was my husband, Anton. He was very practical too, and very loyal. He died in the war." Rudi came back inside, rubbing his hands, and quickly held them over the stove for a few moments.

As Lili had foreseen, dinner was nearly ready. Auntie placed three plates over a steaming pot to get them warm while she carved the chicken. "Sehr gut," she said as she licked her fingers between carving. Rudi, standing beside Auntie, snaffled a bit of chicken and fed it to Lili. He snaffled another piece for himself. Auntie smiled. "Wipe the plates with a tea towel, please, Rudi." Auntie dished out two large servings and one tiny serving of roasted potatoes, carrots, and cauliflower beside the chicken. She set them on the table and fetched a bottle of light Italian red that had been breathing before the deer invaded the backyard.

"Auntie, you have to do better than that," said Rudi, glaring at her plate."

"I don't eat much anymore. You know, you need less as you get older, and I can't afford to get fat, or I'd get too puffed doing the housework. I'll really enjoy having both of you here; cooking is worthwhile then. I made some Kaiserschmarrn too, because I know Rudi likes it so much, and he likes it with Apfelmus," she said to Lili.

They chatted on after dinner until the nine o'clock news. There was no real news, and Auntie became tired. Her eyes began to close, and she began to list from the waist. She put her hand firmly on Rudi's arm. "Thank you for coming, Rudi, and thank you for bringing Lili." She leaned over the table and kissed Lili on the forehead. "Thank you for coming, Lili. Stay as long as you like."

Rudi stood up to give his aunt a big hug and sent her to bed. He attended to the dishes while Lili reflected on how warm Rudi's parents and Tante Marianne were.

THE SMELL OF coffee and fresh Semmel greeted Rudi and Lili as the sun was beginning its daily journey. Lili was given a pair of skis by Tante Marianne, and Rudi was handed his pack, heavier than normal. Auntie waved as they headed to the Kanzelbahn.

"Servus, Rudi. Wie gehts? Zwei Karten Heute?" Rudi was given two tickets and an approving nod. This was the latest Rudi had ever been getting on the Kanzelbahn since he was about six, but he didn't care because he was with Lili, and he was aware she might be feeling just a little wary. She was from the city, after all. You could tell that from what she was wearing: a dark green Pierre Balmain jacket with a dusty red trim around the neck and a dusty red hat with a small dark green rim to match. Black Italian trousers and short laced boots completed the outfit. Rudi's knickerbockers, a Christmas present of three years ago, and a heavy home-knit sweater made up his outfit that day. He had a light waterproof jacket in the pack if he needed it.

The Kanzelbahn rocked to a halt, and Lili looked down the hill with some anticipation. Rudi smiled, took Lili's skis, swung them over his shoulder, and beckoned her to follow. "Where are we going?"

"We aren't at the top yet. Just follow in my steps." Rudi followed some tracks, and Lili followed in his. An automatic response to being in the mountains, Rudi began to hum as he trudged towards the summit. Lili followed joyfully, not quite catching the tune he was humming. After about five minutes, Rudi stopped to allow her to catch her breath. "Are you ok, Schatzerl?" he asked.

A confident "of course" belied her heavy breathing. They looked around them and admired the beautiful day that it was. There was a blue sky with a few whispy white clouds; it was eerily quiet except for the sound of one's own breath and the occasional sound of skis over snow. They stopped once more before reaching the summit. Rudi stuck the skis into the snow and took Lili by the hand.

They gazed out over the Klagenfurt basin below and admired the Karawanken in the distance. He pointed out the Nockberb, the Hohe Tauern, and the Hochalmspitze, which he had pointed out to Lili in the summer. Each time she had been skiing there, it was with Walter, and they had skied close to the lift. Rudi thought for a moment about what route to take down. He decided to avoid the area he used to ski with Franz. He needed to remain happy that day, being with Lili, and he needed to choose a path for "gemuehtliches" skiing, with Lili being from Vienna.

Rudi started off slowly, Lili behind, heading into a gentle but treed slope. Skiing was easy, the snow light, and the powder only ankle deep. Rudi skied a little more quickly so he could stop, look behind, and watch Lili make a few turns. He wanted to gauge her skiing ability to help him decide on the path to take further ahead. *She skies nicely,* he thought, *with good form but a little tentative.* They continued on between the trees, rhythmically and gently carving one turn after another, Lili becoming increasingly confident and pleased that Rudi had caringly chosen a line she could handle.

Rudi came to an abrupt stop, and Lili had to be careful not to plough into him. A tree had fallen and lay directly across their intended track. Rudi herringboned uphill to find a way around the tree and soon called for Lili to follow. *Very nice,* he thought as he admired her technique and strength. Past this obstacle, they skied further into more heavily treed and steeper terrain, Rudi constantly looking behind to see that Lili was comfortably following. Rudi was quite impressed.

A rare rocky outcrop lay before them, and Rudi remembered it as a most suitable place to rest. He skied to a gentle stop, and Lili was momentarily beside him. "How did I do?" she asked, feeling quite proud of her accomplishment so far.

"You were great, Schatzerl. Very nice. Ready for lunch?" Rudi stuck two pairs of skis in the snow, took his jacket out of the pack, and placed it on a rock for Lili to sit on. "I hope you are not sick of chicken," he said as he passed her a chicken and salad sandwich on light rye bread. "Tante Marianne wouldn't like to feed us leftovers tonight. I bet she has beef, venison, rabbit, or fish."

Lunch, including a cheese sandwich, an apple, and some Lebkuchen, tasted delicious, especially after a little exercise. Rudi offered Lili some apple juice, but she declined, both understanding that bathroom facilities were still hours away. *It's easy for a boy*, she thought.

"Let's get going again, Lili, before we get too cold."

A quick embrace and they were again headed downhill. They soon fell back into a nice rhythm, carving wider turns as they came out onto a bit of a clearing. Rudi couldn't resist a few quick turns and a jump from a bump, accompanied by a brief yodel. He waited for Lili, who continued to gather confidence and ski with increasing ease. Soon it was again into a narrow path between the trees, which Lili negotiated with ease. Just prior to a rather steep section, Rudi and Lili stopped; she peered down the slope and grimaced, looking at Rudi. "OK," she said, "I'll try."

"Keep to your left and follow me," Rudi suggested. They both got down in one piece, just with a little panting. "Look, Lili!" Rudi pointed to a deer staring straight at them. "Give me your skis. We're here."

"Is that the same deer that broke into the garden yesterday, Rudl?"

"Yes, you can tell by the number and shape of the pointers." Lili looked surprised as Rudi opened a gate and led her to the back door, where Tante Marianne was waiting.

"My nose told me you were arriving. Did you have a nice day, Lili?" she asked as Rudi and Lili took off their boots on the back porch.

"Yes, it was lovely, Auntie; Rudi is such a wonderful skier, and I think he knows every tree on the mountain."

Auntie smiled. "The hot chocolate will be waiting for you."

Both Rudi and Lili changed into some homey clothes, and they sat where they were the night before for dinner. A Marmorgugglehupf sat invitingly before them. *A slice of Gugglehupf and a hot chocolate with a mountain of cream on each. What could be better than that?* they thought. Tante Marianne had a tiny slice and half a cup of hot chocolate. Rudi described the path down he had taken with Lili and where they had stopped for lunch. Lili thanked Tante Marianne for lunch and reflected on what an enjoyable day she had with Rudi and how pleased she was with her own skiing. She wondered what more difficult skiing terrain she could handle with Rudi as her guide.

"Rudi, could we ski the Grossglockner? I never have, and I think it would be wonderful with you."

"The Grossglockner is one hundred and fifty or more kilometres away, Lili; it would take three to four hours to get there."

"That's OK. We could go and stay overnight, maybe for two nights," Lili suggested enthusiastically. "You told me once what wonderful skiing there is there, Rudi, didn't you?"

"Yes, I did."

The Grossglockner, at 3,798 metres, is a wonderful mountain, and Rudi had spoken of it glowingly to Lili early on in their relationship. It is Austria's highest mountain and the highest mountain in the Alps, east of the Brenner Pass. After Mont Blanc, it is the second-most prominent mountain in the Alps. The glacier, the Pasterze, is nine kilometres in length and is the longest in Austria. It lies within the Hohe Tauern mountain range in Kaernten directly below the Grossglockner. You can reach the Pasterze via the Grossglockner High Alpine Road. This road is the most beautiful panoramic in Austria, in the state of Salzburg. It connects Salzburg with the state of Kaernten and is a very popular bus route.

"Well, why can't we go? You could show me some easy slopes, and we could stay overnight in a hut? That would be so romantic."

"You might be surprised, Lili. There are only quite narrow bunkbeds, men and women in the same area, and the poor ventilation…"

"I can see you just don't want to take me; I'd be too much bother."

"Lili, I'd love to take you, but I can't."

"What do you mean you can't take me?" asked Lili, becoming just a little agitated.

"The Grossglockner and Pasterze Glacier are owned by the Austrian Alpine Association."

"So?"

"Only Aryans can go there."

"What? That can't be possible. You mean to tell me that because I am Jewish, I can't ski the Grossglockner? That can't be true; that's preposterous."

"I'm sorry I am making you angry, Schatzerl, but that's how it is."

"Is that really true, Rudi?" asked Tante Marianne.

"Yes, Auntie, I've been up there many times, as you know, and I only found this out recently while I was doing some research for some articles I was writing. This goes back to the 1870s apparently. The German and the Austrian Alpine Societies merged to form the German and Austrian Alpine Club (DÖAV). Already in the late-nineteenth century, the association's policies were increasingly characterized by anti-Semitism. Now there is an actual Aryan paragraph in their constitution, a clause that says that members must be of the 'Aryan race,' and it excludes non-Aryans, particularly Jews or those of Jewish descent."

Lili fell silent, and tears welled up in her eyes. Then she said, "Tante Marianne, how can it be that everywhere people hate us so much...just because we are Jewish, even if we have nothing to do with the Jewish religion? I could become a devout Catholic, and it would make no difference. I am of the Jewish race, and I am being discriminated against. I am not allowed to ski on the Grossglockner."

"I don't know, Lili. I have never heard of such a thing before. It is truly a scandal."

"You know, come to think of it, I read somewhere that some people seeking shelter from a storm have been turned away from a hut because someone inside said they looked Jewish."

Tante Marianne shook her head. "I look just as Jewish as Lili. Imagine people being turned away because of the way they look. That settles that idea, Lili. Anyway, I want to have you and Rudi here, not being worried about whether you've broken a leg up there in Salzburg."

Lili began to really like Tante Marianne, and she allowed herself a lighthearted thought. *Would Tante Marianne be included in the package if I married Rudi?*

Dinnertime had arrived again, and Rudi and Lili feasted on an onion-heavy rabbit stew. There was a new bottle of wine breathing, and Rudi asked, "What did you do with the wine from last night, Auntie?"

"The bunny drank it." The bunny stew was served with Semmelknoedel and accompanied with a heavier red than the night before. "This is a Knoedel-heavy night," declared Tante Marianne as she placed a bowl of Zwetchkenknoedel in the middle of the table, explaining how she had saved the Zwetchken for many weeks.

Heisse Schokolade ended the evening, with Auntie taking her leave before she began to list. A couple of days more of skiing, and it would be New Year's Eve.

17

New Year Indicators

THE WEATHER REMAINED fine for two more days, with Rudi and Lili enjoying their time together on the mountain as they had done the first day. Trout served with Risipisi (peas and rice) and a Gruener Veltliner provided dinner for one night, while venison, Semmelknoedel, and red cabbage served with a southern Italian red wine made up the other dinner. On that night a deer trampled through the garden to make some point or another.

Rudi and Lili had arranged to spend New Year's Eve with his parents at their local Gasthaus, and several attempts were made to have Tante Marianne join them. Rudi and Lili were dressed up for the occasion and presented themselves for inspection to Tante Marianne as the phone rang and Rudi Senior could be heard imploring her to come as well. Rudi quipped, "We'll even escort you home, Auntie."

She smiled. "Thank you, Rudi, very kind of you. I'm not good after nine in the evening, and I haven't been since my husband died. Have a lovely time. I'll save a dream for you. Let me look at you."

Rudi and Lili left smiling, walked to the train, picked up Rudi's parents on the way, and walked up the hill to their local Gasthaus. It was not yet raining or snowing, but the sky looked rather ominous.

They were cordially met by Herr Wirt and seated away from the door and away from the Kapelle, as they hoped to be able to hear each other even when the music was playing. Rudi's mother admired Lili's sense of style, and Rudi Senior remembered that his wife also liked to dress elegantly. A fixed menu of venison, made the same way as their auntie had made it the night before, was followed by Apfelstrudel. There was ample wine, the waiters having to move seemingly quickly to keep up with the demand. Rudi was beginning to yearn for a Wiener Schnitzel when the venison arrived. It was tougher than the one that his auntie prepared, though it did have good flavor. Rudi wondered where it came from. The Kapelle played all night, mostly Strauss waltzes and polkas, though there was also some Kaerntner folk music, Landler dance music, and some pieces by Mozart.

Though the Auer party was one of the first to arrive, by the time they were enjoying their main course, the Gasthaus was virtually full. There was much conviviality and lots of bobbing up as guests came to say hello and give Lili the once-over. People asked Rudi many questions while looking at Lili. They smiled and nodded approvingly. Rudi felt very proud, and every time someone would look at Lili for more than three seconds, he would put an arm around her and whisper some sweet nothings. Lili liked that. She smiled a lot. After the wine had commenced to take an effect, there was a lot of dancing. Rudi andLili danced a lot together. Rudi also danced with his mother; Lili danced with his father. He was very pleased to dance with Lili, as she was more his height, his wife being a good half a head taller. Lili was very gracious in keeping her feet away from under Rudi Senior's.

As the night progressed there were more waltzes than Landlers and polkas, the bandmaster being aware of the greater difficulty dancers have remaining upright when they have consumed more wine than normal. Slower waltzes were accompanied by dimmer lights, and there was increased togetherness on the dance floor. As midnight approached and champagne glasses were being filled around the room, a storm was quietly approaching on the outside. Dark, ominous clouds, laden with moisture and driven by increasingly powerful winds, were moving in. Would they bring rain, or would there be snow on the first day of 1933? Would there be any thunder and lightning? As the last dance of the current year had nearly come to an end and lovers were in a final embrace, the cymbals clanged, everybody jumped to their feet, and a raucous countdown began. "Zehn, neun, acht, sieben, sechs, fuenf, vier, drei, zwei, eins. Prosit Neu Jahr!" Champagne glasses clinked, kisses and New Year's wishes were generously shared, and the band members paused to share greetings with one another. Lili, Rudi, and his parents were all saying nice things to one another as the first thunder roll of 1933 was heard outside.

Rudi's parents hoped that Rudi and Lili would stay together. They really liked Lili, didn't care that she was Jewish, and would not have cared had she been Budhist or Muslim, for that matter.

There were many greetings on the way out, and as the party reached the door another thunderclap caused them to take a stumbling step backwards. They bundled up as well as they could, and two very contented couples headed towards the stationmaster and his wife's apartment. With the wind at their backs, it did not take long to reach their destination. Several more kisses and good wishes took place, and Rudi's father wished them an additional "noch viel Spaß" as they took the bus back to Annenheim to continue their vacation with Tante Marianne.

There were two other couples on the bus, and everybody wished everybody else "Gutes Neues Jahr." The wind being so very strong and gusty, the bus driver had to concentrate and apply good steering and braking skills to keep the vehicle on the road. Rudi and Lili had to fight the wind to actually get off the bus, there being a strong force keeping them from easily stepping off. There was no rain or snow yet, but it was getting colder; the wind was so strong and gusty that Lili and Rudi had to hang on to one another as they pushed forward. The clouds looked foreboding above, and the Ossiachersee looked and sounded angry on their right as they plodded on, fighting against the elements.

Rudi fossicked for the front door key from atop the wood stack, silently pushed the door open, and pushed Lili inside. They both took off their shoes to tiptoe to their room. "Gutes Neues Jahr, liebe Kinder. Come in." Lili and Rudi stepped into Tante Marianne's room, where she demanded a kiss from each. "I woke up expecting you. Now I can sleep well that you're home safely. Should be a lot of snow before breakfast; it's cold enough now. Sleep well."

All cosy in their little room, Lili and Rudi snuggled up. They were far too excited to fall asleep and had lots of things they wanted to share with each other. It was their first New Year together, and they both knew that they would be together for a very long time, come hell or high water. They promised each other that. "I'll want to sleep in tomorrow, Rudi…sorry, *today*," she corrected herself. "So if you want to go skiing, I'll be very happy staying with Tante Marianne." Lili was already dreaming of someplace far away as Rudi could hear that it had begun to snow. The dense clouds they had observed on the way home and the swirling winds would likely produce a big fall. The snow was driving against the windowpane, and Rudi pulled the curtains slightly open so the first light would hopefully wake him. It did.

He gave Lili a very gentle kiss on the little section of her face that was protruding from under the doona. He didn't notice Lili's smile. On his way out, there was a note: "Rudi, Just in case you go skiing, here's lunch. Bußie, Tante." Rudi took his skis and lunch and closed the back door behind him as quietly as he could.

⸺∞⸺

IT WAS THE first day of the new year, it was Sunday, and it was still snowing lightly as Rudi hummed his way to the Kanzelbahn through half a metre of new snow; only a few birds' footprints disturbed the pristine surface. The sky was now mainly blue, and anything ominous about the weather was not in immediate view. Rudi was first in line at the Kanzel, where men were just finishing the necessary shovelling. "Prosit Neu Jahr, Rudi; schoenes Maderl."

"Danke! Prosit Neu Jahr." The door closed, and the cable car lurched forward. It was a little breezier as Rudi stepped out and trudged slowly towards the summit.

With each step he would sink in nearly to the knees, and progress was very slow. A couple of German tourists, using Rudi's steps, caught up and made some comment about him being slow. Rudi wished them a happy New Year and invited them to go ahead. They made some nice, well-spaced steps in less than five minutes and stopped. Rudi passed them as they were puffing like steam engines, and he wondered how they would feel if this were a mountain reserved only for Austrians and Italians. He wondered what their response would be if at the entrance to the Kanzelbahn there were a large sign that read "Deutsche Verboten." Rudi reached the summit. There alone, he looked out over the valleys and the surrounding peaks and noticed some really omminous weather coming from the northwest, beyond the Grossglockner, in Germany. He wondered whether there was any ill wind in that.

Rudi decided to ski the same route he had last skied with Franz. He took a sip of apple juice, fastened his skis, and skied awkwardly, not able to carve nice turns as he had been able to do in the past. The snow was excellent; he couldn't blame the conditions. He skied to where he and Franz had their last lunch together and stopped for a moment, just enough time for a few tears to well up. Rudi skied on, recognizing a number of undulations that were great for jumps. Suddenly he stopped as if he were required to by a greater force. He burst into tears as he remembered Franz's last jump, the jump where he caught too much air and where his ski pole pierced his heart. When his crying subsided he wanted to say a prayer, but he couldn't. He'd be a hypocrite; he had no faith in God. How could an omnipotent God not have prevented Franz's death? He fondly remembered his best friend and skied away. Rudi again thought about God. *Aren't all people supposed to be the same in God's eyes? Isn't God supposed to be benevolent? How can it be that I will most likely never be able to ski the Grossglockner again? How can it be that God allows Aryans to see themselves as being so bloody superior? Shit, I am Aryan, yet I'm just an ordinary schmuck, lucky to have Lili as a girlfriend. And I can't take her to the Grossglockner. Would we pollute the Grossglockner, God, because she is a Jew and I love her?*

Rudi arrived at the Kanzelbahn and decided he was still too upset to go back home. He needed another run.

———

Lili was woken by the scraping of a shovel on stones as Tante Marianne was just finishing clearing the snow away from near the doors. "Guten Morgen, Tante. I'm sorry I'm so late; I should have helped you do some shovelling."

"Aberwas, Lili; I do it all winter. It's good exercise for me. Come and have some breakfast." A coffee and some Semmel were soon in front of Lili, along with a bowl of cream and some butter and three jars of confiture: apricot, mountain berry, and fig. "I make them all myself," said Tante Marriane proudly. "Did you sleep well, Lili? Did you have a good time last night? Did you dance a lot? Did Rudi's mother and father seem happy? Was the music loud? Did they serve venison? I should have remembered; I would have made something different the night before."

Lili answered the questions, finding she really liked Tante Marianne. *She is curious but not nosy. All she does, she takes seriously but herself not at all. She's not judgemental.*

"I'm so sorry you can't go to the Grossglockner, Lili. It seems so unfair and idiotic, if you ask me. I thought God treated people equally."

"I can't understand it at all, Tante Marianne. Rudi's flatmate is a Jew, and his girlfriend, Ester, lives in Vienna's second district, where there's a large Jewish community. They regularly have their shop windows broken, businesses picketed, and swastikas painted on buildings. You know, the women there even get harassed for wearing scarves."

"That's idiotic. Many women, including myself, wear a scarf all the time. They are Nazis from Germany, Lili. They are very nasty people, arrogant people. I know that Rudi has never liked them. He says they're arrogant and bossy; they behave like bullies. He much prefers the Italians. We get a lot of Italians here. We get a lot of their wine here too. Rudi thinks the Yugoslavs are good as well; their wine isn't so good though."

"You know, Tante, in Germany these Nazis are gaining a lot of power, and it frightens me."

"It also frightens Rudi's father. He reads a lot, and he mentioned not long ago that the Nazis are now the single most powerful party in the Reichstag. He finds this very frightening. Lili, I'm sorry, I must take a little nap. All this political discussion is quite upsetting. I'll have a lie down before Rudi comes back. I packed him some sandwiches, but we can all have a late lunch together when he comes. He'll be hungry. Do you have a book you can read?"

"Yes, thank you, Tante."

"What is it?"

"I'm reading *The Age of Innocence* by Edith Wharton."

"Is it in English?"

"Yes. I don't find it easy, but my English is getting better and better. It was the winner of the 1921 Pulitzer Prize. It's a portrait of desire and betrayal in old New York, where conformity is key, and the uppercrust goes about a life of ritual that has no substance or meaning. It reminds me of a life similar to that which my parents have in Vienna."

"Lili, I must lie down before I fall down." Sleep had always come easily to Tante Marianne, as she had always believed that God looks after all His people. Just over the last year or so she'd begun to have doubts about God's evenhandedness, however. A recent talk with Rudi's father and her discussion with Lili just now had made her uncomfortably skeptical.

Lili read without interruption for quite some time. When she read "Being here is like—like—being taken on a holiday when one has been a good little girl and done all one's lessons," she smiled and thought how lucky she was to be there with Rudi and his auntie.

A LITTLE LATER, Tante Marianne fixed up the bun in her hair, replaced a pin, and added three pieces of wood to the stove. Just then Rudi came through the back door a little out of breath, causing Lili to close her book on a silken Italian bookmark. "Hallo, Rudi."

"Servus, Schatzerl."

"You are all red in the face. Did you have a good time?"

"Yes, it was wonderful skiing—very few people on the slopes. I don't think I had to cross anybody's tracks all day." Rudi gave Tante Marianne a Bußerl, followed by one for Lili, and then sat in his normal place. He leaned over and took Lili's hand. "I hope you didn't mind."

"No, not at all. I had a nice long sleep and a good talk with Tante Marianne, but your hands are freezing."

"That's why I'm holding yours. What did you talk abou—?"

"Rudi, that is our business, isn't it, Lili?" said Tante Marianne with a smile. "A little Eierspeiß or Semmelknoedelsuppe, or both?"

Lili looked at Rudi and shrugged her shoulders. "Eierspeiß would be very nice, Tante," declared Rudi.

They all enjoyed their late lunch. Tante Marianne then made a suggestion. "Rudi, you should take Lili for a little walk while the sun is out and it is not so cold."

The snow was too deep to walk in the woods, so they walked along the road close by the water. The Ossiachersee was now mostly frozen over, but the ice could not obscure the memories of their first days together in the water. "Where's our log?" asked Lili, looking down towards the lake.

"Let's have a look, Schatzerl." Rudi trudged a few steps and started to dig with his gloved hands. "Here it is." He cleared the snow from the top of the log, trampled the snow in front of it, and beckoned Lili to him. Rudi took her by the hand and, with a bit of a tug, encouraged her to sit beside him. They looked at each other with big smiles and gave each other a noisy kiss. They reflected on their first meetings and their first Wuerstel mit Senf together, the sparrows at their feet hoping for a crumb.

Now it was eerily quiet; just a couple of birds picking at something on the edge of the ice caught Rudi's attention. "I think they're late flying south; they should get out of here before the next storm," he suggested.

"I hope it isn't already too late for them. I hope they'll make it safely to wherever they're headed," Lili added.

They trudged back to the road, their boots filled with snow, but they didn't care about that. They wandered around the main parts of Annenheim and couldn't help but notice the quiet and serene afternoon, the sun near the horizon, and the shadows slowly lengthening. It was now quite cold. The church bells tolled for the day's last service as they opened the door to Marianne's house to be greeted by the aroma of Heisse Schokolade.

Tante Marianne turned down the volume of a New Year Day's concert and stood up from behind the table. "Did you have a nice walk? Both of you sit down." She placed a warm tray of Linzerschnitten on the table. "Would you please cut them, Lili?"

Rudi snaffled a little corner of pastry that had broken off.

"Wunderbar, Tante," said Lili as she tasted it. "Rudi, can we take Tante Marianne back with us to Vienna?"

Auntie chuckled. "That won't happen, but you can come and stay with me as often and for however long you want to." Rudi smiled at Lili as he waited for his piece.

Marianne turned up the volume of the radio just a little, and they all enjoyed the Strauss that was playing. It was nearly dark as Rudi noticed the supply of kindling wood virtually depleted. "Tante Marianne, should I cut you some kindling? You've nearly run out."

"Oh, that would be nice, but I use very little in the middle of winter, as I never really let the stove go out."

Lili and Tante Marianne continued listening to Strauss while the splitting of wood provided some dissonance of sound as it was clearly not in three-four time. "I love Johann Strauss," said Tante Marianne.

"I do too," said Lili. "But I wonder if he would be loved so much if people realized he had a Jewish great-grandfather."

"I didn't know that."

"Yes, his paternal great-grandfather was a Hungarian Jew," explained Lili.

"You certainly know your music," said Tante Marianne. "Yes, the Nazis, who love his music, would just deny it, Lili. Rudi is a very nice dancer. You must have waltzed with him last night. Did you dance some Landler with him as well?"

"Yes, it was hilarious, as I couldn't really keep up with him. I'm glad he hung on to me tightly," Lili said with a chuckle.

Rudi came in with a full bucket and put it down by the side of the stove. He filled a glass of water and emptied it just as quickly. "Your deer is behind the back fence again, Tante Marianne; I think he's not all that happy about all that new snow." Tante Marianne took both of Rudi's hands and held them against her cheeks to warm them up. He held her firmly by the waist and waltzed a few steps with her around the kitchen. Everybody chuckled.

It was now quite dark and quite cold outside. It was warm and homey inside Tante Marianne's living room, which was also the kitchen. The lounge room next door was rarely used in winter. Strauss turned to Mozart on the radio as Tante Marianne pulled the curtains across ther window to keep the warmth in. They chatted about nothing in particular, when Lili realized they'd have only one more full day of skiing, as she wanted to be back at work on Wednesday, though Mr. Schwartz said she could start back on the following Monday. "Will you take me skiing again tomorrow, Rudi? On Tuesday we already must be back in Vienna, as I have to be at work the day after."

"Of course. It should be a beautiful day again, just as today."

The aroma of a Rostbraten wafting across the room urged Tante Marianne to prepare some potatoes and carrots. "Can I peel them, Tante Marianne?" She obliged with a smile, passing Lili a small kitchen knife, a thick wooden cutting board, and a bowl of washed potatoes and carrots.

"Would you open this Sangiovese, please, Rudi? It might enjoy a little air." Rudi popped the cork and set it beside the bottle on the table. "Three glasses would be good too, Rudi. Thanks." Tante Marianne poured a little in each glass and pushed one across to Lili and one to Rudi. "We better make sure it's all right. Prosit Neu Jahr, liebe Kinder. I wish you good health and happiness together."

"Danke vielmals. Prosit Neu Jahr, Tante Marianne."

"I think the roast would appreciate some as well." She lifted the lid and sloshed a little wine atop the roast, which was ready quite soon.

Rudi filled up the glasses while Tante Marianne sliced the meat, which was beautifully crisp on the outside and succulent on the inside. Lili jumped up and ladled some potatoes and carrots on the plates, heeding Tante's very careful instructions. "You sound like a German, Tante: 'two potatoes here, one carrot there.'"

"Stop that."

Lili managed to get an extra potato on Tante Marianne's plate when she wasn't looking. Some bread and butter was now also on the table. "Prost, liebe Kinder; don't let it get cold." The three enjoyed the food and each other's company, and Lili was very pleased that Tante Marianne took another slice of roast. "I need it to go with the extra potato, Lili."

There was a wonderful bonhomie at the table as they finished the roast and the wine. Aromas of nutmeg and cinnamon replaced the earlier ones as Tante Marianne took the dish of Scheiterhaufen (bread pudding) out of the oven. "It has a terrible name meaning 'funeral pyre'; I don't know where that came from."

"It smells wonderful, Tante Marianne, but how are we supposed to fit it in?" asked Rudi.

"Ah, you are going skiing tomorrow; you'll need to keep up your strength."

"I have never eaten such a good Ofenschlupfer, Tante Marianne. Do you have a recipe?" asked Lili.

Tante Marianne laughed. "No, I haven't used any sort of recipe in twenty years, but I'd be happy to tell you the details, and you could write them down." Tante Marianne brought three glasses of dessert wine and a Christmas card and a pencil for Lili. "You can write on the back of the card, Lili." Tante, a little tipsy, recited her recipe for Scheiterhaufen.

"What about the Rosinen?"

"Oh, yes, the raisins. Just throw a small handful in between the layers."

Everyone was more than a little tipsy, and the evening and New Year's Day ended joyously, perfectly.

THE SECOND DAY of 1933 in Annenheim and on the Gerlizen was spectacular, with a clear blue sky and hoar frost crystals sparkling in the sunlight. The view from the summit was as splendid as ever, with the storm from the northwest still building slowly and looking to be unmistakenly heading southeastward. Rudi and Lili enjoyed their day's skiing, carving rhythmic turns between the trees. They enjoyed their beautifully prepared lunch from Tante Marianne and arrived home with Lili quite exhausted and Rudi very happy with their skiing. Baked duckling with rice and vegetables was delightful for dinner, and, it being Rudi and Lili's last night with Tante Marianne, a mountain of Kaiserschmarrn became the obligatory dessert.

As Rudi and Lili packed in preparation for their return trip to Vienna, Tante Marianne couldn't hide a little sadness. *Will they visit me again soon? Will they be safe in Vienna? Cities are never as safe as the country. It would be really nice if they came in summer; I'm sure they'll still be together. They are so suited to one another. However, I worry about what's happening in Germany. I hope all the Nazis disappear into a hole in the ground. I hope Lili will someday be able to ski with Rudi on the Grossglockner.* As Rudi moved their bags near the front door, Tante Marianne brought a gift-wrapped box of cake and biscuits to Lili. "Please take these—just some leftovers. I couldn't possibley eat them all. Try to keep them upright, Lili." There were many hugs and kisses and a few tears. There were many nice thoughts but no promises. A couple of small gifts were exchanged. Tante Marianne stood at the gate as she watched Rudi and Lili head towards the train. Lili stopped for a moment, turned around, and waved. Tante Marianne waved vigorously and walked inside. She dialed the phone.

RUDI AND LILI got to the train just in time to take them to Villach, where they'd have lunch with Rudi's mother and father before embarking on their last leg back to Vienna. Rudi the senior was on the platform waiting for the "youngsters," as he referred to them; Tante Marianne had phoned to tell him they were on their way. He led the way home, happily humming and tipping his hat several times with a greeting of "Habidiere" as he passed people he recognized. Maria Auer was standing in the open doorway as they arrived, and she welcomed the youngsters with hugs and kisses. Lili, now much less anxious than she had been when she was first there, noticed and was very surprised at how small the apartment was. It had a decent-sized bedroom but a tiny kitchen, a tiny bathroom, and a living room that could barely fit a table for four. There was a coal- and woodburning heater, a sofa, and a well-worn Persian rug on the floor. A stack of newspapers nearly a metre high was beside the sofa. Rudi's mother knew that the youngsters would have a several-hour train journey ahead of them and therefore needed a hearty lunch. The aroma of onion and paprika introduced a rich Hungarian goulash to the luncheon table. Rudi and Lili both ate amply and, with several glasses of gutsy Italian red, were likely to spend some of the train trip asleep.

As the two women cleared the table, Rudi the senior went to his newspaper stack, leafed through a couple of papers, and returned with one to the table. On a side column there was an advertisement promoting the Grossglockner as a superior skiing destination. He looked at his son. "Rudi, what's this situation where you wouldn't take Lili to the Grossglockner? Tante Marianne mentioned it on the telephone."

"Ja, Papa, it is true: the German and Austrian Alpine Club are not two separate clubs. They own the Grossglockner and the huts on the mountain, and they do not permit Jews. I learned about it doing some research in Vienna."

"How long has that been the case? That's scandalous!"

"I think this rule has existed since the 1880s," explained Rudi.

"I can't believe I didn't know that; did you know that, Maria?"

"No, that's really a frightening thought."

Lili chimed in. "It really is awful that Rudi can't take me skiing to the Grossglockner. I am Austrian; my family...we are Austrian, and we have been Austrians for generations."

Rudi's father picked up the paper in front of him and, pointing to the advertisement, declared he'd write to the DOAV. "It just isn't acceptable that some people see themselves as having the right to exclude others from doing what they want. The mountains belong to all of us. I'll give them a piece of my mind."

"Yes, Papa, it is actually a matter of human rights that people not be discriminated against," stated Rudi.

Rudi's mother, aware of the time and that the Ofenschlupfer needed to be eaten hot, asked everybody to start their desserts; they could talk at the same time. She noticed that Lili seemed to really like the Ofenschlupfer and smiled. "You see, I really enjoy desserts, and this is delicious."

When they were finished eating, Maria Auer gave Lili a big hug and told her how pleased she and her husband were that she and Rudi were a couple. Papa Auer shed a couple of tears as he hugged Rudi and wiped them away before bidding Lili farewell.

Rudi and Lili arrived in good time to board the train for Vienna. As the train gathered momentum north, they both reflected on their very nice vacation and snuggled together in a near-empty compartment. They wondered whether Rudi's father would actually write to the anti-Semitic DOAV and hoped to be able to ski on the Grossglockner together one day. They wondered what the ominous-looking storm they saw a few days ago beyond the Grosglockner was up to. It had been centered over Germany since New Year's Day and was obviously building momentum. What did it have in store for Austria? Where would it inflict its greatest fury? Would the storm head out towards the south or wreak greatest havoc as it marched southeast towards Vienna?

Lili gave Rudi a kiss and put her head on his shoulder. "Thank you for taking me to meet your parents. I think they are very nice and are extremely proud of you."

I wonder whether we'll spend some time over Christmas together again next year, Lili thought to herself. "Tante Marianne is proud of you too. She loves you and would do anything for you. I really like her a lot, but I wish she didn't make so much irresistible food. Do you think we could visit her again in summer, Rudi? Rudi?" Rudi didn't answer; he was already asleep. Lili snuggled into his chest to become even more comfortable, and she too promptly dozed off.

The train was slowing down coming into Vienna when Rudi and Lili woke. They were greeted by a chilling wind and a very dark, expressionless sky when they took the *Straßenbahn (*tramcar) home. They noticed quite a deal of foot traffic, as people were heading home late from work or towards their favourite café, a concert, a ballet, or the opera. Rudi helped Lili get off the tramcar, and they both struggled with their luggage, which now felt miraculously heavier than before. Not unexpectedly, the apartment felt cold, and Rudi's first task was to put on the coal heater. "Even the paper feels moist," he lamented as he set the kindling on top and lit a match.

Lili came out of the bathroom and turnd on the radio. She was greeted by a crackling but unmistakable Strauss melody. Fiddling with the antenna soon reduced the static. Rudi prepared coffee, having had enough hot chocolate for a while, and Lili carefully untied the ribbon on the box Tante Marianne had packed for them. As well as a variety of holiday biscuits, there were two slices of Linzer Schnitten and six pieces of Lebkuchen. "She is such a wonderful lady," swooned Lili.

Rudi agreed as he took his first sip of coffee. "Why do you always feel you need a holiday as soon as you return from vacation? How will you manage at work tomorrow, Schatzerl?"

"I'll be fine, but I'll get my clothes ready for the morning tonight."

———

WORKDAY NORMALITY WAS achieved with Rudi getting breakfast ready while Lili got herself ready. Krapfen, koffee, and a kiss couldn't keep Lili from going to work. She and Mr. Schwartz exchanged New Year's greetings and holiday snippets. Lili told him of her disappointment that Rudi wasn't able to take her skiing on the Grossglockner, the greater disappointment being that it was such a blatant example of anti-Semitism. "That is truly terrible, Lili," he said sincerely. "That is a regulation that should certainly be changed."

"That is highly unlikely, Mr. Schwartz; with anti-Semitism on the rise it is probable that more restrictions against Jews will be implemented, attempts at further discrimination against Jews. I feel a foreboding wind blowing across from the west." A downcast Lili disappeared into her office to phone her brother and mother to wish them "Ein Frohes Neues Jahr." She told her mother that she'd be home for dinner as they had earlier planned.

In the meantime Rudi unpacked, not having bothered the previous night, and he now finished his cold coffee while reading the paper. As was common at that time of year, news appeared sparse, as reporters themselves were just returning from vacation.

Later in the day Rudi escorted Lili home to her mother's place, where she would have dinner. Kafka and Bela were again looking out from between the curtains. There was much barking as they welcomed Lili home.

18

January to April 1933: Winds from the Northwest

Rudi had just returned from escorting Lili home with her holiday luggage when Joseph burst through the door with a great deal of baggage of his own. "Frohes Neues Jahr, Rudi."

"Frohes Neues Jahr. Shalom, Joseph. Let me help you with those bags. Did you you have a good time?"

"Yes, thank you, Rudi. And you?"

"Yes. As you know, Lili met my parents for the first time, and we actually stayed with an auntie. Everybody loved Lili, so that was good. We had a nice New Year's celebration with my mother and father and could barely get back to Tante Marianne's due to a severe storm."

"Was there lots of snow?"

"No, just a terrible wind from the direction of Germany. There was a good snowfall overnight though."

"Did Lili enjoy skiing with you?"

"Yes, she really did, and she surprised me with how competent she is. She was terribly upset though."

"Oh, why?"

"Well, you know that the Austrian and German Alpine Club owns the Grossglockner and all its huts. The club is an anti-Semitic outfit and forbids—"

"Yes, I know about that. Lili would have been very disappointed and angry too, I guess."

"How were your parents, and how was Munich, Joseph?"

"Thank God, my parents are both fine, and there have been fewer incidents against Jews in recent weeks, including over the holiday period. We read that the Nazis are close to being bankrupt. There is some really nasty political wrangling behind the scenes in Germany though, Rudi, and who knows what that will bring."

———

RUDI DECIDED TO spend at least some of the rest of this first week of 1933 catching up on reading some newspapers he had not had a look at since the commencement of his vacation with Lili. He had also been looking forward to eating a good Schnitzel. He took himself to Café Louvre, where he had always been able to catch up on news before, and where he was certain of getting a large piece of bread-crumbed veal done to perfection. "Gutes Neues Jahr, Herr Ober."

"Gutes Neues Jahr. Ein Schnitzel as usual, Rudi?"

"Ja, und ein Pilsner, bitte, Herr Ober." Rudi went to get a couple of papers at once and flicked through them for any headlines that might catch his attention. He had barely had two sips of beer when an oversized Schnitzel arrived, and reading had to be postponed for a little while. *This Schnitzel would be good even cold, but it is wonderful hot,* he thought as he pushed the papers aside. Rudi remembered that in Germany there had been considerable political instability during the months leading up to 1933.

On 2 December, Schleicher had replaced Papen as chancellor, though the government was still most unstable and would likely remain so for some time. From the little reading Rudi had done since his own last article was published, he was aware that Hindenburg, Schleicher, Papen, and others were scheming, wheeling, and dealing with Hitler, who was working feverishly to gain ultimate power for himself. There was a great deal of intrigue, conniving, and double-crossing. The educated classes in Germany understood that, and the well-read Viennese understood that too, although details remained hidden.

Rudi soon replaced two papers with two others. A bold headline of the prestigious *Frankfurter Zeitung* editorial for 1 January 1933 caught his eye, and a smile appeared across his face. The headline read: "The mighty Nazi assault on the democratic state has been repulsed." Rudi finished his beer and ordered another. *Wunderbar,* he thought as he read the editorial, which argued that the Nazi party was now in decline, having virtually run out of money. Rudi's delight was reinforced with the reading of another article in a well-known Berlin paper, the *Vossische Zeitung.* It declared, "The Republic has been rescued." Rudi felt a little relieved as he had been certain that, with so much political turmoil, no good winds would emanate from anywhere in the northwest anytime soon.

The feeling of foreboding mostly disappeared, but Rudi still felt uneasy as the ongoing devious political dealings, the backstabbing, and the clandestine meetings in Germany continued to take place within a huge web of intrigue. This was again confirmed for Rudi when a couple of days later he was back in Café Louvre with the *Taegliche Rundschau,* a Berlin paper, in front of him. The headline read "Hitler and Papen against Schleicher," suggesting some underhand dealings. This was as much as confirmed within the next couple of days with the poor explanatory statements in the Nazi papers. Goebbels's *Der Angriff* and the *Voelkischer Beobachter* both tried to gloss over the meeting between Hitler and Papen, claiming it as part of normal discussion. Much of the intelligencia of Germany and Vienna didn't buy that.

THEIR FIRST WEEKEND back after vacation, Rudi and Lili spent together as they did most weekends from then on. Rudi was heavily into reading and attending lectures, and although he had no plans of wrting anything for the uni paper in the near future, he remained acutely interested in the politics of Germany and Austria, Vienna in particular. He recognized the political instability in both Germany and in Vienna, and he felt that the media were not covering either very well.

Winter had settled in; it was generally cold, and there was a little snow on the ground the last weekend of January. Monday, 30 January, began as a rather dull day with an even, grey sky when Rudi saw Lili off to work. Rudi put a little more fuel on the fire and was reading in preparation for lectures commencing the day after. He was not at all inspired by what he was reading and, by early afternoon, had lost interest. Rudi felt there was an unsavoury smell in the air, so he opened the window and put on an extra pullover. He felt very edgy. He took out the violin and played a little but could not muster any enthusiasm. He thought he'd go for a walk and put on his coat. He thought better of it when he opened the door. It wasn't worth it. He took off his coat, closed the window, and put on the radio. Through the crackling he heard the most disturbing news he had ever heard. *This can't be right; I must be hearing things*, he thought.

He sat at the table as the news was repeated. "Today President Paul von Hindenburg appointed Adolf Hitler as chancellor of Germany. Brownshirts and Communists violently clash in the streets throughout Germany. The SA celebrates Hitler's accession to power with a torchlight parade through Berlin." Rudi turned off the radio and sat there dumbfounded. He was stunned. There had not been any indicators building up to this. The media had been mute. As far as Rudi had been able to ascertain, Germany was in a season of political wrangling, backstabbing, and conniving at a time when the Nazis had lost strength, financial backing, and political momentum.

What was that old geezer thinking, sacking Schleicher and replacing him with Hitler? he thought. Rudi found himself marching around the apartment in circles as if he were looking for a personal strategy to reverse Hindenburg's decision. He was about to sit down when there was a knock at the front door. "Rudi, did you hear the news?"

"Yes, I did. Servus, Lili, come in. Can I take your bag?"

"What will this mean, Rudi?"

"I don't know. It is bad news, obviously very bad news. Now that he has this power, it will go to his head. Those poor Germans!"

"How did so many get sucked into his message?" asked Lili. "I don't understand...the Nazis don't have enough seats in the Reichstag to wield such power; they've recently actually lost seats. I don't understand."

Just then Joseph burst through the door. "Did you hear the news? Shalom, Lili, Rudi." Joseph added to the already somber mood in the room. "Scandalous, bloody scandalous! I couldn't get a news-paper on the way home; they were all sold out. I just spoke with my mother and father in Munich though. My mother was crying, and my father was being brave not to. They were stunned, although there had been some vague rumours over the last couple of days, they said. They don't know what to do. They think there'll be an exodus of Jews starting from tonight."

"Do you think your parents will leave too, Joseph? Where would they go?" asked Lili, putting her hand to her mouth.

Joseph shook his head and was very close to tears. "I think they'll maybe go back to Poland. They have certainly not been welcomed in Germany. They had so much hope of making a good life for them-selves in Munich. How unlucky can you be? They are such good people, hardworking people, polite people; they leave others alone. But they get tormented and have the windows of the shop they work in broken and merchandise stolen. Not fair! No wonder you don't believe in God, Rudi." Rudi slowly shook his head.

"Shall I prepare some dinner?" asked Lili, as it had passed nor-mal dinnertime.

"Yes, please."

"Do you think Jews will leave Germany quickly, Joseph?" asked Rudi.

"I think many will, very quickly; those who have not put down roots, so to speak, and who have maybe already experienced or heard about anti-Semitic actions, they'd be very tempted to leave. They'd be wise to leave too, I think."

"And you really think your parents will leave?" "Yes, I do; I hope so. I will encourage them to. They have enough savings to go. Just enough. Imagine the many people who just haven't got enough money to get out. They'd feel really trapped."

Lili brought some bread, a board, and a knife to the table. "Would you cut some bread, please, Rudi? I'm dishing out now." Lili then brought three bowls of goulash to the table as Rudi opened a bottle of Roter Veltliner. The pleasant aroma of paprika filling the room and the sound of wine filling glasses momentarily relieved the somber mood.

"La Chaim, Lili, Rudi."

"Prost, Joseph."

"How can Hindenburg, that alta Kaka, make such a stupid decision?"

"He owed the Junkers," responded Rudi."

"Dos Shtik drek! Sorry, Lili."

"I can understand how you feel, Joseph, especially with your parents' situation as it is."

"That bastard Hitler, a feier zol im treffen!" Joseph was very angry. "Very good goulash, thank you, Lili," he said, trying to compose himself.

"Just leftovers from Saturday night, nothing special, Joseph. Just added a few extra potatoes."

Shortly after eating, Rudi escorted Lili home on that quiet, foggy, and dreary night with little talk between them. They both felt drained by the afternoon's news and by the discussion with Joseph. They didn't take any notice of various groups deep in discussion at different points along their path.

There was a big embrace at the door, and Lili looked into Rudi's eyes. Tears welled up, and Lili's eyes glistened by the outside lamp. "I guess my dream of skiing with you on the Grossglockner can now only remain a dream, Rudi?"

Rudi nodded his head ever so slightly and gave Lili an enveloping hug. Sadness overtook her, and she turned around and walked inside without looking back. Kafka and Bela were first to greet her, competing to get some hugs.

On the way back to the apartment, Rudi was conscious of several groups out on the street talking about Hitler's appointment. He overheard some man mention his parents already making plans to leave Germany as soon as they could, possibly that night.

THE NEXT FEW days were filled with deep emotion, sadness and anger dominating. A large Jewish minority of students at the uni was generally downcast, whether they thought the change in German politics would eventually affect them and their families or not. In contrast, there was considerable jubilation within the adherents to the mores of the Deutsche Studentenschaft. A group of a couple of dozen Brownshirts, many wearing swastika armbands, some with Nazi flags, marched around the grounds of the university singing "Deutschland, Deutschland ueber alles..." Joseph and Rudi both kept their distance.

Well into the afternoon on a day later in the week, Rudi took himself to Café Louvre again to see what he might learn from the newspapers. As he approached the front door on the corner of Wipplingerstrasse and Renngasse, there was already a mob scene resembling that of a fishmarket. Highly emotional discussion in many different languages and considerable agitation greeted Rudi as he looked for a table. Herr Ober found Rudi a tiny table normally housing a vase of flowers. The vase had been knocked over and broken in the hubbub, flowers flying in all directions. Herr Ober, with a deft eye, spotted a chair that appeared unoccupied and brought it to Rudi. "Sorry, Rudi, no veal Schnitzel left, but we still have a few pork Schnitzel."

"That will be fine, Herr Ober, and a beer, please," said Rudi, having to raise his voice. The place was chock-a-block with mostly local and foreign correspondents and news junkies of various sorts, all trying to make sense of the developing news coming out of Germany. Rudi threw his jacket over the table to save it as he went to get a paper or two. Many papers were missing, but he was able to retrieve a couple, both a few days old.

The Manchester Guardian on 31 January, 1933, reported:

> *BERLIN, MONDAY*
>
> *Hitler's long-cherished ambition to become Chancellor has at last been satisfied. President von Hindenburg appointed him Chancellor of the Reich at noon today—an hour may prove a turning point in the history of postwar Germany, and which at any rate marks another victory for the reactionary forces.*
>
> *The Hitler Government is a coalition of Nazis and Hugenberg Nationalists, and although the latter are more numerous in the Cabinet, three of the most "strategic" posts are held by Nazis, and it is by no means certain that the Nazis will be the "prisoners" in this new Government.*
>
> *The news of Hitler's appointment created a feeling of alarm and confusion almost everywhere.*

Alarm, thought Rudi, *would be the dominant emotion among those who are familiar with the writings of Hitler and Goebbels and other NSDAP officials in publications such as* **Der Angriff** *and* **Der Voelkischer Beobachter,** *and especially among those who are familiar with the rantings in Hitler's* **Mein Kampf.** *Confusion would exist among the great majority of decent people around the world, as it is truly unfathomable how such a misguided misfit, megalomaniac, and criminal could become Germany's chancellor.*

The *Pittsburg Press*'s Frederick Kuh, on 30 January 1933, had this to say:

> *Berlin, January 30. Adolph Hitler rode into power in Germany today on the rising tide of his militant fascism.*
>
> *…Hindenburg entrusted the Chancellorship to the fiery little Austrian from Munich, foe of Jews and Communists and leading exponent of a belligerent German nationalism.*

Rudi was of the view that Communists could readily escape the wrath of the right-wing fascists by denouncing or hiding their allegiance. They could leave the party and refuse to be involved in any future activities that labeled one as a Communist. Jews would find it much more difficult to escape ostracism, retribution, or punishment for being Jewish, he thought. *Being Jewish is not something one is able to choose. It is one's very being, one's very essence. Being a Jew is part of belonging to a heritage, a culture. Many Jews in Europe who had a strong desire to become integrated into a predominantly Christian society had themselves baptized Roman Catholic. So superficially they may have been perceived as belonging to the Catholic Church; nevertheless, this did not diminish their Jewishness. It simply added a dimension in addition to their Jewishness.* Jews of Europe were indeed integrated in every sphere of society—in commerce and industry, in banking and finance, in medicine and dentistry, as chemists, as lawyers. Jews dominated the press and the whole world of the intelligentsia and the arts: education, architecture, interior design, literature, film, the theatre, and music. *To extricate oneself from such a dominant cultural heritage is to go into hiding; one couldn't, just overnight, not be Jewish. In any event, Nazis took the liberty of pronouncing anyone to be Jewish who was not tall, blue-eyed, and blond. That is already how it has been in various German and Austrian sporting associations that have excluded people soley on the basis of their appearance.*

From what Rudi could ascertain, European papers, it seemed, were very careful not to say anything that could possibly be construed as negative against the Nazis for fear of reprisal. Overseas newspapers seemed a little less cautious, relaying the news with a different tone.

Rudi tried to listen to several conversations at once and skim the papers at the same time. He was able to determine that on the day after his accession to power on 31 January, Hitler promised to instigate parliamentary democracy. *What sort of humbug is that, given his declaration from the beginning to push for increased cabinet power?* thought Rudi.

On 2 February, two days after becoming chancellor, Hitler dissolved Parliament. There were many demonstrations, some in favor of the Nazis and some in protest. There were clashes in various parts of the country, some causing considerable bloodshed. On the same day, Hermann Goering banned Communist meetings and demonstrations in Germany. He also apparently banned the social-democratic newspaper *Vorwarts*. An exodus of Jews from Germany had, according to reports, already begun.

As Rudi finished his Schnitzel, he could hear much discussion about the banning of *Vorwarts*. People asked whether this would mark the beginning of limits on the freedom of the press. People asked how foreign journalists would get accurate news as to what was happening in Germany if freedom of the press were indeed restricted.

Rudi's head was spinning. It was difficult to understand the enormity of the events of the recent five days. As he left Café Louvre, journalists were running to transmit telegrams, both the Central Telegraph Building and Radio Austria resembling a zoo, with people agitated, shouting, running. Rudi trudged home wearily under grey skies, catching snippets of conversation, all seemingly about the week's events in Germany.

He arrived home as Joseph was packing to spend the weekend at Ester's, where he also had access to the phone to allow him to speak with his parents. His concern for his parents' well-being eclipsed all other concerns at the present time. Over the last couple of days, they had apparently been vascillating between wanting to emigrate to France or Belgium or move back to Poland. In any event, the atmosphere in Munich at the moment was quite unsettling. Joseph's parents reported jubilant marches by Brownshirts chanting anti-Semitic slogans and clashes between Nazi thugs and Communist groups. Joseph was also aware of the likelihood of demonstrations in Leopoldstadt and of increased Nazi thuggery there, the thought of which frightened Ester and her friends a great deal.

No sooner had Joseph left than the doorbell signalled Lili's arrival. She was pleased the workweek was over and that she would be able to spend quality time with Rudi. She flung her arms around his neck, and he swept her off her feet, spinning her around until they were in danger of hitting the wall. "Servus, Schatzerl."

"Servus, Rudl."

"How was work?"

"Work was fine, but Mr. Schwartz got on my nerves a bit today."

"Why, Lili?"

"Well, I told him about Joseph's parents' desire to leave Germany, and he didn't think that leaving so quickly was necessarily a wise course of action. He thought they should wait to see what further developments the new government might bring. He just didn't seem to have any empathy for them. That's what I didn't like, his apparent lack of empathy."

"When the new situation in Germany touches him sometime via a colleague's family or a business connection, then he'll have a different view."

RUDI AND LILI had a pleasant weekend together, still reminiscing over their vacation. They mentioned how strange it was being in Annenheim in winter after they had met there for the first time only a few months earlier. Lili smiled at the memory of Rudi scraping the snow off "their log" and recalled her surprise at being visited by a deer in Tante Marianne's backyard. She had taken a real shine to Tante Marianne and was pleased to have met Rudi's mother and father, and she hoped Mr. Auer would write to the DOAV. Lili again had tears in her eyes when she speculated that she and Rudi would likely never be able to ski the Grossglockner together. "Who knows where we'll be a year or two from now, Lili? Perhaps we'll ski on Mt. Cook in New Zealand."

"Oh, Rudi, don't say that. I need to be here in Vienna with you, not in some far-distant land."

19

REPERCUSSIONS FOLLOWING HITLER'S APPOINTMENT

CONSTERNATION CONTINUED OVER the next couple of weeks as news via the radio and the daily newspapers reported further restrictions on people's freedoms and further deterioration of parliamentary democracy in Germany. Rudi listened to the news regularly and would return to Café Louvre every few days to read some articles and eavesdrop on conversations. He noted journalists' particular dismay at the news that, on 4 February, German President Von Hindenburg limited the freedom of the press. Rumour had it that many liberal newspapers closed down, while others, under coercion, refrained from publishing certain stories, and a considerable degree of censorship was self-imposed for fear of offending the new regime.

In the meantime, it was understood that the Nazis used every form of media to promote themselves and to provide misinformation about groups and organizations opposed to their takeover. The Communists were their greatest target and were constantly hounded by the *SA*, which functioned as the original paramilitary wing of the Nazi Party, and the SS, the Nazi elite paramilitary formation. A combined force of the SA and SS, under Herrmann Goering, was reported to have gone on a rampage on 22 February, when more than forty people were shot.

The Hitlerjugend (HJ), or Hitler Youth, was also being reinvigorated after it had been banned and lay dormant for a while after HJ groups were fighting with Communist youth. Hitlerjugend was a paramilitary organization of the Nazi Party. It existed from 1922 to 1945 and was made up of males aged fourteen to eighteen; the younger boys' section was named the Deutsches Jungvolk (German Youth) for those aged ten to fourteen. The girls' section, the Bund Deutscher Mädel (the League of German Girls), was the remaining piece of the HJ. On 24 February, it was reported that the Communists had a major demonstration in Berlin. Then three days later, on 27 February, the Communists were blamed for the fire that burned down the Reichstag. Rumours soon spread, however, that the Nazis had set it ablaze in order to blame the Communists. *Would the Nazis have such little regard for their own Reichstag, this grand architectural edifice of German power, that they would arrange to have it burnt down themselves?* queried Rudi.

The response to this event was swift. On 28 February, it was reported that Hitler disallowed the German Communist Party. Rudi was reeling from all this information and was about to leave Café Louvre when a hitherto unknown publication caught his attention. It was *The Literary Digest* of 25 February 1933. It read:

> Israel is dismayed at the Rise to Power of Adolf Hitler, the Nazi chieftain who has rung all the changes on anti-Semitism, and demanded the political and economic extermination of Jews. Jacob Fishman of the New York Jewish Component is quoted as saying: "There have been European Premiers, before this, who were surrounded with an anti-Semitism atmosphere, but never has there such a Jew-baiter sat as Hitler sat at the helm of the Ship of State among modern civilized peoples."

Not before this article had Rudi read such a blunt interpretation of Hitler's intentions. He reread the article before heading home

with a sick feeling in his stomach. *Perhaps all these Germans who support Hitler and the Nazis in the polls are just not civilized people. They surely
can't be ignorant of what he stands for. I wonder how many of them have read*
Mein Kampf *or even some salient anti-Semitic segments in it? I know that it
is difficult to read with those long, awkward sentences and wandering para-
graphs. Have none of them ever read* Der Stuermer, Der Angriff, *or the*
Völkischer Beobachter? *Do people not know what Hitler believes in, what
he stands for, what his desires are? Perhaps there are just a lot of people—mil-
lions of people—who agree with him. How could all these Germans entertain
driving so many of their fellow Germans, their neighbours, out of their communities? Did they think they could get their hands on what was left behind
when Jews and others left? Are they so desperate? Are they without morals?*

Rudi's thoughts turned to Joseph's parents, and as soon as he
got home, he asked about their latest plans. "My parents are terribly
confused; they're very conflicted," declared Joseph. "There has not
been a great increase in anti-Semitic behavior in recent weeks, and
friends have been telling them that it is difficult to emigrate. They
think it might be least difficult to emigrate to France or Belgium,
Rudi, but the process takes hours and hours, and there are very
long lines. It would clearly be easiest for them to move back to
Poland; they have friends there still, and of course they speak the
language. They don't speak French. Father says that going back to
Poland would be going back in life when he wanted to move life
forward."

"So they don't have immediate plans to leave?"

"No, I don't know what they'll end up doing. I just hope that
Mother can handle all the stress."

"You look pretty stressed out yourself, Joseph."

"Yes, I'm worried for them."

WORRY WAS SOON focused close to home in Vienna. On 4 March,
Chancellor Dollfuss suspended the parliament because it had become unworkable. The same weekend, news arrived that the Nazi

Party won an overall majority in the German Parliament. The thought of the onset of Nazism had a sobering effect in Vienna. The cafés were abuzz, especially Café Louvre. Dollfuss was apparently fighting hard to keep the Nazis' influence at bay. The fear was heightened further with the news out of Germany on 23 March that as a result of what was referred to as the Enabling Act, Hitler had now gained dictatorial powers.

This apparently emboldened Nazis in both Germany and Austria, which led to a major Nazi demonstration all throughout Germany and, on 29 March, also in Vienna. There were many SA marches throughout Germany and various incidents of Brownshirt thuggery against Jews. On 1 April 1933, the Nazis carried out their first nationwide planned action against Jews—a boycott targeting Jewish businesses and professionals. The SA stood menacingly in front of Jewish-owned department stores, retail establishments, and the offices of professionals such as lawyers and doctors. The Star of David was painted in yellow and black across thousands of doors and windows with accompanying anti-Semitic slogans painted on signs, saying such things as "Kauf Nicht von Juden!" ("Don't Buy from Jews!"), "Die Juden Sind Unser Unglück!" ("The Jews Are Our Misfortune!"), and "Geh nach Palästina!" ("Go to Palestine!"). Throughout Germany there were apparently only rare acts of violence against individual Jews and Jewish property at this particular time. The boycott was ignored by many individual Germans who continued to shop in Jewish-owned stores that day.

The movements against Jews were, however, again soon accelerating. On 7 April, the Law for the Restoration of the Professional Civil Service was passed, which restricted employment in the civil service to Aryans, hence barring Jews from legal and public services. Jews could no longer be employed as professors, teachers, or judges or hold other government positions. Jewish government workers, teachers included, in universities and public schools were sacked. And for the first time, it seemed, some schools, claiming overcrowding, banned Jewish students from attending. Rudi was quite distraught at hearing of these developments. "The Deutsche Studentenschaft, if it had its way," he told Lili, "would bar all Jewish professors and Jewish students here at Vienna uni."

"Rudi, let's see if we can forget about these things leading up to Easter," pleaded Lili.

"When's Easter, Lili? Is it already Good Friday this week?"

"Yes, and Passover commences tomorrow, the eleventh of April."

"Oh, yes, Joseph mentioned he'd be staying with Ester tomorrow night," Rudi remembered. "It would be nice if you could stay with me."

———

LILI ARRIVED AT the apartment after work, finding it difficult not to think about the recent events in Germany and imagining the angst Joseph's parents must be experiencing right then. Joseph and Rudi were just finishing some dishes from earlier while discussing the pros and cons of his parents returning to Poland versus going to France or Belgium.

"Servus, Rudi. Servus, Joseph. How are you, Joseph? What have you planned for Passover?"

"The same friends we had over for Rosh Hashanah will come over for the Seder feast."

"Does that involve anything special?" Rudi asked.

"Nothing special. We just get together in the evening to read the text of the Haggadah and participate in the customary Seder feast, sharing symbolic foods on the plate—the Passover Seder Plate—drinking four cups of wine, eating matzo, and celebrating freedom. Well, trying to. There's a much greater threat to our freedom now than there was this time last year."

"Perhaps you need to make the cups of wine big ones," suggested Rudi, trying to lighten the mood.

"We will undoubtedly do that. Shalom, my friend. Shalom, Lili."

"Shalom, Joseph. Mazel Tov."

Rudi spent the early part of the night with an ear to the radio, listening for news, but when he ducked into the bathroom, Lili quickly changed channels to some music, which allowed her to coax him into some dancing around the table. With little food in the apartment and Rudi not having been to Café Louvre for some days, he suggested to Lili, "Can we go to Café Louvre for dinner, Schatzerl?"

Lili responded, with a knowing smile, "As long as I don't become a newspaper widow for the night."

"I promise…well, I half promise."

Though a little chilly, it was a pleasant enough evening as they approached the corner of Wipplingerstrasse and Renngasse. "There must be hundreds of journalists buzzing around here. Are they sending telegrams, sharing information?"

"Yes, Lili. Let's see if we can get a table."

Herr Ober immediately spotted Rudi and ducked away. He returned momentarily. "Come with me, Rudi, madam. I found you a table."

"Very nice, thank you." Rudi peered towards the newspapers. Lili tugged on his sleeve and waited for him to pull her chair out. She smiled a thank-you, grabbed his hand, and held it tight in the middle of the table.

"Do you remember our first night together, Rudi? It started here."

"Yes, and I was so nervous, I nearly dropped the champagne glass."

"You were wonderfully attentive."

"I was so nervous. I can hardly remember anything about that evening."

Lili responded, "I was more than a little nervous too, but I remember everything. And I remember how good your Schnitzel was, so that's what I'll have tonight."

Herr Ober approached with a smile on his face. "Ja, liebe Herrschaften?"

"Schnitzel for Lili and Wuerstel mit Senf for me, and two glasses of red, please." Rudi looked in the direction of the newspapers, and Lili tightened her hand over his. He pretended to pull away but didn't. He recalled, in more detail, the progress of his and Lili's first night together and smiled.

"What are you smiling about, Rudl?"

"Just about how awkward I was on our first night together."

"Aberwas," exclaimed Lili as the waiter set the meals on the table. "I think we had a very special evening, thanks to you. Prost, Rudl."

"Prost, Schatzerl."

The meals were excellent, Lili's eyes nearly popping out of her head at the sight of the overlapping Schnitzel. They tasted a little of each other's, and Lili cut a largish piece and put it on Rudi's plate. He didn't mind; the Wuerstel were disappearing rather quickly. Lili uncharacteristically didn't order dessert, the Schnitzel being blamed for that decision, so they just ordered two coffees. Rudi sought and received permission to fetch a couple of newspapers. There was little new news from Germany, just some reports detailing the effects of the Law for the Restoration of the Professional Civil Service. Apparently there were many schools left with insufficient teachers and university lecture halls without professors, many of whom had been respected and loved by their students. The exodus of lawyers and government workers as well as intellectuals, especially teachers and professors, was proceeding at a great rate, and there was a huge backlog of work in government institutions and in private practices as the number of workers quickly diminished. There was considerable unrest among many and jubilation among most of those who considered themselves "Aryan."

—∞∞∞—

IN THE MEANTIME in Vienna, according to various reports, after meeting a number of times secretely with Mussolini, Dollfuss aligned himself with the Italian dictator. And on 2 May, Dollfuss established the Vaterlaendische Front (VF) under the slogan "Austria Awake." In May, the Communist Party was banned, causing a number of acts of defiance, while Dollfuss continued to try to also curb Nazi influence. Many Viennese were concerned regarding the events in Vienna. The apparent instability of the government and of Dollfuss's inclination to rule as a dictator troubled many. This was compounded by the regular news from Germany of the increasing influence of the Nazis in the everyday lives of its citizens. Many Viennese had relatives in Germany; some had business arrangements there, and there was increasing concern building that the actions of the Nazi leadership would affect life in Vienna.

Mr. Schwartz had been only superficially following the recent months' events in Germany, not thinking there'd be any effect on his beloved Vienna. However, one Friday morning in early May he received a telegram that concerned him greatly. It simply read:

Berlin, 5 May s.g. Herr Schwartz,

It is with very great regret that I have to inform you that the project between our two firms cannot go forward. I will send you the money I owe you as soon as I can.

By the time you receive this communication, my wife and I, with our two children, will be on our way out of Germany. It is no longer tenable for us to remain in this country. I cannot have my children live under such circumstances.

M. Braunzweig.

From her desk Lili could see into Mr. Schwartz's office, and she noticed that he was pacing up and down a great deal and obviously was somewhat distressed. Looking up, he saw that Lili had noticed his unusual behavior. "Excuse me, Lili, would you look at this?" He placed the telegram in front of her. "What do you make of it?"

"I am so sorry, Mr. Schwartz. Mr. Braunzweig or someone in his family has obviously been acted on by the new regime in Germany."

"What do you mean by that, Lili?"

"I don't know. Maybe his children were tormented at school or on their way to school, or perhaps he or his wife was. A child may have been barred from entering the school. I heard recently that some Jewish children have been prevented from getting into their school."

"But that is terrible, Lili. That would be terrible. My colleagues here thought his offices may have been targeted."

"Yes, that is quite possible too. There was recently an official 'boycott the Jews day' throughout Germany. And on April seventh there was a law passed in Germany…let me remember now. Yes, it was the Law for the Restoration of the Professional Civil Service. From then on employment in the civil service was to be restricted to Aryans, barring Jews from legal and public services."

"Surely not, Lili!"

"Yes, that's true, Mr. Schwartz."

"How do you know this?"

"Rudi has a constant ear to the radio, and he reads the paper—several papers, actually—every day."

"Really? But Mr. Braunzweig has clients who are mainly Christian."

"That would not protect him, Mr. Schwartz. He may have had his premises barricaded and swastikas painted all over the walls of the building just because he is a Jew. And now he is barred from practicing altogether."

"But he and his wife were both baptized Catholics years ago; they are a well-established family of Berlin."

"That wouldn't make any difference; there'd be some list of Jewish lawyers, and he'd be on it. The telegram says they have already left, Mr. Schwartz. Do you have any idea where they might be headed?"

Mr. Schwartz just shook his head, slowly walked out of Lili's office, and sat back at his desk. *Rudi was right about these Nazis,* he thought. *He's just a boy. How can a mere boy be so right about such matters?* Mr. Schwartz remained somber and obviously upset for the rest of the day. He and Lili exchanged wishes for a pleasant weekend as she left the office.

Both Rudi and Lili had been quite disturbed by the unfolding developments in both Germany and Austria, remaining unclear as to precise events, as there were some conflicting news reports. What was clear to both of them, however, was that Nazism was spreading like a brush fire across the German nation, fanned by strong winds, with most people being somehow caught up in it.

Lili arrived at her usual Friday evening destination, where Joseph appeared in a grumpy mood, packing for the weekend in Leopoldstadt with Ester. She had told him earlier in the afternoon that the telephone lines between Vienna and Munich were not functioning properly. Joseph was anxious to speak with his parents that evening. Lili shared the contents of the telegram Mr. Schwartz had received earlier in the day, and neither Rudi nor Joseph was surprised.

"I am also worried about what my parents might be experiencing in Munich, and I want to know what the status is in terms of their plans," declared Joseph.

Rudi did not seem his usual, positive self either, and when Lili asked what the matter was, Rudi unfolded a letter and handed it to her.

Sattendorf, 23 April Dear Rudi,

Fond greetings from the Ossiachersee to you. You will be interested to know that there has been skating on it for a couple of months now, but boys from school tell me that the surface is rougher than usual because of the stronger than normal winds. I really enjoyed reading your article. I can understand that there would be some groups that took offense and wanted to do you some harm. I am sorry to hear that you were injured in a brawl. You need to be very wary of the Brownshirts; they are nothing but thugs.

My parents have, fortunately, not experienced any anti-Semitic behavior, but some of my relatives in Munich have not been so fortunate. Several work for Jewish firms, and at the beginning of the month they could not go to work for a day because their workplaces were being boycotted. The next day they found windows broken and swastikas painted on walls and on the pavement, and there were pamphlets strewn all around. They had terrible anti-Semitic messages I am unable to write.

Now that Hitler has become chancellor, everything is getting worse. On 7 April, you may have read, two different anti-Jewish laws were passed barring Jews from legal and public services, meaning that Jews can no longer be employed as professors, teachers, or judges or hold other government positions. Jewish government workers, including teachers in universities and public schools, are being sacked left, right, and center. I fear that Nazis in Austria want to follow the same path as Hitler in Germany.

I will try to remain here in Kaernten as long as I am not needed to help my parents in Germany. I am unable to help my other relatives.

Kind regards also from your teachers here.
Best wishes,
M. Birnbaum.

"Things are not looking good, Lili, are they? I wonder how the winds are blowing in Munich right now."

"Things are getting pretty bad, Joseph, when schoolchildren can be barred from attending school and businesspeople are forced to flee their own country, leaving their homes and most of their possessions behind," declared Lili.

"I know," responded Joseph. "Did this Mr. Braunzweig say where he was taking his family to?" Lili shook her head. "I just wish I knew where it would be best for my parents to emigrate to. I must rush. Shalom, Lili. Shalom, Rudi. See you Sunday night."

⸺

RUDI AND LILI had a pleasant enough weekend, despite a general somberness hanging over the city. They did some shopping together and spent some time in a café. Lili was pleased that there were only copies of the *Wiener Zeitung* there. They also spent a couple of hours at the Historisches Museum der Stadt Wien (The Historical Museum of the City of Vienna) located in the Rathaus (Vienna Town Hall). They did not enjoy it all that much, as they were preoccupied. The Gemuetlichkeit of Vienna was not evident; the atmosphere was bleak, and Rudi just wanted to get home to listen to the radio.

The somberness of the weekend turned to concern when Joseph came home on Sunday evening. "Shalom aleichem."

"Aleichem shalom. How was your weekend, Joseph?" Rudi asked.

"Did you have to ask?" responded Joseph with a similar grumpiness he'd had just before he left on Friday evening. "Ester and I had a good enough weekend. It could have been a very good weekend had we not spoken with my parents."

"I'm sorry to hear that, Joseph. What's happening on their end?"

"Mother is in a real mess. She's crying a lot, just wants to be out of there…to press a button and be back in Poland. Oy Gevalt!"

"Anything in particular trigger her despair, Joseph?" asked Lili.

"There were several torchlight marches around their neighbourhood by the boot-stomping SA, which really upset her, and some freshly painted swastikas appeared outside their front door. I think Father threatened to bash a few Nazi skulls in, and Mother got very worried he'd get himself killed instead. And, unfortunately, they heard reports from Poland that there have been increased actions against Jews there as well, with boycotts and other harassment. Tempers are running pretty short, and there is considerable confusion in their thinking. They had also heard a radio broadcast that talked briefly about some planned book burnings, and they instinctively thought of me."

Rudi had heard that from mid-April there had indeed been vague references on German radio and in newspapers that nationwide public book burnings would take place involving publications regarded as "un-German." There were murmurings against it, but nothing was going to stop it. Indeed at eleven o'clock at night on 10 May, in more than thirty university towns, right-wing students, accompanied by brown-shirted storm troopers, marched in torchlight parades against the "un-German spirit." Rituals scripted for the occasion called for professors, university rectors, student leaders, and high Nazi officials to address the spectators and onlookers. At the meeting places, students threw the stolen books deemed "un-German" into huge bonfires. There was much ceremony with bands playing, Nazi salutes, and the reading of "fire oaths" such as:

"*Against* decadence and moral decay,

For discipline and decency in family and state:

Heinrich Mann, Ernst Glaeser, and Erich Kästner.

Against the falsification of our history and disparagement of its great figures,

For reverence for our past:

Emil Ludwig, Werner Hegemann.

Against the democratic Jewish character of journalism alien to the nation,

For responsible collaboration on the work of national construction: Theodor Wolff and Georg Bernhard.

Against literary betrayal of the soldiers of the World War,

For the education of the nation in the spirit of standing to battle: Erich Maria Remarque."

In Berlin, approximately forty thousand people assembled in the Opernplatz for a monster book-burning ceremony and to hear Joseph Goebbels, who declared, "German men and women! The age of arrogant Jewish intellectualism is now at an end! You are doing the right thing at this midnight hour—to consign to the flames the unclean spirit of the past. This is a great, powerful, and symbolic act...Out of these ashes the phoenix of a new age will arise...Oh Century! Oh Science! It is a joy to be alive!"

All the book burnings that had been planned for 10 May did not occur on that day. Rain delayed some, and others were planned by local universities and schools to occur on different days.

The book burnings had all been meticulously planned by the Studentenschaften of universities and colleges around the country from about 6 April. With nationwide coordination, events went off smoothly. An invitation to the book burning in Munich, for example, indicated the level of planning, organization, and the specific order of the events. It read:

> *Invitees must arrive at the designated area at precisely 11:00 p.m., when the torchlight procession of the entire Munich Student Association will be arriving. 1. The united bands will play parade music. 2. The festivities will begin with the song "Brothers Forward." 3. Speech by the leader of the German Students' Association, Kurt Ellersick. 4. Burning of the nation-corrupting books and jounals. 5. Groups singalong of songs.*

On 8 April, the students' association had also drafted its twelve "theses," deliberately evoking Martin Luther, declaring and requiring such things as a pure national language and culture. Placards publicized the students' theses, which attacked Jewish intellectualism

and asserted the need to purify the German language and literature. They also demanded that universities be centers of German
nationalism.

Among the twenty thousand volumes pitched into the flames
were writings of thousands of Jews and others against Nazism, includ-
ing those of Albert Einstein, Lion Feuchtwanger, Friedrich Förster,
Sigmund Freud, John Galsworthy, Ernst Glaeser, Ernest Hemingway,
Erich Kästner, Helen Keller, Thomas Mann, Karl Marx, Hugo Preuss,
Marcel Proust, Erich Maria Remarque, Arthur Schnitzler, Upton
Sinclair, Kurt Tucholsky, H.G. Wells, Emilé Zola, Arnold Zweig, and
Stefan Zweig.

On hearing about this book-burning event, Freud reportedly
quipped, "What progress we are making. In the Middle Ages they
would have burned me. Now, they are content with burning my
books."

20

INCREASING CONCERNS

IT WAS FRIDAY in the second week of May. Lili sat at the breakfast table with her mother and the two dachshunds, Bela and Kafka, perched on cushions, each on a chair. They were patiently waiting for a few morsels, all the while making big doe eyes and letting out little whimpers from time to time. Bela loved anything made of dough: bread, Semmel, Guggelhupf, Krapfen, and especially Kaiserschmarrn. Kafka loved cheese and every kind of sausage.

Quite uncharacteristically, Lili's mother referred to Rudi by name. "Did Rudi mention anything about the book burnings throughout Germany, Lili?"

"Yes, he did, Mother, and he was also aware of a book burning ceremony at Vienna uni."

"Surely not! I didn't read anything about that in the *Wiener Zeitung*."

"Yes, I understand that. The uni administration is very good at keeping these things quiet, Mother. Rudi's actually been very concerned about the rise of anti-Semitism in Germany, especially since Hitler came to power, and he sees this mass burning of books in all major university towns as a hugely ominous sign, and I agree with him. He quoted some lines from Heinrich Heine's play *Almansor* that stated something like, 'Where books are burned, human beings will, at sometime, be burned too.'"

"Disgusting, Lili. That hasn't happened since the Middle Ages."

"And book burnings of such magnitude haven't occurred since then either, Mother."

The maid poked her head around the corner as mother and daughter were at the table for an unusually long time. "Be so kind as to bring a fresh pot of coffee, please."

"The situation is obviously getting really bad in Germany, Mother."

"How Lili, other than burning books?"

"A few days ago Mr. Schwartz received a terrible telegram from a client in Berlin. Mr. Braunzweig is his name, I think. He had just packed the car, left all his furniture in his house, and was leaving Germany with his wife and two children; living there had become unbearable."

The maid came to the table with a fresh jug of milk and poured two steaming cups of coffee.

"Did he say what he'd found unacceptable, Lili?"

"No, it must have been pretty serious though, as he apologized for aborting the project with Mr. Schwartz, which will cost both of them thousands of schillings."

"Mr. Schwartz must have been very upset."

"Yes, Mother, and then Rudi received a letter from one of the teachers he has been corresponding with, and that letter had very disturbing news too. Some of the teacher's relations who work for Jewish firms couldn't go to their jobs for a day because their work-places were being boycotted. The next day they found windows broken and swastikas painted on walls and on the pavement, and there were pamphlets strewn all around with apparently terrible anti-Semitic messages."

"Yes, Lili, since Hitler came to power, the Jews in Germany are not being treated as well as before. Can you imagine? He's a born Austrian."

"Did you read that from April seventh, two different anti-Jewish laws were passed barring Jews from legal and public services? Jewish professors, teachers, and judges are being fired."

"But many are Catholic or Lutheran now."

"Won't help them, Mother. If their parents were married in a synagogue, or even their grandparents, then there'd be some record, and they'll be dismissed."

"That's surely not the case, Lili. There are no such detailed records. All those Jews…rather those who *were* Jews and are now Catholic or Lutheran will be OK. Yes, I'm sure of that. Don't you have to get to work? And here is a letter that came for you yesterday."

Lili took a last sip of cold coffee, fed Bela a corner of a Krapfen, and gave Kafka a scratch behind the ears. She put the letter into her bag and hurried off for work.

Lili was no sooner at her job than Mr. Schwartz came into her office. "Guess what? We've received another telegram from Mr. Braunzweig, the poor devil. Here it is."

Paris, 11 May s.g. Herr Schwartz,

I am really sorry about my previous brief telegram. I am also sorry I cannot yet pay you the money I owe. We are staying with an old school colleague just outside of Paris. On 27 April when I came to work, our offices were barricaded by six to ten Nazis wearing swastikas, and others were schlepping out some of my furniture and papers. The following Monday there were no teachers for my girls, so they were sent home. Their teachers had been dismissed because they were Jews. We tried to argue with the authorites, but nothing was going to get any better. We discussed all our options as a family. There was a lot of crying, terrible crying. We said goodbye to some very good friends. We had the car serviced and filled up with petrol, and on 5 May, we just took our most valuable possessions and drove to Paris.

We hope you and your family are well. I will send you some contact details soon.

Best wishes,

M. Braunzweig "Those poor children! You know, Mr. Schwartz, if I told Mother this, she wouldn't believe me."

"I can understand that. If anybody here told me, I wouldn't believe them either, Lili. It's just that I know Mr. Braunzweig so well. Just take the telegram to your mother. Terrible, terrible," Mr. Schwartz said as he returned to his office.

Lili spent most of the day completing filing tasks left over from the week and thinking about how difficult it must be now for Germans, especially Jews, under the new regime. *I can't imagine what it must be like to just take a few items, leave everthing else behind, abandon all your possessions, abandon your way of life, and just go somewhere else where there is nothing familiar, where you have no roots. I couldn't abandon Vienna. I couldn't just leave behind my wonderful world: my work, the relationships I have, my cosy home, not even the grand piano I no longer play. I couldn't do without the shops, the cafés, the theatre, the Musikverein, the opera, the gardens...oh, the Volkspark, the Burggarten. That would be unimaginable.*

JOSEPH HAD BEEN at a meeting of the Juedische Selbstwehr the evening prior, so he and Rudi hadn't really spoken about the ceremonial book burnings in German university towns. Rudi had just arrived home, having done the food shopping for the weekend, when Joseph and Lili arrived together from different directions. "Shalom aleichem, Lili, Rudi."

"Grüß Gott, Joseph."

"Aleichem shalom, Joseph. Did you hear—"

"Yes, I heard. Der Hitler ist a schrecklicher Mensch. A feier zol im treffen. How he can condone, actually encourage, the burning of books is unbelievable. Einstein, H.G.Wells, our own Sigmund Freud. It's an outrage," declared Joseph, getting red in the face.

"There was a book burning at the uni yesterday, Joseph. Did you know?"

"No, I was at the public library. Were there many involved? None except Brownshirts, I presume."

"Those Studentenshaft bastards organized it of course, Joseph, and no one stopped them."

"The administration folks were out of sight, I suppose. Thought so. Goodbye to your articles, Rudi. I hope you kept a copy." Rudi smiled. Joseph continued, "Can you lovely folks come to lunch at Ester's place on Sunday? We are having some friends over and would be delighted if you could join us."

Lili quickly responded, "We'd be delighted, Joseph; what would you like us to bring?"

"Absolutely nothing, please, Lili. We would be offended."

"Aren't you going to Ester's tonight?"

"No, I won't go till tomorrow morning. She has some meeting that she said would go late. Don't worry, Rudi. I won't make too much noise to keep you from your sleep," said Joseph with a wry smile as he switched on the radio.

The little news that there was was beginning to be repeated, so Lili changed the channel to some music. "Sometimes I feel I'm being bombarded by Strauss," said Rudi.

"You'd probably prefer them to play Landler music so you can swing Lili off her feet," suggested Joseph. Rudi just smiled and raised his eyebrows. "I think I'll go out for dinner and allow you to swing Lili off her feet."

"Aberwas, Joseph," responded Lili. "I can cook something here—"

"Or we can all go out together...to Café Louvre perhaps," Rudi interrupted.

"As long as I can have one of you to talk to while the other has his nose in the paper," Lili said. I'm getting to rather like this café and especially their Schnitzel."

The trio walked to the café together, arm in arm, with Lili in the middle. They were in a surprisingly good mood given the ill winds from the northwest. It was a pleasant, cool evening with a full moon highlighting only a few clouds. Lili pulled a handkerchief from her handbag. *Oh, I still have a letter I haven't opened. I guess it can wait for another few minutes.*

Inside, Herr Ober greeted them warmly and led them to one of the last few vacant tables. "Something to drink perhaps?" he asked.

"Zwei Bier und ein Weisser Veltliner, bitte."

Lili opened her letter. "It's from Tante Marianne."

"Oh, what does she have to say?"

Lili read it to herself, leaning away from Rudi so that he couldn't see. "There might be something private," she said, taking her wine. Her face lit up. "Prost, Joseph. Prost, Rudi." She took a sip. "I'll read it."

Annenheim,

3 May 1933

Liebe Lili,

It was so lovely to have had you and dear Rudi stay with me last winter. It was a delight to have met you and to have been able to get to know you a little. I already look forward to the next time you will come. It is also very nice here in summer, of course.

I am sorry you will have to delay your skiing on the Grossglockner, Lili. I'm sure that with those bandits in power now in Germany, that will not be possible for a while.

You make such a nice couple, Lili. It is none of my business, of course, but perhaps it is time for you and Rudi to think about getting married. I could then begin to knit a few little things for the future. Perhaps the two of you could announce something soon. Your birthday is coming up in a little while, isn't it?

I trust you are both healthy and happy. Viele liebe Gruesse und a tausend Bussi,

Tante Marianne Rudi and Lili looked at one another somewhat adoringly with big smiles. "Perhaps you should take your auntie's advice," suggested Joseph.

"We are waiting for you and Ester to show us the way," declared Rudi as he winked a little wink at Lili.

This was to be a big Schnitzel night as each of the trio ordered the same. The three plates arrived, the waiter looking for the smallest to give to Lili. They were all humungous. They had a wonderful aroma and were served with a potato salad on a side plate, there being no room beside the Schnitzel. Lili began to eat cautiously, while Rudi and Joseph attacked it with gusto. "Looks as if you haven't eaten for a month," exclaimed Lili.

Everyone took a break and clinked glasses for a second cheers. The café was now completely full, and there was a joyous atmosphere belying the serious events within their own city and beyond. There was little time for talking, as there was Schnitzel to be dealt with. Each was momentarily cacooned within his or her own world. Rudi looked around for a moment and thought, *Perhaps all these people are blinded by that full moon and aren't aware of the heavy storm approaching.* Joseph dreamed, *I wish my parents were here to enjoy a meal within such a joyous milieu.* Lili at the same time wondered, *How different would it be if Rudi and I were married? Would Mother accept him then?*

Their focus was interrupted. "Gruess Gott, Lili. I had to say hello. We are just sitting over there."

"Oh, Gruess Gott, Hanna. What a nice surprise." Lili waved at Hanna's husband. "How are you? Hanna, I'd like you to meet my fiancé, Rudi, and Joseph, his flatmate." Rudi and Joseph nearly choked.

"So nice to meet you. Let me not disturb you from your Schnitzel. Lili, we must meet for lunch; give me a call."

When she left, Rudi stared at Lili, and Joseph stopped chewing. "Yes?" said Lili. Rudi and Joseph looked at one another and then together at Lili. She shrugged her shoulders. "I just wanted to let her know that I didn't take her advice."

"By the look on her face, she was very surprised," suggested Joseph as he finished his Schnitzel.

Both Joseph and Rudi received another quarter of a Schnitzel. "Herr Ober, two more beers and another white for madam, please," ordered Joseph as they all seemed to get a second wind.

No sooner had all the Schnitzel disappeared than they were interrupted again. "Servus, Rudi."

"Hi, Friedrich, Gruess Gott. I'd like you to meet Lili and Joseph. Friedrich is a journalist who owns a corner of Mr. Best's Stammtisch. We shared some information for some articles we were writing."

"I think I helped Rudi get beaten up unfortunately. I hope you are keeping your distance from the Studentenschaft thugs, Rudi."

"So far, yes." Lili threw Rudi a look. "Yes, Friedrich, I have no intentions of getting into a brawl with any Brownshirts or police. I have to be responsible now."

Joseph could barely contain himself while Lili made herself a little taller. "I will not spoil your evening by referring to that unmentionable country and their unmentionable leader. Enjoy the rest of your evening. Sorry I interrupted. Servus."

"Servus, Friedrich. Mach's gut!"

Three coffees soon arrived, and Joseph excused himself, coming back with two newspapers from that country that was to remain unmentionable for the rest of the evening. Lili spotted something that piqued her interest, so Rudi sat there paperless. "This would be a wonderful concert to go to if it were only here," she suggested. "Soon they won't have any concerts from Kreisler, Mahler, Schoenberg, Offenbach, or even Strauss. He had Jewish grandparents, if we can believe their rhetoric."

"Idiots," said Rudi. "They'll soon not be able to see the best artwork in the world either: Kokoschka, Modigliani, Schiele, or Chagall. They are about as non-Aryan as they come, as non-Aryan as you, Joseph, my good friend. I hope the idiocy from our northwest neighbours never reaches us here."

Rudi began to twiddle his thumbs, so Joseph handed him the paper he was reading. "Nothing interesting as far as I can see, Rudi."

"Did you read this story?" asked Lili. "It says here that various schools had to close down for short periods so that new teachers could be employed. And in some communities there were complaints that some new teachers were completely inexperienced and couldn't maintain classroom discipline."

"Yes, of course. Discipline, discipline, discipline is most important. Without it there is no learning," mocked Joseph.

"Geh ma bald," suggested Rudi.

They soon left the café and walked home arm in arm, as they had come. The moon, brighter than before, was shining down on them. Unconsciously, Rudi was quietly whistling a melody, and soon Lili sang a few bars. "Dort, wo ich glücklich und selig bin, ist Wien, ist Wien, mein Wien!" Beneath the full moon, Vienna seemed in remarkably good spirits as couples and larger groups, heading to and from cafés, restaurants, concerts, and the like, were light of mood, with people light of step, and with lots of laughter. This was in strong contrast to the downcast mood of the Viennese only weeks ago, when the air was full of foreboding with the knowledge of the repression and restrictions placed on fellow human beings over the border. It was as if that period had passed, and everything north of that border was again back to normal. Things couldn't be that bad.

They arrived home. Rudi pulled the curtains across, and Lili went to freshen up in the bathroom, while Joseph unwrapped the bottle of cognac he had received as a present. He poured three little glasses and turned on the radio.

"Do they have nothing better to play than Strauss?" said Rudi.

"Better than hearing some awful news from that unmentionable land." Lili had come back into the room, and there was a toast. "La Chaim, Lili, Rudi."

"Prost."

"Prost."

"That was a lovely letter from Tante Marianne, Rudi. Do you think we can spend some time with her this summer?"

"Yes, I think so."

"We could also spend some time with your mother and father; I'm sure they'd love to see you. Will you be spending some time with your parents again this summer, Joseph?" asked Lili.

"Yes, Ester and I will try to help them make a decision as to where to go. I'm off to bed. I have to leave early tomorrow so I can have breakfast with Ester. Goodnight. See you both on Sunday at one o'clock. Don't forget."

Rudi and Lili didn't stay up much longer, and both went to sleep thinking what a lovely evening it had been.

Rudi and Lili enjoyed a quiet Saturday together dining and wining, with an afternoon of Spazieren in the Burggarten, the Volksgarten, and the Rathaus Park. Spring had sprung. The deciduous trees, such as oak, beech, and birch, were getting their new foliage, and a variety of bulbs were in full bloom. Daffodils and snowdrops were in abundance, and a few fresias and bluebells added some color. There were even water lilies in the ponds. Some bees were seeking nectar, and birds were seeking bees. The fragrance of lilac had Lili looking for the early blooms, and Rudi automatically began to quietly sing without really taking any notice of the lyrics. "Wenn der weiße Flieder wieder blüht' küß' ich deine roten Lippen müd. Wie im Land der Märchen, werden wir ein Pärchen, wenn der weiße Flieder wieder blüht."

"Did you mean what you were just singing, Rudi?" asked Lili.

"Pardon, what was I just singing?"

"You sang, 'We'd become a couple when the white lilac bloomed again.' That means next May."

"Must have been a Freudian slip," responded Rudi with a smile, squeezing her hand ever so slightly.

On that Saturday, Vienna was an extremely happy-go-lucky place: Wiener Gemuehtlichket everywhere, no one in a hurry; even the trams were going at a snail's pace. Given the bright full moon the night before, Rudi wondered whether the whole population had been moonstruck or had suffered a collective memory loss about the developments in Germany in recent weeks and months. *How could this be?* he wondered.

After a sleep-in on Sunday, a leisurely breakfast, and Rudi whiling a little time away on the violin, he and Lili headed to Ester's apartment, picking up a bunch of flowers on the way. Ester and Joseph greeted them at the door. "Shalom aleichem, Lili, Rudi"

"Aleichem shalom," responded Rudi. "Gruess Gott."

' "Oh, thank you so much for the flowers. How are you, Lili? Joseph said he had a lovely dinner with you both last night."

"Café Louvre is worth going to just for the Schnitzel. Ester; we should all go together sometime."

Just then there was another rap on the door, and two couples entered immediately. "Shalom aleichem."

"Aleichem shalom. Rudi, you know Benjamin and Rivka and Moshe and Rachel. This is Lili, Rudi's fiancé." Lili and Ester threw a glance at each other and another at Joseph.

"Gruess Gott. Nice to meet you," they said as Lili raised her eyebrows at Rudi. Rudi smiled and shrugged his shoulders.

"What happened to you, Moshe?" Rudi noticed a black patch over his eye.

"He looks like a pirate," quipped Joseph. "Let's have a drink first; that could be a long explanation."

After all the toasts of "La Chaim" and Prost," Moshe explained, "It was nothing. My wife hit me."

Benjamin interrupted. "Rachel would never hit him; she's taller than he is. He walked into a doorknob."

"Well, actually, I'll tell you what happened," began Moshe. "You know they had blackmailed me into joining the Selbstwehr, and after I had twice as many training sessions as everybody else had, they gave me a truncheon to wield if I needed to defend myself. Well, I was on duty when I came across three Brownshirts picketing a clothing store...you know, with nasty signs like 'Jews are our misfortune' and 'Jews are dirty thieves.' A couple of ladies were wanting to go into the store, so I stretched myself to a full one hundred and fifty-five centrimetres and moved towards one of these Brownshirts, raising my baton. He hit my baton, and it went into my eye."

"Oh, no."

"Wait, there's more. I fell backwards and kicked him in the balls on my way down. He fainted and fell down himself. So I jumped up and hit him with my truncheon. I missed his head, but I got his shoulder...broke it. He squealed like a pig."

"You mean you hit a man while he was down?"

"Of course. He was too tall when he was standing up. I was aiming for his head when a policeman came and stopped me. I wouldn't have missed a second time."

"Then what happened?"

"The ladies did their shopping."

"No, what happened to you, Moshe?"

"The police interrogated me for about three hours."

"What did they ask you?"

"'Why did you do it?'"

"Anything else?"

"No…oh, yes. They asked how I got the better of him, a man of one hundred and ninety-five centirmetres? I didn't tell them. Are we going to eat, Ester? What's the hold-up?"

Everybody smiled, and Joseph refilled the glasses with a Roter Veltliner as Ester fetched a huge platter of cabbage rolls. Everyone was enjoying lunch. "These are wonderful, Ester," exclaimed Benjamin."

"They could create quite some wind," suggested Joseph quietly. Everybody sniggered.

"What was that?" queried Ester.

"You know I'm more worried about the winds from over the border in the northwest," declared Rudi. "What do you make of the recent events in that unmentionable country?"

"Burning books is a terrible thing," suggested Rivka. "Thousands of them, in more than thirty-five towns all at once! They must have planned this for weeks in advance, the Deutsche Studentenschaft. They should read them, not burn them."

"Yes," said Rachel. "Those Nazi student organizations all over that country became far more emboldened from that first week in April when there was that one day of boycotting Jewish businesses all over the country and shortly afterwards the anti-Jewish laws barring Jewsfrom all legal and public services. It seems that the the young Nazi thugs, with the help of thousands of the SA and SS, began to intimidate and harass Jews as they were being dismissed from their firms and schools by the thousands."

"My boss had a colleague experience all that in Munich," explained Lili. "He had his premises ransacked one day, and his children were sent home from school a few days later, as their excellent Jewish teachers were dismissed and replaced by novices."

"Aha, you see? It will affect us, especially businesses, more and more here."

"Of course," interrupted Joseph. "The Nazis are making it increasingly untenable for Jews to stay in most parts of that country. My mother and fa—"

"Joseph, don't start with your parents' story. We all know it, and it will just get you upset again."

"Oy Gevalt. A feier zol im treffen."

"Joseph, would you please open another bottle of wine?" implored Ester.

"Yes," agreed Moshe. "There's not enough to drown our sorrows here. You know, Lili, there has been an increase in attempts to disrupt life here in Leopoldstadt too. Last week some hooligans ran past an outdoor café, upturning tables and pushing patrons while they were just trying to enjoy lunch."

"Yes, I have not heard of incidents like that in the first district," explained Lili.

"Of course they attack us here because there are so many of us crowded together," suggested Benjamin.

"Can you imagine a time when things got so bad you'd want to leave, Benjamin, like what is happening with Joseph's family?" asked Rudi.

"I think so, yes, Rudi. Jews have often experienced intimidation so that they have felt obliged to move. I heard of a case in Poland just recently where the Catholic Church has supported the expulsion of Jews." Benjamin took a sip. "Rivka and I want to get married and have children, but things are getting more and more unsettled here, and we are not certain we will be able to stay."

"Where would you go?" queried Rachel.

"We don't know; we'd love to get married in our temple here."

"We've also talked about getting married here," explained Rachel. "Haven't we, Moshe?"

"Pardon?"

"Yes, that is terrible, feeling obliged to delay getting married and having children," agreed Lili. "You know, my parents were married here in the Leopoldstaedter Tempel in 1904."

"Well, you and Rudi could show us the way, Lili," suggested Moshe.

"Oy vey. Rudi's a goy and a heathen," explained Joseph.

Rudi chimed in. "I agree with Benjamin. The situation has already become very difficult for Jews and will surely become worse there in Germany. It will only be a matter of time before life will be made more difficult for Jews here in Vienna as well."

"You seem very certain about that, Rudi."

"Yes, Hitler has made it clear in many of his writings that he intends to annex Austria and get rid of all 'impurities.' He wants to exterminate all Jews. Sorry."

"Oy Gevalt. Anything else to eat, Ester?" asked Joseph.

A large apple and cinnamon cake, baked in a Gugglehupf form, was soon set in the middle of the table. "Would you like to cut it for us, Moshe?" asked Ester. "You're the nearest," as she passed him a large knife.

"You're kidding. I'd probably cut a finger off. Here, you have it, Joseph," he said as he passed him the knife. Ester poured coffees all around, and a bowl of whipped cream was shunted among them.

"Perhaps we should all leave together," suggested Moshe. "None of us has got that much. We don't own apartments; some of us don't even own all our furniture. I could fit most of my belongings in a couple of suitcases, including my chess set."

Benjamin agreed. "It would be much more difficult to leave if you owned a beautiful house with grand chandeliers, many rooms of furniture with Persian rugs, a large library and tapestries, and a grand piano."

"Yes, I am sure my mother, my boss, and all their acquaintances would absolutely resist leaving all their worldly goods behind," suggested Lili.

"But there is a different dimension too," Rudi chimed in. "Many well-established Jewish families have in a sense renounced their

Jewishness; some have even been baptized Catholic and would never refer to themselves as Jewish. They see themselves as Viennese."

"As invincible, Rudi?" asked Benjamin.

Rudi looked at Lili, who nodded. "Nearly invincible. The first-district Jews rarely witness, let alone experience, any harassment and cannot imagine being dislodged from their comfortable existences."

"Yes, Rudi is right; there is a huge self-confidence within my mother's and my boss, Mr. Schwartz's, circle of friends and acquaintances. They've worked hard to build nice lives for themselves, and now, I think, they work hard to ignore what is happening around them," explained Lili.

"See?" said Moshe. "When it comes to some things, it's better to be an ordinary Shmuck than an extraordinary Shmuck." Everybody smiled.

"My parents are somewhere between being ordinary Schmucks and extraordinary Schmucks," declared Joseph. "They own their own one-bedroom apartment; they own all their furniture; Mother even has her own piano. They both have work when about twenty percent haven't got work; they consider themselves lucky. They can't sell their apartment; no one is buying them. They have enough money saved up to keep them going for a few months were they to leave. But if they left, they realize they would likely never own an apartment again. And there they are in Munich, being called terrible names, having their places of work picketed, trampling on swastikas on their way to work, and always feeling the need to look over their shoulders. They believe they are being forced to leave their own country."

"What advice do you give them, Joseph?"

"I think they should leave so that they can maintain their dignity." There seemed to be general agreement. "When they do leave though, the reality is that they will not be able to help me with my costs here in Vienna. I will have to find work. I may not be able to finish my degree."

"Don't worry, Joseph," assured Moshe. "We'd pass the hat around for you." The funny thing was Joseph knew that Moshe actually would.

Soon there was an exodus to the kitchen, where Rivka and Rachel alternated washing the dishes while Moshe ordered everybody else about to take turns drying them. "I've only got one eye, you'll appreciate," he said. Everybody smiled; they all loved Moshe.

The time came when everybody wished each other farewell and left. Another full moon dominated the early evening sky as a formation of birds squawked and headed north, avoiding Europe altogether.

As the full moon slowly waned, so did Vienna's Gemuehtlichkeit of the last few days, with the realization that the Austrian government, under Dollfuss, remained in a precarious situation, and Nazism was strengthening daily, leading to a constant stream of Jews departing for friendlier and saner environments.

21

ANTI-SEMITISM INCREASES, SUMMER 1933

LILI HAD ARRANGED to have lunch with Hanna, so they made a reservation at Demel. It was a pleasant spring day, sunny with barely a breeze, as both Lili and Hanna arrived virtually simultaneously; neither liked being late.

"Gruess Gott, Hanna."

"Gruess Gott, Lili."

There was no need to hurry, as Hanna's children were at school, and Mr. Schwartz told Lili she could take as long as she wanted. They were led to a quiet table, as had been requested. The waiter took their light coats and pushed in their seats behind them. He returned momentarily with the menus, and two glasses of champagne were quickly requested. "Would your preference be Perignon or Monopole, ladies?"

"Perignon, please, Herr Ober." When the waiter left, Lili asked, "Well, how have you all been, Hanna?"

"We have all been very well, thank you, Lili. Michael is very busy with work, travels a little too much, and the girls are doing well at school. And you, Lili? That Rudi is a handsome man and certainly has a very becoming voice."

"We are both well, thank you, Hanna. Yes, he has a beautiful speaking voice and beautiful singing voice too."

The bursting champagne bubbles tickled their noses as they took their first sips. Both smiled and looked at the menus, feeling a little awkward, Hanna because she wanted to ask Lili some serious questions and Lili because she knew Hanna would ask them. They ordered a selection of mini sandwiches, including asparagus with chicken, ham and mustard, beef with horseradish, and cheese with pickles, along with two glasses of rose from the Cote D'Azur. Hanna took several sips to help with courage. "Now I can imagine that Rudi to be a very gallant and attentive young man, but he is very young, Lili." Lili took a sip. "He wouldn't make twenty, would he?"

"He's about twenty," answered Lili, a little on the defensive.

Hanna finished her champagne, and her face became the color of the rose they had ordered. "With Rudi being so young and still being a student, what does he really offer you, Lili? He is a country boy and not sophisticated like you. You are used to having all of Vienna at your disposal: the cafés, the Musikverein, the opera. With Rudi you will have to forsake a lot of this, won't you? An American friend whom I told about your situation had a very good expression. She said, 'I think she has hitched her wagon to the wrong horse.'"

Lili smiled. "That may all be correct, Hanna." She took another sip of champagne as the sandwiches and rose arrived. While Hanna was expecting a continuing response, Lili slowly perused the sandwiches, formulating in her mind what she would tell her friend. Hanna got impatient and took a sandwich. "I think Rudi and I would make beautiful babies."

Hanna nearly choked on an asparagus spear.

"At least we'd have children because we really wanted them."

"What are you implying, Lili?"

Lili took a bite of a cheese and pickle sandwich. "Very good," she said. "From the Savoir, I think. All those men Mother wanted me to try out with, so to speak, only wanted children as commodities, Hanna, to show them off, beautifully dressed, to their business colleagues, to recite a poem before dinner perhaps, and then to disappear and leave the adults to discuss serious matters." Hanna half smiled as she recognized the characterization, words momentarily eluding her. "Your Michael should have had a brother; that might have worked, Hanna." They both smiled. "You know," Lili continued, "for all his lack of sophistication, Rudi understands the world so much better than men nearly twice his age. No, he does not understand the financial world, and he does not understand how business is transacted, but he does understand the feeble political situation here in Austria and the threat of the Nazis in that unmentionable land to the northwest."

"Germany, you mean?"

"Yes, he understands the extent of the anti-Semitism in Germany and the threat its likely development poses for us here in Vienna"

"Oh, Lili, we are not in danger from the Nazis here. There have been a few isolated incidents of thuggery here over the years, but—"

"Hanna, I spent last Sunday having lunch with friends in Leopoldstadt—"

Hanna interrupted, "In the second district? Why would you go there?"

"Rudi and I had lunch with Joseph's girlfriend and two other couples. In their neighbourhood, they experience regular boycotts of their shops, have windows broken, and have swastikas painted over their buildings and some terrible graffiti painted on walls and footpaths, terrible, horrible slurs that I can't say."

"Yes, please say."

Lili took a deep breath and blurted out, "Things like 'Weg mit dem Judendreck,' 'Jews are thieves and liars; they are our misfortune,' and 'Jews belong to Palestine.'"

"Enough, enough, we must speak quietly about such things." They looked around; Hanna drank half a glass of wine at once. "But these things don't happen every month, Lili," she whispered.

"Once every month would be depressing enough. But, no, Hanna, they happen every week. Young women wearing scarves get harassed nearly every day by Nazi thugs."

"That wouldn't happen to us ever. We are different. We are secular and well integrated into Viennese society."

Lili interrupted, "And most of us don't care what happens to other Jews. We in the first district don't care. We knit a few pair of socks for the poor each year and take no further responsibility. We don't support them, take a political stance, and have the harassment against them stopped. They have had to develop their own Juedisches Selbstwehr, for God's sake, because there is no political will to help them, and the police turn a blind eye and are actually in cohoots with the Nazis."

They both nervously looked around as they realized that Lili had again raised her voice to where others might hear. Lili told the story of Moshe assisting women to enter a picketed shop and getting a black eye for his troubles. Hanna felt a twinge of guilt, finished her glass of rose, and, excusing herself, went to the bathroom. In the meantime Lili took another sip and composed herself.

Hanna returned. "That's better," she said as she sat down. There was a further pause.

"Rudi cares," said Lili. "He cares about those people in Leopoldstadt; he cares about all human beings. He cares about human rights, the right of everybody to live in safety and peace. All those men who Mother and Father wanted to set me up with don't give a damn about the rights of human beings in general. They are all selfish, self-absorbed, and self-important. Boring, boring, boring. Well, one wasn't, I guess, but most were."

Lili and Hanna ordered some mini cakes and biscuits that the Demel was famous for and, of course, some Heisse Schokolade.

Lili was just getting wound up. "Rudi is not boring; he's never boring, not for one minute. He is exciting to be with. He makes me feel alive. He cares for me a lot, never forgets anything, remembers flowers every weekend. He sings to me; we sing together. He plays violin for me; we dance in the kitchen. Imagine those boring farts dancing! They woudn't know the difference between a polka and a waltz." The Demel specialities arrived, including the Heisse Schokolade, but Lili was not to be stopped. "On Sunday at lunch we talked about what it would mean to be so harassed, so tormented, that you felt obliged to leave, Hanna. Each of the three couples is delaying having children because of the uncertainty of their existence here in Vienna."

"But it isn't uncertain, Lili."

"Really? Would you like to be harassed walking to work, Hanna, have the windows of Michael's business broken, glass chards in the cuffs of his trousers at night when he undressed? Have nasty signs and graffiti greet you nearly every morning as you arrive at work, some actually threatening you?" Lili took another sip of hot chocolate. "It's as wonderful as always, Hanna. Joseph's parents live in Munich, have lived there for a very long time, and they are not just thinking about leaving; they are actually planning to leave. Joseph's mother spends most of the time crying. The anti-Semitic actions have become so bad there and in the rest of Germany that Jewish families are emigrating by the hundreds every week. Hitler has begun his Reinigung, cleansing Germany of all Jews. And Hitler has designs on Austria; he wants to annex it. Then he'll want his cleansing to be carried out throughout Austria; that's what Rudi thinks, and I agree with him."

"Hitler wouldn't be able to; Dollfuss is against Nazis. That I know."

"No, Dollfuss and the whole Austrian government wouldn't be able to stop Hitler. His SA and SS—" Hanna looked blank. "His personal army consists of tens of thousands and is growing every day, and the Hitlerjugend is recruiting future soldiers by the hundreds, if not thousands, every week."

"Our men would rise up against any such threats," suggested Hanna.

"Not a chance," interjected Lili. "Our men are finance and business people, lawyers and doctors, film directors and editors. They are not fighting people. They wouldn't have a clue. Rudi says that they wouldn't know if a country convenience fell on them."

Hanna smiled. "Oh, Lili, you have obviously made up your mind about Rudi. I wish you both all the very best and a perfect pigeon pair of beautiful children, of course. He is very handsome."

———

SOMEWHAT FATIGUED DUE to the intensity of the discussion and the fine food and wine, Lili arrived back at work at precisely 3:30 p.m. "You could have taken longer had you wanted to. Did you have a good time?" Mr. Schwartz asked. "We've received another telegram from Mr. Braunzweig."

"Oh, what did it say?"

"It just said that his brother and family left Germany and had now joined them in France, seven of them altogether staying in just two rooms. Apparently there is a steady exodus out of Germany. His brother was a teacher, I think. Terrible, just terrible, Lili." Mr. Schwartz returned to his office, and Lili was focusing hard on her tasks to prevent her from snoozing off. The phone rang. It was Walter.

"Hallo, Lili?"

"Ja, Walter, what a nice surprise. How are you?"

"Very well. How are you, my dear sister?"

"I am very well; we are both very well."

"Yes, Mother has told me that you are with Rudi normally three days per week. She misses you very much she said."

"Yes, I'm aware of that. She'd miss me even more if I had married one of her choices."

"Bela and Kafka miss you too."

"I know; they are wonderful. They even know when I come home after being with Rudi and are there at the window barking and wobbling their heads. And how is it in Paris, Walter?"

"It's good. Work keeps me very busy, and my French is nearly perfect now. There is some heated debate going on here, though, about the Jewish emigrants coming from Germany, whether France can absorb all these Jews. There are hundreds, maybe thousands, every week. Many come with barely more than the clothes on their backs. Poor beggars, probably just left the house and furniture and everything behind them."

"Yes, that's exactly what happened to a business partner of Mr. Schwartz's."

"Germany has become a disgrace since Hitler gained power."

"You heard about the book burnings, I imagine, Walter."

"Yes. Hasn't happened to that extent since the Middle Ages. People who do such things are just uncivilized. Has there been any increase in anti-Semitism in Vienna in recent weeks, Lili?"

"Not in the first district, but in Leopoldstadt, on the very block where our parents were married, there has been a steady increase of all sorts of nasty anti-Jewish behavior perpetrated by Nazi thugs."

"Thank God there is very little of it here. Lili, I'm sorry. I must go. I'll let you know when I can next get to Vienna. Servus, Viele Bussi."

THE END OF May was fast approaching, and the Viennese remained conscious of but not all that clued into the details of the Austrian national government wranglings. They were more interested in the latest films to hit the screen, who was playing the lead role in the State Opera, or who was currently conducting at the Musikverein. Most understood, however, that there were tensions between the left- and the right-leaning parties vying for influence. Some people were aware that the Christian Social Union was converted to the Patriotic Front, which was heavily Roman Catholic and vehemently anti-Marxist. On 27 May, the Kommunistische Partei Österreichs (the CPA, the Austrian Communist Party) was banned, as were several other groups.

Various demonstrations occurred at this time, many Viennese not knowing who was demonstrating for or against what. The Viennese were mostly pleased that the Nazis didn't get more than 25 percent of the votes in local elections in most areas. They felt generally sorry for the Jews in Germany, and they perceived Hitler as a bit "narrisch." Perhaps they thought he'd disappear as quickly as he had arrived. Or perhaps it was just wishful thinking as the NSDAP was quickly gaining adherents and Jews were emigrating from Germany by the droves, their existence in Germany being made less tenable with the passing of each day.

Lili was thinking about Tante Marianne and felt a little guilty that she hadn't yet replied to her recent letter. One afternoon when there was no work that was really pressing, she penned a few lines:

Wien, 12 Juni 1933

Liebe Tante Marianne,

Thank you very much for your recent letter. It was a lovely surprise to hear from you. It was also lovely to get to know you last winter and to try out the recipe you gave me. The Ofenschlupfer turned out very well but not as good as the one you made for Rudi and me.

Rudi and I gladly accept your kind invitation for us to stay with you over the summer. I haven't told him yet though. We are looking forward to it already very much.

In summer I won't be reminded of not being able to ski the Grossglockner with Rudi. I'm sure we'll enjoy the lake though, and we look forward to you coming swimming with us.

Rudi will be in touch with you closer to our coming.

Thank you again for your dear invitation,

Viele Liebe Gruesse und Bussi,

Lili

SOON IT WAS Lili's birthday, which she requested be celebrated at Café Landtmann. Rudi made a booking for the actual Friday of her birthday and requested that at eight o'clock two glasses of Perignon and thirteen red roses be on the table at which they had sat several times before. Elegantly dressed, they arrived at the Landtmann as planned, and Herr Ober showed them to their table. Several table groups spontaneously and quietly sang "Happy Birthday." Lili and Rudi both blushed a little with embarrassment but managed to smile at various groups. "Thank you, Rudi. You shouldn't have."

"Of course, Schatzerl. This birthday can't happen again. After all, it is your first birthday I am celebrating with you." Rudi pushed Lili's chair in behind her, and they soon drank a little toast, Rudi wishing her a happy birthday. Leaning over, he gave her a firm kiss on the lips. A couple of girls giggled. He took a small gift-wrapped box, a little larger than a matchbox, from his pocket and placed it beside the vase. Lili looked at it, looked at Rudi, and smiled. *Could it be an engagement ring?* she wondered for a moment. *Of course not. Rings need to be measured,* she concluded. *Interesting, I wonder what it is.*

Lili and Rudi sipped champagne, intermittently holding hands across the table. Herr Ober brought the menus. Soon Rudi odered Tafelspitz for Lili, Gulasch mit Semmelknödel for himself, and a bottle of red wine suggested by the waiter. The bottle was brought to the table and opened with appropriate protocol. Rudi took a moment to mentally add up the cost of the items so far ordered and ones they were likely still to order to make sure he had sufficient Schillings in his pocket. His additions suggested he'd have enough and some left over for the rest of the weekend. He smiled to himself. In the meantime Lili was reflecting on her prevous birthday. She remembered that she was with her mother and brother in some classy restaurant. The food was very good, as was the wine, and Walter was in particularly good spirits. She remembered, though, that she was not all that happy. She had not met any man who excited her and only one she could recall whom she even respected, while many of her girlfriends and aquaintenances were already married, some with children. Today she felt happier than she had felt in years, all those things she told Hanna being true. She had also learned a great deal from Rudi and Joseph. She had learned to be much less insular, and she really appreciated Rudi's caring for others. Their age difference was of no real significance; she was now rarely conscious of it. She loved Rudi and wanted to be with him.

As Lili again caught a glimpse of the small gift box and was wondering what it might contain, the waiter arrived with their meals piping hot, the aroma of paprika dominating. Rudi and Lili clinked glasses and took a sip. "That's very nice," declared Lili. "What are we drinking?"

"The waiter just said it was from the Veneto region. As long as you like it, Lili." They both enjoyed their dishes and enjoyed feeding one another until some of the goulash dropped, in transit, onto

Lili's plate. They were lingering over their red when Rudi noticed Lili's eyes on the little parcel. "Why don't you open it before dessert? You might then enjoy it better."

Without hesitation Lili untied the bow, throwing Rudi a glance, and lifted the lid from the box. She took out a silver bracelet to match the necklace and locket Rudi had given her for Christmas, which she was wearing. Lili beamed and leaned forward to give Rudi a kiss. She handed him the bracelet and her left hand. As he fastened it to her wrist, the two previously giggling girls, who were about to leave, clapped. They looked as if they wanted to come over, so Lili invited them to have a look as she gave it a few twirls. The girls said thank you, grinned from ear to ear, and left.

Rudi and Lili each had dessert. "Thank you, Rudl, for the lovely gift. It's so nice that it matches my necklace. And thank you for the first of my birthday dinners together. It was very special."

Herr Ober handed Rudi the bill and took the vase of flowers, promising to be back in a moment. He soon returned with the thirteen roses nicely wrapped in paper with a bow and handed them to Lili. He helped her with her chair and bade them both farewell and goodnight. They indeed had had a good night, as pleasant as both would have wished.

<hr />

NOT ALL PEOPLE were having as good a night as Lili and Rudi. In various parts of Austria there were skirmishes among various political factions. Members of the recently banned Austrian Communist Party were still smarting and continuing to fight clandestinely with the increasingly confident Nazis. That's all it took for Dollfuss, on 19 June, to ban the Austrian Nazi organization. That was, of course, seen as a provocation in itself, causing further widespread skirmishes for a while. This mostly did not affect the Viennese, who went about their daily lives with their characteristic Gemuehtlichkeit.

There was clearly less Gemuehtlichkeit throughout Germany, however, where the movement to Nazification and Aryanization seemed to be occurring apace and in every direction. The SS and the SA were expanding their presence with torchlight marches and much foot stomping. Some people liked the precision of the marchers and the show of strength; others found the arrogant display not short of scary. The Hitlerjugend groups were developing quickly from one end of the country to the other under the influence of sophisticated propaganda, including promises of glory. The SA and the SS were spreading fear far and wide—harassing, frightening, intimidating, even beating people who were in their path. Political oponents were often brutalized and executed. The media was being purged as quickly as possible of all outlets, print or radio, that were not sympathetic to the NSDAP. Some media owners had fled immediately when Hitler came to power; others left more slowly and of their own accord, while still others accommodated Nazi wishes for the necessity of their very survival. The media was being used extensively to frighten people against the existence of all groups who were not of the Nazi persuasion, especially the Communists. With considerable resolve, the process of the Aryanization of schools and universities was also in full swing. Jewish teachers and administrators were sacked and replaced frequently by less able substitutes. The curriculum was also quickly purged of all aspects considered non-Aryan. The purging of Jewish businesses had also commenced; many lawyers and doctors as well as most government employees were sacked if they were Jewish. All this led to an exodus of thousands of academics, professionals, business personnel, and others, mainly to nearby countries that would take them, including France and Belgium.

It seemed that a great majority of the German people supported this expulsion of the Jews, having no care at all as to their well-being, though they had often been neighbours, sometimes for generations. Many believed the propaganda that their own circumstances would soon be improved. There were some non-Jews, of course, who sympathized with their Jewish friends and even went out on a limb, some risking their own lives, to support them. By and large, however, there appeared to be majority support for Aryanization across the land. The Nazi power elite marched forward relentlessly to achieve their goals, and on 14 July 1933, the NSDAP became the only political party in Germany. Autocracy had been achieved.

The Austrians seemed to take little notice of the fast-moving developments in Germany in summer of 1933, seemingly also taking little interest in Dollfuss's processes to consolidate as much power unto himself as possible. Vacation time had arrived for many Viennese, the wealthier of whom headed for the beaches and lakes of Italy and the many mountains and lakes in southern Austria. Rudi and Lili would also soon be on their way.

22

VACATION IN ANNENHEIM, SUMMER 1933

LILI TOOK DAYS to pack, being quite excited and careful not to forget anything. She and Rudi took the train of the Österreichische Bundesbahnen, BBÖ, to Villach on a Tuesday in August, as the fares were less expensive than at other times. Rudi the elder was on the platform to greet them. "Ja servus, meine liab'n Kinder." He gave both a big hug. "You look wonderful, Lili," he said with dancing eyes. "How are you both? Mother is eagerly awaiting you." Rudi's father took one of Lili's bags, leaving her with the smaller and lighter one, and the three crossed over the Drau bridge, Rudi remarking that the water level seemed a little low. Rudi the elder led the way, happily humming and tipping his hat several times with a greeting of "Habidiere" as he passed people he recognized.

Rudi's mother stood, arms outstretched, in the open door as they approached. She gave both her visitors such a strong hug that they became red in the face. She beckoned them to sit on the couch, one beside the other, as she pulled up a chair opposite them. She held each by a hand, looked them in the eyes, and asked about their trip, their health, their friends, the weather in Vienna, their diet, and if they had been getting enough sleep. The elder chuckled. "Is something the matter, Rudl?" his wife asked.

"No, not at all," her husband replied as he winked at Rudi.

Rudi's mother got up and went into the kitchen, Rudi the elder taking her place, smiling a lot and asking mostly the same questions. "Ein moment." as he picked up the phone. "Marianne, they are here, and they'll see you at about five. Servus." He replaced the receiver and asked, "Did you hear about Hitler's latest outrage?"

"Which one was that, Papa? There have been so many."

"I just read the other day that he banned all trade unions in Germany on the second of May, I think. Can you imagine? I've belonged to my union since I was eighteen years old. He should soon have the greatest part of the population against him."

Mrs. Auer served scrambled eggs with rye bread and butter as Mr. Auer poured four glasses of a lighter red from a bottle opened the previous evening. "It's very good…from Italy," he declared. The elder looked at Lili with adoring eyes he couldn't hide. He remembered her dark eyes and shiny hair. "So when are you getting married?"

Lili dropped her fork, and Rudi nearly choked. Mother apologized, "He's always direct, Lili; he doesn't know any other way."

"It's better like that; people know exactly what you are thinking," the elder said. "They don't have to wonder."

"Soon," replied Rudi as he glanced at Lili.

"I can tell by the way you look that you haven't even asked her yet," his father said. "It's time. You should ask her before she gets to know you completely. She might have second thoughts. Often happens. I knew this fellow—"

"Enough, Rudl."

"Ja, perhaps you could ask her by the Ossiachersee, Rudi," he continued.

Lili smiled at Rudi and his father. Rudi's mother knew how to change the subject. "What do you think of Dollfuss, Rudi?"

"I think he's a poor leader who cannot get people to work together."

The elder interjected, "Couldn't work with those Nazis, so he banned them. Good for him."

"Yes, Papa, but he's banned virtually every other group as well, and that could lead to terrible unrest."

"How do you think the people of Vienna are responding to Dollfuss, Lili?" she asked.

"I think they are happy that he is clearly against the Nazis and—"

The phone rang. It was Marianne, wanting to know if they had left yet. Rudi and Lili finished a coffee and a couple of butter biscuits then left with the understanding that they would bring Tante Marianne to their Gasthaus on Friday night at eight sharp.

It was a very warm afternoon as they walked towards Tante Marianne's house. Some people were returning from the lake; some were going for a late-afternoon dip. Marianne was standing at the front gate, looking for Rudi and Lili. She wore a simple, floral summer dress, midbrown sandals, and a big smile. Upon spotting them, she walked as quickly towards them as she could, given her arthritis. She threw her arms first around Lili and then Rudi. She had been looking forward to seeing them from the moment they left her in winter. Never having had any children of her own, she adopted Lili and Rudi as her surrogates. They had no choice about that. They were told they must be tired and should sit at the kitchen table. A tall glass of lemonade was placed in front of them. "So, how are you both? You look wonderful, just a bit pale."

"We are both well, thank you, Tante Marianne."

"Tell me everything you've been up to. I'll just listen. I want to hear about everything, everything."

Rudi began to give quite a detailed account as Tante Marianne reached beside her, took up her knitting, and began to knit. Lili's inquisitive look quickly turned to a smile. "A little something for the future; knitting is good for my arthritis." Rudi continued to tell Tante most of what he and Lili had been up to, and indeed the only sound from Tante Marianne was the clashing of the knitting needles as she knitted two plain, two purl. "I wish I knew if the first will be a boy or a girl…knitting with a color is much easier than knitting in white," Tante Marianne explained. Rudi was at the end of his tale, and Tante got to the end of a section. "Why don't you two youngsters go for a walk and reacquaint yourselves with the lake, and I can do what I want here in the kitchen without any eagle eyes watching? Dinner will be on the table at eight, and I'll be hungry."

Lili exchanged her shoes for some sandals, Rudi trousers for shorts and shoes for sandals. They headed off to the lake as Marianne watched them and smiled contentedly as if they were her pride and joy.

The lake was as calm as a millpond; the only ripples being made were by children pretending to be ducks. For the moment they were quiet; the only noise was the gentle lapping of the water at the lake's edge and the crunch of sand beneath Rudi and Lili's bare feet, both having taken off their sandals. The reflection of the sun shimmered brightly across the water, highlighting a couple of waterbirds landing to catch their evening meal. "Ibises," said Rudi.

"How do you know?"

"They are the only birds on this lake with a black neck and head and a very long, curved beak."

Rudi and Lili reminisced about the time they met about a year before. "Remember how we met, Rudi? You were so daring, climbing up the ladder and knocking on my window."

"I succeeded. Had I not been so persistent, we wouldn't be walking here together now." Lili smiled; she was delighted he'd been "daring," then. As the sun was beginning to hide behind trees, Lili and Rudi headed back to Tante Marianne's home.

They brushed the sand off their feet before they entered and gave Tante Marianne a hug. She returned the favor with strength. "How was your walk?" she asked.

"Very nice, thank you," replied Lili. "The water was quite warm, so you must come and swim with us, Tante."

Auntie smiled and returned to the stove, where three brown trout were gently sizzling in butter. "Here, you make a dressing for the salad." She passed Lili the olive oil, a pot of mustard, and vinegar. "From Italy," declared Tante Marianne, "and the wine too. Would you open it, please, Rudi?"

Trout and salad made a perfect dinner for a summer's evening, and there were more excellent dinners, as Tante Marianne was not only a very good cook, but she also loved to cook, especially for Rudi and Lili. She was meticulous in applying her skills. Chicken, duck, quail, sausages, cheeses, and salads were all part of the coming week's fare, and all meals were eaten with enjoyment and gusto as the mountain and lake air can make one quite hungry.

Tante Marianne made excuses on the first day of their stay not to go to the lake, but on the second day Lili was able to persuade her to join them. Lili made sure she had on her bathing costume and a good pair of sandals, and she handed Rudi a couple of chaisse lounges to carry, while Lili carried a bag with towels, some food items that Tante had put together, and other sundry items. They walked to a nice flat sandy area, threw off excess clothes onto a chaise lounge, and coaxed Tante to the water's edge. She put a toe in the water. "Jesus, Maria, it's cold." Rudi gave her such a look that Tante Marianne marched into the lake to just below her knees. "Rudi, do you want me to have a heart attack?"

"Oh, Tante, I'll go with you." Lili on one side and Rudi on the other, they edged ever so slowly into knee-deep water. Tante went under to above her waist and bobbed up again quickly. "Jesus, Maria." Rudi and Lili just smiled and waited for Tante to become accustomed to the water's temperature. She soon did and smiled for the first time since leaving home. "It's actually quite warm," she said as she swam out with a perfect side stroke. Rudi and Lili shrugged their shoulders, smiled at one another, and swam out beside her. They swam out maybe fifty metres when Auntie held herself up by holding Rudi's arm and motioned back towards the shore. The slight sound of rhythmic breathing and three birds squawking overhead accompanied them to the shore.

Lili hurried ahead upon reaching the sand, fetched a towel, and held it out for Tante Marianne. She smiled. "Thank you for letting me swim with you, Lili," she said, sitting on a chaise lounge. "Pass me the bag, please, Rudi. I can eat something now." Lili sat on the second chaise lounge, and Rudi sat on a towel on the sand. Tante

Marianne unfolded a tea towel on her lap and laid out some sandwiches and a paper bag of cherries. "Cheese with cornichons or ham with cornichons? I have a good selection today," she said, tongue in cheek. "You first, Lili…Rudi." They munched away on some sandwiches and ate some cherries. With some cherry pits still in her hand, Tante Marianne fell asleep. Rudi and Lili were a little surprised and continued to speak in whispers. Rudi went for a swim, while Lili, lounging beside Tante Marianne, watched three children building sandcastles just twenty or thirty metres away.

THE NEXT FEW days were much the same, with Tante Marianne preparing lunch and accompanying Lili and Rudi for a swim and snooze each day. As planned on Friday, Rudi and Lili took Tante Marianne to the Villacher Gasthaus, where they met up with Rudi's mother and father at exactly 8:00 p.m. It was still quite warm, and many people were glowing from having spent at least some of the day under a browning sun. There was only the slightest breeze, without much cooling effect. The ladies wore light summer dresses, and the men were all in shirtsleeves. Rudi the elder was in fine form, effusively paying Marianne and Lili compliments, Rudi and his mother rolling their eyes at each other.

Rudi's father took Lili by the hand and walked with her to four or five tables where he knew people, proudly, and with dancing eyes, introducing her as his future daughter-in-law. Lili was not really sure of this herself, as his son had not formally proposed to her, but she enjoyed the attention being paid to her at the moment. By the time they returned to their table, the Kapelle had begun to play, menus were being distributed, and a bubbly, probably from Italy, was being poured. Rudi the elder proposed a toast to the continuation of everybody's good health. Lili began chatting with Rudi's mother, so Rudi whisked Tante Marianne onto the dance floor before she could become self-conscious. He waltzed her forwards and backwards, in perfect circles and figure eights, with such energy that she could only hang on to him tightly and enjoy the exhileration. There was no time to remember her age or her rheumatism or arthritis. When the music stopped, Tante Marianne was flushed and beaming all over. Rudi carefully took her back to her chair and sat her down, her head still spinning.

The other Rudi was now deep in discussion with Lili, so Rudi whisked his mother off to the dance floor, where she had to hang on to him equally tightly as the beat of the Landler quickened. She too returned to the table all energized and needing to dab her brow.

The food was good, as was the wine, and plentiful to boot. The bandmaster, as usual, was able to select the music to be played for the appropriate mood. Everyone appeared really happy; there seemed not to be a care in the world.

Lili couldn't help but wonder, *What is this reality? Is this carefree attitude, this bonhomie, existent only here? Are these people not aware of the general anxiety in Vienna? Are they not aware of the existence of the increasing anti-Semitism: women being harassed, shops picketed, swastikas painted on footpaths and windows and walls? How can they be so ignorant? Or are they free, just free of the everyday worry of the city? Something isn't fair. Perhaps people here are right. Perhaps things will not develop as nastily as in Germany. Perhaps the ill winds will subside and even Leopoldstadt will return to some civility. Perhaps I should extinguish the thought that one day we might have to leave our beloved Vienna. I wish I could know what will be.*

Lili was whisked off her feet and brought back to a nice reality as she smooched with Rudi to a slower tempo. The bandmaster gave an approving smile to Rudi, who had been at this venue for years but mostly dancing with his mother and local young ladies, generally to Landler and polka music. Rudi had always been less fond of the courtly Strauss waltzes, which he thought rather pretentious.

The evening ended very pleasantly, the wine contributing to the joyousness of the night. Tante Marianne, Lili, and Rudi had a nightcap at his parents' apartment before taking the bus back to Annenheim.

THE WEEKEND WAS a little hotter and a little more crowded than the previous days. Rudi and Lili decided to allow Tante Marianne her own space on Saturday, and they took themselves off to the Ruine Landskron, a pleasant walk from Annenheim to these ruins of a castle with a long and checkered past. The expansive view from the top, though slightly hazy, overlooked most of the Villach countryside and town. Rudi and Lili were happy to be there on their own, to enjoy each other's company and feel free from the pressures of living in Vienna and away from family, though they enjoyed Rudi's family a lot. It was still very hot as they wandered back down the hill, Rudi humming most of the way.

When they returned midafternoon, Tante Marianne was clearing out some old newspapers. "Oh, I hadn't expected to see you quite so soon. Don't I get a kiss?"

"Of course, Tante; we're a bit hot and sticky though." There were kisses nevertheless. She had laid one paper aside with an article she thought might interest them. It read, "July 1: German Nazi regime declares that married women shouldn't work." Rudi read the article while drinking a glass of lemonade Tante had put in front of him. He pondered a moment, passing the paper to Lili. "You know, the NSDAP has become so autocratic now, it wants to totally control the lives of the people it is not driving away. Did I tell you, Tante, that my flatmate's parents are in the process of deciding which country to emigrate to from Munich because it has become quite uncomfortable for them to stay there?"

"Yes, you told me, Rudi. It's really scandalous. Ja, Kinder, it would be nice to go for a little swim. What do you think?" Tante Marianne didn't wait for an answer; she went to put on her swimming costume and expected Lili and Rudi to do the same. They did. A few pieces of fruit were added to the towels in her beach bag, and Tante asked Rudi to take the two chaise lounges.

There were many groups at the lake's edge and in the water. "Look, the two ibises are there again, Rudi," commented Lili. She sat in a chaise lounge, smiling at Tante Marianne as she took Rudi by the forearm and slowly led him towards the lake. Tante lowered herself cautiously into the water, and soon she and Rudi were swimming sidestroke, facing one another. Lili couldn't stop smiling, thinking about the wonderfully warm relationship she had developed with Auntie, who had embraced her as if she had been one of the family all her life and now even knitting baby's clothes before she and Rudi had even married. Tante Marianne and Rudi soon emerged from the lake, disturbing a couple of small birds fossicking for insects at the water's edge.

Just then, a small group of locals passed by. "Gruess Gott, Marianne. Ja, Gruess Gott, Lili. I hardly recognized you," said Mrs. Stein. "How are your mother and your Tante Mizzi? And how are you, Rudi, and your parents? Thank you for returning the ladder to where you had found it last summer, Rudi."

Lili developed a broad smile and Tante Marianne a most quizzical look. Lili burst into laughter as soon as Mrs. Stein's group had passed beyond earshot. "Well, what was all that about a ladder, Rudi?" asked Tante Marianne.

"'Twas nothing," responded Rudi.

"Rudi?" Tante prompted.

Lili burst out laughing. "I'll tell you, Tante Marianne." And Lili did, in complete detail, to Tante Marianne's delight as Rudi got up and went for a walk.

"Meine Guete, was he that persistent, Lili?" Lili just nodded with a smile. "He must have been lovestruck as soon as you pressed a few coins into his hand and he looked into your eyes. It is a wonder I haven't heard about this incident before, as I am sure a number of neighbours wouldn't have missed that little episode, however late in the evening. They miss nothing around here. They live for little incidents they can gossip about in this village."

Rudi returned from his little walk.

"You are as romantic as that father of yours, Rudi. No one risked their lives up a ladder to court me. Help me up before we all fall down laughing at the image of you tippy-toeing around with that long ladder. Here, give me your arm, you rascal." Tante Marianne grabbed Lili by the other arm and whispered, "I'm very happy he was so persistent."

They all walked home with that same Romeo and Juliet image, Lili attempting to sing a little from Gounod's opera. Rudi gave her a bit of a look, and she wasn't sure whether it was because she was so off key or because she was mocking him. They were all still smiling when they reached home and had lemonade.

Tante Marianne prepared a large platter of cheeses, sausage, and ham with salad items and asked Rudi to open a bottle of wine. "Red or white, Tante Marianne?"

"I don't mind; why don't you ask Lili?"

"A red is better with cheese, don't you think, Tante Marianne?" Lili asked.

"You are right, Lili. Rudi, why don't you open the Lambrusco from Northern Italy?" They had a hearty and joyous meal, Tante Marianne continuing to chuckle at the image of Rudi at the top of a ladder. "You should have demanded that he sing to you before agreeing to meet him, Lili."

"I should have," she agreed. "Had I known he has such a wonderful voice, I would have." Lili smiled at Rudi. They were all soon beginning to nod off at the table, so they called it a night.

THE FOLLOWING MORNING Lili decided to give the beach a miss, as it was extremely hot, and she thought a little reading and quiet time with Tante Marianne would be a good break from the sun and sand. Rudi would be at the lake all morning, so she took out her book and began reading straight after breakfast, while Auntie continued knitting something for the future. Tante Marianne looked at Lili quizzically. "I'm reading *A Room with a View* by Forster...E.M. Forster. He is an English writer. It's a story set in Italy and in England, and it's about a young woman. It's a romance. It's very good so far." Lili kept reading for some time, until Tante Marianne put down her knitting and rubbed her left hand. "Tante Marianne, would you take me shopping in the village? I need to buy some chocolates or something to celebrate the anniversary of Rudi's and my first meeting."

"That was a year ago?"

"A ha, this week."

"Well, of course we should get something. Come, let's go." Tante Marianne went to the door to put on her sandals.

It was late morning, wind still, and very hot. "Pity there isn't a little breeze to provide some relief," suggested Tante Marianne as she led Lili straight to a chocolate shop. Lili selected a box of Italian zwetchken in dark chocolate and had them wrapped in an extra layer of paper for protection against the heat. She took Tante Marianne's arm, and was steered in the direction of a café known for its excellent ice cream. They sat at a table furthest from the door. "Ja, Maria," Tante Marianne exclaimed at the size of the ice cream as she attacked it with gusto nevertheless. She smiled. "Did you notice Rudi is losing his hair, Lili?"

"Yes, I'm probably the cause of that. He doesn't care, and I certainly don't, as he is so handsome anyway." They returned home, cheerily chatting about Rudi and without wasting any time. They had just sat down to a cold lemonade when Rudi walked in.

"Ach du liebe Zeit; you're as red as a beetroot, Rudi," declared Tante Marianne. "Have a lemonade."

Rudi downed his lemonade then took a shower only to emerge redder than before. "You really are as red as a beetroot, Rudi; are you OK?" asked Lili.

"This is normal for me. My distant relations were red Indians."

Tante Marianne had prepared a plate of cold cuts with some semmel and a variety of breads for lunch. Lunches were normally at home after a morning at the lake, Lili and Tante Marianne staying at home several mornings because of the heat. They were happy to chat, knit, and read. On late afternoons the three invariably went to the lake together.

On a day forecast to be the hottest yet, Lili and Rudi decided to go up into the mountains. Lili requested they go back into the Gerlitzen, where they had skied last winter and where Rudi had taken her a year before, nearly to the day. As they got ready straight after a heartier breakfast than normal at the insistence of Tante Marianne,

Lili burst out laughing. "I look ridiculous with these boots and a dress. Do I really have to wear them, Rudl?"

"Ja, Schatzerl; I promise I won't laugh. You are less likely to slip with those boots." They hurried out to try to gain some altitude before the heat of the day, carrying a lunch Tante Marianne had prepared. Rudi decided on a less strenuous route, and they wandered hand in hand, first along the Ossiachersee shore and then up a moderately gently slope. Just before they were about to emerge onto the plateau, they were both startled as they looked straight into the eyes of a Gamms, statuesque and only metres away. Lili quickly took a step back and behind Rudi. "No fear. She's more scared of us than we of her. Isn't she beautiful?" whispered Rudi, cupping his hand over his mouth.

"Speak for yourself; he's huge."

"It's a she."

Lili shook her head. "She's huge; why won't she go away?"

"She's saying the same thing about us. 'Why won't they go away?'" Rudi started forward abruptly, and the chamois leapt to one side and noisily disappeared downhill.

"Why did you do that, Rudl?"

"I thought you were frightened."

"I was just beginning to like her."

As they reached the gentle grassy slopes humming with bees, they felt the hot sun on their backs. They trudged towards the summit, reaching the outcrop of rocks where Rudi had last picked an Edelweiss for Lili. There were none to be found. "Must have all been plucked by those German and Italian tourists who have already visited this season," he suggested. Lili smiled and led Rudi to the summit, where he was peering towards the northwest. He named several peaks that Lili enquired about and remarked that there were foreboding clouds in the same direction as there had been the last time they were there. On the way down, Rudi, humming a tune, steered Lili to the same spot by the stream where they had picnicked before. There was a big embrace before Rudi took his pack off, revealing a large wet area on his shirt. He had Lili help him spread a large tablecloth on the grass, and they had a hearty lunch. Lili rummaged through the pack and found two pieces of Streuselkuchen and a small paper bag with some other items. They ate the cake happily, and Rudi opened the paper bag and pulled out two chocolates in the shape of small eggs.

Lili laughed her head off and took them from Rudi. She then wished him a very happy anniversary, gave him a passionate kiss, and said, "These are to celebrate our anniversary. Happy anniversary!"

"What anniversary?"

"Eat this and think about it, Rudl," she said as she had him bite into a chocolate-covered prune, although a little softer than ideal. Lili had the other half, and they spent the next minute laughing and licking fingers as Rudi figured out it was just a year before that he and Lili had first met. They each had a second chocolate and just looked at each other as they reflected on the year that had passed. Rudi thought about how much he had experienced and learned during the last year, while Lili could barely believe how happy and contented she'd been since meeting him. Rudi also thought about his last ski run with Franz only fifty or so metres away, and he had to clench his teeth together to prevent himself from crying. He did not want to spoil the moment for Lili.

Using the pack and pullover as pillows, they both fell asleep. Lili had a wonderful dream of plunging naked with Rudi into a bracing stream and both holding each other tight to keep from being swept away. Rudi dreamt of Joseph's parents packing to leave, but instead of getting ready to leave Munich, they were preparing to leave Vienna.

Keeping their dreams to themselves and holding hands, Rudi and Lili skipped their way downhill, quietly singing, with Lili also trying to imitate Rudi's whistling with little success and a lot of laughter. They arrived at Tante Marianne's hot, happy, and hungry and just in time for Rudi to help her water the garden. Watering time was always during the half hour prior to it getting dark, when plants had already cooled down a little and would recuperate before the next day's heat. They all soon found themselves sitting around the kitchen table with ein Gesprizter (white wine and soda water) and shared their day's adventures, however small.

Tante Marianne jokingly scolded Rudi, "What, you didn't remember your anniversary? You'll have to do a lot better with your first wedding anniversary."

"You could write to me every year to remind me," suggested Rudi. Lili squeezed his arm hard. "Ouch, you hurt me."

"Good," responded Lili as she took another sip and winked at Tante Marianne.

Rudi poured himself another drink and left out the soda. Lili and Tante Marianne were quickly poured the same, and they were all soon seriously having a dinner of gebratene Wildente- wild duck, which a neighbour had brought back from a recent hunt and given to Tante Marianne, knowing she had guests. The neighbour had suggested that the visitors not be told of the source of dinner as a city girl might be a bit squeamish about such matters. Tante Marianne apologized that fruit salad was the dessert that evening, as she was not up to baking anything, it being so hot. Lili soon produced the remainder of the chocolate prunes, which prompted Tante Marianne to pour a little liqueur and propose a cheeky toast directed at Rudi, suggesting he need not be so shy. "After all, how long can a young lady be kept waiting?"

THE FOLLOWING MORNING Lili and Tante Marianne shared several tears as they said goodbye, Rudi and Lili being expected for lunch at his parents' house on their way back to Vienna. Tante Marianne washed the tears from her face and phoned to let Rudi's parents know they were coming. The Auers had spent quite some time getting ready for their guests, the stationmaster cleaning the apartment and his face of whiskers, and Mother carefully preparing a platter of charcuterie and cheeses. Rudi the senior was always particular about his appearance and put on his best suit and tie; the only concession he was prepared to make because of the heat was to forego wearing a waistcoat. Mother, being much more sensible, changed into a light summer frock and open sandals a short while before Rudi and Lili's expected arrival.

The four had a very nice lunch, the open window allowing a breeze, though not as cool as Mr. Auer would have preferred, as he needed to frequently mop his brow. There was no political talk or reference to any threatening weather, just some comparison about cultural offerings between Villach and Vienna. Lili felt really bad when Rudi's mother stated that they would love to visit Vienna but could not afford the expense. Rudi's father immediately contradicted her and stated he'd been regularly saving a little extra for a trip quite soon. Mother raised her eyebrows, which Rudi and Lili interpreted correctly. They also interpreted correctly the intent of her asking, "Did Tante Marianne show you the lovely things she has been knitting for the future?"

"Yes, Mother. She told us that knitting was good for her arthritis," Rudi said as he and Lili both smiled and rolled their eyes in unison.

There were many hugs and kisses before Rudi the senior escorted his son and Lili to the station. He marched ahead, and there were several greetings of "Habidiere" as he raised his hat several times at passersby. Lili could barely contain herself as she immediately conjured up an image of Charlie Chaplin in *The Tramp*, which she had seen at home during one of several cinema evenings her father had organized a couple of years ago. Lili was concerned for the welfare of her ribs as she received bear hugs from the stationmaster. A few tears welled up in his eyes, and he turned and waddled off in Chapilnesque fashion.

23

RUDI'S WRITINGS POORLY RECEIVED

RUDI AND LILI arrived back at the apartment without incident. "Shalom, my friends."

"Servus, Joseph. How is Ester? How are your parents? How was Munich?"

"Ester is fine, thank you very much. My parents are not in good shape; my mother is still crying a lot. Munich seems confused. There are many people in support of Hitler, especially if they think their economic circumstances will improve, and there are many others who see freedoms taken away and recognize the party propaganda for what it is. Since the middle of July, the Nazi Party is the only party in Germany, so thinking people see this as a real concern."

"How are the people handling the actions against their Jewish neighbours?" asked Rudi.

"People think mainly about themselves, I'm afraid."

"So are your parents still preparing to leave, Joseph?" asked Lili, somewhat concerned for Joseph's mother.

"Mother wants to leave, but Father is not so sure. They both have work in Munich and are getting by, and he is not so confident of finding work should they move somewhere else." Joseph shrugged his shoulders.

"But the harassment against Jews must be becoming quite unsettling," suggested Rudi. "I read of two hundred Jewish merchants being arrested in Nuremberg and paraded through the streets just recently."

Joseph shrugged his shoulders again. "What can you do?"

———

JOSEPH AND RUDI spent the next several weeks concentrating on their uni work, and Rudi spent considerable time in Café Louvre to keep up to date with matters political, as he had a request from the uni paper editor for another article. He was rather reluctant but was encouraged by Joseph. "Yours is a very important voice at the uni," he declared.

One afternoon Rudi was quietly walking up Wipplingerstrasse on his way to Café Louvre when he heard a lot of noise: pounding footsteps and yelling. He could see several young men being chased by police. Wanting to get out of harm's way, he ran into a side street and down some steps and found himself in a semi-dark passage that stank pungently of horse manure. Curious as to the extent of this underground world, he wandered around many curves and followed steps up and down and around. There was not a horse to be seen, nor any people. The air was dry; shafts of light were coming in through small, dirty windows, and it was quite dry underfoot on a clay floor. Rudi was lost. He had lost his bearings completely and was very surprised when he saw direct daylight at the end of steep steps leading into a courtyard. He looked around. He was two blocks away from where he went underground, and there was no longer any smell of horse manure, nor the sounds of police in pursuit. He continued to Café Louvre, as he had planned, and spent several hours reading and formulating the contents of his next article.

"Bitte sehr, Rudi?"

"Ein Paar Wuerstel und ein Bier, bitte, Herr Ober."

Rudi decided the focus of his article would be on what had been happening in Germany and how this might impact Vienna in the future. He wrote himself some notes:

Germany moving toward securing an autocratic state,

All opposition parties have been eliminated,

Media has been turned into a very effective propaganda machine for the Nazis,

Many people sucked in by the propaganda and promises of a better economic future for them,

Aryanization a powerful movement,

Jews severely discriminated against in most spheres of life,

Hitler has designs to annex Austria and extend the Aryanization to Austria with the negative impact not only on the whole Jewish community but on all of Austria,

Anti-Semitism will be rife.

"Was that good, Rudi?" asked Herr Ober. "Another beer perhaps?"

"No, thank you."

Rudi went home and discussed the proposed contents of the article with Joseph. "Your audience, Rudi, is university people, so you could make greater reference to uni attitudes and likely effects on university life in the future."

"I was steering away from that because I don't want to be hit over the head again by any Brownshirts."

"Yes, but you can't allow yourself to be intimidated by the right wing. You must write what is relevant and true for your whole audience."

Rudi completed his article and really worried about a section he believed would bring trouble. He had written:

The evidence suggests that at least some of the university administration supports the Deutsche Studentenschaft in its campaign to thwart the progress of Jewish students at the university. The administration does little to prevent the anti-Semitism around campus. There are regular acts of intimidation, harassment, and even actions to prevent Jewish students from attending lectures.

Evidence also exists of Jewish lecturers not being appointed when they are clearly the outstanding candidates and of Jewish professors not having their positions renewed, while non-Jewish lecturers and professors gain preferential treatment.

"What a Mensch, Rudi! That's exactly as it is, and it's incumbent on you to state the truth in this regard."

"I've made similar statements before and now wear several life-long scars to prove it."

"Don't worry, Rudi. Lili will still love you even with an extra few scars. In any event, any goy with a few scars is superior to a blemish-free Jew," said Joseph with a smile. "You have no choice, Rudi. Didn't the American president Lincoln once say something like, 'The press is the greatest instrument for enlightening the mind of man and improving him as a moral and rational social being'? Something like that."

Rudi showed his article to the editor, Heinrich, who was very pleased and made just a few minor alterations. The article, titled "Political Developments in Germany Spell Bad News for Austria," came out in late October 1933.

On Thursday afternoon Rudi was enjoying a lecture when a young man walked in and interrupted the professor. The professor looked up at Rudi. "Herr Auer, bitte. You are excused from class; you must report to the main administration office at once." Dozens of eyes followed Rudi out the door. Unlike the last time Rudi was summoned to the administration, also on a Thursday, he had no doubts as to why he might be summoned this time.

"Herrein…what is your name?" Rudi was asked when he arrived.

"Rudi Auer."

"Rudolf Auer?"

"Ja."

"Sit down, please. We seem to have met with you before."

Three stern-faced men, all grey at the temples and beyond their middle age, sat at the table opposite Rudi. The one seated in the middle carefully and slowly opened a folder in front of him and took out the latest edition of *Die Universitaet's Zeitung*. He picked it up, turned the page, creased it down the middle, then held it up and handed it to the person on his right. He walked it around to the other side of the table and placed it in front of Rudi. *Here we go again,* thought Rudi.

"Did you write this?"

"Ja."

"Did anyone help you write it or contribute to it?"

"Nein."

"You wrote this by yourself?"

"Ja."

"Did you have a mental breakdown when you wrote this?"

"Nein."

"You realize these allegations are very serious?"

"Yes."

"Where is the evidence for these allegations?"

"I have evidence. You have the same evidence: the recording of incidents against Jews and the statistics about the employment of and promotion of Jewish professors in comparison to non-Jewish professors."

"Quatsch!"

"No, it is true. The statistics are available for anybody who wants to dig for them."

"You should give up digging, Auer, and concentrate on your studies. Do you wish to make trouble?"

"No, I do not."

"You must promise not to write anything that reflects poorly on members of the university."

"Of course."

"Do you understand?"

"Yes."

"If there is another infraction, you will be summoned to appear before the UBD…the University Disciplinary Board."

Rudi heard a side conversation: "They would not want the publicity that such a hearing would attract right now, alles klar?" The three grey men nodded in unison.

"Herr Auer, do you understand?"

"Yes."

"That would be very serious. Do you understand?"

"Yes, I do."

"The next time you will be in extremely serious trouble for undermining the good standing of our beloved university. Do you understand? You are dismissed. Use the door on your left."

As had occurred before in the same situation, Rudi did not breathe until he was outside. He left the uni grounds and soon headed down Wipplingerstrasse. When he got to Café Louvre, Rudi hesitated, thought the better of it, and went straight home, looking over his shoulder every few steps until he turned into Salzgasse.

"Verdammt noch a mal, Joseph; they want to hide their own statistics that show them to be anti-Semitic. They warned me again, just more severely than last time."

"Of course, Rudi. That they didn't send you immediately before the University Disciplinary Board suggests they are guilty of the behavior you accused them of."

Unexpectedly, Lili came to the door and was let inside immediately. "Sorry, I had to see you, Rudi; I had this feeling that something terrible happened to you."

"No, nothing, Schatzerl; everything is OK."

"Servus, Joseph, how are you?"

Joseph wanted to hide the latest uni newspaper that was lying on the table. He was too slow. Lili picked it up and began to leaf through it.

"You didn't tell me, Rudi."

"What, Schatzerl?"

"That you had written another article." Lili read Rudi's article; she turned red in the face and began to fume. "Are you crazy? Do you want to ruin your university career and our relationship? Have you gone out of your mind, Rudolf Auer? It is not possible to attack the administration without suffering severe consequeces. You surely know that."

"I already met with the administration today," he responded.

"You are so stupid, Rudolf Auer," Lili said as she got up and marched around the room. "Do you not see how you jeopardize our relationship? This will probably convince Mother, Mr. Schwartz, and probably Walter that you are too immature."

"Lili, Lili," interrupted Joseph, "it is incumbent on Rudi to write it as he sees it; and what's more, he's correct. Rudi is a man of principle, a real Mensch."

"To hell with you too, Joseph, egging Rudi on. You don't write this stuff and put your neck on the line." Joseph and Rudi both turned red in the face. "Well, what happened at the meeting with the administration?" asked Lili, a little less hot under the collar. Rudi went through the whole meeting in detail. "Well, I'm going home now. I'm fed up with both of you. A relationship has to be open, Rudi, and you told me nothing about this article. I can find the door myself." With that, Lili marched out, Rudi and Joseph dumbstruck and still red in the face.

There were no repercussions from students or staff for Rudi's article, just a few complimentary comments from fellow students and a couple of professors. Rudi continued to look over his shoulder rather frequently nevertheless. One evening he was sure someone was lurking in the shadows near his apartment. He decided that if he was ever to write for the paper again, he would certainly discuss it with Lili first.

—※—

WEEKS WENT BY as Rudi continued with his university work, managing to keep up but only just. He was more interested in following political developments in Germany and in Austria, and he spent some hours at Café Louvre most days, keeping abreast of the news. Nazis continued to consolidate their power in Germany, Hitler ridding Germany of many opposition characters through intimidation, imprisonment, or murder. The media, the theatre, the opera, the music, literature, and art displayed in galleries were increasingly restricted to what Hitler approved of. Yet he seemed to progressively improve his popularity ratings.

Rudi read about the death penalty being imposed for anti-fascists in Germany, absolutely marking the end of any semblance of democracy. He had just read a back copy of the *New York Times*, which relayed the information that Albert Einstein was one of the thousands of Jews who had already fled Germany and arrived in the Unites States in July. The *Times* went on to explain, "At the request of the International Relief Association, headed by Albert Einstein, an American committee has been formed to assist Germans suffering from the policies of the Hitler regime."

Rudi was also worried about the attacks on democracy in Austria. Dollfuss was, as was Hitler in Germany, amassing dictatorial power and gleeful at getting rid of "parliamentarianism," as he called it. Rudi was not at all pleased with the events of the December tenth Catholic Day celebrations either, when the justice minister called Austria "a Catholic country," providing a smack in the eye to Jews and other non-Catholics. Rudi was also quite dismayed when he read that in the November elections in Germany, the Nazis had received 92 percent of the vote. *How ignorant or thoroughly hoodwinked can the German people be?* he thought.

RUDI'S BIRTHDAY CAME and went with a very nice dinner in his apartment, cooked by Lili. She insisted. Joseph was staying with Ester on that Friday evening, and she had never prepared a celebratory meal for Rudi. There was as much cuddling as there was cooking. Lili prepared Rudi's favorite meal of Wiener Schnitzel followed by Kaiserschmarrn and Apfelmus. She had asked Mr. Schwartz for advice about an appropriate wine, and after lunch he presented her with a bottle from Bordeaux. "It would give me great pleasure for you to share this wine with Rudi; it is lighter than the normal Bordeaux and should be perfect with Schnitzel."

Lili had Rudi open it to let it breathe, while she opened a half bottle of champagne and poured it into two newly purchased glasses, as she wasn't able to remember whether there were any suitable in the apartment. They drank a toast and kissed. Lili also presented Rudi with a gift-wrapped package, so large that he could not possibly guess what might be inside.

"It's big enough for a collapsible table or perhaps a chair…no, a picnic hamper. Perhaps a new eiderdown, as the one I have has seen better days."

Lili smiled. "No, but it is something to replace something that has seen better days." Rudi had no clue. "Open it, Rudl. I'm curious as to what you'll think."

Rudi took great care in unwrapping the parcel, and a big smile appeared across his face as he admired a new violin case with his initials in gold lettering. "Well, open it, Rudl."

"Wait a moment. I must fold this nice paper so that I can use it to wrap Christmas presents. Thanks so much, Schatzerl. So you noticed a hinge being held together by some wire?" Rudi jumped up to give

Lili a passionate embrace then went to the bedroom to fetch his violin. He took it out of the old case and set it down ever so gently in the new one. "I'm sure it has a better tone already," he remarked as he leaned the old case against the wall near the front door for early disposal.

Rudi was about to start playing when Lili invited him to sit at the table as she lit the candle and asked him to pour the wine. "Prost, the Schnitzel is perfect, Lili. The wine is excellent too; pass on to Mr. Schwartz a big thank-you from me." The Kaiserschmarrn was a little burnt, but Rudi didn't say so.

After dinner Rudi played a little violin. "That's Schubert," declared Lili.

"Yes, and this?"

"Johann Strauss."

"And this?"

"Mozart."

They both smiled, and Rudi put the violin away, taking a cloth to first remove the dust on the top of the wardrobe. He sneezed three times and thanked Lili again for her gift.

They discussed the possibility of spending some of the Christmas holidays skiing in Italy, but due to Rudi's lack of funds and Tante Marianne's insistence, they decided to virtually replicate their previous Christmas holiday. Lili was very happy about that, as she had developed a very warm relationship with Tante Marianne. She also enjoyed spending time with Rudi's parents. While Rudi was to travel to Villach on Thursday, 21 December, Lili would travel there the following Wednesday, 27 December, when Tante Marianne would expect them in the late afternoon that same day. This would also allow Lili to spend Christmas with her mother and Walter, who planned to be in Vienna until the end of December. Lili was really looking forward to spending more than a couple of hours with Walter, as she sensed considerable unease, if not upheaval, in Europe, and she had not really spent any significant time with him for more than a year.

24

CHRISTMAS 1933 AND BEYOND

RUDI AND LILI went Christmas shopping alone and together and spent an afternoon wrapping presents in the Salzgasse apartment while singing carols, as they had done last year. Lili wouldn't allow Rudi to use the secondhand paper from his birthday present, declaring it was not festive enough, though really being of the view that the idea itself was tacky. She bought him a fountain pen and included a little personal note, while Rudi purchased tickets for the premier of "Giuditta," a musical comedy by Franz Lehár, at the Vienna State Opera for 20 January of the following year. Jarmila Novotná and Richard Tauber were to play the leading roles. Rudi was really excited to hear Tauber live.

On the day after the last candles were lit on menorahs throughout Vienna, most of them in Leopoldstadt, Rudi took the train to Villach, as had been decided, and Walter arrived in Vienna a day later. Walter and Lili spent a great deal of time together chatting, playing piano duets, and singing. Lili went shopping with her brother to help him purchase a gift for their mother, and they spent considerable time in cafés, chatting about all and sundry. Rudi came up in the conversation quie a lot, and Walter pronounced, "You are obviously meant for each other, Lili, for every time his name is mentioned, your whole face lights up."

"Oh, thank you for saying that, Walter, for until we are actually married, there are still little doubts that creep into my head."

"Is Rudi still following politics to the same extent as the last time we spoke, Lili?"

"Yes, he is, and he's really very worried about the developments both in Germany and in Austria."

"Why is he worried about Austria? Dollfuss is severely against the Nazis and has recently banned the party in Austria, hasn't he?"

"He sees Dollfuss as very weak and likely unable to stem the increasing anti-Semitism here. Anti-Semitism has clearly been worsening, especially in Germany."

"Rudi is right; it is getting worse."

"You know, Walter, no one believed Rudi when he was first warning people against the increase in anti-Semitism."

"Yes, I think that many people increasingly understand the rise of anti-Semitic actions now and an attempt, at least in Germany, to Aryanize everything. I just read the other day that Erich Kleiber resigned as conductor from the Berlin Opera. He apparently conducted Alban Berg's opera 'Lulu,' which was branded as degenerate music by the Nazi Party. Do you know 'Lulu,' Lili?" Lili shook her head. "Kleiber," continued Walter, "is not even Jewish and could have easily continued his career under the Nazis, but he resigned from his post in protest."

"Good for him."

On Christmas Eve in the apartment on the Ringstrasse, there was a very pleasant dinner, a happy exchange of gifts, and some joyousness as Lili and Walter played some duets on the piano, which their mother just had tuned on the off chance that it might be used. Kafka and Bela were noisy until they received their presents and a cuddle. Lili smiled a big smile as she took in the details of Rudi's gift and passed over the opera tickets for Walter to see. He passed them on to their mother. "Very nice," she declared. "I loved his 'Merry Widow.' And to go to the premiere, with Tauber singing, will be very special, Lili."

The next morning a phone call came for Walter.

"Have you heard? Yesterday a Paris express train was derailed, and there are more than one hundred and fifty people dead and close to three hundred injured."

"Ach du liebe Zeit. Um Gottes Willen, nein!" The caller was a work colleague, and the news saddened the rest of the Christmas period as accounts of the accident dominated the radio news for days.

It was cold and gently snowing as Rudi the senior met his son on the platform in Villach on the afternoon of 21 December. Rudi the junior found himself saying "Habidieri" several times along with his father while walking back to the apartment through several inches of powder. He smiled inwardly, recollecting Lili's Charlie Chaplin impersonations that she had tried several times in recent months.

Maria Auer opened the door as they walked up the steps and gave Rudi a big bear hug and several kisses on the cheek. "Ja, Rudi, you look good. Did you have a nice trip? How is Lili? Have you been getting enough sleep? Are you hungry?" she asked as she led father and son inside without giving them sufficient time to shake off all the snow.

"Look at the mess you made!" Rudi quickly took a broom and shovel and collected the loose snow and returned it outside. "Are you not hungry?" asked his mother. "Have at least a little something." She placed some old Apfelstrudel and some fresh Lebkuchen in front of Rudi at the small table in the living room. "Kaffee oder heisse Schokolade, Rudi? How is your university work? Have you been eating properly? Does Lili cook for you often? Is she a good cook? Does her mother cook a lot too? Have you been able to keep warm?"

Rudi's father rolled his eyes in harmony with the rhythm of his wife's questions then asked his own. "Are you married yet, you and Lili?"

"No, but who would it be if it were not Lili?"

Smart-arse, thought his father, who just smiled.

The following evening Rudi accompanied his parents to the local Gasthaus for dinner and dancing, which they had done regularly for as long as they could remember. Herr Wirt greeted them immediately and sat them at their normal table, furthest from the door and away from the band. Father took Mother onto the dance floor, as it was nearly empty. "Come, Mother, before there's no room to move." They danced well together, as the regulars always got a kick out of watching Maria towering over her husband, who was a good head shorter.

Several young local women noticed Rudi sitting on his own and giggled. One went over to him. "Can we dance with you tonight? Next time your fiancé might be here, and we'd have no chance." Rudi danced off with the young lady, and her friends giggled again.

The Gasthaus was soon full, and the evening was very pleasant, the band playing as well as normal and the band leader's quips also the same as usual. They left close to midnight, Herr Wirt looking forward to seeing them on New Year's Eve, and they trudged home through a few centimetres of new snow, Rudi's mother's arms hooked into her husband on one side and son on the other.

———

RUDI SPENT A very pleasant and relaxed short week with his mother and father. He slept on the couch in the living room, and hence the responsibility for keeping the apartment warm fell on his shoulders. Whenever the cold woke him, he would add some more coal to the stove. He easily fell into the rhythm of his parents' daily comings and goings. He helped his mother with the shopping and father with the housecleaning, which was invariably interrupted as he'd find a newspaper article he hadn't read or finished.

On Christmas Eve, his mother went to much trouble to prepare a very nice meal, and there was much anticipation and joy when it came to gift-opening time, parcels having been delivered the previous week from Onkel Julius, Tante Frieda, the Railway Workers' Union, Onkel Max, and various others. Rudi carefully unwrapped his gift from Lili, his father's and mother's eyes ever attentive. He took the fountain pen out of its box. "The instrument of a professor," declared Father, as Rudi read the accompanying greeting and smiled. "For My Love, Merry Christmas. May you never run out of ink for important jottings, including an occasional love letter to me." Father snatched the note from Rudi, smiled, and passed it on to Mother, who also smiled.

They spent the next few days doing lots of eating, a little drinking, and a little walking, always together. They talked about most things and naturally about politics, as both Rudi and his father were alarmed about the leadership in Austria, both agreeing that Dollfuss was becoming as much a dictator as Mussolini to the south and Hitler to the northwest. Rudi predicted difficult times ahead, and his father agreed, suggesting that all three leaders were up to no good and that the Church in Rome had a lot to answer for as well. Rudi talked with his father about the growing influence of the right wing within the university, and his father was about to give him some advice but, on a hunch, thought better of it.

RUDI AND HIS father went to fetch Lili from Villach station just after noon on 27 December, Rudi's father suggesting he'd benefit from the air. Rudi nearly lost his footing as he embraced Lili and twirled her around in a couple of circles. "Be careful, children," warned his father. "How are you, Lili? You look wonderful."

Lili gave each Rudi a bag and took each by the arm. Father found it quite difficult to perform his "Habidieri" greetings, both hands occupied, as he recognized several people on the way home. Mother stood at the open door as they approached the steps and warmly embraced Lili. "You look wonderful, Lili. The three of you please shake the snow off," she said as she ushered them inside.

Lili opened a bag and presented Rudi's mother and father each with beautifully gift-wrapped boxes. Father folded the wrapping paper very carefully and set it aside. Each had a pair of warm leather gloves inside. They beamed from ear to ear as they said thank you, gave Lili a kiss, and tried them on. "Perfect, thank you," said Mother.

"Perfect," agreed Father as there were more kisses.

The phone rang. "Is she there yet?"

"Ja, Marianne, they'll be with you late afternoon," Father said.

An assortment of freshly baked biscuits and some Lebkuchen were put on the table as everybody accepted their hot chocolate. Mother gave Father a look as he sloshed a little cognac into his and offered the others the same. "It was only a drop, Mother."

Mrs. Auer had questions: "Does Rudi look after himself in Vienna, Lili? Is the apartment warm? Does he sleep enough?" Father raised his eyebrows. "Does he eat properly? Do you cook for him sometimes? Does your mother cook too?"

Time was getting on, and Mr. Auer was beginning to nod off, when there was another phone call: "Have they left yet?"

"No, Marianne, they are getting ready to leave now," Father said.

———

MARIANNE COULD HEAR the whistle as the train pulled into the station. Six minutes later she looked out the window and opened the door. "Ja, meine Lieben! You look wonderful. Bussi." There were several noisy kisses. Lili presented Tante Marianne with a small gift-wrapped box and some biscuits from Rudi's mother. Rudi took out six bottles of wine from his pack and put them on a counter in the kitchen then sat at the table as Tante Marianne was carefully folding the wrapping paper. She admired a pair of leather and woolen gloves. "You shouldn't have, Lili. I've never had such a fancy pair. Thank you so much. You are so kind."

Marianne ensured the table was clean by sweeping her pullovered arm across the top and, with a gleam in her eye, produced several items of knitted baby clothes. "But now I'm knitting in yellow; it's easier than white," she explained as she produced a half-completed nightshirt. "Rudi, what's holding you up? I'm getting impatient," she said as she smiled at Lili.

Just then there was a crashing noise outside. Lili jumped, and Rudi ran to the window. "Ah, don't worry," suggested Tante. "It's only our friendly deer. And it has a baby with her, only a few months old."

"Very nice, Tante; perhaps you could knit something for the baby," suggested Rudi, causing Lili to nearly spill her drink. "I'll let you know if it's a boy. Then you can knit in blue."

Tante Marianne shook her head as she continued, two plain, two purl. *Cheeky possum*, she thought.

Some appetizing food aromas were soon developing as Rudi took the hammer and some nails to repair the fence. "Ah, don't bother, Rudi; it's good if mother can find some food for her baby. We can fix the fence next summer, not that that keeps the foxes out. It's venison you can smell; I wanted to cook it tonight so that I won't cook it for you on Saturday because I'm sure you'll be having it on New Year's Eve at the Gasthaus."

Rudi and Lili smiled. "Is there anything I can do, Tante?" asked Lili.

"You could peel and cut the potatoes and carrots, and I can do a little more knitting. My arthritis is better at the moment. In fact it is much better when you are here than when you are not."

The venison was excellent, and so were the other five dinners that Tante Marianne would prepare. No one could complain about the weather either, although the snow was a bit sparse at first, as were German tourists. "One is a blessing, the other a pity," according to Rudi. He had recently read that Hitler had placed such a heavy tax on Germans wanting to vacation in Austria that it deterred many, hence depriving the Austrian tourist industry of revenue.

It was indeed pleasantly quiet on the Gerlitzen as Rudi and Lili spent their first day on the mountain finding their ski legs. As luck would have it, it snowed twenty or so centremetres that night, so the cover next morning was quite good, and there was less danger of them scratching the bottom of their skis. Rudi woke at first light. "Lili, we have fresh snow, lots of it; shall we go up early this morning?"

"Oh, Rudi, why don't you go? I'd only be a hindrance to you wanting to get as many runs on untracked snow as you could." Rudi was off and out in no time as Lili rolled over to continue her dream that Mussolini decided to instigate a rule in Italy that only non-Aryan Germans could ski on their mountains because the Nazis had forbidden so many Italian opera stars from performing in Germany. *That'd be fair.*

"Lili, where are you?" came a question from Tante Marianne.

"I was in Italy in my dreams, Tante Marianne."

"Can I pour your coffee?" Lili got dressed in record time. "What would you like for breakfast, Lili? Did you sleep well?"

"Just some toast, thank you, Tante Marianne; I can get it."

"Aberwas, sit down. I'm here already. So you slept well, Lili?"

"Yes, thank you, like a baby."

Tante Marianne took out her knitting and resumed two plain, two purl. She suddenly stopped and looked directly at Lili. "Is there anything wrong that you and Rudi haven't had a baby?" Lili turned a little red in the face. Nobody had asked her that before, and she was a little taken aback. "Sorry, I shouldn't have asked. I'm so sorry, Lili, but I am curious, of course."

"No, that's all right, Tante. We need to be married first, and the time isn't quite right yet."

"Well, how have you been able to avoid having a baby? I'm sure you're not a nun, and I know Rudi isn't a priest, healthy young things like you." They both laughed.

"I have an excellent doctor, a leading specialist in such matters."

"Oh!" Tante was satisfied and returned to her two plain and two purl. "With all your good planning, I'll have a cupboard full of these little items before you need any of them, Lili." Lili smiled and finished her coffee.

She went to her room to get a book. Tante Marianne noticed the cover. "Edith Wharton? Isn't that the same book you were reading last time, Lili?"

"No, Tante. The book is by the same author though, but it is a different story. It's about a woman by the name of Lily; that's why I picked it up. I haven't started it yet. It is *The House of Mirth,* and it supposedly tells the story of a Lily Bart, a woman who is torn between her desire for luxurious living and a relationship based on mutual respect and love…something like that. I thought it could be interesting." Lili read while Tante's needles continued to clink rhythmically to two plain, two purl, except when Tante paused to sip her cold coffee or to shake out her fingers to prevent them from cramping. After a while, the rhythmical sounds of knitting ceased, and Tante Marianne listed to her right and fell asleep. Not long after, Lili's book fell shut, she listed left, and, as her head touched the wall, she too promptly fell asleep.

Lili returned to her dream of earlier in the morning: Hitler, in retaliation against Mussoloni, decreed that all Italian operas were to be sung in German. However, they sounded so terrible sung in German that the opera buffs were outraged and stayed away in droves, and the opera industry across Germany fell into decay. The only way to restore order in the operas throughout Germany was to employ Jewish management.

Just then the clatter of skis returning to the back porch woke the two ladies, who were still in a daze as Rudi poked his head through the door. "With both of you out of it like that, a whole band of robbers could have come in and taken everything that is not screwed down."

"Close the door, Rudi. It's cold, and you sound more like your father every day." Marianne transformed herself within seconds, stoked the fire, and put on scrambled eggs. Lili barely had time to wash her face and Rudi to take off his boots when Tante Marianne sprinkled some chopped chives on each plate. "Mahlzeit," she declared. Tante could not think of anybody who did not love her scrambled eggs with butter on rye bread.

The afternoon turned to evening, and after a couple of days of pleasant skiing, the evening was New Year's Eve. As Lili and Rudi were about to depart, Tante Matrianne took Lili by both hands. "Let me look at you." Rudi looked handsome in the same grey suit he wore exactly a year before, and Lili was beautifully dressed in an ankle-length black dress, round neckline, tight around the hips and then full, designed for flowing movement. A short, green, double-breasted jacket matched midheeled, buttoned shoes.

"Do I pass?" asked Lili.

"With flying colors. Rudi, come here again." She adjusted Rudi's tie and farewelled both with a big kiss. "Make enough noise when you come in, so I can be sure you are home safely."

Rudi and Lili stepped into the crisp wintry evening, a little powder falling, and the fresh snow squeaking beneath their feet. They had to hurry their last few steps, as they heard the train approaching. They made it in good time to Villach to meet Rudi's parents, both ready to put on their coats. Rudi and Lili followed Rudi and Maria up the hill, Lili cheekily doing a little mimmicking of Rudi the senior's natural Charlie Chaplin interpretation. Rudi joined in the fun, and he and Lili giggled as they competed with each other to master the Chaplin waddle. Rudi the senior didn't notice as he marched Maria uphill at a good clip, arriving at the Gasthaus thirty metres ahead. "Did you get lost?" asked Rudi's father jokingly.

Herr Wirt greeted them warmly, especially Lili, whom he hadn't seen since summer. He showed them to their table furthest from the door and took their coats, Rudi the senior reminding everybody to take all valuables from their coat pockets.

"Is there something to drink here?" he asked. "One can develop a right thirst walking up the hill." Four glasses of white wine arrived immediately. "Prost, alle Lieben. Do you know in the past we were offered a selection of wine and even champagne? Yes, even champagne. That was before the economy went down the sewer; too many crooks in the banking system, of course."

The band was just warming up for the commencement of proceedings when Rudi's father led his wife onto the dance floor. "Better here now; it'll get too crowded soon." Strauss soon had the couple waltzing around the whole available floor area, but it soon became increasingly restricted as other couples joined in. Rudi spun Lili onto the dance floor as soon as the first Landler was played, and they were soon hot and hungry.

Venison was served, as had become the traditional main course, and the color of the wine changed from white to red. Herr Wirt came and asked the elder Rudi whether he could announce that Rudi and Lili were married. "They are not, but that wouldn't be the worst lie told in this establishment." At the next lull in the music,

Herr Wirt announced: "Dear guests, it pleases me greatly tonight to tell you that our most regular and loyal patrons, Rudi and Maria Auer...please stand...announce the recent marriage of their son, Rudi, to Lili Gruen, whom he met in Vienna...please stand. And we all thought Rudi was going to Vienna to study." Everybody in the hall chuckled, the Auer party looked at one another in astonishment, and the chuckling turned to applause.

"Give me your ring, Mother," asked Rudi. She hesitated but handed it to her son, who quickly slipped it onto Lili's finger, nearly getting the fingers mixed up. Mother smiled; she understood. "I wouldn't want them to think your son was too stingy to get his wife a ring." Everybody smiled, and there was soon a line of diners wanting to congratulate Rudi and Maria as much as Rudi and Lili. *What a circus,* thought Rudi and Lili, but they enjoyed the good wishes nevertheless and the champagne that now replaced the red. The band played the bridal waltz, and Rudi and Lili took the cue and were somewhat embarrassed as maybe a hundred pairs of eyes were on them. *Thank God Lili taught me to waltz so well,* Rudi thought as they waltzed backwards and forwards in perfect unison and error free. Lili whispered she was getting tired, so Rudi waltzed her back to their seats.

Though this was not a wedding ceremony, Lili and Rudi found themselves the center of attention and dancing with strangers for the next couple of hours. Lili was exhausted and Rudi nearly so as midnight approached. The champagne glasses were being filled around the room as Rudi reflected on this time the previous year, when a storm was quietly approaching from the northwest, and he wondered then as to its possible impact. He now knew it was an evil, wicked storm that spread not only across all of Germany but was impacting Austria as well.

As the last dance of 1933 had nearly come to an end and lovers were in a final embrace, the cymbals clanged, everybody jumped to their feet, and a raucous countdown began: "Fuenf, vier, drei, zwei, eins...Prosit Neu Jahr!" Champagne glasses clinked, and kisses and New Year's wishes were generously exchanged. The Auer party stood to leave, and Herr Wirt brought four coats and a wrapped bottle of champagne for the "newlyweds."

After many more wishes of good luck, the two Rudis, Maria, and Lili laughed all the way back to the apartment. "Not like last year, when there was a terrible storm in the making," declared Maria. Lili returned the borrowed ring as soon as they were inside, and everybody was again in stitches. As soon as they had all composed themselves, Rudi and Lili walked the short distance to the bus that took them back to Tante Marianne, fellow travelers wondering why they were giggling to each other for most of the journey.

Tante was awake as they entered, still chuckling. "Did you have too much to drink? You are both so red in the face and all giggly."

"We got married tonight."

"What? What do you mean you got married tonight?" asked Tante Marianne as she sat bolt upright in her bed and turned on the light.

"Without our consent," added Lili.

"What happened? Bussi first. Happy New Year to both of you. I wish you both a healthy, prosperous, and productive New Year." She gave each a big kiss and hug. Lili and Rudi both contributed to telling the tale. "And you had to dance with all these strangers? Some are not strangers to your mother and father, Rudi, but to you, Lili... you must both be exhausted."

"Shall we open the champagne now, Tante?" offered Rudi, a little less than sober.

"No, don't be silly," said Lili emphatically.

"Oh, it's a good bottle too. I think it can wait for a few more hours. I'm sure your bed is anxious to see you. Goodnight, meine Lieben."

Rudi and Lili couldn't stop giggling and recounting the evening's bizarre events for more than an hour before sleep found them.

POWDER SNOW HAD been falling for some time with excellent accumulations and the Kanzelbahn running for hours before Rudi and Lili surfaced. "Oh, we were very tired from last night; sorry we are so late, Tante Marianne."

"Here, have some coffee; it will do you good." Tante Marianne also produced some toast, Semmel, and a whole Guggelhupf. They all began to giggle again at the breakfast table. "Do you think Herr Wirt misunderstood, or was he having some fun at the expense of your father, Rudi?" queried Tante Marianne.

Rudi shrugged his shoulders as he wrapped his hands around the coffee mug and smiled at Lili. "Are we going skiing, Rudi? We only have today and tomorrow left." Rudi nodded in the affirmative, and Tante Marianne bounced up like a jack-in-the-box.

"Where are you going, Tante?" enquired Rudi.

She sat down again and shared a second slice of Gugglehupf with Lili. "We are in no hurry, Tante," said Lili, "but I need some exercise after all the good food I've been eating here."

It was not quite midday when Rudi and Lili headed to the Kanzelbahn with a lunch packed by Tante Marianne, including two insulated flasks. *No wonder this pack is heavier than usual,* thought Rudi. It was colder than usual for that time of year too, as light snow gave way to a clear sky. Lili replaced her gloves with a pair of mittens on the way up in the cable car, and they immediately stomped uphill to the summit, getting quite warm from the strenuous exercise. Rudi led Lili down a gentle slope for their first few turns of 1934 then selected increasingly steeper pitches that provided greater challenges.

When he led her to the rocky oucrop for their lunch break, she declared, "I was beginning to think you'd never stop." He gave her a kiss and unloaded the pack: a thin jacket for Lili to sit on, a paper bag with three Semmel, a tea towel with two bowls and two soup spoons, and two insulated flasks. "Tante Marianne is wonderful," declared Lili as Rudi screwed the top from the wider flask to reveal the aroma of a paprika-heavy goulash. It was splendid, the Semmel used to mop up the last skerrick. Several pieces of Lebkuchen and some piping-hot Gluehwein were next, and Lili wished she were sitting at Tante Marianne's table. She didn't let on, and they soon skied off again between the trees, Rudi finding several sections of untracked powder, which were always greeted with a brief yodel.

They took another trip up on the cable car and again trudged to the summit to check out their surroundings. The sky was blue above, but there was a distinct mist in surrounding valleys and heavier weather threatening from the direction beyond the Grossglockner. They skied basically the same route as the previous run, with Lili in the lead. She carved beautiful, rhythmic turns that led Rudi to admire how well she skied. She was constantly aware of Rudi, as he was continually humming behind her. Rudi took over the lead for the last, short, steep descent that brought them to Tante Marianne's back fence, which was now more down than up.

"Did you have fun?" asked Tante, poking her head into the back porch, where some derobing was taking place.

Lili rushed in, rubbing her hands. "Thank you for the wonderful lunch, Tante Marianne. Feel my hands." Tante Marianne gave Lili a kiss and her hands a rub as Lili moved toward the stove for increased warmth.

The next day was much like the one before—cold with a clear sky and crystals suspended in the air, providing a magical quality—as Rudi and Lili again enjoyed skiing on the Gerlitzen. The evening came too soon, especially for Lili, who needed to be back at work on Wednesday. She had a strange feeling in her gut that caused her to worry whether she would ever see Tante Marianne again, the weather from the northwest looking dirtier that day than it had the day before. Was that an omen?

Rudi soon popped the cork from their champagne wedding present, and there was again some mirth at the recollection of the events of the night before. They all wished each other a happy New Year, and Lili was pleased that no mention was made of when they'd see one another again. Rudi and Lili slept like logs and enjoyed their usual sumptuous breakfast with Tante Marianne, who was knitting when they made it to the kitchen.

They were soon packing in readiness for the journey back to Vienna when they heard the phone ring. "Das ist Marianne. Yes, they are still here. They will leave shortly and be with you in less than an hour. Servus."

There were hugs and kisses and a few tears at the door before Rudi swung his pack on his back, and he and Lili headed off, each with a large bag. Tante Marianne wiped tears from her face with her apron, waved a last goodbye, and closed her door.

Rudi and Lili walked up the steps as his father was shoveling some remnants of snow, a little having fallen earlier that day. "How is the young Auer couple today?" he queried with dancing eyes and as hugs and kisses were exchanged. Mother greeted Rudi and Lili equally warmly, her apron still in her hand.

They had a wonderful lunch of gebratene Ente and ein Gruener Veltliner, and Lili, with some concerns in her heart, suggested to Rudi's mother that she wished she could stay in Kaernten. Father said he also wished they could both stay. "With that triumvirate of fascist bandits—Mussolini, Dollfuss, and Hitler—we have no idea what will happen with our beloved Austria, but it is certain to affect you in Vienna before it affects us here in the country."

Mother pleaded that they write more frequently than Rudi had in the past as she and her husband waved goodbye to them from the doorway.

25

Vienna, Early 1934

THE TRAIN TRIP was uneventful, sleep making the journey seem shorter than usual. Vienna looked more beautiful even than normal, with a dusting of light snow over the rooftops, as Rudi and Lili arrived at the apartment.

Joseph had walked in not all that much earlier, as indicated by footprints leading to the front door. He was still unpacking. "Gruess Gott, Joseph."

"Shalom, Lili. Shalom, Rudi. How was your trip?"

"Very nice, thank you, Joseph. How are your parents? Anything changed?" enquired Lili.

Joseph looked up. "No, we had a very nice time, and Mother stopped crying after the first day. We kept filling her wine glass when she wasn't looking, making sure she was never sober. Father was in on it, of course. A happy drunk is always more pleasant company than someone unhappy and sober. She turned out to have a sense of humor I hadn't seen before," he declared.

"Are they still planning to emigrate?"

"I think the idea is on hold at the moment, as life has seemed a little more normal of late. There was the stabbing though of a couple of Jewish students in the neighbourhood just a little more than a week ago."

"Perhaps they are also getting used to so many attacks against Jews that it's becoming quite a normal part of life now," speculated Lili.

Rudi recounted the tale of the innkeeper, declaring that he and Lili had married, and Joseph thought that was just a great story. "Did you have anyone ask you, Lili, to change your mind and to run off with them instead?"

"No, but I realized the next morning that many men don't dance all that well because both my feet were quite bruised. How is Ester, Joseph?"

"She is well, but she is quite sick of the Nazi activities over there in her neighbourhood."

"Oh, that's terrible!"

"Just before we went away there were leaflets all around the streets warning people not to buy from Jewish shops, and fresh Hakenkreuzer appeared on the footpaths."

"Better tell Moshe he hasn't been doing his job," suggested Rudi. "How are he and Rachel?"

"I haven't seen or heard of them since halfway through Hanukkah. As I remember, he won most of the chocolate money playing the dreidel game. We should all get together again soon."

IT TOOK A few days to get back into a normal routine, and before Rudi and Lili realized, it was the 20 January, the night of the premier of "Giuditta" at the Vienna State Opera, a musical comedy in five scenes with music by Franz Lehár. Rudi was really excited to be hearing Richard Tauber live. "Who's playing the leading lady's role?" he asked as he put on his jacket."

"Jarmila Novotná. I know nothing about her," declared Lili, who was wearing the same outfit she wore on New Year's Eve.

Rudi put his gloves in his pocket and helped Lili on with her coat. It was a very cold evening as they stepped out, buttoning up as well as they could, complete with scarves and gloves. "Lehar wrote this especially for Tauber's voice, didn't he?" asked Lili as she grabbed Rudi tighter by the arm, feeling a little cold.

"Yes, that's why I particularly wanted to hear Tauber. He should be at his very best tonight."

They walked arm in arm up the grand staircase; the usher bid them a wonderful evening and opened their second-tier box door. They stuffed their gloves into a pocket of a coat and hung scarves and coats on the hooks behind their seats. Rudi had purchased front-row seats to ensure good visibility for Lili. "Nice seats," she declared as she kissed him on the cheek. "A wonderful present, Rudl." Lili had watched the conductor, Clemens Heinrich Krauss, many times before, she said, as he appeared at the lecturn. She didn't think he was anything special, though she couldn't say exactly why. Tauber's voice though was special—resilient and vibrant with wonderful resonance and on a par with that of Jussi Bjoerling, they both agreed.

But the show that night was not Tauber's...not that night. The night belonged to Jarmila Novotná, not just for the quality of her soprano voice but also the lyrics of the title aria. It began:

Ich weiß es selber nicht,
warum man gleich von Liebe spricht,
wenn man in meiner Nähe ist,
in meine Augen schaut und meine Hände küsst.

I don't understand myself
Why they keep talking of love,
When they come near me,
Look into my eyes and kiss my hands.

There were several encores with the most rapturous applause following the stanza that ended with the line: "Meine Lippen sie küssen so heiß!" When the last note was sung, Rudi and Lili bundled up for the cold and headed across the road, which Lili had done so many times before with her brother, Walter. Rudi was humming the "Giuditta" aria as they reached the café's front entrance. "Gruess Gott; fuer zwei?"

"Ya, bitte, Herr Ober." Lili and Rudi were led to a cosy table in Café Sacher. Rudi couldn't get the melody out of his head.

"This 'Giuditta' will become a big hit, I think. It will appeal to a lot of people, though it hasn't the tragic quality of a true opera," suggested Lili.

Rudi agreed just as the waiter returned to take their order. "Zwei Glasserl Champagne und einmal Esterhazie, bitte, Herr Ober." They enjoyed their cake, feeding each other a piece or two without anybody noticing. Lili took another sip then poured half a glass into Rudi's and had Rudi order her eine Heisse Schokolade. They talked about the performance, comparing their perceptions. They reread part of their program. It wasn't a real opera, but it was a pleasant enough comedy and beautifully, if not brilliantly, sung, they both agreed.

After leaving the café, they held on to each other's arms tightly to keep warm as they headed down Kaerntnerstrasse towards home. Rudi kept humming the same melody over and over until Lili recalled one of the aria's stanzas and began to sing with a little assistance from Rudi, who could not recollect the lyrics all that well though.

Meine Füße sie schweben dahin,
meine Augen sie locken und glüh'n
und ich tanz' wie im Rausch den ich weiß,
meine Lippen sie küssen so heiß!
My feet, they glide and float,
My eyes, they lure and glow,
And I dance as if entranced, because I know!
My lips kiss so hot!

"Meine Lippen sir küssen so heiß," Lili repeated as they closed the apartment door behind them.

DURING THE COMING days and weeks, Rudi again spent considerable time listening to the radio news and reading whatever foreign newspapers informed him of what was happening in Germany and there in Austria. Unfortunatly, newspapers coming out of Germany were severely sanitized, editors dictated to as to which stories they were allowed to write and how they were to be told. The whole world knew that. Rudi was utterly dismayed at the Germans' apparent acceptance of Hitler at the very time that their freedoms were obviously being curtailed, their culture heavily diminished, and fellow citizens—political opposition figures and Jews—being harassed, brutalized, and even expelled from their own homeland. He couldn't believe the rumours he had heard that even the Protestant churches were being pressured to accept the Aryan paragraph and expel converted Jews. *How is it that people accept these developments so freely?* he thought. *How can it be that the majority of the population can stand by to see the best teachers and professors being expelled, government workers being dismissed just because they are Jewish, and businesses—legal and well-run businesses—being closed down because they were owned by Jews? Do these Germans have no hearts? Do they have no sense? Do they not care as long as it does not happen to them? Is the whole population, the population at large, perhaps anti-Semitic? Where would such a sentiment come from? Have they no sense of what's fair and decent? Have they not heard of basic human rights? Perhaps they have become drunk with their own sense of superiority. Hitler has been constantly and incessantly pronouncing that Germans are superior beings on earth, the master race. Has it caused them to lose their sense of perspective? I don't know. I'm perplexed,* thought Rudi. He was not happy.

Heinrich had seen Rudi a couple of times in Café Louvre, and he suggested it was time he wrote another piece for the uni paper. "No, thank you, Heinrich; I haven't got time, and, in any event, it gets me into too much trouble. The uni administration is—"

"I hear you, Rudi. If you change your mind, we always like your slant on things. Servus."

Political developments in recent months at home in Austria had not impressed Rudi either. The government seemed to be in competition with the growing Austrian Nazi Party, although it had been officially banned. The party, of course, wanted Austria to join Germany. Dollfuss, to his credit, resisted fiercely, emphasizing that Austria was culturally and fundamentally Roman Catholic, while Germany was predominantly Protestant. Violence was always threatening, though, it seemed, and soon it escalated among the Nazis, the socialists, and Dollfuss's Austro-Fascists.

On 12 February 1934, trouble apparently broke out in Linz. A force led by Emil Fey, commander of the Heimwehr in Vienna, it was reported, searched Hotel Schiff, a property belonging to the Social Democratic Party. Linz Schutzbund commander Richard Bernaschek actively resisted, sparking off armed conflict among a group of the

Heimwehr, the gendarmerie, the police, and the regular federal army against the outlawed, socialist Schutzbund that had gone underground. Skirmishes between the two camps spread to other cities and towns in Austria, with a major confrontation occurring in Vienna. Members of the Schutzbund apparently barricaded themselves inside city council housing estates, the symbols and strongholds for the socialist movement in Austria. Karl-Marx-Hof was one of them. Police and paramilitaries took up positions outside these complexes, and the parties shot at one another, at first only with small arms. Fighting also occurred in industrial towns such as Bruck an der Mur, Ebensee, Graz, Wörgl, Steyr, Sankt Pölten, Eggenberg, and Kapfenberg.

There was apparently a pivotal moment when the Austrian military entered the conflict. Chancellor Dollfuss ordered Karl-Marx-Hof to be shelled with light artillery, endangering thousands of civilians and destroying many apartments. The socialist fighters surrendered. Fighting in Vienna was reported to have ended on 13 February, though in other cities it continued until the fourteenth or fifteenth of February, particularly in Bruck an der Mur and Judenburg. By 16 February 1934, the hostilities had ended, but hundreds had died, and more than a thousand had been injured. It was reported that eleven Schutzbunders were hanged with the encouragement of Dollfuss, causing an international outcry. The Social Democrats were now left very weak, and there was to be no stopping fascism's rise to power in Austria, as had occurred in both Italy and Germany.

These few days had a profound effect on Rudi. What occurred in Vienna, in particular, was so antithetical to the concept of "Wiener Gemuehtlichkeit" he had embraced that he had a series of bad dreams that continued night after night. One night the essence of his dream was that he had run away from earth and found himself on a different planet with different creatures but no human beings. On another night he dreamt, very vividly, that he and Lili were quietly working on a farm in New Zealand. Rudi talked with Lili about the possibility of them leaving Vienna. Where to, he didn't know, but the thought of being in Vienna with Mussolini in the south and a raging lunatic gaining acceptance in Germany frightened him a great deal. Dollfuss, thought Rudi, was far too weak and stupid to be relied on not to have Vienna overrun by the fascists from the south or from the northwest or being fought over by both in a violent conflagration.

Lili became very depressed. She understood Rudi's view, was even in agreement with his concerns, but didn't feel ready or prepared to run off. She loved Rudi dearly and had thought she'd go wherever he wanted to go, whenever. Now she had her doubts. *I can't leave Vienna*, she thought. *I love my life here...our life here. I can't give up my good work, my independence, the few very dear friends I have. I love this city. I have a roof over my head. I love the good food, the shopping, the opera, the music, the gardens, the parks. Rudi might be able to cope, but I may not be able to...to become a gypsy overnight, a Bedouin. I don't think so. Please, Rudi, be happy here. We are so happy here.*

Rudi was not so happy there right then, with people killing each other in the streets of Vienna because of ideological differences; Karl-Marx-Hof partly destroyed; blood on footpaths that people used every day to go to and from work; and groups of people with placards yelling and displaying ugly signs. *No, the signs are inappropriate, but the people are ugly. Too many ugly people here in Vienna now.*

26

ENGAGEMENT, MARRIAGE, AND TROUBLE, MAY - JUNE 1934

RUDI COULD NOT understand the details as to what was occurring at the parliamentary and constitutional levels, but he understood there was a great deal of wrangling going on. From 1 May, he read with near disbelief that Dollfuss created a one-party state with an authoritarian constitution. *Just like the authoritarianism in Italy and in Germany,* he bemoaned. *Nothing good could develop from this situation. The one positive aspect of the present government developments was the continued crackdown on pro-Nazi and pro-German-unification sympathizers.*

Rudi read, and hence was reminded of the fact, that it was also the first anniversary of the Concordat with the Roman Catholic Church in Italy and that the Church now had greater influence on the state than earlier. *I have never read of any good coming from a Church, any Church, meddling with the affairs of state,* he thought.

Rudi was now so disenchanted with Vienna that it was affecting his studies. Lili was less disenchanted, but she was worried about Rudi's uncharacteristic downcast disposition. Her disposition, however, was also to be dealt a severe blow. The news came via a letter that arrived at work early after lunch. Mr. Schwartz gave it to her to read:

3 May 1934,

Dear Mr. Schwartz,

It is with great difficulty and sadness that I convey this information to you. I cannot foresee a time when I will be able to pay you the money I owe you. You will remember I told you my brother with his family came to join us here in France, it no longer being tenable for them to stay in Germany. My brother had, unfortunately, not been able to find any work here despite very considerable efforts. This made him very depressed. He took his own life a couple of weeks ago. I now have the responsibility of supporting two families.

I hope you understand,

M. Braunzweig

Lili had tears in her eyes as she bit her bottom lip. "It is really terrible," said Mr. Schwartz, "that people are driven to such desperation because of the way they are treated in Germany by the Nazis. Mr. Braunzweig's whole family had lived in Germany for generations, as far as I know, and then were forced to scurry away…like cockroaches. Lili, let us go home. We'd both likely not get any work done this afternoon anyway."

Lili walked down Wipplingerstrasse much in a daze before she knocked on the apartment door on the Saltzgasse. "What a nice surprise, Schatzerl. Why are you not still at work?"

Lili was delighted to have found Rudi a little more upbeat than he'd been in recent weeks, and she tried hard not to project any gloom herself. "Who is this letter from on the table?"

"It's from my old science teacher. He's such a nice man. Here, read it."

Sattendorf, 28 April 1934

Dear Rudi,

I came across your father recently, and so I enquired about you and your studies. He spoke so proudly of you, telling me you were doing well at university. He also said you were engaged to be married to a very nice, young, cultured lady from Vienna—a real pearl, he said—and that you had together been skiing on the Gerlitzen.

I am still enjoying my teaching—must be more than fifteen years at the same school now. I am also very happy to have my sister and her husband staying with me for the time being. My sister and I always got on very well, and we hadn't spent any significant time together for years. She is a nurse, and her husband is a teacher, and both recently lost their jobs in a town just outside of Munich. They have both already found work here and seem to be settling in well despite considerable anger at having been driven out by the Nazis.

I think we should all be very worried about a government that can expel whomever it wants, and I understand that Hitler wants to take over Austria at his first opportunity.

I would love to hear from you if you have a few spare moments.

Stay safe, stay healthy, and stay vigilant, Rudi.

M. Birnbaum

Lili looked up and smiled. "Everyone seems to want to have you married, Rudl, whether it be to a cultured pearl or a real pearl."

"I wonder how many people in Germany actually know of or have heard of people who've been sacked from their jobs.

"You'd think there'd be some backlash against the Nazis." Lili shook her head.

"At least Mr. Birnbaum is happy to have his sister and her husband living with him," said Rudi. Lili couldn't contain herself any longer and had to tell him the reason she left work early. "Those Nazi arseholes have no conscience, Lili. Can you imagine how many people, how many families, they destroy every day? What's wrong with these Germans? Their support for Hitler is over ninety percent. And I fear there is huge support for him here in Vienna as well, Lili. At least Dollfuss is good for something. He's determined to keep those Nazi bastards down," declared Rudi, who was again visibly deteriorating into a serious funk. "You know, Lili, if Hitler were to take over Austria, and there are many people here who would want that, you would lose your job because Mr. Schwartz would no longer be allowed to practice. He'd be out of business like all those Jews in Germany who have lost their jobs and been driven out of Germany during this last year. I couldn't live in an Austria like that, an Austria that resembled the Germany of today."

Rudi held his head in his hands and squeezed both eyes shut as if he were in pain. "Lili," he started and then stopped, taking both of Lili's hands across the table.

"Yes, Rudl, what is it?"

"Would you run away with me if things got so bad here that I just couldn't stay any longer?"

Tears welled up in Lili's eyes, but she could not respond. She squeezed Rudi's hands very tight, but she had no answer. She was also embarrassed because she could not find it within her to clearly say yes. She loved Vienna; she loved her life there. She was independent there. She had a home there. Yes, she loved Rudi, but they were not married. He had not even proposed to her. Lili let go of Rudi's hands and declared that her mother was expecting her, which was only partly true. She took her bag and coat so quickly that Rudi had no time to object. "I'll see you tomorrow night, Rudi," said Lili, trying to perk up, and she quickly left.

Rudi felt most unsettled. He had very mixed feelings towards Vienna ever since all that fighting had occurred there in February, and increasingly he was becoming more and more disenchanted with Dollfuss. Rudi's mind was wandering. *No wonder someone from the* New York Times *referred to him as a "jockey." But he is not just physically short; he is also short of ability. He can't cobble together any sort of government; he is not his own man. He is influenced by Mussolini, also a jockey, and he allows himself to be sucked in by the Catholic Church. I can't see him as...*

"Rudi, are you home?" came Joseph's voice as the door banged shut. "I don't know what to do, Rudi. Can you grab a couple of beers? My mother and father are definitely going to leave Munich. Mother feels she can't stay there any longer; the negative energy in their neighbourhood—the leaflets, the Hackenkreuzer, the harassment—is getting too much for her. She spends so much time being depressed and crying that Father has agreed to leave. Father wants me to provide support to him and help them secure their papers."

"Where will they be going?"

"Brussels or somewhere in France but not Paris. Father says that Paris will be too expensive for them."

"How long do you think you'll be away, Joseph?"

"Maybe a month."

"A month?" queried Rudi in astonishment.

"Maybe even longer; who knows how long it'll take for me to secure their papers?"

"And uni?"

"Bugger uni. It'll have to wait." They both took a sip.

"Shit, I'm so sorry, Joseph. I hope it will all work out, but I'll miss you."

"You don't look so good yourself, Rudi. You look like something the cat dragged in."

Rudi relayed how he was feeling about Vienna, he related the contents of the letter Lili's boss had received, and he showed him Mr. Birnbaum's letter that had arrived earlier that day. Rudi mentioned the conversation he had with Lili and the circumstances under which she left.

"Oy vey, Rudi. It's clear. Go get another beer."

"What's clear?" queried Rudi.

"You must propose to her. You must propose marriage to Lili, pronto. You love her. Your parents love her. Tante Marianne loves her. Everybody at the Villacher Gasthaus loves her. She's been referred to as your fiancé by all and sundry. Why should she be sure of you? Do it tomorrow. Be a Mensch." Rudi stared at Joseph, who wasn't yet finished. "Yes, yes, I know you are young; she is older. She is a Jew; you're a goy. She is sophisticated; you're a country Schmuck. Just do it, Rudi. It's long overdue. You'll be just fine. Goodnight, Rudi. I'm off to Ester's to make plans of our own. See you Monday." Joseph grabbed a bag and rushed out the door.

It was Friday, 11 May, and Lili arrived directly from work as usual. She was just a little apprehensive as to what sort of mood Rudi might be in. "Servus, Schatzerl," he said as he embraced her and twirled her around, her feet in the air, nearly scraping the wall. Rudi appeared very happy. *Is he a little tipsy?* thought Lili. She put her bag down and took a breath. She noticed things were a little different. It took a moment to register. Rudi was dressed in a shirt and tie, a shirt she had not seen before. *Had we planned to go out this evening? Have I forgotten?* The table had a freshly pressed tablecloth, and there was a vase of expensive red roses nicely displayed. The kitchen area was pristine; pots, which were usually on the stove, were stowed away. The floors looked as if they had just been mopped and the cushions on the sofa freshly plumped up.

"I want this to be a very special evening, Schatzerl," he said as he took both her hands and looked directly into her eyes. "Will you please marry me? Dear Lili, will you please marry me?"

Lili was not expecting that, not this evening, not right then, although she had been hoping Rudi would propose to her for several months now. She hesitated for what was probably less than three seconds, although it seemed much longer than that to Rudi. "I would love to be married to you, Rudl." She flung her arms around his neck, and they lingered in a long lovers' embrace. Lili knew that her mother would be disappointed, that Rudi's parents would be very pleased, and that Tante Marianne would be delighted. Walter, Tante Mizzi, and Mr. Schwartz would be pleased for Lili, as they were all convinced she'd make whatever decision was best for her. The Leopoldstadt sextette would be delighted for them both.

"I see you're all dressed up, Rudl; let me freshen up a bit, and let's go somewhere close for a little celebration." Lili took a little longer than she'd first planned and emerged from the bedroom in a dress she'd purchased some time before but had never worn. *Perhaps it was meant for this evening,* she thought as she carefully buttoned it up. She liked how she looked in this dusty brown, high-waisted, chiffon dress by the designer Shiaparelli. She put on a little matching bolero jacket with sleeves that flared out at the wrists. "I'm ready," she announced as she proudly showed off her new outfit with a little pirouette.

"Wow, you look stunning—as if we're about to be married right now."

"OK." She smiled in agreement.

Lili was extremely happy, as was Rudi. He threw on his jacket, and Lili gave his pocket handkerchief a little tug as they locked the door. There were many excellent restaurants and cafés in Vienna, and Lili had been to the most highly regarded. Her choice for the night was Café Central. It was only minutes away, had a grand ambiance befitting their special evening, and, with a bit of luck, they might be able to secure a very nice spot in a semicircular, open booth.

Herr Ober, himself immaculately dressed in a dinner suit, detected from Lili and Rudi's attire that this might be a special evening, so he found them a perfect spot. He showed a little patience while they settled in. "Meine lieben Herrschafften, something to start perhaps?"

"A bottle of champagne, bitte, Herr Ober."

"Perignon," Lili whispered to Rudi. Rudi just nodded as the waiter got the message.

Soon the cork was popped at the table and two glasses instantly poured. Each proposed a toast, and both sipped, intermittently wiping away tears. There was a lot of talk, much happy talk. They held hands across the table and didn't really notice their glasses being topped up intermittently until the empty bottle was taken away. Only then did the waiter ask them for their order. Rudi ordered Tafelspitz for Lili and a Wiener Schnitzel for himself. It was generally his favorite meat dish, and he ordered it for most special occasions. It was not as large, nor as good, as at Café Louvre, he thought, but it was good nevertheless. Lili's taste was more varied than Rudi's, and she'd liked her selection there before. A glass of French red rounded out their main courses very nicely, barely leaving any room for dessert. Yet they had plenty of time to let their food digest as they also tried to digest the decision they had made that Friday evening.

They were momentarily interrupted by Heinrich, who spotted Rudi on his way out. "Rudi, we need another article from you soon, especially with all the present developments in Vienna. Verzeiung, Madam."

"Who was that, Rudi?"

"That was Heinrich, the uni newspaper editor without any sense of timing."

They shared some Palatschinken and had a coffee as they saw most people leave before they decided to do the same.

———

THEY WERE BOTH deliriously happy during the weekend, and they were itching to tell people. Lili would tell her mother on Monday, though she knew she'd be disappointed. *That's just bad luck,* she thought. *My parents have disappointed me a lot too, over many years, especially my father, who only ever cared about appearances and making money, and then he killed himself, not caring at all about Walter or me.*

Rudi and Lili agreed that they would not have a religious service, neither one caring for any sort of institutionalized religion. They began to talk about a possible wedding date then decided that the registry office at the Vienna Rathaus (City Hall) might have some restrictions, so they would wait until Monday to find out available dates and times.

On Sunday evening, Lili was happily preparing a little dinner, while Rudi was fiddling with the antenna of the radio to try to reduce the crackling. Suddenly Joseph burst around the corner. "Well?" he asked, looking at Rudi. Rudi nodded. "Congratulations, Lili. Congratulations, Rudi. Mazel Tov, Mazel Tov." Joseph, very excited, kissed Rudi on both cheeks.

"What about me?" asked Lili. She got some kisses and a hug. "Excuse the apron," she said, returning her attention to the stove.

"God, you look married already—the little woman with her apron and bent over the stove and the handyman making sure things work. What a Mensch, Rudi!"

"Make yourself useful, Joseph, and open that bottle on the bench."

"You'll stay for dinner, right, Joseph?" asked Lili. "Could you cut the bread, please?" Lili set the table for three.

"It smells wonderful, Lili. What are we having?"

"I'm not really sure. It started as coq au vin as our cook at home used to make. Then I found a carrot and three lonely little potatoes, and I couldn't leave them out." It had a luscious, rich aroma and tasted splendid, not a skerrick being left unmopped with the bread.

Joseph excused himself and rummaged high in a cupboard. He returned to the table with three little glasses of unequal size and a bottle. "Perfect," he said as he poured each a Marillenschnaps. "My previous flatmate sent me a bottle from Krems, and I'd forgotten all about it. La Chaim, Lili. La Chaim, Rudi. Mazel Tov."

⟞⟐⟝

LILI WAS EXCITED on Monday morning as she told Mr. Schwartz the news. He was very pleased for her, just a little concerned as to what their living arrangements might be. Lili quickly explained that Joseph was about to return to Munich to help his parents "escape," as he called it, and, in any event, he'd been spending most of the time in Leopoldstadt with Ester because of the near omnipresence of anti-Semitic activity in recent weeks. Lili had become very fond of the humble apartment in the Saltzgasse and was looking forward to establishing herself there with Rudi. She'd just want to change the drapes in the living room and bedroom, as they were severely faded and drab.

Lili phoned her mother, who politely congratulated her, wished her well, and told her she would always have her bedroom should she ever need it. Lili informed her mother that she'd not be home for the rest of the week; she had enough clothes in the apartment. Not five minutes went by when there was a phone call. It was from France, from Walter.

"Lili, congratulations…congratulations to you and Rudi. I had been expecting the news for quite some time. I wish you both all the happiness in the world."

"Yes, we are very happy. Thank you, Walter; we're very excited."

"Please keep me posted regarding arrangements. I must away; I am between meetings. Servus."

Lili tried to settle down to some work, but her focus eluded her. Mr. Schwartz knowingly smiled into her office intermittently, genuinely feeling very happy for her. In the afternoon, Lili phoned Hanna. She too was very happy for her and offered congratulations and help, whatever she might need.

Lili had finally settled down to some meaningful work when the telephone rang. "Ein Moment, Annenheim on the line," the switchboard informed. "Liebe Lili, liebe Lili. Congratulations to you and to my dear Rudi! I'm so excited for you. At last, at last! I am so excited. His father just phoned me. Rudi phoned him from the café. They are very happy, very happy. All the best, all the very best. A thousand Bussi. Servus." Lili replaced the receiver with a big smile, not sure whether she was exhilarrated or exhausted.

She was about to leave the office when Mr. Schwartz presented her with what was obviously a bottle of champagne, elegantly wrapped and ribbonned. "Till I think of something more suitable, Lili. Congratulations again and pass on my heartiest congratulations also to Rudi."

THERE WAS MUCH excitement in the air during the next couple of weeks. Rudi visited the Rathaus and sought advice and some alternative dates he could discuss with his wife-to-be. Hanna went with Lili to buy a dress for the occasion, and Rudi and Lili went together to select the rings they planned to exchange. Inside the simple, fourteen-carat-gold bands they had inscribed "Rudi 30 May 1934" and "Lili 30 May 1934."

And so it was to happen. It was Wednesday, 30 May. Lili would dress at Hanna's place, from where she would escort Lili to the Rathausplatz. It was a beautiful spring afternoon, a little warmer than normal and the air lightly perfumed as Rudi crossed the Ringstrasse from the Burgtheater and began to walk through the Rathaus Park. He could see Lili and Hanna chatting about eighty metres ahead at the edge of the Rathausplatz.

Rudi soon stood beside Lili, and Hanna offered him her congratulations before leaving with a kiss on Lili's cheek and a hearty smile for both of them. Rudi and Lili engaged in an ever-so-gentle embrace as to avoid crushing clothes or the bouquet Lili was carrying. They took each other by the hand and headed across the Rathausplatz towards the magnificent and imposing neo-Gothic Rathaus, the Vienna City Hall. They were both a little nervous, and Rudi got a severe case of the goosebumps. "You're shaking all over, Rudl. Are you having second thoughts?"

"No, no…no, Schatzerl. I'm very excited, and this building is so spectacular. And, anyway, I haven't done this before." They both smiled nervous smiles.

They stood beside each other next to a small, elegant, leather-topped table before a Rathaus official. He was arranging papers as Rudi was admiring Lili. She was dressed in a long and beautifully cut rich brown dress of midcalf length with a camisole top and many round, dark brown buttons down the front. A lightly scalloped deep V-necked jacket was draped loosely over the top. She was carrying a bouquet of white roses with a little greenery. Rudi was in a simple brown suit Onkel Julius had made for him, with a white shirt, a brown patterned tie, and a white pocket handkerchief.

The city official looked up and greeted them. He smiled an approving smile and had them hold hands and repeat the simple oath to "love one another" until death do them part. They exchanged rings, signed the formal document in duplicate, and discreetly kissed each other on the lips. A Rathaus photographer introduced himself and took a few photos inside with the couple variously sitting on a bench and standing. He then led them out into Rathaus Park, where he took a few more photos. Selections could be made at their offices any time a week later. With the official ceremony over, there was a long embrace that ended when Rudi twirled Lili around as he had so often done before. They skipped away as happy as could be and left the park the same way as they had entered. They crossed the Ring over to the Burgtheater and left into Café Landtman.

Herr Ober met Rudi and Lili at the door and led them to a booth where there were a few of their closest friends: Mr. Schwartz; Hanna and her husband, Michael; and Joseph and Ester, who had all introduced themselves. A large bouquet of red roses was brought to the table with an announcement that they were from a Walter Gruen in Paris with best wishes. People looked at each other, wondering how that had been arranged. There were kisses and hugs all around for the newlyweds. Before anyone had time to sit down, Mr. Schwartz elegantly offered a formal toast wishing Mr. and Mrs. Auer a long, happy, and fruitful life together. A second bottle of champagne soon topped up glasses, and a chef came to personally offer the finest delicacies from a large silver oval platter. There was a second and a third such platter as savory items gave way to desserts. It was a very pleasant afternoon.

"I've never been here," Joseph whispered to Rudi. "I could get used to this, especially it being so close to uni." Ester agreed, also appreciating this sophisticated café.

As the after-work crowd began to filter in and the air was cooling outside, the wedding party dispersed, everyone going their separate ways. Joseph planned to spend the evening with Ester and then take the train directly to Munich to be with his parents. Rudi and Lili wished him luck in his mission, promising to keep their fingers crossed for him.

Each with a bunch of roses and arms around each other, Rudi and Lili, who were very happy and very light of step, found their way home. Rudi was humming, as he often did. "Do you realize what that melody is, Rudi?" Rudi thought a little and shrugged his shoulders. "Yes, you do," continued Lili, who began to sing. Rudi joined in.

Wenn der weiße Flieder wieder blüht,
küß' ich deine roten Lippen müd'.
Wie im Land der Märchen, werden wir ein Pärchen,
wenn der weiße Flieder wieder blüht.

"You sang that to me a year ago, Rudl. You sang it to me in the Stadtpark, I think. I then sensed it was predictive, and you said it was just a Freudian slip."

"I remember that day, Lili. The Wiener Gemuehtlickeit was so pronounced; no one had a care in the world, and I wondered whether anyone in Vienna had a clue as to what had been transpiring in Germany. I remember beng very concerned at that time and thinking all Viennese must be deppert (dopey)."

"It was a full moon, Rudl, I recall," said Lili. "Yes, that would do it."

⸺⊗⊗⊗⸺

RUDI AND LILI thrived as "ein Pärchen," immediately settling into a comfortable routine: breakfast together, Lili off to work, Rudi off to lectures or the library, and a pleasant evening of cooking and canoodling. There was a little shopping on a weekend and lots of Spazieren in the parks inside and ouside the city. They loved each other, they loved the very idea of being married, and they began to think of the future.

Rudi was much more attuned to what was happening in Austria and its neighbours than was Lili. He was well aware of the instability of the region. Nazism was galloping forward in Germany, Hitler was making overtures about wanting to annex Austria, and Italy had Mussolini wanting to avoid any expansion of Nazism and wanting to curry favor with Dollfuss. Dollfuss seemed less than optimally competent and had ostracized major political groups in Austria. While he had banned the Nazi Party, he had also crushed the Democratic Socialists, and there was evidence of his own anti-Semitism. It had been reported in recent months that more than five thousand Austrian Jews had lost their jobs because of Dollfuss's anti-Semitic policies. It was also a considerable worry that the *Oesterreichische Beobachter*, one of the main newspapers in Vienna, promoted the removal of Jews from all important positions in Austria.

Rudi had really been shaken by what had been referred to by some as a civil war in Austria in February of that year. He had also been affected by the personal story of his flatmate's parents, who felt obliged to emigrate from Munich due to the rising anti-Semitism not only in that town but right across Germany. He was appalled by the behavior of Nazi thugs in Vienna itself, especially in Leopoldstadt, where there were frequent incidents of harassment, thuggery, windows being broken, and threatening graffiti, in additition to the media barrage attempting to set Christians against Jews. While Rudi often wished he did not read international newspapers, the fact was he did, and he had become very knowledgeable about the political developments in Germany, which he believed would sooner or later impact Austria and other neighbours of Germany. He'd read excerpts of *Mein Kampf* and was aware of Hitler's hatred for Jews and others, for his intentions to rid Germany of all Jews, and to annex Austria and implement severe anti-Semitic policies there as soon as the opportunity presented itself.

Several international newspapers warned against the scourge of Nazism, but in Germany itself it seemed that Hitler was gaining support, and anti-Semitism was on the rise across the country. Viennese Gemuehtlichkeit was one thing, thought Rudi, but a nonchalance or an ignorance as to what was happening on your borders was quite another. How could the Viennese, for example, be so ignorant of what was happening in Germany and even about what was happening in its own second district? Rudi had doubts as to the leadership and strength of the Austrian national government and of the role the police were playing in keeping law and order, especially in the Jewish areas of the city. He was also offended that, in his own university, the Deutsche Studentenschaft seemed to retain a presence with the knowledge, if not the acquiescence, of the university administration. It had also become general knowledge, certainly within the university, that non-Jewish professors were being given preferential treatment over their Jewish counterparts. There were also blatant instances, spoken about on campus, where Jewish students were graded more harshly than their Aryan counterparts. Such discrimination offended Rudi's sense of fairness, and he could barely believe how such behaviors could be prevalent in an establishment that should epitomize all that is fair and idealistic. It was now difficult for Rudi to feel proud of the institution that he referred to as his university.

Lili was less deeply affected by these matters. She was very happy that she was now married like most of her school peers and to a man whom she actually loved, respected, and even admired for the importance he placed on human rights and human decency. Rudi was a very compassionate and caring human being, shown by the weekly letters he wrote to his parents. Lili was most concerned about her husband's sense of well-being in Vienna, a city in which he had become increasingly uncomfortable, for he now saw it as vulnerable, not only economically but also politically, culturally, and socially. Lili was just looking forward to living a nice life with Rudi, independent of her mother, and enjoying all the attributes of Vienna with which she had grown up. She didn't need to sit in the most expensive seats at the Musikverein, however, or at the opera; she was equally content to be in the standing-room area as long as she was with Rudi. Not only did he understand the difference between a waltz and a polka; he actually played music, danced really well, and had a singing voice she loved and that many admired. Lili was just as content having a Wuerstel from a Wuerstelstand and enjoying it sitting on a park bench as being in a fancy café or restaurant.

Rudi was also happy at home, helping with the preparation for dinner. That was never boring, as there were frequently a few waltz steps in the kitchen, a toast to all and sundry, and an occasional gift for no particular reason. Lili could not remember ever being as happy coming home as when it was coming to that little, basic apartment on the Saltzgasse.

Lili and Rudi couldn't help but miss Joseph occasionally, and they were wondering how much success he was having in helping his parents, when a letter arrived from him.

Munich

11 July 1934

Shalom, Rudi und Shalom, Lili,

I hope you are both enjoying your life together and enjoying the little apartment. I cannot foresee my coming back within a month as the process of gaining the appropriate papers for Mother and Father is neither easy nor speedy. They have made contacts with people in Lyon and will migrate to that city as soon as all the paperwork is in order at this end.

I also just learned that in April there was a major boycott of Jewish shops with lots of noise and intimidation that nearly frightened my mother to death. There have been regular reports of harassment, distribution of anti-Semitic leaflets, and various forms of Nazi thuggery. My parents have had enough. Ester tells me that such activities have also increased in Leopoldstadt.

Look after yourselves.

Very best wishes,

Joseph

"I'm not surprised, Rudi, that getting the appropriate papers for his parents is taking considerable time. Walter told me that the French are requiring stricter procedures for people to emigrate now. I hope the anti-Semitism doesn't become so bad here that people will feel the need to flee."

I fear it won't be long, thought Rudi, but he said nothing. He did say, though, that he'd again been approached by Heinrich to write another piece for the university paper.

"Do you think you should, Rudi?" asked Lili. "The last two times your articles got you into terrible trouble."

"Yes, Schatzerl, but this time I'm thinking about writing something that could not be construed as controversial at all. I thought I'd call it 'Can Vienna Avoid Becoming Like Berlin?'"

"That doesn't sound as though anybody could take offence."

"Anway, I'll get you to read it before I submit it."

Rudi took several days between lectures to write the article, and he double-checked that all information was verifiable and accurate. Lili read it a couple of times and said, "Why not?"

───◆───

A COUPLE OF weeks later, during the very same Thursday class from which he had been summoned before, Rudi was again fetched and escorted to the office of the administration. *Now what?* he thought.

"You are being informed that you are appearing before the Vienna University Disciplinary Board? What is your full name?"

"Rudolf Auer."

"Sit down, please, Auer."

Rudi was aware of his heart pounding, but he also noticed he was in large, imposing, wood-panelled room with an oversized oval table with twelve chairs. Five stern-faced, grey-suited, and mostly bespeckled men looked straight at him from about four metres away at the other end of the table. "You have been sent to us by the office of administration. We are told that this is your third offence making untruthful allegations against our esteemed Vienna University." The one seated in the middle carefully opened a folder in front of him and took out what seemed to be a report. He then took the latest edition of *Die Universitaet's Zeitung* and opened it to page two. "Did you write this article, 'Can Vienna Avoid Becoming Like Berlin'?"

"Ja."

"Did anyone help you write it or contribute to it?"

"Nein."

"You wrote this by yourself?"

"Ja."

"Do you realize these allegations against our university are very serious?"

"Yes, I understand they are."

"Where is the evidence for these allegations?"

"I have evidence—the recording of incidents against Jews and the statistics about the employment of and promotion of Jewish professors in comparison to non-Jewish professors."

"The details you cite are not true."

"With deepest respect, sir, they are available for anybody who wants to dig for them."

"You were told to give up such digging, Auer. You have been told not to concern yourself with matters that are only the administration's concern, not the concern of students. Unfortunately, this is the third time you have not done as requested by your administration and the third time you have undermined the good standing of our beloved university. You will have to bear consequences for this…severe consequences." The five men moved towards one another into a huddle and had a brief conversation. Then, without saying as much as one word, they left the room. The door clicked closed, and a second click could be heard as the door was locked from the outside.

Rudi just sat there. *What will happen now?* he thought. He looked at his watch. It was 2:45 p.m. on this Thursday afternoon. Rudi kept looking at his watch every few minutes, and he soon became agitated. He remained agitated for quite a while, for it was not until nearly five o'clock that the door was unlocked, and two large men in some sort of uniform he did not recognize beckoned him to follow. Rudi followed one man, the other officer behind him. Not a word was spoken. Rudi was led down two corridors; the second one, at right angles to the first, was quite a lot longer. He was led down stairs and along three more corridors, narrower than the earlier ones, before he was ushered into a small room.

"I would like to speak with my wife, please," said Rudi. There was no response. "What is happening here?" he asked. Again there was no response as the door was locked behind him. Rudi began to worry. *I need to talk with Lili; I need to find out what is happening. Lili must have the right to know what is happening, even if they won't tell me. I want to go home, damn it.*

Rudi began to pace around the room, and it soon dawned on him that he was in a cell, a lockup. There was a narrow bed against a wall, a small table with a chair opposite, and a toilet and a sink opposite one another in two corners. A single light swayed gently from the ceiling, but there was no light switch he could see. A very high, small window let in only indirect light. As Rudi spied a grey, folded blanket on the bed, he began to panic. *Jesus, Maria, am I now in a police precinct or still in uni territory? Are they planning to keep me overnight? They can't do that. Lili will be beside herself. We haven't been apart even once since we've been married. She will be so worried. It's not fair to do that to her.* Just then the door was pushed open, and a bowl of soup, ample bread, and a spoon were placed on the table just around the corner from the door. Rudi was about to ask some questions when he heard "mahlzeit,"- bon appetit and the door was closed and locked.

Rudi ate the lukewarm broth with a few floating vegetables but ate little bread, as it was stale and tasteless. He really had no appetite anyway, as his stomach was churning, and he was becoming increasingly worried about Lili. The door was opened again, and the same man who had brought dinner was now clearing the table. "You may be sorry tomorrow that you did not eat the bread tonight. Goodnight."

What the hell might that mean? he thought. Rudi again wanted to ask questions, but he was too slow. He nervously paced around the room until he was becoming dizzy. He sat down momentarily and then paced around the room in the other direction. Rudi was so worried about Lili that he was nearly physically sick. She would have arrived home and expected him, but he wasn't there. And now a couple of hours later, he still hadn't shown up. Rudi wanted to scream. His head was throbbing; he felt he was about to vomit. He needed answers, but there was no one to ask. There was only a deathly silence.

He desperately wanted to escape, to be with Lili, but there was no apparent way out. He tried the door several times. Locked. *Could*

I bash the door in? he asked hiself. *Could I get out through the window?* he wondered. *What if I turned the bed on end? Could I then reach the window?* Rudi did the arithmetic calculations. He'd still be a couple of metres short. He felt a little dizzy from looking up, so he sat on the chair. He was now certain he'd be there for the night. He kept worrying about Lili. His being kept from her was so unfair to her. She did not deserve the angst being inflicted on her.

The light suddenly went out. It was pitch black. It took minutes before his eyes could sufficiently adjust to make out the shapes within his room for the night. He lay on the bed and could barely make out the lamp as it was gently swaying. *Like a slow metronome,* he thought. Rudi was beginning to feel cold, so he awkwardly unfolded the blanket and pulled it over himself. He just lay there thinking about Lili, worried for her. The fluorescent arms of his watch allowed him to tell the time: 11:23 p.m. He must have looked at his watch at least a dozen times before it was even midnight. Rudi began to toss and turn, for he was tired, but he could not sleep. His mind turned to speculating about the next day. Whatever the authorities planned, he had better be alert and functioning properly. He decided he needed to get at least a few hours of sleep. He had heard of the expression "counting sheep," but he had no idea how that would work. He decided he'd try to count the mountains he'd skied on to get him to sleep. *The Gerlitzen, of course. Nockberg, Ankogel, Moelltal, Katschberg, Turracher Hoehe, the Grossglockner. I guess I'll never ski there again. I wish Franz were here. What would he say? I bet he would...*Rudi fell asleep.

27

ESCAPE

WHEN RUDI AWOKE by the light of the bulb, he was momentarily disoriented, but only momentarily. He washed his hands, which felt sticky, and his face. There was no towel. He heard the door being unlocked, and soon the two officials who had brought him there the previous afternoon stood at the entrance. Without a word they beckoned him to follow. Rudi was again escorted with one man in front, the other behind. He was led only a few doors down and locked into what seemed to be a meeting room. He sat there until ten precisely, when the door opened, and three uniformed men entered and sat at the table.

"Rudolf Auer?"

"Ja."

"Whom can we contact?"

"My wife. What is happening?"

"Quiet. What is her name?"

"Lili Auer. Could you tell me what is happening, please?" Rudi's heart was pounding so loudly he had to concentrate to hear what was being said.

"Quiet. She will be informed. What is her phone number…at home or at work?"

Rudi gave them her work number.

"You will be transferred momentarily for sentencing." As the three men stood up and walked out, Rudi distinctly heard, "Thirty days…he'll get thirty days." His heart nearly jumped out of his chest. Did he understand correctly—that he'd be sentenced to thirty days, locked up for thirty days? *No way,* he thought. *Shit, no time for being indignant. Too late for that. What to do?* The same two officials reappeared and beckoned Rudi to follow. "To sentencing," one declared.

Rudi's mood was decidedly solemn as he feared the worst, but he was also as alert as he'd ever been. He was keenly aware of his circumstances. He was about to be led into yet another room and face another group of stern-faced men who would tell him how serious his crimes had been and that he'd serve thirty days. *That is what will happen. Nothing clearer!*

His heart pounding heavily, he was being led down a corridor when a small man with a large bin on wheels entered via a side door. In two steps Rudi was parallel with the large bin. He gave it an almighty shove, spilling its contents as it bounced off the opposite wall. The little man fell over the sprawling bin, and Rudi made a dash for it out the door. He ran across some lawn as he had never run before. He heard whistles and the word "halt" being yelled several times. He came to a main road he did not recognize and ran across, dodging heavy traffic. He continued to hear "halt, halt" and frantic whistles. Then he heard car tyres screeching and horns blaring. He got to the other side and ran down the first side street; he turned every corner he came to and ran down some steps.

He was in some cellar. It was quite dark, and there were many large sacks. He paused for a moment to catch his breath. He heard more of the same whistles. Rudi ran along an underground corridor then another. There were benches in what seemed to be a wine hall. He crawled under a bench in the darkest corner, lay there, and just waited. His heartbeat began to return to normal, and he started to feel cold. He had been there for what must have been half an hour; there were no more calls to stop and no whistles to be heard. Rudi wandered along underground passages that opened into larger storage spaces then, without apparent reason, narrowed again. He walked further down some stone steps when he was greeted by the smell of horse manure, and he found himself in a large underground stable. There were four or five horses peacefully munching at some hay in a trough. "Anybody there?" he heard. As stealthily as he could, he returned the way he came for a while then, after ascending a flight of steps, again found himself in a narrow passageway with a distinctly different aroma. He'd come across sacks of Eastern spices, the smells less familiar to Rudi than the ones he'd encountered a few minutes earlier. He wasn't sure which he preferred.

An hour or more had passed since Rudi had heard any whistles or calls to stop. He made his way to the surface and headed cautiously toward the Hauptbahnhof. He needed to leave Vienna if he did not want to be captured and serve thirty days and then some more for escaping. He wanted to check out the timetable for service to Trieste or Constantinople or somewhere from where he and Lili could get themselves overseas—not just another land but to another continent. After looking over his shoulder at every corner, Rudi finally arrived at the Wiener Hauptbahnhof. He was just about to enter when he noticed three uniformed men looking for something, somebody. *Are they looking for me?* he wondered. *It can't be a coincidence that men in a uniform I recognized from earlier today are at the Bahnhof. They are looking for a fugitive, and that is likely me.* Rudi, somewhat stressed, stepped behind what was obviously a transport truck to be out of the sight of the uniformed officers. The driver asked, "Are you OK, young man? Is there a problem?" Just then Rudi noticed a large sign on the truck that read "Constantnople-Wien: Kräuter & Gewürze Betrieb."

LILI WAS ABSOLUTELY beside herself. She had received a call from the police department. "Is Rudolf Auer your husband?"

"Ja."

"You are being hereby informed that he is to be sentenced to thirty days' imprisonment, commencing immediately, for sedition against the Vienna University."

Lili had a thousand thoughts rush through her mind. *What happened? Where's Rudi? I need to see Rudi. What's he done? Can I help? Who could help? Where will I live? Should I stay with Mother? Hanna? Will my job be in jeopardy? What sort of shame will this bring? How will I manage without Rudi? How will he be treated? Will he get enough to eat? Will he be able to remain healthy? Are there bugs in the bed?* Lili sat in her office, head in her hand, sobbing. Mr. Schwartz was making phone calls to whomever he could think of to try to have Rudi released. There was a lull in outgoing calls, and the phone rang.

"Liebe Lili, Rudi hier. Listen to me carefully. I am free."

"Oh, wonderful. How did that happen?"

"I'll explain later. I have to leave Vienna at once. Will you leave with me?"

Lili burst into convulsive sobs. "What is it, Lili?" asked Mr. Schwartz, standing beside her.

"Rudi wants me to leave Vienna with him immediately."

"Ei yei yei. Well, um…will you be with your husband, or do you wish to stay behind?" asked Mr. Schwartz as Rudi began to become impatient.

"Lili, are you coming?"

"Of course!"

"Leave the office at once; be careful you are not being followed. No one recognizes you as my wife, but we can't be careful enough. Outside the Hauptbahnhof there's a truck parked at the entrance. It has a large sign; you can't miss it. It reads Constantinople-Wien: Kräuter and Gewürze Betrieb. I'll be there. Wear comfortable shoes and bring all the money you have. I'll expect you in about half an hour. Do you understand all that, Lili?"

⸺⸺

A SWARTHY, SMALL, nuggety man, about middle-aged, stepped onto the road. "Where do you need to go? Trieste or Constantinople?" The driver pointed to the sign. "I wouldn't mind the company; it gets lonely on the road. What's your story? No bullshit. I can smell something fishy from a thousand metres."

Rudi explained his role as a subeditor for the university paper and the substance he had been writing about; then he said that he'd been locked up overnight and escaped. "But you're not a Jew."

"No, but my wife is, and I wonder if we could both—"

"I don't see why not. I'm Italian, but many people think I'm Jewish. Perhaps I have got some Jew in me somewhere. I work mainly for Jews. They are good people; they always pay…and on time."

"She should be here in less than half an hour," Rudi informed the driver, looking at his watch.

The driver asked, "Can you drive??"

"Yes, I can drive," said Rudi, a little hesitantly.

"Good. I will be able to make better time that way."

LILI ARRIVED AS expected and flung her arms around Rudi's neck. The driver looked towards where the uniformed officers had been stationed for some time, opened the cabin door, and commanded, "In, young lady. Both of you, in; keep your heads down." The truck pulled away, and it was not very long before they were on the open road. Lili found the smell of Eastern spices a little unpleasant, but to Rudi it was the best smell he could ever remember.

Lili was at first very quiet and visibly distressed as Rudi recounted the events of the past two days. "You have a brave husband, young lady, and one with principles," the driver declared. Lili could barely raise a smile; she was exhausted. She had not slept at all the night before, and the events had absolutely drained her.

At first a little wary, Rudi became far more upbeat and positive as they headed towards Budapest. It was very late when they pulled into an inn on the outskirts of the city. "Give them a good rate," implored the driver as he wished them goodnight. "They make a good breakfast here. We'll leave at eight. You'll do some driving tomorrow, Rudi."

LILI FELL INTO bed exhausted but could not sleep. She felt utterly frustrated. Rudi, beside her, had fallen into the deepest sleep, and she began to think. *What crazy situation do we find ourselves in? Why are we running away? What are we really running away from? Did Rudi not tell me everything? Did he just act impulsively? Mother, Walter, and Mr. Schwartz all warned me about Rudi's possible impulsiveness before. What will happen to us?* Lili's thoughts turned to practical matters. She needed at least some basic clothes: some socks, some knickers, a blouse. How and where could they change money? How much did Rudi have? Mr. Schwartz had given her some in an envelope. She hadn't opened it yet.

Lili snuggled up to Rudi, and he let out a contented groan. She cried a lot before finally succumbing, until the innkeeper knocked on their door at seven, as they had requested.

Breakfast was good, as had been promised, and they indeed hit the road again at eight in the morning. The innkeeper handed the driver three packages and wished them safe travels as they climbed into the Opel truck. "She makes lunch, so we don't have to stop; it's good too."

They filled up the tank with diesel soon after they left and headed back onto the open road. Leaving Budapest behind, Lili began to feel a bit strange as she reflected that she had never been that far east before. Rudi didn't care about that; he just wanted to be as far away from Vienna as possible. The trip to just outside of Belgrade would take all day, and time seemed to pass quite quickly, as the driver kept everyone pretty engaged with his questions.

He knew a lot about Rudi and Lili by the end of the day. When the driver thought it was about lunchtime, he pulled over and requested that Rudi drive while he and Lili ate their cheese and salami sandwiches. Rudi managed well, and Lili was astonished, as she had never seen him drive. *Took to driving like a duck to water,* she thought. The driver was also impressed with Rudi's driving. "Tomorrow we drive a long way, so we will take it in turns, driving two hours each at a time or until someone falls asleep at the wheel." Lili didn't like the sound of that much but soon forgot about the comment, as her backside began to hurt. *I thought I was better padded than this,* she thought.

They pulled into a Gasthaus not far from Belgrade, and the greeting was much the same as it had been the night before. "Give them a good rate. They are very nice people but not so rich. They make good dinner and breakfast here," the driver said quite loudly on purpose. "We'll leave at seven. We have a long way to go tomorrow."

For dinner it was recommended they have Cevapcici, the most popular dish in the region, they were told. It was very rich and inexpensive and washed down well with a full-bodied local red. As soon as they had finished, they went to their room, and Lili washed her knickers and blouse, while Rudi washed his shirt, knickers, and socks. They must have looked quite comical. "Hope nobody knocks on the door to invite us out dancing," said Lili.

———

RUDI AND LILI went to breakfast with their fresh items of clothing, and they were again soon in the truck on the road to Bucharest. It would be a long day's driving, with Rudi doing his fair share. The road deteriorated for quite a stretch, and whoever was driving had to concentrate hard to avoid bouncing from one pothole to another. They stopped briefly for a salad at a roadside café to break up the trip before completing their journey to a small town just south of Bucharest. They pulled into an inn to book a room. "Give them a good rate. They are very nice people, and are on their honeymoon. They make good dinner and breakfast here" was again stated rather loudly. "We will leave at eight sharp in the morning. Goodnight, Lili. Goodnight, Rudi."

It was quite late when they sat down to dinner. Lili shuffled in her seat a little, and Rudi asked her whether something was wrong. "My backside hurts; the seat in that Opel isn't all that well cushioned." They were pleased when they were offered a dish of stuffed peppers deemed a speciality of the house. The next day was to be their last to get them to Constantinople. The weather had been very pleasant on the previous three days, and Rudi and Lili were hopeful that the next one would be the same.

Knickers were again washed and hung over the bath to dry before they climbed into bed.

As THEY HEADED south to southeast, the day was becoming warmer than the previous ones, and Lili, especially, wished the trip were over. She was still in somewhat of a daze; she did not think of what might lie ahead, but she had had enough of sitting many hours in the cabin of a truck, being bounced about kilometre after kilometre. They arrived in Constantinople when most people were out having dinner on a beautiful early summer's evening. The atmosphere was quite different to that which either Rudi or Lili had experienced before. The pungent smell of Eastern spices, mixed with that of tobacco, was not all that becoming, and it was somewhat disconcerting to hear only Turkish being spoken. Rudi and Lili thanked the driver very much, and he in turn farwelled them and thanked them for their company and Rudi for his share of driving.

Rudi and Lili walked down towards the sea hand in hand and looked out over the Bosporus. They found an outdoor café and ate lamb kebab on pita bread before heading overnight to the pension the driver had pointed out. Freshly washed knickers dried overnight on a rack hanging from their window.

AT THE SAME café at which they had had dinner, they found themselves having *kahvaltı.* (breakfast). They ordered what the people beside them seemed to be enjoying. It was quite good, but it wasn't Viennese. They had white bread and white cheese, green olives and pink sausage, coarsely sliced tomato and cucumber. They had two coffees, but Lili couldn't drink hers. She wasn't aware it was designed to grow hair on one's chest. They were in a deep mental fog. They knew what they had had just four days before, all that was theirs in Vienna. A four-day bumpy journey later, halfway across Europe, they still had each other. Other than that, they had the clothes on their backs, a little money, and soon a bag containing a little lunch.

Not really having any clue what the day might bring, they bought some rolls for lunch and wandered down to the waterfront to see what ships might be headed for wherever. Lili mostly still in a daze and Rudi not really sure what he was doing, they wandered along several wharfs and watched the varied activities. A group was fishing at one end of a pier where a dozen noisy birds seemed to be having more success than they were. There were several extended families, with umpteen pieces of luggage, excitedly walking onto a liner; a man with chickens in a cage was boarding a smaller vessel that was rocking to the swell, and cargo was being loaded onto a lower deck of a brightly painted ship.

The pieces of cargo had labels with "fragile" written on them. Ever inquisitive and, when necessary, opportunistic, Rudi led Lili for a closer look. They followed some large containers into the hold of the vessel. It was eerily quiet as Rudi and Lili sat unnoticed on a wooden box. The shaft of light from the open door narrowed until it was quite dark. There was a metallic clunk as the lower door of the brightly painted ship was tightly shut. There were no windows and no portholes to provide a clue as to what was happening. But they knew. The vibration of engines, a couple of whistles from the starboard bow, and a sensation of movement told them they were headed to sea. Where they were headed, they did not know.

Prologue for the Next Book

The next book, about the lives of Rudi and Lili, commences with the following pages:

Cargo Hold

Sitting in the dark on a hard wooden box in the cargo hold of that brightly colored ship, Rudi didn't know what to say. There were strong smells of oil, tobacco, leather, and grain and a continuous vibration that travelled from their backside to the top of their head. Lili stood up and walked around in a circle and sat down again while Rudi scratched his head. Lili broke the silence with some sobbing.

"Where are we headed, Rudi? Where are we…going? Why did we really have to leave Vienna? Did you tell me the truth, Rudi? Did you tell me everything? I couldn't even say goodbye to my mother." Lili stood up, her bruised backside hurting.

"I'm so sorry, Lili. I should not have written that article. I now realize those uni authorities were determined to shut me up…even though they all knew that I was not making anything up. I didn't think."

"You didn't think; and look where it's got us." Lili's sobbing became ever louder. Rudi stood up and put his arm around Lili, but she pulled away.

"You got us into this—now you get us out of this. You're a fugitive from justice, a criminal. Do you realize…We are both illegally on a ship and don't know where the shit we are going. Where? Where the hell are we going, Rudi?"

Lili soon became exhausted and sat beside Rudi, putting her head on his shoulder. The vibration from bum to brain seemed to awaken some remorse, as Rudi thought about how stupid he had been. *I didn't need to write that article. I should have known that the uni authorities would have pulled all strings to shut me up and not further expose the anti-Semitism within that administration; after all, it had been entrenched for several years if not longer. Eminent professors and citizens had tried to change the mindset within the uni and they had no success. How the hell did I think I could have made a difference—just a second-year law student? Shit, I was arrogant. Shit, shit, shit! I know I'm not yet even twenty-one and it's easy to make mistakes. Yes, it's easy to make mistakes; but I'm married and should have been more responsible. What a stupid arsehole! This will likely jeopardize my relationship. I'm so lucky to have Lili; she's twenty-eight and could have married any number of well-established and mature men who wouldn't make goddamn stupid decisions. What an immature idiot I've been. I let her down so badly. No wonder her mother thinks I'm a poor match and neither her brother, Walter, nor her friend Hanna are over the moon about me. I should have been much more caring; I should have thought much more about Lili. In Villach, my mother and father, who love Lili dearly, will be furious. Tante Marianne, who adores her and is proudly knitting for the future, will never forgive me. We had such a good life in Vienna. Our apartment was small, but it was adequate and my stipend was paying for that. And Lili earned good money, enjoyed her work and loved her boss—Mr. Schwartz—who has always been generous, even to me. What an idiot. I didn't leave much behind—just a few clothes and my violin, but Lili had an extensive wardrobe. Christ, what will my flatmate, Joseph, think when he comes back, the apartment all cold and all Lili's and my things still there. He won't know what the hell's happened.*

The boat began to pitch as it found the open sea and some wooden boxes began to creak to the rhythm of the waves. Rudi began to feel a bit queasy and Lili needed to go to the toilet, she told Rudi.

"Go have a wee behind those big metal crates, Lili."

"I have a more serious need," said Lili, standing up.

"Perhaps we should have lunch now and you'll have some paper then, Lili." They had lunch and Lili went behind the big metal crates.

"How long will this journey take, Rudi?"

"I really don't know," said Rudi somewhat sheepishly. "Some of the boxes are stamped 'Perishables,' so it can't be more than two or three days."

"Two or three days, Rudi…how could you have done this to me? Are you out of your mind?" Lili burst into tears. "My mother knew best; your decision-making skills are lousy." Rudi felt really bad. "We didn't even have a honeymoon, and now we're on a ship to God knows where. Have you really no idea where we could be headed, Rudi?"